Secrets in the Shadows

HANNAH EMERY

Harper*Impulse* an imprint of
HarperCollins*Publishers Ltd*
77–85 Fulham Palace Road
Hammersmith, London W6 8JB

www.harpercollins.co.uk

A Paperback Original 2014

First published in Great Britain in ebook format by HarperImpulse 2013

A catalogue record for this book
is available from the British Library

ISBN: 9780007584901

Automatically produced by Atomik ePublisher from Easypress

For my family: past, present and future

PART ONE

Chapter One

Grace should be with Eliot.

Grace should be the one to take a bite of Eliot's toast in the morning, to text him and see what he fancies for dinner, to carry around a solid weight of certainty that he is hers and she is his.

But Grace isn't the one with Eliot, and doesn't know how to be.

She sighs shakily and glances up as she walks along the promenade to Ash Books. She can barely see Blackpool Tower for the autumn mist. It's a blue, cool morning and her icy breath streams behind her as she clatters down the glittering concrete. The tide is in, and to her left is the wide expanse of grey sea that she knows so well. Salty spray spits at her and she wipes it quickly from her face, disturbed by what the sea contains. By the time Grace reaches the shop an hour later, her face is stinging with the bite of cold air.

Even today hasn't taken her mind off Eliot. She is tired of thinking about him, but her thoughts are pulled to the image of him like pins to a magnet. When Grace sleeps, which isn't often, Eliot's face floats through her dreams and his voice weaves around the jumbled stories of her subconscious. When she wakes, she can think of nothing but her connection to him.

Grace's mother called it a gift.

There is only one person who has the power to make Grace think of something else. He is the only person who can make her feel as though the future might be different somehow. But he is not here.

After a slight pause, Grace tugs off one of her blue woollen mittens with her teeth so that she can find her keys in her bag, unlocks the heavy green door and shudders as she enters the bookshop.

As Grace enters Ash Books, she looks around and takes in her new business venture. Opening a secondhand bookshop with her twin sister Elsie seemed straightforward at first. Grace loves books, and Elsie loves books. The business loan application went through easily. It all seemed too simple to be the wrong thing to do.

There are new pine shelves lining each of the ivory walls, mostly filled with second-hand novels. Grace thought that they should sell only children's books and Elsie argued that they shouldn't narrow their target customer. The rainbow of creased spines is the result of their spat: a mixture of men's black crime, women's powder-blue romance and a colourful burst of children's books piled up at the back of the shop. Grace runs a finger along the spines of the books on the shelf to her left, careful not to move them from their perfectly lined up positions. Her eyes wander to the stray leaflet on the counter.

ASH BOOKS OPENING DAY
COME AND SEE OUR NEW SHOP! DON'T LEAVE IT TOO LATE!

As she stares at the exclamations that scream out at her in acid yellow and thinks about the day ahead, a surge of panic fizzes through Grace's blood and into her stomach, where it sits like a dissolving tablet. Hopefully Elsie will be here soon.

The scent of yellowed paper that has been thumbed through a hundred times hangs in the air like nicotine. The counter is to the left, cluttered with boxes of pens and lists of things to do before the grand opening. Grace moves over to a pile of stock behind the counter and picks up a stuffed owl that Elsie bought them as a good luck gift. Elsie has a thing for owls. She places him on top of the counter, then stands back to take in the view.

'Perhaps you could be our lucky charm?' Grace asks the owl, who glares at her with his frozen black eyes in response.

No, he doesn't look right at all. And he might scare small children. Grace glances at the door uneasily, her nerves easing a little when she sees her sister appear behind it. Elsie is laden with tote bags and wearing a royal blue beret that Grace immediately recognises as her own.

'You're here already!' Elsie says to Grace as she unwraps her gigantic yellow scarf from around her neck. She tosses the scarf on the floor next to where she dumps her bags. 'Shall we make a coffee and then straighten up? We've got an hour until we officially open.'

Grace holds the owl up. 'I'm worried he'll scare the children,' she says.

'He won't. He's cute.' Elsie snatches the owl from Grace and plonks him back in his rightful position next to the till.

The twins are quiet as they unpack the final boxes of books and gifts that they ordered last minute to try and fill up their shelves. As the boxes dwindle, the shelves begin to look a little more cluttered with choice and the counter and surrounding floor become tidy.

'It's finally starting to come together,' Grace says, pushing a strand of black hair from her face. 'It looks better than I thought it would when I first arrived.'

'And still fifteen minutes to spare,' Elsie says as she folds down the last empty box.

'Yes,' Grace frowns, 'so why is somebody already at the door?' As the tall figure behind the glass motions to be let in, Grace walks over to the front of the shop.

'Oh, Mags! It's you!' Grace unlocks the door and ushers Mags in. 'I'm so glad you made it. You're our first customer! Come and have a look around.'

Elsie makes some more coffee in their little staff room at the back of the shop and Grace walks Mags around, pointing out the novels that she has given them to sell. Mags smiles at Grace and squeezes her arm as they return to the counter.

'I'm so happy for you girls. It's about time something good happened for you both, after everything you've been through.'

Elsie returns with three potently scented coffees and puts them down on the counter. 'I hope it works out. We just kind of went for it without thinking it through in too much detail,' she says, taking a sip of coffee and wincing when she realises it's far too hot.

'Well, that's exactly what you have to do. People get far too wrapped up in what they think they should do, rather than what they want.'

Grace stares at Mags for a moment, thinking of her own mother. There's a short silence, peppered with blows on coffees to cool them. After a few moments, Mags takes her oversized handbag from where she dropped it behind the counter and swoops out a bunch of roses wrapped in bright pink paper.

'I brought you these. But I've just realised that you probably don't have a vase here. I'll pop and get you one later. Or I might send someone in my place.'

Just as Mags says this, the bell above the door tinkles again and two elderly women enter, cooing over *The Wizard of Oz* window display, which Grace assembled late last night after stumbling upon a 1960 edition of the book amongst their stock. Dorothy is a doll borrowed from the toyshop next door, and the yellow brick road is gathered crepe paper. Paper poppies surround the road, and in them nestles *The Wonderful Wizard of Oz*.

It's October, the last week of the illuminations, which always means that Blackpool and the surrounding towns are swelled with families who are there to see the flashing show of lights that dangles along the whole length of the promenade before the end of the season in November. The till is constantly beeping and at 2 p.m. they run out of paper bags. It's the silly things that are sold first: the extras that Grace bought on a whim and Elsie didn't think would match the shop of their imagination. Teddy bears wearing Ash Books hoodies; bundles of marshmallows in cellophane tied with curling ribbon; cheap children's books with gaudy covers are all grabbed without much thought, paid for, probably forgotten soon after.

Towards the end of the day, when the buzz of new customers has died down, Grace is in the small office at the back counting through the money they have taken when she hears Elsie call her.

'Somebody has brought us a vase for our flowers,' Elsie shouts from the front.

Grace smiles as she piles the notes neatly on the desk and stands up, expecting to see Mags in the shop again, brandishing a vase. But when she turns around and sees who has just come through the door, Grace feels all the blood in her body rush to her head.

'My mum said something about you needing a vase?' Noel says, smiling at the twins and setting the vase on the counter.

'When did you get back here?' Grace asks, trying to dismiss the instant confusion that swarms around her mind, the warmth that blasts through her body at the sight of him.

'Just now. I had a couple of days' holiday to take, and I couldn't miss the grand opening, could I?'

Elsie beams. 'Grace, why don't you show Noel all our stuff?'

'I think he's capable of looking himself,' Grace says, suddenly sullen. Elsie shouldn't try to pair her with Noel. Elsie has no idea. It's just not that easy.

Noel touches Grace's arm. 'Come on, Grace. Give me a tour.'

Grace softens. 'Okay.'

They wander around the shop, arm in arm to the back, where there are more boxes piled like bricks, two old office chairs and a small desk. The desk is crammed with the notes that Grace was counting when Noel arrived, piles of books and magazines, cups, a jar of cheap coffee, some powdered milk and a kettle.

'So you came all the way from London just to see our shop on its opening day?' Grace asks.

'Yeah. I've heard how hard you've both been working, and I wanted to come and see how your first day was going.'

Grace flicks the little kettle on the desk on. 'That's really nice of you. Has Bea come here with you?'

'No. She's had to stay and work.'

There's a silence, which is softened by the bubbling kettle. Grace glances across at Noel. He has been a part of Grace's life for as long as she can remember, since those early, bright days that seem so out of reach.

'How is Bea?' Grace asks him, busying herself with cups, not really wanting to think about Bea at all, cursing herself for asking.

'She's okay.'

And then, because she has had a big day, and because it's been so long since she has seen him, and just because she wants to, Grace puts the cups down, moves forward and hugs Noel.

A long time ago, the worst time in Grace's life, a time filled with screams and horror and nightmares and loneliness, Noel made things slightly more bearable for Grace. She was only sixteen then, and full of jagged emotions that made her feel as though she might tear open at any moment. Grace hasn't hugged Noel for a long time, but now his solid, strong arms are around her again, his clean, musky scent transporting her back in time, she remembers that when she did hug him all those years ago, she felt safe and still for that moment, as though nothing was moving.

With Eliot, everything is moving, all the time.

Grace sighs, and breaks away from Noel. 'Come on. It's almost time to close.'

Chapter Two

Louisa, 1960

Louisa was in her bedroom when it happened.

She hadn't been thinking about her mother to start with. She'd been lying on her bed with her feet up on the wall reading *Bunty*, when the strips on the pages before her became fuzzy as though they were hot.

This had happened before: it always happened before a vision. Louisa's sight became silver around the edges and her head ached, as though what was in it was too big for her mind. And then she would see something that was about to happen. Louisa was the only girl she knew who had such premonitions. She delighted her friends by telling them what would be for school dinner before it had even been served, or what colour Miss Kirk's dress would be before she came into the classroom.

So now, as Louisa's head began to pulse with pain, she knew that she was about to see something that would happen shortly. *It won't be anything of interest*, Louisa thought, for it never was. She shook her head, wanting to continue reading her strip about *The Four Marys*, but a stubborn image floated before her eyes, as though she was watching television. She scratched her leg idly as the vision began, but her body stiffened when, in her mind, she saw her mother wander out of their tall house, across the cool sand and into the roaring sea beyond. Louisa felt a suffocating pain in her chest as the sharp picture in her mind showed her mother's skirt billowing out with water, as she moved further and further out to sea until she had vanished completely. The image disappeared as quickly as it had arrived. Louisa tasted salt and fear, and then nothing.

She flung her magazine onto the floor and sped downstairs to the kitchen, where she had heard her mother clattering about a few minutes before. Her mother had been more and more distracted lately, and Louisa had felt as though something might be the matter with her. There had been more of the nightmares than ever before. Twice in the night, Louisa had heard her mother moaning and crying. Those blue, anxious hours came back to her now, as she stood alone in the kitchen.

'She's *fine*. What I just imagined meant nothing,' Louisa said to herself, her voice too loud in the empty room. She tried to make herself calm down a little, but her breaths had become short and sharp, and her heart was light and trembling.

Louisa called her mother, but there was no answer. She looked all around the kitchen for a note, a sign that her mother might be back any moment, but all she found was a half-finished cup of tea and an uncooked blackberry pie. She thudded upstairs, into all the empty rooms, and then fled back downstairs to the kitchen, knocking the pie from the kitchen table as she flew past it and out of the back door into the whipping, salty air.

'Mum,' she tried to call. Her limbs dragged along as though they were being pulled back, and her shout for her mother was sucked back into her mouth. She could not speak. She could not yell. *Come and find me*, she pleaded silently.

Louisa searched and searched and searched; she waited until her voice returned and bellowed for her mother over and over again; she wandered up and down the beach until her feet were numb and prickled with sand. Eventually she gave up and walked from

9

the beach to Dr Barker's house.

Dr Barker lived a few streets down from Louisa and her mother. *Dr Barker tells me what to do too much*, her mother used to say. But Louisa liked him. Something about him made her feel safe.

Louisa rapped on the blue front door. There was an immediate fumbling coming from within: a shift in sound and movement. Louisa tensed as Dr Barker loomed towards the glass window. She had never visited him alone before.

'Louisa, what can I do to help you?' Dr Barker said as he appeared in the doorway. A single white crumb of bread, or perhaps cake, dangled from his beard like a charm from a necklace and Louisa wondered how long it had been there. She didn't imagine Dr Barker was the type of man who looked in the mirror very often so the crumb could have been there for hours, perhaps even days. For a very short moment, this thought eclipsed Louisa's day so far. But as soon as it passed, the bright, burning memory reappeared.

'I'm sorry to bother you. I didn't know who else to go to. It's my mother. I think she might be in trouble. I think she might have gone into the sea,' Louisa said, noticing when she had finished speaking that her face was wet and that she was crying.

It was as though Dr Barker knew exactly what had happened. He didn't make an urgent attempt to reach for his big leather bag that he kept by the door. He didn't swoop his big brown cloak over his gigantic shoulders. He just held out an old, papery hand and stroked Louisa's head kindly, and gave her a grey handkerchief to dry away her seawater tears.

Louisa stayed in Dr Barker's living room whilst he went out to try and find her mother. She sat alone with his half-eaten cheese sandwich (that explained the crumb, then), his ticking clock and his scratchy carpet. She kicked her heels against his fuzzy green chair, and realised that whenever she saw a cheese sandwich from now on, she would think of her lost mother wading into the sea.

She lifted a leg and kicked the plate from the table so that the sandwich split and fell to the ground.

Had her mother seen that from wherever she was now?

Louisa sprang to her feet and reassembled the soft spongy bread and waxy cheese. She put it on its plate and back onto the table, muttering something about kicking it by accident.

Just in case.

When Dr Barker returned, his face was puckered into a strange, sympathetic bundle of features. He took Louisa's hand in his.

'Louisa, my dear.' Louisa waited for him to say more, for more words to come out from the depths of his beard. But none came. He shook his head and his eyes filled with grey water and turned pink around the edges. She looked down at his paper hands and at hers inside them.

'You shall sleep here tonight,' Dr Barker eventually said. 'I'll find you a blanket.'

So Dr Barker found Louisa a blanket and she found herself thinking about how much her mother would have liked the blanket because her mother loved colours and the blanket was made of hundreds of different colours, all wrapped around each other.

Louisa's mother used to speak in colours. She used to ask what Louisa's mood was, and Louisa would answer in a colour. It was a game Louisa liked and was good at. 'Red', she might say, if her day had made her angry; 'blue!' she would shout if she was cold; 'yellow!' she would holler if she felt happy and the sun was shining.

As Louisa lay wrapped in all the colours of the blanket on Dr Barker's couch, she tried to think of a colour to describe how she felt now. But no colour came. Her mind and her thoughts were clear, like ice.

The next day, Dr Barker took Louisa back to her house. As they walked towards the front door, Louisa looked up at the grey building. It seemed different somehow: taller and more intimidating. Louisa could hear the sounds that she had always heard from the Pleasure Beach, but the squeals of joy now sounded more like screams of terror. They came in waves, like the waves of the sea.

The pie that Louisa had knocked over the day before was the only thing out of place. Its purple innards spewed out over the grey stone floor in a bloody mess and its sour scent drifted up around Louisa like a ghost.

'Get together anything you want to bring with you, dear Louisa.' The way Dr Barker spoke made Louisa want to cry. A lump of pain appeared in her throat. She tried to swallow it down as she climbed upstairs to her bedroom. The summer holidays had filled the small, square room with shells and books and socks, and Louisa had planned to tidy it up before she returned to school. Her copy of *Bunty* lay on the floor where she had dropped it after the vision of her mother the day before, making her feel sick and hot.

'I don't know what I'll need.'

Dr Barker didn't seem to know what a twelve-year-old girl with a missing mother might need either. But that didn't matter. He knew to take Louisa's hand, and to offer her his handkerchief and to walk beside her as she left her house behind.

Louisa stayed with Dr Barker for a time. She couldn't remember how long. Those days were misshapen and blurry in her memory, as though they had been left outside and rained on. One day, while she was sitting in Dr Barker's lounge, there finally came a moment when suddenly she felt a tiny crack of space opening between that terrible day when she had lost her mother and her life now. Dr Barker's eyes twinkled when Louisa told him that she felt a little better and that she might be hungry. He slipped out of the room, leaving his newspaper and his reading glasses to peep at Louisa from the little table next to his chair. When he returned, he handed Louisa a plate with daisies around the rim and a ham sandwich stacked together in the centre. Louisa took a bite and focused on the daisies.

It was soon after the sandwich that Louisa found herself in Dr Barker's car, which smelt faintly of leather and fish. Dr Barker was very quiet for most of the journey. It was after almost an hour when he turned to Louisa, his big hands settled on the steering wheel, and said:

'Louisa, today is a very special day. Because today, you're going to live with your father.'

Chapter Three

Grace, 2008

'A toast is definitely in order!' Grace says as she struggles with the cork of a champagne bottle.

It's the evening of the opening of Ash Books and the twins and Eliot are at Rose House, the old guest house that Elsie lives in by herself. The three of them ate at the pub across the road from the shop for dinner, Elsie warning them that they wouldn't be able to eat away their profits every night and Grace rolling her eyes and pointing out that they deserved a treat.

'Was it a huge success then?' Eliot asks.

Grace avoids eye contact with Eliot. Tonight needs to be simple. She nods and allows herself a congratulatory 'whoop!' as she finally manages to pop out the stubborn cork.

'Yes. A lot of people came in and looked at the second-hand stuff. And the head of English from a high school in Lytham came in and we did a deal with him on a collection of the classics we'd put on offer. He ordered about two hundred pounds' worth of stock.'

Eliot strokes the peppering of stubble on his chin as though he has a full beard. It makes an unpleasant scratching sound and Grace wants to prod him, to make him stop.

'Two hundred pounds is great,' he says. 'If you make that much every day you'll be heading for world domination in no time!'

'World domination?' Elsie says, and grins at Eliot. 'You're ambitious.'

Eliot smiles back. 'I'll bet the free cupcakes had something to do with it. Good work on those, by the way, Grace.' He bites into a leftover cake, and Grace sees a faint trace of pink icing line his mouth.

'More champagne, anyone?' Grace asks loudly as she fills up her own glass. Elsie doesn't answer, but looks at her own glass, which sits on the battered coffee table, untouched.

'Go on then, Grace. I'll have a top-up,' Eliot says, leaning forward and jostling Elsie, who sits up and rearranges her hairclip.

'I think I'll go to bed actually,' Elsie says.

'Bed?' Grace asks incredulously. 'You've hardly had any champagne. I thought we were celebrating?'

'Yes, bed,' Elsie answers simply as she stands and stretches. 'Night.'

There's silence for a few minutes after Elsie has clomped upstairs. Grace and Eliot hear Elsie's bedtime ritual float downstairs and through the open lounge door: aggressive teeth brushing, cupboard doors opening and clothes being tossed onto the floor.

Grace sighs and downs her champagne. It's cheap stuff, not even really champagne, and tastes woody and too sweet.

'I'm so relieved that the opening day went well,' Grace says after a moment. 'I started to worry this morning.'

'About what?'

'About opening the shop. It all seemed a bit overwhelming. I was worried we'd perhaps done the wrong thing.'

Eliot shakes his head and loosens his tie. Eliot always wears a tie, even if he's not at work.

'Taking a risk like this is never the wrong thing. You've both been talking about opening a bookshop for a while, so it was the obvious thing for you to do. You can't have any regrets about that.'

'I hope not,' Grace says. She shivers. 'It's always freezing in this house. Don't you make Elsie put the heating on when you stay over with her?'

'I hate being too hot. I'd rather be cool,' Eliot says. Grace sees him start to reach for the blanket on the arm of the sofa to give her, then watches as he thinks better of it. If only things weren't this complicated.

'Elsie's the same as me. She hates being too hot as well,' Eliot finishes. Grace thinks she detects a look of defence in his slim, stubbled face.

'So you're staying over here tonight?' he asks.

'Yes. Elsie and I are going into the shop together tomorrow. She's made one of the spare beds up for me.'

'You've not slept over here for ages.'

'I know. I don't like sleeping here. But Elsie wanted me to stay over so that we could celebrate our first night and go in together first thing tomorrow. I'm trying to do things right at the moment. I want us to feel like a team again. I barely even feel like we're friends at the moment. And that's surely bad for business,' she finishes with a weak smile. An unexpected lump lodges in her throat like a boiled sweet.

'Yeah. She said things were a little tense between you both.'

The reason for the tension hangs in the air, between Grace and Eliot. Grace won't say it. Eliot doesn't know it.

'Let's have another drink,' Eliot says, filling their glasses.

The next morning, Grace shuffles further under her blanket as wisps of her sister's voice drift into the lounge like smoke. She wonders where she is for a moment when she opens her eyes, then remembers that she is in Elsie's lounge.

When Grace and Elsie were younger they were never allowed in this room. It feels forbidden to Grace, even now. This was the guest lounge, only to be used at Christmas. Grace can still feel the visitors in the air. It's like they never really left. Elsie has redecorated, trading the 1970s velour orange curtains and swirling gaudy carpet for classic beige carpet and blinds and chocolate brown leather sofas. But in the weak winter light of the morning, the new decor changes nothing. Grace can hear the sea here, and, for some reason, can't bear it. She can hear it now: the clashing of the monstrous grey waves against each other. The more she tries not to listen to it, the more she hears it, until it feels as though the shards of water are crashing against her head.

Elsie is shouting at Eliot in the kitchen. The words blur into meaning. Grace can't help but listen.

'I'm not asking much, am I? My boyfriend in my own bed instead of downstairs with my bloody sister!'

There's only a silence in reply.

So Eliot obviously didn't make it upstairs to Elsie's room last night.

Bad move.

Grace feels a tug of guilt. They got through quite a bit of champagne in the end, and Eliot had meant to go upstairs to Elsie. Grace remembers asking him to stay until she fell asleep in the lounge. She didn't want to be alone in a spare room upstairs. She remembers her eyes closing slowly as they talked, the room in a blur around her. She wouldn't have asked him to stay with her if she'd been sober.

The front door slams, the stained glass rattling in its splitting frame.

Sleeping here was a terrible idea. From now on, Grace will only ever sleep in her brand new flat, surrounded by brand new furniture and brand new other flats. There are too many memories here at their old home, creeping into Grace's body and mind like damp. And it's too cold. Rose House has always been horribly cold in winter. Even though the central heating clunks and bangs its way around the rooms like a metal snake, the old windows let all the heat out and all the outside air in.

Grace can remember being cold every single winter of her childhood in this house. She shared Room 5, the smallest, with

Elsie. Their mother never came upstairs to bed until the very middle of the night. She would often come into Room 5 instead of her own room. Grace would wake as her mother banged around the bedroom, knocking over the twins' things and whispering to herself. There would be further noise and cursing as their mother tried to undress; sometimes she didn't bother, and Grace would wake to the sight of her mother, fully clothed, complete with jewellery and shoes, lying open-mouthed on top of her sheets.

Those nights, in the early days, had been quite easy to bear. It was the later nights that were the haunting ones. Elsie always claimed that she couldn't remember, that she must have slept through it all. But how could she have slept through such potent alcohol fumes, such sickening screaming as their mother awoke from yet more nightmares?

Grace gets up and stretches her long pale limbs.

'Eliot?' she shouts.

He appears in the living room, his wavy, dark brown hair still crumpled on one side from where it has rested on the arm of the sofa all night. 'Elsie's gone to the shop—'

'I know. I heard,' Grace interrupts as she pulls her creased cardigan over her shoulders. 'I'm going now. I just wanted to say sorry about last night. I shouldn't have said I'd stay over, because I never feel relaxed in this house. It was my fault we both fell asleep down here.'

Eliot shrugs and looks at the table of empty bottles and toast crusts. Eliot always makes toast when he's drunk. Grace remembers him fiddling with the toaster in the early hours and burning the first two slices. The sickly smell of charred crumbs still lingers in the air.

'I know Elsie's mad with you now but she'll get over it.' Grace says, then sits back down on the jumble of blankets and cushions.

'I hope so. I told her nothing happened between us. But she won't believe it.'

'Well, I'll tell her later as well.'

'She'll believe you even less than she believes me.'

Grace stares into space. She supposes that's true. Is this what things have come to? There used to be a time when Elsie would believe anything Grace said, and vice versa.

But not now. Never, now. The time when things were straight-forward between the twins glints beyond the darkness of the past, and Grace can't work out how to grasp it.

She stands up, suddenly unable to stay in the house any longer.

'See yourself out,' she says to Eliot as she grabs her handbag and heads out to the hallway.

When Grace arrives at the shop, Elsie is standing stiffly behind the counter.

'So did you have fun with Eliot last night?' she asks as soon as Grace has closed the door behind her.

'Yes. I did. Surely you don't think I should apologise to you for that?'

Grace watches as Elsie drops her eyes to the wooden counter. They have splashed out on oak. The joiner who made it for them claimed that oak was a hard wood and would be able to survive a little better over the years. If only their sisterly bond was made from oak, too.

'For God's sake, Elsie,' Grace replies. 'We had a few drinks and crashed on your sofa. Honestly, you should be pleased that we get on. It's you who Eliot wants, you know,' she continues, her tone softening a little. 'I'm his friend. That's all. You were the one who went to bed. We wanted you to stay up with us.'

Grace moves forward and traces a line along the oak counter with a purple fingernail as she speaks. She thinks back to last night as she waits for Elsie's answer. Surely Elsie doesn't blame her for staying up. Early nights aren't for everyone. Old ladies and children. But not Grace. Not Eliot.

Elsie follows Grace's finger with her eyes and sighs, relenting. 'Okay. I'm sorry. Let's forget it. Do you want a hot chocolate?'

'I might have a coffee,' Grace says, relaxing at Elsie's truce. 'Ugh, I won't be drinking champagne again for a while. I hope I don't look as rough as I feel.'

'You're so gorgeous that you couldn't possibly look anything but amazing,' Elsie assures her twin with a smirk.

'It's funny that you of all people should think that,' Grace laughs, returning an identical smile. 'I'll make the drinks, shall I?'

As Grace stirs cheap coffee granules into two new mugs, she sees the vase of flowers that Mags brought the twins the day before. She wonders if Noel will come and see them again today. Her stomach tightens at the thought. She squints out of the window to the square beyond as she wanders back to the front of the shop. Noel never wanted to stay in Blackpool. Grace remembers him reading about other worlds, other people, for the whole of their lives. Wherever they were when they were all young, Noel was usually tucked away in a corner, head deep in a book full of facts. The moment he could, he bolted from Blackpool to university in London. Grace was mad with him, for a time. She was mad that he had left her alone with a sullen Elsie and a distracted mother. She was mad that he was seeing new places and meeting different people, while Grace was stuck in her green bedroom that she knew every single inch of. She was mad that Noel suddenly wasn't always just there, reading in the corner, in case Grace wanted him.

But then, as Noel phoned Grace every week and sent her cards and the occasional gift: a keyring, some sweets, she began to forgive him for leaving. She began to miss him a little, and look forward to his phone calls and visits home.

But somewhere, somehow, between Grace wandering around town with her friends, being in plays after school and being out when Noel made his phone calls, and Noel getting his first job in London and wearing shirts and suddenly being important, the cards and gifts faded. Their phone conversations became less frequent, and when Noel visited Blackpool, Grace felt like she knew him less.

And then her mother disappeared, and it all changed again.

Chapter Four

Louisa, 1960

Along the bumpy road they went. Dr Barker didn't say any more and Louisa didn't ask him to. She had never met her father before, and the news that she was going to live with him made the ham sandwich she had eaten hours before at Dr Barker's house feel heavy in her stomach, as though she had eaten a dollop of glue. It swerved around the corners as the car did and threatened to come up into her throat.

And then suddenly, the car stopped. Dr Barker tugged at his handkerchief until it came loose from his pocket, and wiped his face with it. Louisa felt a sudden urge to take the handkerchief and keep it forever, but she didn't tell Dr Barker this and she didn't tell him that she almost loved him, and that if she had been allowed to stay with him and his daisy plate with ham sandwiches on it for longer she would have been almost happy. Instead, Louisa looked up at the house that loomed over them.

Maybe, just maybe, Louisa's mother had known all about this house, and had sent Louisa here. Maybe it was all planned. Maybe her mother would be inside.

Louisa let herself be pulled from the car by Dr Barker. He held her hand as they ascended the steep, green hill. The front door was shiny and tomato red. When it opened, Louisa stared at the man behind it.

Her father.

He was a grey man: grey hair and grey clothes and grey skin. He looked down at Louisa and gave her a half-smile. She gave him a grim smile in return. He would, she decided, have to work for a real smile.

'Well,' Dr Barker said brightly. The word hung in the air like a sheet out to dry, flapping this way and that, getting in the way of things.

'Well,' Louisa's grey father repeated after a while.

They stood for a few moments.

'It happened, then. You knew it would,' her father said to Dr Barker, looking over Louisa's head and directing his words only at him, as though that would make Louisa unable to hear them. Dr Barker bowed his head slightly, his hands held together in a steeple.

They all shuffled through into the hall. It was a pretty hall, with an umbrella stand and a huge framed painting of a girl and a dog on the wall. Louisa looked up at the girl. She looked sad, and Louisa wondered why. Louisa's mother would have been able to tell her. If her mother was here, she would stare into the painting and hold Louisa's hand and tell her a rich, beautiful story filled with colour and happiness and sadness. But Louisa could tell by now that her mother wasn't here after all. Tears burned the backs of her eyes, but she would not let them fall. Not now.

'So, you're all ready for her then?' asked Dr Barker.

'Yes, yes. I have a bed made up. Thank you, Gregory. For everything.'

Louisa watched Dr Barker's face droop in a sad smile as her father said this, and knew then that Dr Barker liked her father, and had met him before, that he knew him more than Louisa did. Then she looked at her father. Did *she* like him? The man who had an umbrella stand and grey hair and grey skin?

Not yet, no. But she knew that one day, she would.

Just a year after Louisa had gone to live with her father, a silent, steady drift of snow began to fall one Monday afternoon and continued on and on, until nothing could be seen from the highest window of the house but a blue-white world with no boundaries.

The day Louisa had arrived at her father's the previous autumn, he had enrolled her at the local school that smelled of scrubbed potatoes and old shoes. Louisa had liked school in Blackpool and she'd had good friends there who adored the fact that Louisa could see into the future, and who had given her sweets in return for a clue about what might happen that day. But in her new town, with her new father and her new school, things were different.

Oh, how different, Louisa thought each night as she lay underneath a cool eiderdown and listened out for the sound of the sea that never came. Louisa's gift was stronger than ever: she knew exactly what the teacher would be wearing every day, and she knew whose knuckles would be rapped and what would be served for lunch. But she said nothing now. If she ignored the visions, then perhaps they would eventually go away. Her vision of her mother had been too late. No good could come of them.

So, because Louisa had apparently nothing to offer them, and perhaps because her face was plain and her hair a little too dark for her pale complexion, the other girls at her school made no real attempts to befriend her, or to poke fun at her. They simply let her be.

At weekends, Louisa and her father took little outings. They walked to the park, the duck pond, the high street. Her father spent more money than her mother ever had done and Louisa's tummy swelled ever so slightly with a weekly bag of fudge from Spencer's sweet shop. The outings were strange at first, and Louisa and her father spoke little. Words seemed to be difficult to find now, and when Louisa did push a word from her lips, her father might simply nod, or shake his head, or give a small smile.

After a year, Louisa's life still seemed to be colourless. And the snow that fell that Monday made it even whiter, even more unreal. School was out of the question, Nancy the maid said that morning as she cleared away Louisa's toast crumbs. And Louisa's father would stay at home too.

Louisa sat and watched her father eat the last of his eggs. He ate slowly, and neatly. Her mother had always made eggs that oozed orange onto the plate and the bread. Her father's eggs were more like foam and he cut them carefully so that there was no mess on his plate. He could, Louisa supposed, have just eaten them off the table.

'What will we do, then?' he asked Louisa once he had swallowed the last of his breakfast.

Louisa shrugged. She didn't think they would be able to go for a walk in this weather.

'Come with me,' he said, as he stood and pushed his chair back. He took Louisa's hand, led her to the coat stand in the hallway, and offered her the red wool coat that he had bought her a few weeks ago. Louisa put it on. The buttons were gold, and made her feel as though she was a queen.

When they both had their coats and shoes on, Louisa's father opened the front door. The snow was piled so high that they could see nothing beyond it. Louisa's father pushed at it with both of his hands and then, as though he was a boy of ten, launched himself on top of it. Snow puffed out from underneath him, and his face turned red.

He's gone mad, Louisa thought.

And then she threw herself into the snow too.

Freezing water raced through her shoes and her wool coat, and Louisa shivered. She felt a strange laugh escape her mouth. Guilt coursed through her immediately: she had vowed that she would never laugh again, not unless she found her mother.

But then her father laughed: a deep, loud laugh that made Louisa giggle more. She choked and wiped her eyes with her cold, wet sleeve.

'I'm not used to snow. We hardly ever get any in Blackpool,' she said.

Her father didn't correct Louisa's present tense. He smiled and wiped a piece of ice from his rounded jaw. 'It's because of all the salt near the sea. It stops the snow from settling.'

Louisa nodded, her face frozen and all her words used up, for now. But it had been a start. A very good start.

When they had thrown snowballs, and made a tall snowman with currants for eyes, a stone nose and a shoelace mouth that insisted on falling and dangling on one side, Louisa and her father went back inside. Louisa changed into some dry clothes and her father asked Nancy to make them some hot chocolate.

'I don't often have hot chocolate,' Louisa's father said as they sat sipping.

'It's nice,' Louisa said.

'Nancy is good to me.'

'Yes. She's nice.'

There was a stretch of silence dotted with sipping. Louisa looked out of the window. The sky hung down heavily, yellow grey. The snow would continue forever, it seemed.

'Mum talked about somebody,' Louisa said all of a sudden, leaning forward a little, her heart racing. 'She talked about a boy with purple eyes. She talked about finding him. But I don't know who he was.'

Louisa's father scratched his chin and shook his head. 'No,' he said sadly, 'I don't know who he was, either.'

'Perhaps if I could find him, he would be able to tell me where Mum went?'

Louisa's father put down his hot chocolate and Louisa saw that he hadn't finished it. 'Perhaps.'

'Is somebody else living in my house now?' Louisa asked. Her toothbrush and clothes and a couple of dolls she had outgrown had been parcelled up and sent to her a few weeks after she had moved into her father's, and she still hadn't looked in the box properly.

She felt that if she did, a sorrow too deep to recover from would pull her in. So the things that had been sent were still untouched, in Louisa's big fancy wardrobe next to her new, soft bed.

Her father sighed sadly. 'Yes. It's being used as a guest house now.'

Louisa swallowed a big gulp of chocolate and scalded her throat. So that was it. She couldn't go back. 'It feels strange to think of somebody else brushing their teeth at my sink,' she said, wondering if her father would understand.

He nodded, and sighed again.

'I can't sleep at night,' Louisa said next. It was as though her words were suddenly dripping out with no control now, like her mouth was a broken tap. 'I can't seem to sleep without the sounds of the sea.'

'I see. And a girl needs her sleep.'

Louisa nodded, pleased that her father appeared to be listening to her and thinking about what she had said. It seemed so long since she had had a conversation, a real one where she felt like something had happened at the end of it.

'You know,' her father said after a little time, 'if you hold a seashell up to your ear, then you can hear the sea.'

Louisa raised her dark eyebrows, interested. The idea reminded her of something her mother would have said, and made Louisa's insides tremble a little with grief.

'I'll try to get you a shell so that you can listen to it each night before bed. We need you to sleep well.' Her father stood and left the room, and Louisa finished her hot chocolate, and when she was sure that her father wasn't coming back, had the rest of his too.

That night, even though going out was out of the question, and even though Louisa and her father were goodness knows how many miles from the coast, Louisa saw that there was a small, shiny seashell on her pillow. It was cream, with tiny pink veins running through it. It was beautiful.

Louisa held the shell to her ear to hear the crashing of the sea, and wondered how her father had managed to find it for her.

And as she sank into bed, and listened to the waves, a little bit of colour seeped back into Louisa's world.

Chapter Five

Grace, 2008

'I'm going to go and get us some lunch,' Grace says.

Ash Books has been busy on its second morning of business, making the whole venture seem real and feasible. Two groups of Eliot's students have already responded to an email from him promoting the shop by turning up and wandering around the small section of plays, giggling and jostling each other and fighting over the only copy of *Talking Heads*.

'Tuna salad sub for me please,' Elsie says, rooting in her purse.

'Don't worry about the money. I don't think we need to split things down to the penny now that we have a business together.'

Elsie looks up at Grace and smiles. It's an excited smile, full of the promise of success. Grace smiles back, seeing her own face reflected by Elsie's: pale skin, an angular cat-like grin, dark arched brows over kohl-lined violet eyes.

Grace tugs her coat around her tightly as she steps out of the shop to protect her from the icy whip of the sea air. She has lived near the sea all her life and still the salty wind can take her breath away. People used to visit Blackpool for this clean, fresh air; it was good for their health and their souls. The stretch of promenade a few miles north of Ash Books is still stuffed with the same old attractions as it was in the 1960s. Blackpool Tower stands over the promenade that it has spawned: the south of the promenade is filled with the sounds of clicking, whirring Pleasure Beach rides and the screams of tourists' rickety descents down roller coaster tracks. In the summer season, Central Pier is gaudy with lights and colour, and amusement arcades and cheap food shacks squall for custom. From north to south, a string of giddy illuminations hover over the line of cars that queue to see them.

Grace squints into the distance and sees Blackpool Pleasure Beach. When half term is over, the rides will stop and the park will fall silent. There is always something dead about Blackpool in winter. Grace's whole life has peaked and fallen with Blackpool's peaks and falls, as the town has breathed in and out over summer and winter. The dazzling attractions and pleasant weather used to make Rose House bustle with loud, excitable overnight guests for the first few summers of Grace's childhood. But the guests dwindled over the years. Eventually, they stopped coming altogether. Grace's mother didn't seem to care.

'It's all too much trouble. We're better off with no guests. We're better off just us,' she said to the twins when they were about fifteen, an empty brandy glass beside her.

Of course, it wasn't running the guest house that had caused trouble. It was the other thing their mother did for the guests, night after night, behind the closed door of the dining room. The twins listened sometimes, kneeling on their bedroom floor, ears pressed to the musty-smelling, swirling green carpet and hearing nothing but muffled voices. Their mother used to come upstairs afterwards, clinking coins and smelling of smoke and grown-ups. That's when she'd come into their room, and think that they couldn't hear her. Grace will always remember the sound of her mother's sleep. It's mixed in with the sounds of the night sea. Shallow breaths, hoarse with alcohol.

Grace and Elsie never understood what their mother was doing in the dining room until the day of the car crash. That was the day that changed everything.

'Yes, love. What can I get you?' Grace's memories are interrupted by the deli assistant, poised over her clean white chopping board.

When Grace arrives back at the shop, a tall, chubby man in a green waterproof jacket is just leaving.

'Another cold day, eh?' he says politely as he lets Grace pass. As she does so, she sees him rapidly scanning her face, hesitation clouding his own. She smiles.

'I think we confused that customer who just left,' she grins at Elsie as she plonks the sandwiches down on the counter. 'I don't think he was expecting to step out of the shop and see a carbon copy of you.'

Elsie smiles weakly. 'He wasn't a customer,' she says as she pulls a sandwich towards her and begins to unwrap it.

'Who was he then?' Grace asks over the rustling of the sandwich paper.

Elsie shrugs. 'A salesman.' She wrinkles her nose. 'This one's yours. I don't know how you can eat prawns. Didn't you know that they are the maggots of the sea?'

'A salesman of what?'

Elsie shrugs and bites into her own sandwich neatly. 'Books and stuff.'

'So, did he have anything good? Did he give you any ideas of any other stock it might be worth ordering?'

'No. He wanted to sell us a load of old stuff.'

'Like what?'

'It was just old stuff. Not really what we're going for.'

'I would have liked to have seen it. Did he leave a number?'

'No,' Elsie replies simply as she pops a piece of cucumber into her mouth. Just like that, as though the matter is closed. As though she is the boss.

'Elsie, we're meant to be a team! Why didn't you at least take his number?'

'Why don't you trust the decision that I made? Who would buy horrible dusty books from a hundred years ago?'

'They were from a hundred years ago? There could have been all sorts in his collection, Elsie. There could have been first editions that we could have made actual money from! Why do you think that you are the one in charge? Why can't we both be the adults here?'

Elsie shrugs and screws up her sandwich paper, soggy with tomatoes that she has delicately removed.

'I thought I made the right decision. People want new stuff these days. Even if they're buying second hand, they want it to look new.'

'No, they don't *all* want new stuff. Don't be so narrow-minded,' Grace shoots back.

Elsie scowls at her sister as she grabs the ball of tomato-smeared paper and pushes past her. Grace picks up her own sandwich and bites into it. She frowns as Elsie's words are finally processed in her mind. *Maggots of the sea.* She swallows her first mouthful uneasily, poking at the remainder of the sandwich's pink, veiny innards before pushing it away.

The apology comes the next day, just as Grace knows it will.

'I really am sorry.'

Grace looks up from her pile of pound coins to her twin's apologetic saucer eyes. 'It's fine, Elsie. Honestly, I'm over it. As long as you promise we can decide things as a team in the future.'

'I will, I will. I promise. I was just feeling stubborn yesterday. I thought I could handle things on my own. But today I can see it all a bit more clearly. I know I was out of order,' Elsie says, her voice slightly high-pitched as though she has sucked an old helium balloon. 'So, I'm going to leave you to it for the afternoon. To show that I trust you.'

'You're taking the afternoon off?'

'Well, not exactly. I'll start some stuff for the tax return. Boring stuff.' Elsie gives Grace an impulsive hug over the counter, her earrings catching on her sister's glossy black hair. 'I'm not skiving. I just want you to know that I trust you.'

A few minutes after Elsie has left, Grace drums her fingers on the counter. She takes a sip of the hot chocolate she has made herself, even though it's too hot to taste the sweetness. She watches a lone man in a brown suede coat browse the small selection of biographies they have stacked near to the doorway. When was the last time Elsie hugged Grace before today? She can still smell her sister's perfume: a leathery, almost manly scent. A scent that makes her seem like the boss. She has been worse since their mother left. Elsie seems to think that telling Grace what to do might fill in the horrific, inexplicable gap in their lives that they are forced to step over each day. Elsie seems to bound over the gap easily, like an exuberant Labrador, and has done since they were sixteen. But Grace, even now, constantly finds herself edging over it cautiously, trying not to fall.

The twins' mother vanished on their sixteenth birthday: a day when she should definitely have stayed until the end. In many ways, she had gone long before the day she disappeared, but the traces of her at least made Grace feel as though they had a mother. Sticky hairspray wafting through the hall. Perfume. Brandy. All toxic fumes, seeping into their skin, making the twins' faces grey and their thoughts jumbled. She had been even more distracted in the days leading up to the twins' birthday, and Grace had felt as though something might be the matter with her. There had been more of the nightmares than ever before. Twice in the night, Grace had heard her mother moaning and crying. Those blue, anxious hours of thirteen years ago came back to her now, as she stood in the shop.

Grace had woken up suddenly on her sixteenth birthday. She'd had a frightening dream that she was drowning, pulling for something to grab onto, her mouth and eyes and nose filling with stinging seawater. She had clawed at her duvet, gasping, and shot up in bed, disorientated and dizzy with breathlessness. She'd looked over at Elsie, who lay still as a corpse, breathing deeply and steadily. Although the curtains were shut, Grace could tell it was still early.

But not early enough.

She sat up, feeling a suffocating pain in her chest, tasting salt and fear and loss. When she went downstairs to find her mother, she found sixteen fairy cakes with silver balls on top, two glasses of cloudy lemonade, a blood red bottle of wine from a neighbour, presents wrapped in pink foil paper, cards stacked up in the hall. A lone balloon.

But no mother. Grace remembered her dream: remembered being pulled into the slicing waves, water filling her lungs until there was nothing but blackness.

'She's *fine*,' Grace said to herself, her voice too loud in the empty hall. She tried to make herself calm down a little, but her breaths had become short and sharp, and her heart was light and trembling.

She called her mother, but there was no answer. She looked all around the kitchen for a note, a sign that her mother might be back any moment, but all she found was a half-finished glass of brandy in the kitchen. She thudded upstairs, into all the empty rooms, into the one where Elsie still lay sleeping. Elsie couldn't know that their mother had tried to leave them. She would never forgive it. Grace had to find her. She fled back downstairs to the kitchen, knocking the brandy from the worktop as she passed so that it crashed onto the stained stone floor. She rushed out of the back door into the whipping, salty air.

'Mum,' she tried to call. Her limbs dragged along as though they were being pulled back, and her shout for her mother was sucked back into her mouth. She could not speak. She could not yell. *Come and find me*, she pleaded silently.

Grace searched and searched and searched; she waited until her voice returned and bellowed for her mother over and over again; she wandered up and down the beach until her feet were numb and prickled with sand. Eventually she gave up and walked from the beach, back home to Elsie.

Now, Grace looks at her watch. Nearly half past two. She picks up her phone from the counter and pauses slightly before tapping into her caller list. Eliot finished work for the half term break the other day. He went on to a teacher training course after his degree and now he teaches Theatre Studies in a sixth form college. He is probably still in bed. Grace pictures his bare chest rising and falling with sleep, his mouth slightly open, his face immersed in a dream he won't remember when he wakes.

Her hand hovers over his number, until she remembers the hug from Elsie, the feeling of their hair and earrings and scents being entangled. She locks her keypad and places her phone back on the counter. As she does, she glances up at the door, which has opened.

'Eliot! I was just thinking you'd still be in bed, enjoying your break.'

'Thought I'd come and check in here. How's it going? Good day?'

'Yeah. Pretty quiet, after a surge yesterday.'

Eliot nods then looks round. 'Isn't Elsie here?'

'She's taken the tax stuff home to work on,' Grace says, not wanting to go into the reason why Elsie has left Grace to it. 'She'll be back in a bit. She won't be able to stay away, although it seems to be going quieter this afternoon.'

'I suppose with this kind of shop it will always be a little up and down. Have you had many students in? I was thinking if you did some kind of student discount then it might work in your favour.'

'Yes, we've had a few, thanks to your promotional email. Student discount is a great idea.'

'If you decide on the discount then I can email my students again, in case they're thinking of buying anything.'

Grace laughs. 'Did you used to spend your college holidays buying books?'

'I certainly did! You know I did!'

Grace bites her lip. 'I remember. You were always reading.'

'Reading or drinking,' Eliot shrugs. 'But drinking's a student's prerogative.'

'And what's your excuse now?'

'It's a teacher's prerogative too! Some of the banal things I have to teach and the misery that some of the students put me through are both enough to make me reach for a drink.'

'I can't imagine your lessons being banal.'

'My lessons aren't banal!' Eliot retorts. 'It's the bloody curriculum that's the problem. Bores the students to death. If I followed the lesson plans that I was meant to, as well as sticking to the set plays, then everybody would have slipped into a tedium-induced coma by the end of the lesson – me included.'

'Have you got much marking to do over half term?' Grace asks, remembering that Eliot normally spends most of his time off lamenting what he should be doing to keep in the head of department's good books.

'Nah. A bit of planning. Nothing that I can't do on the day before I go back. So I'll probably help out here a bit. I like the idea of reading all day.'

'We don't just read all day! We're actually very busy,' Grace says in mock outrage. 'In fact, I have a load of new stock to put out. Mags found some of Noel's old books we could sell at her house the other day, so I need to catalogue them and decide where to place them. I'm considering changing the window display at some point so I need to think of some ideas for that. And I have to cash up, too.'

Eliot rolls his sleeves up. 'Well then. We'd best get started.'

Chapter Six

Grace, 2008

When the phone rings in the shop, Grace knows who it'll be. They have had a landline installed but it hasn't rung, apart from now. Grace can't even remember hearing the ring before, and the noise shocks her at first, a shrill shriek straight through her body. She takes a moment to register what the sound is, then picks up the receiver.

'Grace? How's it going there?'

'It's going well,' Grace says perkily, 'how's your afternoon?'

'Oh, you know. It's fine.'

'So what's up?'

'Nothing. I just wanted to check you're okay. I could have come back to help if it was busy.'

'Elsie, please. I'm fine here. In fact, I have some brilliant news. You know the teacher who bought all those books on our first day?' Grace doesn't wait for Elsie's response before continuing. 'Well, he came back in about an hour ago and bought a load of novels! So I've taken over £50.'

'That really is brilliant!' Elsie's voice lifts.

'So I was thinking we could go out tonight to celebrate. Dinner? On me?'

'I'd love to!'

Grace smiles. 'Great. Let's go to that new tapas bar, you know the one—'

'It's called Sombra,' Eliot interrupts cheerfully, as he places books on an empty shelf.

There's a silence. 'Is Eliot with you?' Elsie asks Grace, her voice tensing.

'Oh, um, yeah. He was looking for you, actually.'

Elsie relaxes a little. 'I've been trying to call him.'

'I think he left his phone at home. I'll put him on.'

Grace hands the phone over to Eliot and tries not to watch him, tries not to take notice of whether his face lights up, or tenses, or changes at all.

'Sorry,' he says, 'I didn't realise I'd left my phone at home until I got to the shop. I was just going to ring you. I could come to yours now? We could watch a film or something?'

He smiles as he speaks again. 'Yes, Grace seems to be doing rather well, actually. If you'd have seen her make that sale on those novels before, you would have been really impressed.'

There is a pause, and then Eliot swallows uncomfortably. It is a sickly sound. 'Yeah. I'd just arrived when the guy came in. Yes, I've been here an hour.'

Silence. Then:

'Elsie, you're overreacting to this. I came here to see you! Elsie, I—'

But she's gone, and Eliot is left holding the buzzing receiver.

Grace holds her head in her hands and groans. 'I don't know if I can take much more of this. I thought this morning that we had made some kind of progress. It actually felt like we were sisters again.'

'I know, I know. And now you're back to square one. Because of me.'

'It's not because of you. Not really. If Elsie trusted me properly, then she wouldn't be so quick to jump to conclusions.'

'I think we should try to spend less time together,' Eliot says quietly. 'I don't want to lose Elsie.'

'And I don't want to lose you!' Grace explodes. 'She's *got* you! You're *hers*! And it's still never enough.' She opens the till and snatches out some notes before banging it shut again. 'I've had enough of being good, of going against what I should actually have, just for her, and it *still* not being good enough, her *still* not trusting me.'

Eliot watches Grace as she rants her way through the shop, to her jacket at the back, and to the front again, where she stuffs the notes from the till into her pocket.

'Well, I'm still going out for dinner,' she finishes. 'And I think that you should come with me. What do you say?'

Eliot scratches his head, probably to stall time, to give himself a bit longer to think of an answer.

He glances at Grace, almost guiltily. Then he glances at the phone, as though Elsie is still in it, trapped in the shiny coiled wires.

There are stinging tears in Grace's eyes now.

'I don't want to lose you,' she repeats. 'You're my friend, Eliot. Just because Elsie's going out with you, it shouldn't mean that I can't ever see you.'

'Okay. I'll come out for dinner. Elsie probably needs some time to cool off anyway. I'll compensate for all this with her tomorrow. But it'll have to be just dinner, Grace. I don't want to cause any further problems, and I don't want to hurt Elsie.'

'Fine. Just dinner,' Grace replies hotly. 'God, I need a drink. Come on. This shop is now officially closed for the day. Pick me up at eight. I'm going home for a hot bath and a vodka.'

She hears Elsie's voice in her head: *Vodka? The things you drink are disgusting, Grace.*

She sees their mother clinging to an empty bottle, hears her demented wailing.

'I'll pick a bottle up from the shop on the way home,' she says to herself, shaking her head slightly to shuffle the images to the back.

As soon as Grace reaches her flat, she runs a scorching bath and lowers herself in carefully. She plunges her head under the water, hearing the blurred clunking of pipes. Even underwater, the feeling of tightness in her stomach does not disappear. She considers calling Elsie to apologise, to explain that nothing has ever happened.

She opens her eyes, water stinging them, her black hair floating above her like smoke. Elsie wouldn't believe her. So what's the point?

The day of the car crash was the day that Elsie started to change. The twins had been invited to Rachel Gregory's twelfth birthday party. Elsie had wanted to wear a dress that Grace had never liked. It was red: a dirty, blood red. Elsie always wanted to stand out as the most grown up. Grace didn't mind that Elsie was growing up before her. She was, after all, five and a half minutes older.

'Mum, where's my red dress?' Elsie hollered as the twins stood in a rubble of discarded clothes. 'I can't find it anywhere!' She lowered her voice and frowned as she rooted through the pile of tangled items that she had tossed from her wardrobe. 'Everyone else will be wearing something new. I just want to look nice.'

'I don't have a new outfit,' Grace pointed out. She didn't want Elsie to feel as though she didn't look nice. She decided that she would try to get Elsie to wear the same as her. She loved dressing the same as her twin.

'That's not the point. I have absolutely nothing to wear.'

'Just wear your jeans,' Grace suggested. She was wearing her favourite white jeans that Mags had bought her for Christmas. Elsie had been given a bright pink pair.

Elsie looked at Grace and pretended she was horrified, even though Grace knew she was just trying to be dramatic. Rachel Gregory was turning twelve before anybody else in their year. She looked older than all the other girls, and always had new clothes and hairstyles. Elsie always tried to copy Rachel, and tried to make herself look older as well. Grace could tell that Elsie wished they

40

were twelve now too: that another six months of being eleven was too long for Elsie to bear.

'Jeans are fine for you. But I want to appear as though I have made an effort for this party.'

Grace shrugged and looked at her watch. 'Well, if we're any later, then it won't look like you've made an effort. The party started ten minutes ago.'

Elsie shook her head as though she didn't know what to do any more. She wiped a tear that was sitting on her cheek and beckoned for Grace to join her in their bedroom.

'The consequences of this are going to be catastrophic,' she said, shutting the door behind them.

Once the door was closed, Grace laughed. 'You're so funny, Elsie.'

Elsie tried to look adult, but Grace could tell she was struggling to stay serious. A little smile was trying to break through her sister's lips. It won in the end, and Elsie let out a giggle.

Elsie found her dress eventually. It had been crumpled up in the guest lounge, which, Grace supposed, seemed strange, but she didn't think much of it at the time. She just wanted to get to Rachel's party. She saw her mother frown as they pulled away from the kerb, as though something had gone wrong. A few minutes later, their mother jolted the car to a stop and turned round, staring at them in a way that made Grace wish they were already at the party, safe, and where they were meant to be. Her mother's eyes were wide and scared, and Grace felt a shiver curse down the whole of her body, even though she wasn't cold.

'Grace. Come and sit in the front, please,' her mother said. Even her voice sounded strange, as though she was being strangled.

Elsie obviously hadn't noticed her mother's bizarre stare, because she sighed and said, 'Mum, we've already established that we're late. We haven't got time to start playing silly games.'

But their mother ignored Elsie. 'Grace. Now. Otherwise we're turning around and going home.'

'Okay, okay.' Grace clambered out of the back and sat in the front seat, sneaking a glance at her mother and seeing that she already looked much calmer. It was minutes later, when they had reached Rachel Gregory's wide, pretty street, when a gold car whizzed beside them, and suddenly came closer and closer until there were the horrible sounds of metal on metal and glass on glass, and Elsie screaming.

After the crash, after they had ruined Rachel Gregory's birthday by making it all about them, and after Elsie had been checked over and given a lollipop that she had pretended to be too old for but crunched on anyway, the twins went home.

Elsie slept when they got back to Rose House, and everybody said that it was for the best, to leave her. But Grace couldn't rest without thinking about the crash and how they had ruined Rachel Gregory's party. She was worried about Elsie's arm, which she had seen soggy with burgundy blood. She tried to watch the comedy programme that her mother had put on for her, but she couldn't concentrate. So she wandered into the hall, where the telephone was, and dialled Mags's number.

When Noel answered, he couldn't tell if it was Elsie or Grace.

'It's Grace. I'm glad you answered. I wanted to talk to you.'

She told Noel about the car accident.

'I know,' he said when she'd finished. 'Mum told me. She'll be coming to see your mum soon.'

Grace told Noel that her mother had made her move seats in the car.

'That's strange,' he said.

Grace nodded, then remembered that he couldn't see her. 'Yep,' she replied.

'But you're both okay?'

'Yeah. Elsie's worse than me. I'm worried about her arm. It was bleeding a lot. The people at the hospital said it would be fine.'

'Well, then it will be.'

'What if it scars? We won't be the same as each other anymore.'

'Yes, you will. A scar doesn't change anything. Not really.'

They chatted some more. Noel told Grace that he had a scar on his right knee from when he fell off his bike when he was six. There had been a lot of blood that day, but the scar was only small now. That made Grace feel better. Perhaps she'd ring Noel again soon.

As she was hanging up, Grace saw Elsie edging down the stairs, wincing with every step. Her face was even paler than normal, and her hair, which was normally plaited or twisted into clips or bands, was hanging down like a pair of dusty black curtains. Grace leaped up the stairs and helped Elsie down to the lounge. They switched over from the comedy and watched cartoons together instead, mocking them and pretending to hate them. The light dipped in the room until the television was the only brightness. The twins heard Mags arrive and bustle into the kitchen. There was always a lot of noise when Mags was around.

'I'm going to see Mags,' Elsie said, and disentangled her legs from Grace's before limping out into the hall.

It was after that day, after the few moments that followed, that Elsie changed: hid in her own shadow and refused to come out into the light.

Now, Grace picks up her shampoo from the side of the bath. Cold water drips from the bottle onto her skin, making her flinch. Elsie will be angry about tonight. But she is the one who is choosing not to come. She could be in her own bath right now, getting ready for dinner, wondering which dress to wear, if only she would trust Grace like she used to, before things changed.

Chapter Seven

Louisa, 1965

Tomorrow, Louisa decided, she would go for a walk. She would set off after her father's breakfast, when he was having his morning doze, and she would walk down the hill, to the very bottom. She would call into the shops and buy the things she never bought: fresh flowers, shampoo, and some meat for their dinner. Nancy always bought these things. But tomorrow, Louisa would tell her not to.

And if the morning was taken up with buying fresh flowers and shampoo and meat for dinner, then an afternoon sitting in her brown chair next to her father in his blue chair would seem a little more bearable. All she needed was some exercise, and more purpose, and Louisa would be fine.

The next day, Louisa woke early. The promised fuzzy heat of the day shimmered through her curtains and she wiped a faint line of perspiration from her forehead as she sat up in bed. After a few moments, she remembered that she was going out today and her heart fluttered.

'Dad?' Louisa said quietly as she descended the staircase that she still felt was rather too grand just for her and her father.

There was no reply, only the sickly scent of fried eggs lingering in the hall to confirm her father's presence. She took her coat from the stand next to the front door, lifted it around her shoulders and crept into the piercing May morning.

Louisa meandered as much as she could, but it was her habit to walk quickly, to rush as though she was late. But she wasn't late; she had nowhere to be. That was the problem, she thought as she chose a bunch of wilting roses from the meagre selection on offer at Pilkington's. She stuffed the roses into her basket and continued along the street to Geoffrey and Sons, where she thought she might buy some sausages.

As Louisa stood and stared into the cabinet of pink flesh, she felt a tug on her arm.

'Is that you? Louisa?' Hatty Kennedy, one of Louisa's old school friends, stood beside the counter, some pork chops cradled like a baby in the crook of her arm. She smiled as Louisa turned to face her. 'I thought it was you! And to think I didn't want to come to the butcher's. Such a chore, isn't it?' Hatty rolled her eyes as she gestured towards her pork chops.

'Yes, a chore,' Louisa repeated, feeling herself turn pink with embarrassment at the thought of her excitement about her walk.

'I normally try to get out of coming to the high street, don't you?'

'Oh, yes,' nodded Louisa, feeling the rude tingle of the blush staining her cheeks.

But Hatty didn't seem to notice Louisa's pink cheeks. 'I wouldn't mind shopping so much if there were some interesting things to buy. If there were great big shops with dresses and handbags I'd come every day! But I don't have too much longer to wait until I can buy more exciting things than meat. This time next week, I'll be in Hill's buying all the dresses I want.'

'Hill's? In Blackpool?' Louisa asked, the stench of the raw meat suddenly making her feel quite sick.

'Yes! I'm off to Blackpool! With my parents, worse luck. But they'll leave me to it, I hope. It'll be sunbathing, shopping and dancing. Hopefully I will meet some boys. There are none round here,' Hatty said with a scowl. 'None.'

There was a silence as Louisa scrambled for something to say. But the only thought in her mind, and the only word on her lips, was 'Blackpool.'

'Hey!' Hatty suddenly exclaimed as the silence grew to an uncomfortable length. 'You should come with us! Mum offered to take a friend of mine, but between you and me, I couldn't really think of anybody. Everybody is either already going to Blackpool or staying here to do some silly shorthand course. But you'll come, won't you Lou? We haven't spent any real time together since school! Think what fun we'll have!'

Louisa thought of the week to come. Her stomach lurched, and the smell of meat and blood drifted down around her. 'Yes. I'll come to Blackpool.'

As Louisa said goodbye to Hatty and paid for her sausages, she remembered the last time she had planned to go to Blackpool. Since that day when Dr Barker had brought her here to live with her father, she hadn't been back.

Louisa had planned to return to Blackpool on her fourteenth birthday. Three weeks before her birthday, she had written a list of things to take with her. Two weeks before, she had cracked open the piggy bank that her father had given her and transferred the coins to her new red velvet purse. One week before, Louisa had asked her teacher, Mr Marlowe, how she might best travel to Blackpool. She was going to take her father there as a surprise, she told Mr Marlowe, bits of the lie trickling down her throat like poison and settling heavily in her stomach as she spoke.

The night before her birthday, Louisa counted out her money. There was definitely enough to buy a train ticket for the 9.47 that Mr Marlowe had told her about: her father had been generous during the time that she had been there. When Louisa arrived in Blackpool, she would surely find somebody who remembered her from when she lived there with her mother. Perhaps they would help her to find out what had happened and piece together why her mother might have disappeared. Perhaps she would find out if she really had wandered into the sea, her skirt billowing out with the grey waves. Perhaps she would find out if there was anything her mother had wanted to tell Louisa, something that Louisa had missed.

Perhaps, perhaps, perhaps, Louisa thought as she drifted into sleep.

And then it was morning. Louisa had dressed quickly and stepped out of her bedroom, expecting her father's bedroom door to be firmly shut as it always was early in the morning. But the door was flung wide open, and she heard the clattering of pots and jars coming from the kitchen. Louisa followed the sticky smell of flour and eggs until she was standing in the doorway of the large, upturned kitchen, watching her father whip a grey mixture in a bowl. He looked up, and his face fell in despair.

'Louisa,' he said. 'This was meant to be a surprise. Nobody was meant to see me...'

Louisa had thought how odd it was to see a man holding a spoon. She pictured her father getting out of bed early to make her goodness knows what kind of birthday cake on Nancy's day off. And then she thought of the 9.47 train, and how she would not be getting on it.

That, Louisa recalled now in the bloody air of the butchers, was the day she had decided that Blackpool could wait.

Until now.

'So your father didn't mind you coming along with us, Louisa?' Hatty's mother, Mrs Kennedy, asked the following Monday as their train began to amble along the tracks.

'No. He doesn't really notice whether I'm there or not, these days. So he didn't mind,' Louisa murmured, noticing as she spoke that Mrs Kennedy's face was a shade darker than her neck.

'Ah, Doctor Ash is a busy man. I am sure he does notice you, even if it doesn't *feel* as though he does,' Mrs Kennedy offered, misunderstanding.

She must have known my father some time ago, Louisa thought, *when he was busy and important.* Time seemed to have washed away his importance like a tide. Each day, Louisa would sit with him and talk to him about his life, his house, their happy times together. As dusk fell, he would be shining with the knowledge of his life, but with the morning sun his face and mind would be blank again.

'Yes,' Louisa sighed, not wanting to explain. 'Maybe you're right.'

'So!' Hatty said rather more loudly than she needed to, eyes wide. 'Let's get into the holiday spirit! What do you want to do when we arrive? There's the beach, and it's a gorgeous day so we could sunbathe. Or we could go dancing in the Tower, or we could go to the Pleasure Beach, although we're probably best waiting until tomorrow for that so we have a full day there, or we could...'

Hatty's voice drifted away as Louisa stared out of the train windows into the fields beyond. Had she done the right thing coming on this holiday? Perhaps she should try to get a train back somehow, and explain to the Kennedys the truth about why she had come and why she definitely shouldn't have.

'Louisa? What do you think? I don't feel exposed in it, so I don't see a problem. Sally Smith has a bikini, and she's fatter than me. If she can wear one, then I certainly can.'

Louisa nodded. 'Hatty,' she began, 'I think that I've perhaps made a bit of a mistake. I don't...' Her words stopped abruptly as she thought of what she was speeding away from. She looked at Hatty, who sat waiting patiently for the rest of Louisa's words. 'I don't remember packing my sunglasses,' she finished, embarrassed by the sad little ending to her sentence.

'Well, that's not a problem. I've packed three pairs,' said Hatty.

When the girls were finally settled on the swarming sands, Louisa lay back. She draped her arm lazily over her eyes, having yet to receive an offer of sunglasses from a rather bikini-preoccupied

Hatty. Eventually, the sun managed to glare through the crook of Louisa's arm, and she sat up. Hatty was splashing about in the sea with some boys who were staying at the hotel next door, her headscarf tied carefully over her rollers and her new bikini showing off her lean legs and flat stomach. Louisa glanced down at her own stomach, and pulled it in, suddenly self-conscious, then looked away again, not wanting to dwell on her old-fashioned bathing costume.

I can't believe I'm here, she thought, as she drank in the sights of the beach and the promenade. The last time she had smelled salt and skin and sun had been so long ago. Those smells had belonged to her old life, and had been replaced by the meaty, heavier smells of soup and wood fires and her father's cologne, and later, his sweet medicines.

Smelling her old life reminded Louisa that it hadn't left her. She had left it. Hadn't she? After her failed plans to return to Blackpool three years ago, the idea that her mother might be dead lay untouched in a shaded corner of Louisa's mind. The thought was sharp and Louisa never took it out to inspect, for fear of the pain of handling it. Her father never mentioned her anymore; he never mentioned anything. But now, here, with the thought of what was about to happen to her father trapped in her mind too, Louisa's mother seemed to float out, freed with the evocative sights and sounds of the sea.

Louisa scoured the beach for anybody who might look like her mother would now. But after a few minutes of gazing into the crowds, of seeing horribly stiff hairstyles and velvet lapels and wide smiles and sultry frowns, Louisa covered her eyes with her sand-dotted palms. It was too much. Her mother wasn't here. She wasn't anywhere. All because Louisa had been too late to save her.

'Lou! Lou!' Hatty shouted, her dampened scent of hairspray preceding her grip on Louisa's arm. 'What's the matter with you?'

Louisa allowed her hands to be peeled from her face. 'Nothing. Nothing's the matter.'

'Then why on earth are you sitting there like that? Join in the fun for heaven's sake! I didn't bring you on holiday to mope. Now,' Hatty continued, her tone changing promptly and effortlessly, 'what do you want from the van over there? There's tea, or ice cream, or oysters, but my friend Anita came to Blackpool last summer and got some oysters and she had the most terrible stomach problems for months after. She puts it all down to those oysters, you know, and she said that she bought them from a little blue van. So with that van being blue, I think we'll give the oysters a miss. What do you think?'

Louisa looked over at the blue van, a snake of people queuing right into its mouth. 'Ice cream,' she said, trying to cram as much joy into those two words as she possibly could. She winced as she heard her voice: too high-pitched, too false. But Hatty didn't seem to care. She gave a firm, single nod, and stood up.

'You know,' she said, as she brushed flecks of sand from her golden thighs, 'I think we should find ourselves some men tonight.'

'Yes,' Louisa agreed, her merry tone much improved second time around, 'I think you're right.'

Later, when Hatty had carefully backcombed her hair and applied plenty of eyeliner on herself and Louisa, they followed Mr and Mrs Kennedy down to the hotel bar. The Fortuna was a very grand hotel, Louisa thought as she descended the rather regal staircase. She wished she had on a long, sweeping dress rather than her short blue dress, a dress that she could swoosh along the red carpet.

'Mother,' Hatty was grumbling as they reached the bar, 'I don't see the harm in just one drink. After all, we're eighteen on our next birthdays.' She turned and rolled her eyes at Louisa.

Mrs Kennedy fiddled about with the clasp on her cream leather handbag. 'Okay, darling.'

Hatty squeezed Louisa's arm excitedly. 'Knew she wouldn't put up a fight,' she hissed in Louisa's ear.

And so, one drink turned into two drinks. Two drinks gave

Hatty the courage to ask her parents if she and Louisa could leave the hotel bar and go to Yates's, and gave Mr and Mrs Kennedy the courage to say yes.

Louisa and Hatty stumbled along the promenade, the summer wind fresh on their faces. Louisa licked her lips and tasted salt, sand and loss.

Yates's was just as Louisa had imagined it would be when she had stared up at it as a little girl. It was smoky, hazy and hot. Hatty bought them a glass of wine each, but the woman behind the bar misheard the order for two glasses of white wine and slopped two glasses of deep purple wine down in front of them. It tasted of wood and winter, not summers on the beach, and it burned Louisa's throat as she swallowed. But after their first glass, they found they had a taste for it. So when a tall, rather hairy man wandered over to them and offered to buy them a drink, they asked for more of the same. Louisa stared at the man as he queued at the bar, waiting to be served. His shirt was unbuttoned at the top and his chest looked almost as though it wanted to leap out of his clothes. Hair sprouted from his chest, his neck, his face and his head. Later, when he stroked Louisa's cheek and smiled at her, she noticed that he had hair on his fingers too.

'What's your name?' Louisa asked the man, over the hum of voices and laughter and music.

'Nicky. Yours?'

Hatty cleared her throat and leaned forward, stubbing out her cigarette. 'Never mind that. I think we'd better be getting back.'

'I don't want to get back,' Louisa frowned. 'What is there to get back *for*?' She liked how philosophical this sounded, and laughed. Nicky smiled appreciatively.

'My parents. They'll kill me if we're much later.'

Louisa groaned as Hatty stood up.

'Tell you what,' Nicky said in Louisa's ear, his yeasty scent floating around her as he spoke, 'I'll meet you under Central Pier in a bit.'

It was this thought that kept Louisa going as she stood up

and the room lurched towards her, as Hatty dragged her back to the hotel, as there was a knock at the door of their shared room.

'Yes?' Hatty asked as she opened the door, her eyes wide at the unexpected drama of somebody visiting them in their hotel room. Louisa couldn't see past the door, but knew exactly what news was going to come from behind it.

'Yes, yes, she's in here,' Hatty said. 'Hold on. It's the manager. He's asking for you,' she said to Louisa, frowning in confusion.

Louisa clambered over the bed to receive the news that she was waiting for, the words that she knew would be spoken at this precise time, whether she was at home or in Blackpool, or drunk or sober.

'Miss Ash? I'm afraid to say that I have some rather bad news for you. It's your father,' said the manager. 'We've had a telephone call from your maid. I'm very sorry to tell you that he's passed away.'

Louisa said very little and focused on not vomiting on Hatty's unmade bed, on the jumble of clothes and bikinis and make-up. She thanked the manager, and then swung the door of Room 35 shut abruptly. The click as it closed seemed to mark the change in direction of Louisa's life.

'My father is dead,' she said simply. 'I'm going for a walk.'

Hatty wailed. 'Oh Louisa! I'm so sorry!' She fumbled in her bag for the room key. 'I must come with you. Or do you want me to wake up my parents?'

'No. Please. Just let me walk,' Louisa said, and left the room.

At first, Nicky was more gentle than Louisa had expected him to be. He stroked her cheek again, and then he kissed her forehead. Louisa thought how strange this was, and remembered her mother kissing her forehead before bedtime. Nicky kissed her cheek next, and his fingers moved to her thigh. The sand beneath them was cool and uncomfortable: it seemed less welcoming than it had done during the day. She wondered what she should do with her hands, so decided to run them through Nicky's hair, like she had seen in the film at the cinema last year. Nicky didn't seem to like this. He swatted her hand away as though he was angry. Then he began tugging at her dress and all of a sudden Louisa remembered her father and wanted to cry. She pushed against Nicky with all her weight, but he just grunted and forced her back into the sand. The grains prickled into her like glass.

'My father's just died!' Louisa shouted after a minute of grunting and pushing. 'Please get off me! I feel sick, and I—'

Nicky straightened up for a moment and knelt above her. He looked as though he was about to say something, and Louisa felt relief flooding through her, mixing with the wine and sadness already coursing through her blood. But then Nicky lurched towards her again, even more fiercely this time. Louisa heard her dress rip and felt Nicky's hands grip and burn her waist, and then she felt another pair of hands on her, gentler ones, and she saw Mr Kennedy above her and Hatty's pale face floating somewhere behind him.

Chapter Eight

Louisa, 1965

The next day, as Hatty and Louisa waited in the reception of The Fortuna Hotel while Mr Kennedy checked them all out two days early, Hatty patted Louisa's hand.

'I'm so glad that I brought my dad with me to look for you last night. I had a feeling you'd run into that awful man. I'm just glad that we caught him before he...' The sentence skulked away, its content apparently unsuitable for the finery of the hotel's foyer. 'I know you'd had a terrible shock, Louisa, and so I don't blame you for doing something silly. But the thing is, you were quite taken with that man before you'd even found out about your poor father, and it was clear that he was bad news. We were all lucky that nothing worse happened to you last night under that pier. You need to be more careful.' Hatty saw that her father had finished at the reception desk and was heading towards the girls, so quickly wrapped up what she was saying. 'You won't always be lucky enough to have somebody to rescue you.'

Louisa thought of how Dr Barker had rescued her years ago, thought of her father, thought of Mr Kennedy's gentle grip last night. She looked up from the red swirling carpet, at Hatty's smooth clean skin and her sleek hair and neat black eyeliner.

The thing about being lucky enough to always have someone to rescue you, she thought, *is being unlucky enough to always need rescuing in the first place.*

It was as they were waiting for the train back home that Louisa saw her.

She had soft brown hair that hung down over her face, and a rounded jaw just like her mother's. She stood alone in the midst of all the shrieking groups and families and couples. She held a fashionable rounded suitcase in her hand and her dress was bright, almost garish. She looked, Louisa realised with a creeping nausea, just like her mother would do now. Louisa banged her suitcase down on the platform and raced over to the woman, hearing vague calls from Hatty as she did so. The woman didn't notice Louisa charging towards her. She stared down the empty platform, lost in her own world: a world that Louisa was certain she had once shared.

As Louisa reached the woman, she slowed down. She tried to stretch out that last glorious moment when anything was still possible for as long as she could by sidling up to her mother gradually. But closer, Louisa could see that she had been mistaken: that the woman's hair was not soft, but hung in waves that would be sticky to the touch. As she moved closer still, she could smell a dark, exotic perfume. It wasn't unpleasant. But was it how Louisa had imagined her mother would smell now?

Oh, how Louisa had imagined.

The woman turned, then, and the heavy scent wafted over Louisa, drenching her aching body. All at once, as nausea swept over her and the woman gave her a cool, unknowing glance, Louisa knew: it was not her. With sudden ferocity, the certainty that her mother was dead crashed over Louisa, and all the hot, sharp pain that she had tried to lock away for so many years engulfed her, burning and pinching her whole body. She began to sob: huge, heaving sobs that were too big for her lungs and choked her, twisting air out of her chest and making her shake.

'Louisa,' Hatty appeared then, grasping at Louisa's elbow gently. 'What are you doing? Our train will be here any minute.'

'I don't want to leave,' Louisa wept.

Hatty took a deep breath, a breath which seemed to say *I've been expecting this.* 'Darling, I know that the idea of going home must seem a little overwhelming. I know how close you were to your father. But there is so much to sort out, and we're all going to help you. Once the funeral is over, perhaps we could return to Blackpool, if that's what you'd like.'

'But I need to find out what happened to my mother,' Louisa said, noticing that she was crying. How long had she been crying for? She couldn't remember.

Hatty's pretty face crumpled into a frown. 'Your mother?'

'Yes. My mother. I lived here in Blackpool with her, before I knew you. She disappeared.'

Hatty's features blurred with confusion. 'Louisa, I don't understand. You've never mentioned living in Blackpool before. I thought that your mother was...well, I thought she was dead,' Hatty finished in a whisper. 'I'm worried that you're confused,' she said finally, her face suddenly snapping back to perfection. She steered Louisa towards Mr and Mrs Kennedy and spoke conspiratorially into their ears. They looked at Louisa with inclined heads and matching frowns.

'You all think I'm mad, don't you?' Louisa wailed. 'Well, I'm not! My mother disappeared, and I want to know why, and so I need to find the boy with the purple eyes! I know you don't believe me, and that you think I'm shocked by my father's death, but the truth is that I knew he'd die, I could see it all in my mind before it happened, and that's why I came here with you. I knew he'd die after eating his fish supper last night, and I know that the plate he had his fish on will still be in the kitchen stinking the house out when I get home because the maid's gone now that he has, and I knew that I'd get a visit from the hotel manager, and that I would be wearing my blue dress with the white belt. I knew it all!'

'Let's get you home, Louisa,' Mrs Kennedy said. 'Here comes the train, see, and we all have a ticket to get on it. Perhaps you could have a little nap when we are settled, and then before you know it—'

'You're treating me like a child!' Louisa screamed.

The station stopped. The people stared, their conversations frozen by the hysterical teenager and the possibility of one last Blackpool spectacle before the dreary trip home. Well, Louisa wouldn't give it to them.

'I'm sorry,' she said quietly.

Mrs Kennedy, her face flushed by the slap of Louisa's outburst, nodded silently, gesturing for Louisa to step a little closer to the platform; a little further away from her.

And so Louisa didn't remain in Blackpool that day. She returned to the house on the hill, now hers, and dealt with papers and letters and stiff visits from people her father had known, and finally it was time for his funeral.

The first time Louisa met her father, his face was grey and his hands were grey and his life was grey. But slowly, as Louisa grew and ate side by side with him and walked with him and chattered to him about colours and stories and painted him pictures and asked him questions, he began to have more colour. His cheeks became pink with lively conversation, his hands brown from walking in the sun, and his life coloured in.

Now, as Louisa stood before his imposing coffin, and looked down at his sunken cheeks and that Roman nose she knew so well, and those kind eyes closed in final resignation, she noticed that her father was grey once again.

Things had come full circle.

PART TWO

Chapter Nine

Rose, 1921

The last heat of the summer had made the train to Blackpool smell of other people's sweat. Rose could still smell it when they stepped out of the carriage onto the swarming platform. She looked up at the sharp blue sky, wondering if the whole holiday would smell brown and dirty, until her worries were melted away by what she saw.

Past people's hats, past people's faces that were blurred from Rose's jerky movements through the crowds, and up, up in the sky, was the place she had wanted to see for all of her eleven years. It was just as wonderful as the picture her father had shown her: Blackpool Tower stared down at Rose proudly, calm amongst the hullabaloo of the station.

Rose, who had only ever been to Scarborough on her holidays, stared up at the Tower all the way to their hotel. She didn't look at anything else. She tripped over twice and was scolded by her mother four times for not watching where she was going. But she didn't care. It would take something very, very special for Rose to want to look anywhere except way up above her, to the tangle of iron crisscrosses that stretched high, high up into the sky, to the beautiful peak that floated in the clouds.

It wasn't until the middle of her holiday that something very special took Rose's mind and eyes from Blackpool Tower.

Rose and her parents had been walking along the promenade, from the north to the south, for what felt like a very long time. Rose kept glancing backwards to look into the sky, and every time she did, Blackpool Tower bore down upon her. The crowds of people moved slowly along the promenade, for everybody was gazing at something: the endless roaring sea, or the sands crammed with families, or the fairground rides that soared round and round. The walk to the Pleasure Beach was taking so long that when Rose's mother spotted a space on a bench, she pulled Rose and her father over to it so that they could all rest their aching legs.

They had been sitting on the bench, the early September sun blazing down on them, for only a few minutes before Rose's father spotted a friend of his walking by. Rose's father jumped up and patted his friend heartily on the shoulder as they exclaimed about the chances of spotting each other away on holiday, and Rose's mother smiled politely at the man's wife, who wore a fancy yellow hat.

As her parents stood and laughed about things Rose didn't understand, she stared up at the Tower some more. When the sun began to make tiny white dots on her eyes, and her neck became sore, she dropped her gaze and looked along the colourful promenade that was shining with people. She looked at the green trams and the stalls selling salty seafood. She looked up towards The Pleasure Beach, at the row of hotels opposite a man holding some donkeys, and it was there that she spotted the door.

A tiny handwritten sign above it made every little hair on Rose's body stand on end in excitement.

Gypsy Sarah. Fortunes Told Here.

Rose knew that her mother would scold and her father would frown if she moved from her spot on the bench, but something inside Rose made her stand and wander over to the door. The door was blue, which was Rose's third favourite colour. Rose pushed at it, wanting to know what was behind it so much that her insides seemed to quiver a little as it gave way.

Colours and shapes that Rose had never seen before in her quiet Yorkshire life dangled and jingled behind that door. And amongst all the purples and pinks and golds and crystals and gems sat the oldest woman Rose had ever seen.

Gypsy Sarah's crinkled face puckered as she saw Rose hovering in the doorway.

'Are you here for a reading?' she whispered, gesturing to Rose with a hand that looked as though it was made of the brown paper Rose's dresses were sometimes wrapped in when they were new.

Rose tore her gaze away from Gypsy Sarah, and turned to see her mother and father still deep in conversation with the people near the bench. She could quite possibly have her fortune told before her parents even noticed that she'd gone.

She turned back to the room. 'Yes, please,' she answered quietly, her words flying out amongst the exotic colours.

Rose knew little about fortune tellers: she knew little about anything. She did not expect her life's story to be told, or for Gypsy Sarah to smell of a strange combination of burning wood and lavender and raw meat, or for her hands to be grabbed and squeezed, or for Gypsy Sarah to cry out in a scratchy voice:

'You must find the boy with purple eyes, for he will give you your life! He will give you a gift!'

'A gift?' Rose asked, intrigued and wide-eyed.

A gift, Rose thought as she carefully placed every coin of her holiday pocket money into Gypsy Sarah's quivering hand, as she shuffled out of the shadows of the room and blinked in the bright sunlight, as she sneaked back to her place on the bench and sat as though she had never moved while her parents continued to talk to their friends, as she slept by the side of her snoring mother and father in Room 35 at The Fortuna Hotel.

Puppies and hair ribbons and books and dolls filled Rose's mind each time she thought of Gypsy Sarah and the boy with the purple eyes. For what else, to an eleven-year-old girl, could a gift mean?

Rose thought of the boy with the purple eyes as she was swept along the crammed promenade, as she ran her hands through the gritty beige sand on the beach, as she sat up straight in the hotel restaurant. She looked into the eyes of the boy who helped the man holding the donkeys, of the boy selling oysters in the little white hut, of the boy who was staying in the room next door at The Fortuna Hotel. But she saw no purple eyes.

On Saturday, Rose bathed in the sea as her parents snoozed on the sand. She paddled at the water's edge for some time, and then walked out until the water reached her shoulders. Although Rose wasn't a very good swimmer, she managed to propel herself a little by kicking her legs haphazardly and waving her arms against the cool waves. The water was calm and lulled her gently out to sea. The swarms of people bathing and splashing and shouting became more diluted as Rose moved away from the water's edge. The silver water blurred around her.

And then, everything shot into a burst of magnificent colour.

He was swimming towards her, shooting through the water like a fish. His eyes were not the purple that Rose had imagined. They weren't a pale, striking lilac as she had thought they would be, but a deep, velvet violet. When he smiled at Rose, she began to tremble and lost her momentum beneath the water. She fumbled, her legs kicking wildly, bitter salt flying into her mouth and making her want to spit and cry out.

'Well! What's the matter with you?' the boy giggled, treading water expertly. His voice was a twinkling bell, light with laughter.

Rose frowned. 'Nothing's the matter, you just frightened me.'

The boy held out his hand, which was brown, and shiny with water. Rose took it, and they moved towards the shore. She continued to kick and the boy pulled her along, so that she moved almost gracefully through the waves.

'What's your name?' the boy asked as they felt sculpted sand appear beneath their feet.

'Rose. What's yours?'

The boy laughed again, his dark face screwing up in pleasure. 'I'm not going to tell you.' He stuck out his tongue, then smiled. His teeth, although crooked, looked white against his skin. He rubbed his black hair from his face as they walked away from the water.

Rose stiffened, and wished that she hadn't told the boy her name. She felt hard little goosebumps prickle her skin as the sea breeze washed over her, and wondered again what her gift from him might be.

'What are you doing tomorrow afternoon, Rose? I have something exciting planned,' the boy said, wiping his nose with his hand and leaving behind a streak of water on his cheek.

'I'm—' Rose squinted over to where her parents lay on the sand. Tomorrow was their last day: their train home was at 6.30 tomorrow evening. She thought about how long and bleak the day would seem, knowing that it was their last. 'I'm not doing anything, really. But we have a train home to catch tomorrow evening, so my parents might want me to stay with them all day.'

'Stay with them all day? But you're not a baby,' the boy, who didn't look much older than Rose, said.

Rose puffed out her shiny wet chest. 'No, I'm not. What have you got planned?'

The boy shrugged and moved closer to Rose conspiratorially. 'I'm going to sneak into the Pavilion. You should come.'

'On the North Pier? But won't it be closed in the afternoon?'

'Yes, that's why I have to sneak in. If I manage it, we'll have it to ourselves.'

Rose frowned as she thought about this strange boy's plan. She had watched a concert in the Indian Pavilion on the North Pier a few nights before with her parents. It was a beautiful, exotic hall full of blue and green and red decorations that reminded Rose of other worlds, ones she would probably never even see. The Pavilion had been filled with people and perfume and hats and music when

Rose had visited. She imagined being there when it was still and quiet, and a delicious shiver coursed through her body.

'I'll come. Where shall I meet you?'

The boy leapt with joy, high into the air, and Rose smiled, glad that she had made him happy.

'I'll meet you on the pier at 4 o'clock. Outside the sweet kiosk. We'll take some fudge in with us.'

Rose nodded, wondering what she could tell her parents, and thinking that she had perhaps made a terrible mistake, but before she could change her mind, the boy with the purple eyes had shot off through the crowds.

At 3.30 on Sunday, Rose's mother was folding clothes very carefully back into the suitcase, and Rose's father was sitting in the hotel lounge reading his newspaper. Rose sat on the bed, swinging her legs forwards and backwards. She stood up, then sat down again. The boy with the purple eyes would be expecting her soon. Rose didn't want to let him down, and she didn't want to get the train back home to Yorkshire's black streets without her gift.

'Mummy?' she said after a little while, her legs kicking furiously against the bed. She had practised her speech in her head over a hundred times in bed last night, but now that she had to say it, she didn't feel very confident.

'Yes, Rose?' her mother replied, as she held up a stained blouse to the light and shook her head.

'I made a friend yesterday. And I'd like to see him again before we leave. He has something for me.'

'I see. I wonder if this is vinegar?' Rose's mother lay the blouse on the bed and scratched at the stain gently with her rounded fingernail. 'I don't remember spilling anything.'

'So, can I visit my friend?'

Rose's mother turned, distracted from the blouse for a moment. 'He's staying here, is he?'

'I'm not sure.' Rose remembered the boy's tough skin and long hair, and doubted that he was staying anywhere like The Fortuna.

'Ah!' her mother said, her eyes suddenly becoming wide. 'I remember! It's a wine stain! My glass was a little too full and I spilt some. Well, that should wash out without too much of a problem.'

'Mummy?'

'Well, that is a relief. This was new for the holiday. Yes, Rose?'

'Can I go and see him? Quickly?'

Rose's mother folded the blouse, and placed it in the case. 'Yes, yes. But be quick.'

Rose sped out of the huge front of the Fortuna Hotel, clattering down the wide steps and tearing along the promenade towards the North Pier. She wound in and out of jostling bodies, past the refreshment rooms and the portrait studios. When she reached the end of the pier, she saw the pink and blue sign hanging above Seaton's sweet kiosk. There were two girls who looked about Rose's age waiting to be served, and Rose hung back, feeling as though she didn't want anybody to see her. She watched the girls take their paper bags from the man in the stall, and then looked around her. Everybody seemed to be in a group, bouncing from one person to the next, and Rose suddenly felt very alone.

And then, past Seaton's sweet kiosk, past the ticket kiosk and next to the closed doors of the Indian Pavilion, Rose saw the boy, his face a shadow amongst the bright, swirling colours of the pier. He smiled and beckoned her, and although there was a flurry of noise around her, Rose's world fell into a blurry, underwater silence.

As Rose moved nearer towards the boy, she noticed that he was holding a small, glistening box. Could this be her gift? Her heart fluttering with all kinds of ideas about what a small silver box could contain, she broke into a run. When she reached the boy, she was breathless and laughing, although she didn't quite know what she was laughing at.

The boy didn't speak to her. He took out of his pocket an odd, gold key, and without looking like he was doing anything he shouldn't, unlocked the grand, high door of the Indian Pavilion.

Rose stared at the boy, wondering how he looked so confident when he was doing something he wasn't allowed to. Rose knew that she would have dropped the key and been caught red-faced straight away. The boy turned to her and grabbed her arm.

'Quickly!' he hissed, and they tumbled into the giant room, the door blowing shut behind them with a bang.

The Pavilion looked different in the daytime. Although Rose had thought it beautiful when she had visited the other night, the crowd of people and roar of the orchestra had hidden much of the extravagant decoration. It was even grander than the Winter Gardens. Rose lay back and rested on her elbows so that she could stare up at the huge glass skylight that ran along the centre of the roof. She could make out gulls circling ahead of them, their grey wings bouncing on the blustering winds.

'You know, I am going to live somewhere like this one day,' the boy announced, making Rose sit up and look at him.

'It's true,' he said, seeing Rose's doubtful expression. 'It's meant to look like an Indian temple. And I have Indian blood.'

'You can't be all the way from India,' Rose said, wrinkling her nose in confusion.

'Well, my grandfather was. I could be an Indian King for all we know. And one day, I'm going to travel there, and I'm going to find out. And my palace will look just like this.'

'Can I come and visit?' Rose asked.

The boy shrugged as though he didn't care either way, and Rose wondered, not for the first time, if she had found the right boy after all. He flicked open his silver box, but before Rose's heart could begin fluttering again at a possible gift, he picked out a drooping cigarette and lit it with a matchstick.

'What on earth are you doing?' Rose said, suddenly feeling very much like her mother.

The boy stared at her with his violet eyes, smoke floating out of his mouth and curling around Rose's face. The smell was heavy and almost pleasant in a way, and Rose took in deep breaths until her head was filled with grey, making her cough delicately into her powder blue sleeve.

I don't think you're allowed to smoke in here, Rose was going to say. But something stopped her. Not the fact that the boy might be an Indian King, or the fact that Gypsy Sarah had told Rose to find him, but because Rose wanted this moment to last. She wanted to be in the Indian Pavilion in Blackpool with smoke curling around her ears and weaving through her hair and her mouth, with the boy and not with her parents. She felt as though she had left a grey world behind and had stepped into a world of power and movement and colour, and she didn't want to leave it. Not just yet.

And so they sat, with the colours of India all around them, yellowed and hazy with smoke.

After a time of sitting, the boy jumped to his feet, tossing his cigarette end away. 'They'll be coming in to set up for tonight's concert soon. You'd better go. I'll lock up again.'

They walked to the doors of the Pavilion and Rose looked out to the sea which was glinting with the dipping sun, and then back at the boy.

'You can come and visit me, if you like,' he said after a few seconds. 'When I'm King.'

Rose smiled at the boy. 'Goodbye.'

She skipped a little as she headed back to the north of the pier. She liked the idea of seeing the boy again, in a land as exotic as the Pavilion. She pulled her collar up to her nostrils and inhaled the smell of cigarette smoke, smiling as she did so. She surely hadn't been with the boy for too long. She would be able to get back to the hotel in plenty of time for the train home.

But as Rose neared the end of the pier, she saw that the swarm of people in front of her had swelled. There were screeches and wails floating out from the crowd, and Rose felt a prick of fright at trying to find a path through it. People were gesturing, clambering over one another. They all seemed to be looking past Rose, behind her.

She turned, and what she saw in that moment haunted her forever.

The end of the pier was a terrifying orange. Flames roared up into the sky, shooting higher and higher with each second. The dark smell of burning wood was suddenly thick in the air.

'The Pavilion!' she heard someone wail.

At that moment, a burst of sparks flew from the pier and shattered the sky into fragments.

'Good thing the Pavilion is empty,' the man next to Rose murmured.

And suddenly, Rose was running towards the pier, snaking through the gasping crowd, the flames pulling her like a magnet. She thought of nothing but his purple eyes as she moved closer and closer towards the rumbling pavilion. The crowds trickled to nobody but two pier officials, who launched buckets of water towards the flames in panic. They didn't see Rose: didn't see her pause for half a second for fear of being eaten by the flames; didn't see her sneak down the side of the crackling wooden sweet kiosk. They didn't see her pull a boy underneath the tangled iron of the pier, into the safety of the sea. Everybody watched the frightening, flashing sky, mesmerised by the cloud of black smoke dancing above their heads.

The water tasted black, and Rose struggled to swim and clutch the boy's bony body at the same time. He seemed to be dozing, his eyes half closed in a sort of dream. Rose tried to shout, but the sound of her voice was washed away with the waves. She pounded her legs against the heavy water, trying to move away from the splitting pier. Shards of glowing wood floated around her and slices of fire hurtled beside them.

She pounded, and moved, slowly, slowly, until the boy's eyes began to open.

'Swim!' Rose shouted as his eyelids flickered. 'Swim!'

And soon, his weight became lighter, as he began to move

beside Rose in the littered waves. The tide was working with them and carried them towards the shore. Rose felt her legs give way as they reached the sand, and she felt herself retching, her body forcing black water from her stomach out onto the sand. She felt his arm around her and his smoky breath next to her face as they lay together. Still, nobody saw them, nobody noticed their entwined bodies, for everybody was staring up at the flashing sky.

'My train,' Rose moaned, and tried to shuffle herself up on the sand. She lifted her hand to her hair, which was slick and cold. 'My parents,' she said next.

'I'll come with you. I'll tell them what you did for me,' said the boy.

Rose looked at the boy, who, even after almost drowning in water, was still filthy. She looked at his nest of knotted black hair and his jutting collarbone and his clever smile.

'No. You mustn't do that. They wouldn't like you.' She stumbled to her feet, which squelched beneath her like two jellies. 'I have to go.'

The boy lay on the sand and stared up at her. 'Come back to me one day, won't you.'

Rose smiled and thought that she might love him. 'Of course I will.'

She climbed the stone steps up onto the promenade and made her way through the sighing crowds.

It was only after she had told her parents that she had gone in the sea to rescue a little girl's dog, after she had joined them in the dash to the train station, after she had flopped down on her seat on the train in a dry lemon-yellow dress, that Rose remembered.

She remembered as their train huffed through the damp green countryside, over steep hills and past glassy lakes.

She still didn't have her gift.

Chapter Ten

Grace, 2008

Eliot is late picking Grace up.

'I wasn't ready anyway,' Grace waves Eliot's apology away with her hand, bracelets twinkling and jangling with the movement.

'Did you book a table?'

'No, but it'll be quiet, it's a weeknight.'

Eliot shrugs. 'Okay.'

They walk from Grace's flat into Lytham square. The grand, tree-lined houses they walk beside gradually give way to small, independent shops, much like the one Grace and Elsie have just opened. Towards the square, the gold light spilling from the restaurants and wine bars twinkles with the movement of people.

When Grace and Eliot arrive at the new tapas restaurant, a troubled middle-aged waiter with a faint smear of sweat on his forehead greets them at the door. 'Name?'

'Oh, we didn't book. Do you have a table for two?' Grace asks.

'You didn't book? Not a chance. We've got an opening special, and it's gone down a storm. You'll be waiting hours,' the waiter sneers, apparently cheered a little by his bad news. 'Should've booked,' he smirks, as Grace and Eliot turn to shuffle out of the door.

'Sorry. I didn't think. Shall we go somewhere else for a few drinks and see if they have room for us in a bit?' Grace suggests.

'Can do. Look, Grace, I feel guilty about not having Elsie with us. She's my girlfriend...your sister. She should be here with us.'

Grace looks down to the cobbles, feeling sick. 'You're right. Phone her.'

As Eliot wanders away, shoes crunching on the ground, phone to his ear, Grace wonders what it would have been like if she had told Elsie the truth in the first place. If she had told Elsie her secret, then Eliot wouldn't be phoning Elsie now. Grace wouldn't be wearing a heavy necklace of resentment around her neck. And Elsie, most probably, would have met someone else.

But then, Grace reminds herself, Elsie would never have forgiven her. That's why she could never tell her.

'She's not coming,' Eliot says abruptly as he walks back towards Grace. 'She's still angry.'

Grace sighs. 'Come on. Let's get a drink.'

As they queue at the bar, jostled by people who are ordering pints, Grace remembers when she first met Eliot.

'Shakespeare is a genius,' Eliot had been insisting in the student union. A few of Grace's friends from her English degree were having drinks there, and Eliot, who was studying some English modules as part of his Drama course, had joined them. 'Imagine writing something now that people still care about and can still relate to hundreds of years in the future!'

'But his writing doesn't make any sense!' Grace had cried before swigging from her alcopop bottle. Elsie was working on a presentation with a group of people from her course that night so wasn't there. Grace had been tense to start with; it felt strange to be without her twin. Since they had started at university, they had been inseparable. They had chosen mostly the same modules, and at every social event, Elsie sat next to Grace, a silent observer. For the first half hour of the evening, Grace had found herself turning to her side on more than one occasion to try to bring her sister into the conversation, surprised to see an empty seat. But now, feeling light-headed from her Bacardi Breezers, and in the full swing of conversation, she realised with a sticky sensation of guilt that she was enjoying being alone with these people.

'Of course it makes sense. Love, death, murder, friendship! What more is there?'

It was as Eliot threw out these words, carelessly as though he had better things to do, that Grace's head had suddenly split with pain and an image of a wedding had flown into her mind. It was her own wedding. People threw confetti that was carried away by the wind. Grace wore a heavy wedding dress with lace daisies stitched onto the sleeves. And Eliot stood by her side, wearing a suit, his hair a little longer, his stubbled jaw a little wider.

Grace had paused, her heart shuddering. She had her mother's gift to see into the future. This was a vision. Although it was the first premonition Grace had ever had, she knew exactly what it was, and she knew exactly what it meant.

'I bet Shakespeare didn't even write half of the plays he is famous for,' Grace said, after taking a few minutes to pull herself together. Her heart hadn't slowed yet, and she placed a hand on her chest to try and steady it.

Eliot threw his head back and laughed: a deep, throaty laugh that somehow managed to imply that he was sure of himself, affluent and popular.

'I can't believe you're throwing that in! Nobody has ever proved that theory. Everybody knows it's a load of bollocks.'

Grace shrugged, feeling a little fluttery and nervous, like a moth trapped under a glass.

'I'm not going to defend the theory, because I haven't done my research. Yet,' she smirked. 'But when I have, I'll be in touch.'

The group of friends she was with went to a house party after that. Grace went with them and drank primary-coloured strong drinks that she hadn't even known to exist before that night. She saw Eliot a couple of times. Once, in the kitchen, she dared herself to go up to him and kiss his cheek. She edged towards him slowly, through shards of conversation and a net of cigarette smoke. She caught his eye. He had green eyes, like a cat. She smiled. He smiled back, his face fractured by people moving around in front of him. Somebody called his name. He turned. And the moment was gone.

So that was all Eliot was for now. A new friend.

But Grace knew that he was meant to be so much more.

'I'm not even hungry anymore,' Grace announces now, as Eliot tips the last of their second bottle of wine into her glass. 'I think we should go into town.'

'Now?' Eliot looks at his watch. It's not a nice watch. It has an ugly tan-brown leather strap which is fraying around the buckle. 'It's nearly ten o'clock.'

'Oh, come on! That's a ridiculously boring thing to say and you know it.' Grace snaps her clutch bag shut and stands. The bar they have come to has settled and is dotted with full, tired people who all seem to be having quiet after-dinner drinks. 'I want to go somewhere a bit more lively. I haven't been out in Blackpool for ages. It'll be fun, and you're coming with me, and I won't take no for an answer.' Grace clamps her hand over Eliot's arm and leads him out into the freezing night.

'Okay, okay, you win,' Eliot laughs as Grace flags down a taxi with steely determination, and clambers in next to her.

'Let's go to The Coaches,' Grace says. 'Do they still do amazing cocktails there?' she asks the taxi driver.

The driver mumbles in response, suggesting that he isn't interested in any kind of small talk, or cocktails. Grace finds his hostility surprisingly amusing and giggles quietly into her clenched fist, her head warm and hazy with wine.

When they arrive at the pub, Eliot tosses a note into the taxi driver's lap. 'Keep the change,' he says casually.

'That's one of the things I really liked about you when I first met you,' Grace says as they push open the heavy, clouded glass doors to the bar.

'What?'

'I thought you were generous. You bought me a drink at the student union bar. And I have liked you ever since,' she laughs as she says this. As soon as the words leave her lips, they seem naked, embarrassing. She bites back all the other words that she wants to say: all the other things she is thinking, she leaves lurking in the darkness of her mind.

'What are you drinking? A cocktail?' Eliot asks.

'Oh, I'm not sure. It doesn't seem the same in here as it used to be,' Grace replies, looking around at the tired bar. 'It's probably changed owners or something. I'll have wine.'

They drink at the bar, jostled by people who slosh more of their beer onto the bar and the already filthy carpet with each minute. As Grace drinks her sweet, yellow wine, the jostling becomes pleasantly familiar, like the lapping of waves against her skin. The music thumps down on them like rain. Grace sets her glass on the bar and turns to make her way to a bit of sticky linoleum which appears to be the dance floor. As she gestures for Eliot to join her, she feels something brush against her hand and sees her glass suddenly tumble to the floor. It shatters around her feet. She takes a tentative step forwards and feels her heel crunch against the glass. Shards stick to the sole of her shoe with a glue of spilled drinks and make her topple slightly as she walks.

'I want to go on the beach,' she says to Eliot suddenly.

Eliot's face breaks into a wide grin. His teeth are pointed and narrow and his smile somehow gives him a look of intelligence. 'You're so spontaneous, Grace. I can't keep up with you.'

Grace tuts impatiently. 'So, do you want to come with me?'

'Do I have a choice?' Eliot smiles.

'No,' Grace replies as she drags Eliot out into the freezing night.

'It's too cold to be walking on the beach.'

'It's always cold here. I'd give anything to move away, you know.

74

Somewhere warmer, somewhere different. I really don't want to start my thirties in Blackpool.'

Eliot shakes his head as they head for the promenade. 'Well, then why are you still here?'

His words are unexpected, and sting. Grace pulls her jacket around her and turns her head so that Eliot doesn't see he has upset her. Across the road, a tramp huddles on a wet concrete step, surrounded by dirty blankets and cider cans. He doesn't ask Grace and Eliot for money, but simply stares across at them. Grace wonders how his life has reached this point. Where did he start, and how did he end up in a doorway in Blackpool on a freezing night? She thinks of her mother and suddenly feels sick.

'Eliot,' she says, grabbing his arm and knowing she shouldn't. She shouldn't touch him, but at this moment, she has to. 'If I ask you a question, will you answer honestly?'

'That's a ridiculous thing to ask me before you've even asked me the question. How do I know if I'll be honest?'

'Oh, Eliot,' Grace snaps, frustrated. 'Just say yes. Be simple for once.'

'Okay,' Eliot says, putting on a slow voice. 'Yes, I'll be honest.'

Grace stares down at her feet as she walks. 'Do you think my mum is still alive?'

There's a pause.

'Grace, I can't possibly know that.'

'I didn't ask if you knew. I asked what you thought.'

'Well let me ask you something. If she is alive, would you still want anything to do with her?'

Grace stops walking. 'Of course. She's my mother.'

'She left you, Grace. You were sixteen. Just sixteen.'

'I know that. But I don't think she was very well. I think she was struggling. I understand that.'

'Do you?' Eliot has stopped now too and faces Grace. She no longer clutches his arm.

'Yes, I do. I know that Elsie doesn't understand, though.'

'Elsie won't ever mention your mother. She barely acknowledges her. It's very sad.'

They begin to walk again.

Grace looks back at the homeless man, still huddled in the doorway. 'I hope that wherever she is, she is happy and at peace. Do you think she is?' she ventures.

Eliot sighs. 'I can't tell you that.' He turns and sees Grace's pinched face. 'You told me to be honest,' he reminds her.

'I know, I know. Forget it. Come on, let's get to the beach.'

The beach is deserted and black, the waves hissing against the sand. Grace has an urge to take off her shoes and walk barefoot but she knows that the sand would be frozen and sharp with fragments of shells and litter. She nuzzles her chin into her coat, buttoned up to the very top.

'I feel a bit sick,' she says to Eliot after a few minutes of walking.

'Me too,' Eliot admits. 'We haven't eaten. That's probably why.'

'Let's not tell Elsie that we didn't go out for dinner in the end. She won't like that we just went drinking.'

'Only because it worries her. She doesn't like drinking, and she thinks we always end up drunk every time we see each other.'

'Well. We kind of do,' Grace replies, and for some reason, after feeling so melancholy only moments before, suddenly finds everything hilarious. Eliot walking alongside her, the crash of the waves, the way her head feels as though it is wobbling, all make her want to laugh. She begins to cackle, and loses her balance, and Eliot has to steady her with his arm, and when he does, she stands, and just for a moment, feels his touch through her coat. She wonders what Elsie thinks of his touch: if it feels like it should be hers and nobody else's.

It was the day after Grace had first met Eliot, after the party where Grace had wanted to kiss him but had left it a moment too late, after she'd had the vision of marrying him, that Elsie met Eliot too.

'Grace! Guess what?' Elsie had called, .entering their lounge in a flurry of jangling keys and denim, and interrupting Grace's thoughts about the previous evening's party. 'I'm going on a date tonight!'

Grace looked up from the modernism study guide she was working through. Something about Elsie was different. Her movements were quicker than usual, her face bright. Grace smiled as she thought of Elsie having a boyfriend too. Perhaps this was all Elsie needed to be happy. And perhaps, as soon as Grace had managed to arrange something with Eliot, they could all double date. 'That's so exciting! Who with?'

'A guy I met in the bookshop on campus. Grace, he's gorgeous. He seems so...adult. Does that make sense?'

Grace thought of the small sample of men that, between them, they had associated with. Sadly, none of them could have ever been described as 'adult'.

'It makes perfect sense. So where's he taking you?'

'To the Grand Theatre. We're seeing a play. He's doing drama and some of the people on his course are performing so he wants to support them.'

'That's so nice. I'm really pleased for you. Makes my night of reading about Virginia Woolf seem even more dull than it did before,' Grace said, a little pebble of resentment plopping down into her stomach. A few of her new friends were doing Drama. She wondered if she knew the guy Elsie was talking about. He must be something special to get the usually silent, aloof Elsie to even talk to him. 'So what's his name?'

'Oh, it's a gorgeous name. And it goes really well with mine. He's called Eliot.'

A second passed where Grace was unable to say anything at all. She busied herself with underlining a meaningless section of her study guide with a pink highlighter. 'That is a nice name,' she said eventually, her insides twisting in dread.

Grace had seen Eliot in the student union bar the day after he had dated Elsie. Elsie had been typically evasive that morning, simply saying that Eliot was fun to be around and that they'd had a nice time. Grace had fought the urge to shake her, to try and get the old Elsie out, the one who would tell her twin exactly what he had worn and how he had smelled and what he had said and how he had said it. Instead, Grace had said she was pleased and had climbed up to bed, where she stayed awake for hours, replaying the scene of her future wedding day in her mind.

'Eliot! How was the play?' Grace had asked Eliot the day after. He wandered over to where Grace was sitting in the student union. He looked slightly different to how he had the other night. His features seemed sharper, his manner a little calmer. Or maybe he didn't look different, maybe Grace had just remembered him all wrong.

'Ah, so your sister told you all about me, did she?' Eliot asked unashamedly.

'She did. So how was it?' *Just get it over with. Tell me you're with her and get it over with.*

'I liked her. I can't believe you're identical twins! It didn't even register when I met Elsie, because you have different hair, and to be honest I didn't really think...'

'Ah.' Grace turned and watched some people playing pool. The white ball swung into the pocket, clicking against the sides and tunnelling its way under the table. She wasn't going to beg him to tell her about it. She'd have to ask Elsie again tonight. But for some reason, she'd rather hear it from Eliot.

'Your sister's an interesting girl. We had a good time.'

Grace sprung up. 'Want a drink?'

Eliot looked at his watch: tan with a leather strap. 'I have a late lecture. At five thirty.'

'Well, then you definitely need one,' Grace said and headed to the bar.

'So how's your course going?' Eliot asked as they waited for the student behind the counter to serve their lagers.

'I like it. We're doing modernism at the moment, and it's a bit confusing. A lot of the stuff we're reading sounds like nonsense. But I kind of like it.'

'Ah. "Friendship between man and woman is impossible because there must be sexual intercourse,"' Eliot replied.

Grace had been staring at the student behind the bar, who wore carefully arranged red chopsticks in her hair. Now, she spun around to face Eliot.

'What?'

Eliot shrugged, a wide smile breaking out on his face and making him look quite pleased with himself.

'It was a James Joyce quotation. He's the master of modernism.'

Grace sighed and pulled her lager towards her. 'Well, it sounds like he talks nonsense too.' She eyed Eliot from underneath her fringe. He was swigging his beer casually, but his expression was thoughtful.

'Nonsense is actually a very measured form of art, you know. It takes a lot of skill.'

'Maybe. Although I still think what you've just said is nonsense. Anyway,' she said, wanting to change the subject all of a sudden, 'how's your course?'

'I like it. It seems like there will be a lot of opportunities,' Eliot had said. Grace watched him as he talked, his gesturing becoming more animated, his pint placed down on the bar to free up his hands. What Elsie had said was true: Eliot was more adult than any other males they'd associated with. Apart from Noel. He seemed adult too, although it was a different kind of masculinity to Eliot's, Grace realised as she watched Eliot.

Noel. Grace thought of Noel's arms wrapped around her when she had felt so scared after her mother had vanished, of the card he had just sent her to wish her luck at uni. Then she thought of the image of marrying Eliot, and a shiver coursed through her body, even though the bar was warm. She shouldn't ever compare Noel and Eliot.

'That's great,' she said when Eliot finished describing the play he was going to perform in. 'I always thought I wanted to do acting, but I love books too, and I wanted to be on the same course as Elsie, so English won in the end. I might do some drama modules next year though. I would like to do some acting too. I did some at college and I loved it.'

'Well then you should definitely consider the drama modules. You can get into all sorts here. Even though I'm an acting student, I'm going to be directing a performance next semester.'

'That'll be so cool. Imagine if I can get a part in the play you're going to direct!' Grace said, just for a moment the thought of being on stage eclipsing her thoughts about Eliot.

It was seven thirty when Grace and Eliot finally stopped talking and left the student union bar. Eliot had missed his lecture. They were both drunk.

'So, can we still be friends even though I'm your twin's boyfriend?' Eliot asked as they wandered out of the campus.

There it was. *Boyfriend.* And although Grace had been waiting for it, expecting him to say it, it still stung.

'Yes, Eliot,' she replied, trying to walk steadily, trying to speak steadily, 'we can still be friends.'

Now, Grace stands on the beach, deserted apart from her and Eliot, and holds onto him for another moment before letting his arm drop to his side. For the first time tonight, she suddenly wishes Elsie were with them. Being on her own with Eliot is too difficult. She stares up at the sky, its blackness interrupted by the flashing lights of Blackpool Tower.

'You know, I've never been to the top of Blackpool Tower?' Grace says, suddenly feeling quite sad.

'That's impossible. You've lived here all your life.'

'How many times have you been up there?'

There is a short pause. 'About eight,' Eliot eventually says. 'We had cousins who used to visit and wanted to do the touristy stuff every summer.'

'Have you been up there as an adult?'

'Just once.'

And as he says it, Grace remembers that she knows he has. She remembers Elsie returning home, glowing with the happiness of a perfect day, commenting that she and Eliot had decided to 'be tourists' and do the Tower and the prom and the Pleasure Beach.

'You should go up there. You'd love it. It's quite thrilling in its own tacky little way.'

'I don't want to. I bet it's horrible going up on your own.'

Eliot stops walking and lights a cigarette. The smoke drifts around Grace, seeping into her skin and warming her.

'Don't be so melodramatic. You don't have to go up on your own. Go with friends. Or with Elsie. Or me.'

'I want to go up there with someone who loves me,' Grace says mournfully, finding herself suddenly on the brink of violent tears.

'I love you, Grace. You know that. And Elsie does.'

'Yes. But you love each other more.'

'Oh, Grace, don't.' Eliot's voice hardens. 'You sound like a child.'

'It's true,' Grace chokes, still staring up at the tower, her tears blurring with the glimmering lights.

'What do you want me to do?' Eliot asks quietly, before taking a long drag of his cigarette and puffing out the smoke into the darkness.

'Nothing. I don't want you to do anything,' Grace says, swallowing her abrupt tears. She casts her eyes down from the Tower and looks ahead of her, to North Pier. The shapes of the various bars and amusements loom over the sand, casting black shadows. The image in front of Grace is still for a moment, then seems to rear in an ugly blur. She puts her hand up to her mouth as she watches a luminous flame rip into the end of the pier nearest the sea. The horrid reflections of fire twinkle in the water as the sudden flames crash through the pier. People spill out into the road from the orange pier, their screams engulfed by the roar of flames and cracking of wood.

'Eliot! Eliot, look!' Grace shouts, her stomach swirling in fright.

He says nothing, just looks beyond them. 'Look at what?' he says after a few moments.

'The pier! It's—' Grace stops abruptly as she motions to the pier. Her arm drops to her side and she frowns in confusion. 'It was on fire,' she says slowly. 'I saw it.'

There is a moment's silence.

'Come on, Grace. It's fine, there's nothing to worry about. You're hallucinating after all the dodgy wine we've had. Let's get you home.'

Eliot takes Grace's arm and guides her away, away from the Tower and the pier, and the black sea which twinkles with reflections of nothing but the moon.

When Grace clambers out of the taxi to her flat, she wants to ask Eliot to come in, but doesn't. As the taxi flies off into the night, Grace imagines phoning him and asking him to come back. They would probably drink even more, and smoke. Grace only ever smokes with Eliot. She might tell him about her visions and that she has her mother's gift to see into the future. She might tell him about the biggest vision of all, the one that makes her unable to think about anything but him.

She peels off her shoes as soon as she is in her flat and flings her keys on the couch. She looks around her lounge as she slumps down onto her loveseat. Grace's flat is always immaculate. Her mother was messy, and late, and all the things that suggested that she wasn't in control. Grace had decided a long time ago that she would be different. Her coffee table is home to four precisely placed red coasters and a neat pile of magazines. Her shelves are bare, except for a couple of photos, and polished every other day. Her bed, when she crawls into it shortly, will be freshly made with white sheets that are cool and stiff.

Grace wouldn't live any other way. She doesn't know how Elsie bears it in the draughty old house in South Shore, amongst her mother's clutter and memories. How does she sleep every night, Grace wonders, in their mother's old bedroom?

As Grace leans her head back on her sofa and pictures her sister, she feels a familiar thud of guilt in her stomach, and knows that she won't ring Eliot and ask him to come back, not tonight. Not ever.

She wants to crawl into bed fully clothed, make-up still on, teeth unbrushed, but if she does this then she will be plagued through the night by images of crumbling teeth and poisoned skin. Plus, she still has her contact lenses in. There's no way she can leave them in overnight.

She drags herself into the bathroom and pops out her lenses, the room around her snapping into a watery blur. Elsie has perfect sight, but Grace's eyes have failed her for years. She splashes water onto her face, which drips down her chin and onto her chest. She reaches lazily for her toothbrush and brushes slowly, feeling her mood lift now that it is almost time to squash herself down amongst her pillows.

Sleep comes easily. It winds itself around her, lulling her, pulling her from the day and into the night. She breathes deeply, her thoughts finally breaking away from reality, fragmenting into pleasantly bizarre images.

Then there is fire, and pain. Grace tries to take a breath but the room is full of smoke, and the air is too thick to pass down into her lungs. She gasps, but still nothing enters her mouth. Her heart panics and flaps about. Air! Air! She tries to move, but without air she is dead and still. Flames jump up at her like excited dogs, licking her face and burning her with their heavy orange paws. She is dragged down, still fighting for breath.

Just one breath.

She struggles, and struggles, and suddenly she can breathe: clean, white air.

She sits up in bed, her lungs satisfied but her heart still whipping around in panic.

Chapter Eleven

Louisa, 1965

After her father's funeral, Louisa asked the guests if they wanted to return to the house for some refreshments. She had pushed pine-apple pieces onto cocktail sticks and cooked some cocktail sausages that Mr Geoffrey, the butcher, had given her as a goodwill gesture. She didn't care for most of the people at the funeral. She imagined that her father was with her, his eyes crinkling, his mouth giving nothing away, as Louisa made remarks about each of their habits: Mrs Harris barking commands at her scrawny husband; Mr John huffing and puffing for at least half an hour after his walk up the hill; Rebecca Whitely smoking without actually inhaling anything from the cigarette that dangled casually from her long fingers.

As it turned out, there weren't nearly enough sausages to go round. Once they had all gone, people began picking at the squelching pieces of pineapple, juice running down their hands, which, in the absence of napkins, they all wiped on their black clothes when they thought nobody was looking. When the table was bare, Louisa remembered a square of cheese in the fridge: people gobbled up the little cubes that Louisa diced within seconds of her putting them down.

'I feel like a waitress,' she'd have said to her father, if he had been here. Or perhaps, if Hatty had come, Louisa would have said it to her. But Hatty had a 'rotten cold' and unfortunately couldn't make the funeral. She had telephoned Louisa that morning to tell her. But Louisa didn't think Hatty sounded at all ill. She knew that, really, Hatty was avoiding her, and that her parents had probably told her to. Louisa knew that she wasn't meant to be friends with Hatty, or anybody like Hatty. But she couldn't help but want to be like her. Hatty would have served the right amount of sausages. Hatty's father would have served the gentlemen brandy, because Hatty's father wouldn't have gone mad and then died.

Brandy. Louisa stood a little straighter. Brandy was better than sausages, or pineapple, or cheese.

Soon, the room was spinning gently, and the smoke from people's cigarettes brushed over Louisa. She took one from somebody and inhaled lightly, coughed, inhaled again and did better. She took another cigarette, and another. Her head felt light, as though it might fall off her shoulders. If it did fall off, she thought, she could pop it onto the table, onto the empty sausage tray.

What a silly thought. Louisa shuddered. Hatty wouldn't ever have a thought like that.

Four days after the funeral, Louisa took the train to Blackpool. She glanced up as she left Talbot Road station, sticky and creased from her journey. It was a hot day, and the oppressive air hung heavily from the deep blue sky. Louisa wiped her forehead and pushed her damp hair from her skin. She paused for a moment when she reached the gaudy promenade, her suitcase falling against her legs like a devoted dog. Louisa pulled at it to stand it upright and wished she had packed a little more lightly.

She and her suitcase ambled on, through the haze of colours and people. South Promenade and the Pleasure Beach was a dot in the distance when Louisa first wandered from the station towards the bustle of the Golden Mile. But after almost an hour of winding between the slow-moving crowds, past Mr Bee's Amusement arcade, past the horses who rested between their stints of pulling landaus along the packed road, past the screeches and jingles of the Pleasure Beach, Louisa reached her destination.

Louisa had expected the place she stood in front of to give her goosebumps and make her tremble; she had expected it to do to her all those things that long-lost places always did to the heroines of the stories Louisa had read. But Louisa's insides felt still, and her heart continued to beat calmly and quietly.

She looked up, taking in the sight of the house she used to live in with her mother.

It was a boarding house now, like most of the other houses down Burleigh Road. The houses around it remained as they were when she had left. They still stood tall and grey, brightened here and there by a yellow hood over the door or a red sign by the front window. Her old house had a neat burgundy hood over the front door, and the stained glass windows that Louisa remembered so well were scrubbed and bright. With a surprisingly still hand, Louisa pushed forward the gate, lifted her suitcase onto the garden path with her aching arm, and took four neat steps towards the front door.

Even when the landlady opened the door and the scent of roses and green carpets and *home* that flew out to greet Louisa stirred something inside of her, it was more of a twinge than the full wave of emotion that she had anticipated. She had thought of this house so many times since she had moved to her father's in Yorkshire: she had dreamt about it and daydreamed and wondered. There was a part of Louisa that thought she might not even be able to stand in the house; a part of her that expected her body to crumble to the ground like ash. And yet, here she was, making polite little sounds as the landlady, Mrs Williams, showed her around and spoke briskly of the rates per night.

The house wasn't altogether different to how Louisa remem- bered it. The dining room was the most changed, with its lines of mahogany tables shrouded in white linen. The room at the front was the guest lounge now. Louisa felt another little twinge as Mrs Williams spoke.

'You're most welcome to use this room. It has a television,' she said, pointing to the little brown table in the corner. Louisa remembered sitting in the lounge night after night, listening to her mother's colour-filled stories about Blackpool and love and loss. She wondered, as Mrs Williams ushered her to Room 1, which used to be her mother's bedroom, if she should tell her landlady that she knew the house: knew its breaths and moans and sighs as intimately as she possibly could.

'You can see the sea from Room 1. And the noises from the Pleasure Beach won't bother you so much from this end of the house,' Mrs Williams said, her powdered face smiling carefully.

'Ah,' Louisa said. The noises, she knew, were the splitting screams, the freakish laugh of the famous clown in his glass case, the eerie silence of the closed night. 'Ah. I see.'

'Well. Teatime at five,' Mrs Williams said as she bowed out of the room, the scent of face powder following her.

Teatime was what did it. Sandwiches, made in the very kitchen with the blackberry stain on the cool stone floor, brought on the trembling hands and the shortness of breath that Louisa had waited for and missed when she first arrived at the house.

'I was wondering if I could perhaps have a little glass of wine with my meal?' Louisa asked.

A disapproving crack appeared in Mrs Williams' face. 'I have a bottle of red if you would like a drop of that?'

Louisa nodded and stared through the gap in the door as Mrs Williams swung into the kitchen. Was it the same? She wondered if she could somehow go into the kitchen. She wondered if she wanted to.

As Mrs Williams poured Louisa's wine into a cloudy glass with an ugly short stem, Louisa closed her eyes for a fleeting moment, blocking out the room and the house, and instead focusing on the face that hovered in her mind: a kind, sad expression and a wiry beard.

'Do you know a Dr Barker?' she asked, her eyes flickering open and focusing on Mrs Williams.

'Dr Barker from around the corner? Yes, I knew him a long time ago, but he moved. I'm not sure if he's still in Blackpool, or alive.'

Louisa didn't answer. She could hear the thud of the wine bottle as it was set down on the table, and the ticking of the clock in the hall, and the tedious hum of the other guests' chatter.

'I have a telephone directory, if that's any help?' Mrs Williams offered.

'Yes!' Louisa stood straight up, knocking the table with her thighs so that the red wine sloshed out of the glass and bled onto the white linen.

'It's just in the hall,' Mrs Williams said, eyeing her tablecloth sadly.

She passed Louisa the volume for the north-west of England and Louisa fumbled hungrily for the B's. 'Barker,' she mumbled.

There was no Dr Barker in the book.

'I wonder why he's not in there?' Louisa asked, the answer stinging her. She picked the book up and checked for his name again. Nothing.

Mrs Williams shrugged. Louisa sat down at her table, shaky and disappointed, trying to banish the image of her mother walking into the sea from her mind. Without Dr Barker, she didn't feel as though she would know what happened in those lost, shadowy days.

'Well, wherever he is, he's better off. Blackpool's changing, if you ask me. And not for the better,' Mrs Williams replied eventually, eyeing Louisa's wine glass as she spoke, as though it was to blame.

That night, Louisa lay in her bed and thought about the past. The curtains that Mrs Williams had hung at the window didn't quite meet in the middle and a sliver of light sliced through the blue-black of the room. Louisa was silent. After frequent night-mares, she used to sit up in her own crumpled bed, tiptoe through the velvet black of the landing and tap on her mother's bedroom door. Her mother would peel back her blankets and cocoon Louisa into the folds of her nightdress until the morning. The room was the biggest and the coldest of the whole house and Louisa would lie shivering until the heat from her mother seeped into Louisa's own skin and warmed her.

The night around Louisa was still: the noises from outside had died. Louisa wondered if any part of her mother still lingered in this bedroom. She listened hard, trying to hear her mother's breathing, until she could no longer decipher between her own breaths and her mother's and those of the sea; until she was dreaming that she was cocooned and safe once again.

The next morning, Louisa walked along the promenade to the police station in the centre of Blackpool, the ugly scent of eggs from Mrs Williams' dining table clinging to her hair and her favourite electric-blue dress.

'I was wondering if you could help me,' she asked the man at the front desk. His hat, Louisa noticed, looked rather too small for him, as though it would fly off his head with the slightest move-ment. He seemed aware of this too and moved only very slightly as he gestured for her to sit and wait.

'Got a pile of papers to go through, miss. I'll be with you shortly, if you'd like to take a seat on that bench.'

Louisa had never been in a police station before. She wondered now, as she sat on the bench, what would have happened if she had gone to the police station on that day when her mother died, instead of Dr Barker's house. She supposed she should have done. But Dr Barker had always told her to go to him if anything ever happened. He'd always said it in hushed tones, so that her mother couldn't hear. But she had only been a child, and not quite at the stage to question why he might do that. Now that she was, there was nobody to question. Louisa kicked the side of the bench softly with her shoe.

After around twenty minutes, the man with the small hat cleared his throat with a tight little sound. He employed a small, plain smile and Louisa stood and made her way back to him.

'How can I be of help, miss?'

'It's my mother. She went missing quite some time ago, and I have been unable to find out what happened to her until now, because I have been out of the area.' Louisa's words sounded clipped as she spoke, as though somebody was trimming them into neat, clean shapes. 'I wondered if you could check your records from 1960 and see if anything happened to a woman called Rose Ash.'

The man turned, and his hat wobbled precariously with the movement. He clutched at it and turned around to enter a little office behind his desk. Louisa heard the shuffling of papers and the rolling of cabinet drawers. After a few minutes, she took her seat on the bench again and allowed herself to indulge in a short daydream of what might follow. The policeman might re-emerge from the office clutching a pile of papers, a photograph of her mother perhaps, and a nearby address for somebody who would take Louisa's hands in theirs and tell her why her mother had gone. Louisa closed her eyes and leant back, resting her head on the hard, polished panelled wall until the policeman returned, his hat more secure and his smile sad.

'I'm afraid there's absolutely nothing on your mother.'

Her heart sinking, Louisa stood, nodded in thanks, and rushed out into the hot blue Blackpool morning. She walked and walked until she reached the glittering promenade, walked through the sweating crowds until her steps sank into the sand. Her breathing, which had been quick and shallow when she left the police station, began to return to normal. She bent and took off her shoes so that her toes sunk into the gritty, warm sand.

She was beginning to feel calm again. She would find out what had happened to her mother. She had only tried two ways of discovering why Rose had vanished into the slicing waves. Two out of thousands. If Dr Barker wasn't here, and there was nothing recorded about her mother at the police station, Louisa would have to dig a little further into the soil of the past. She squinted across the beach at the barefoot teenagers and the squawking children and the chattering parents. She would have to look for the boy with the purple eyes who her mother had talked about so much before she disappeared. Someone, somewhere would know where to find the boy, and he would be able to tell Louisa what had happened to her mother. He would be able to tell her that there was nothing that Louisa could have done.

As she mulled over this and walked along with her shoes swinging in her hand, a running child stopped Louisa in her tracks. She went dizzy for a moment as she watched the child, almost transparent, run through the swarms of people, into the sea. It was a girl in a red bathing costume, her hair in pigtails. Louisa watched, mesmerised, as the little girl crashed into the water, being carried out further and further by the waves. She watched everybody else ignore the girl as though she wasn't there. And she watched as the girl was suddenly a flash of red, flipped under the water by a brutal wave. Horrified, Louisa screamed.

'Help her!' she cried. A few people turned to look at Louisa; not with looks of concern or fright, but looks of confusion and scorn, as though she was making things up. She gestured wildly to the water. But the red, and the wave, and the horror, had all gone. The water twinkled calmly, clear and hiding nothing. The people who had looked at Louisa turned away again. Everything was as it had been before.

Louisa scrambled away, towards the promenade and away from the sea.

She should have known straight away. That sickly, dizzy feeling; the transparency of the girl, the blur of everything around her. She scrambled through the crowds, squinting in the sharp glare of the sun for the little girl she had seen in her vision. Eventually, Louisa found her. The little girl in the red bathing costume was playing on the sand while her family dozed nearby. Louisa watched as the girl said something to her father, who dug in his pocket and gave his daughter a coin without opening his eyes. Before Louisa had reached the little girl, she had darted away from her family. Louisa hurried her pace.

'Excuse me! Excuse me!'

The father sat up slowly and glared at Louisa.

'Yes?'

'I'm sorry,' Louisa said breathlessly. 'Your little girl is about to go in the sea and it's far too strong for her. She'll get into trouble if you let her swim out there.'

The two women looked up now.

'I beg your pardon?' one of them said, fingering her carefully constructed curls.

'I can't explain how, but I just know. She's going to get herself into trouble, somebody needs to go after her and make sure that she's safe.'

The woman who hadn't yet spoken glanced at the man.

'Jack, do you know this lady?'

'Never seen her before.' He looked up at Louisa again. 'Our little Suzie's gone to get an ice cream. She's nowhere near the sea. I don't know who you think you are, coming over here telling us how to parent.'

'Jack!' the woman suddenly yelped, clutching his arm. 'Look! She's right! Suzie's over there, wading into the sea! Oh, please, go and get her! She's too little to go in the water on her own!'

Darkness clouded Jack's face as he gazed out into the sea and saw Suzie. He jumped up and sprinted off, leaving a salty scent of sweat behind him. Louisa watched as he threw himself into the waves and pulled Suzie towards him. They bobbed closer and closer to the shore and reached the sand just as a huge grey wave swooped behind them.

'Suzie!' one of the women yelled as Jack came into earshot,

dragging the dripping little girl behind him. 'What on earth were you doing?'

'I saw something sparkly in the water and I wanted it for my Blackpool box,' Suzie said, her voice babyish and scared. 'I'm sorry, Mummy!' she finished, before exploding into sobs.

Suzie's mother eyed Louisa as she began rubbing ferociously at her daughter with a towel.

'How did you know? Did you set us up? Did you tell her to go in the sea?'

'Sheila! Why would she do that?' the other woman interjected. She held out her hand. 'I'm Mags. This is my sister Sheila. What you just did was amazing. And we're all thankful.'

Louisa shook Mags's hand and was lost for a moment in the woman's firm grip.

'I'm Louisa,' she said eventually, as Mags let go of her hand.

'So,' Mags said, lighting a cigarette. 'You're psychic?'

'Yes,' Louisa answered. 'I am.'

It felt like someone had let go of an invisible thread running through Louisa. She felt light and free. She hadn't told anybody about her gift since she had moved to her father's as a child.

'Brilliant. I want to know what's going to happen to me. Come out with us tonight. A load of us are going to the pub.'

Sheila tutted and plonked Suzie down on the sand next to her. 'I'm sure Louisa has better things to do than watch you lot drink.'

'Oh, I don't know. We're pretty good fun to be around. You're just jealous because you're stuck at home ironing,' Mags retorted, and winked at Louisa. 'We'll be in Yates's at eight-ish. You should come. I'll tell them all what you did today and you'll never have to buy another drink again.'

Chapter Twelve

Louisa, 1965

At dinner, Louisa chewed on an indestructible piece of lamb and considered Mags's invitation. She pictured her room upstairs, her suitcase in the corner, her single book, which she had finished, on the bedside table, and the invisible, silent ghost of her mother all around.

'May I have a key for tonight?' Louisa asked Mrs Williams as soon as the lamb had finally struggled down her throat. 'I'm going to meet some friends.'

'I don't give keys out. Be back for eleven.'

Louisa ached with the heavy thought of Mrs Williams being the sole owner of the key to a front door she used to think would always, always be hers.

'Oh,' she said, pushing her plate away from her and standing. 'Eleven is fine.'

In her room, she tipped out the contents of her make-up bag onto the bed. Blusher spilled from its pot and was lost in the creases of the bedding. She plucked her eyeliner out from the sparse selection and wandered over to the mirror. She thought of her old friend Hatty as she applied thick strokes to her eyelids. Louisa still hadn't heard from her. But then, Hatty probably had no idea where Louisa was now. Louisa would just have to make new friends. She stood back from the dim mirror to check her work. Her eyes hung heavily in her face, draped in black cloaks of kohl. She needed something to brighten things up. Some red lipstick, perhaps. She would buy some tomorrow. For tonight, this would have to do.

When Louisa entered the wine bar, she looked for Mags, but couldn't see her. She stood at the bar, wondering if people thought there was something wrong with her overly black eyes. Nobody seemed to be looking at her, though. They carried on with their business of drinking and talking and smoking. She ordered a white wine and sat on the end of a long bench full of rowdy men. The memory of the night with Hatty loomed in her mind, and Louisa tipped the alcohol into her mouth in a bid to cleanse herself of the image of Nicky's hairy fingers and his forceful, heavy body on top of hers. Eventually, she saw Mags at the bar, and pushed her way over to her, the wine glass, now empty, in her hand.

'Louisa!' Mags gave Louisa a quick hug and a kiss on her cheek. Her lipstick left a slimy residue that Louisa thought would be rude to wipe off. 'I'm so glad you came. I still can't get over what you did today. I've told my cousin Jimmy all about you.'

A man with a curly beard winked at Louisa.

'Intriguing,' he said, apparently pleased with himself for summing her up in one word.

'So, do you save people's lives all the time?' Mags handed Louisa a drink of something dark and thick.

'No.' A stab of pain shot through Louisa as she remembered her mother wading into the sea. Her father in his chair while Louisa was in Blackpool with Hatty. 'Not all the time.'

'But you are psychic?' Jimmy asked, the foam of his bitter sticking to his beard.

'Well, yes I am.'

'A rare gift,' Jimmy said, wiping the foam away with the back of his hand. 'So what's going to happen to me?'

Mags elbowed Jimmy. 'Oi, it's my turn first.' She turned to Louisa, her eyes gleaming. Louisa noticed that her eyeliner was immaculate, like Hatty's always was. How did they all do it, and why couldn't Louisa? 'Let's find a seat and then you can tell me.'

Louisa followed Mags and Jimmy to a sticky booth.

'Right,' Mags said as she sat down. 'Go on.'

Louisa wondered what she should do. She closed her eyes, trying to conjure up an image of Mags in the future, but nothing came.

'I'm not sure I can do it on command. I've never tried to,' she admitted after a few minutes. She took a swig of her drink. She had no idea what it was, but the taste burned into her throat.

'Course you can. After today, you can do anything,' Mags commanded, and gestured frantically for Louisa to close her eyes again and continue.

Louisa obeyed. She shut her eyes, and thought of her kohl eyeliner, and wondered if she could perhaps buy a better brand of eyeliner and a new lipstick the next day. She thought about maybe buying a new dress too. She would go to Hill's tomorrow and spend as much money as she liked. She opened her eyes.

'You're going to have a baby boy,' she said.

Mags wrinkled her nose, revolted. 'I most certainly am not!' she snorted.

Louisa shrugged. 'It's just what I saw.'

Mags relented a little. 'So does this mean I'll meet a nice man then?'

'Oh yes. Definitely. A very nice man.'

'With a nice car?'

'A lovely car,' Louisa confirmed.

Mags sat back. 'Well. I must say, I'm surprised at that. I had always thought I'd never have kids. Suzie drives me potty and she's not even mine! But a son might be different. A little boy, and a nice husband. That'll be fine, I suppose.'

Louisa smiled from behind her glass.

'So,' Mags sighed, obviously tired already at the thought of having a child, 'how much do I owe you?'

'Oh, nothing,' Louisa said, with a wave of her hand.

Mags's eyes widened. 'Nothing? But the gypsies on the prom charge a fortune for their fortunes!' She giggled loudly at the play on words.

'Nothing at all. We're friends, aren't we?'

Mags gave Louisa a wide smile. 'Course we are.' She rolled her eyes. 'Until I'm up to my eyeballs in filthy nappies, that is. Right, Jimmy. Your go. Let's see what's in store for you.'

He grinned at Louisa and held his hands out. 'Maybe it'll help you if you have some contact with me.'

Louisa smiled back, and took Jimmy's hand. She closed her eyes, but before she could think about dresses or eyeliner or Hill's again, she saw an image of Jimmy's naked body wrestling with her own, saw a tattoo of a snake on Jimmy's bare shoulder, and felt as though his lips and his breath were on her, touching her skin.

'Do you have a tattoo of a snake on your shoulder?' she asked, her eyes flying open.

'How do you do it?' Jimmy asked, and gave a small applause.

Louisa flushed. 'I...I'm sorry, can we finish your reading another day? I'm feeling a bit worn out. I don't normally do two in a row, and I—' she felt Jimmy's hand on hers.

'Don't worry,' he said. 'I understand. We'll finish off another time. And just so you know—' he peeled away his shirt to reveal a snake swirling over his shoulder, '—you have a real gift.'

Mags nodded. 'You really do. You could make so much money doing readings for people in here. We have loads of friends who would love to know their future.'

'I don't know if I could charge for it,' Louisa said.

Mags smiled. 'Relax! We know that. I think you need another drink. Jimmy? Same again?'

Jimmy nodded and turned back to Louisa as Mags left to go to the bar. 'So, where are you living at the moment?'

'I'm staying at a boarding house in South Shore.'

'Ah, so you're not a permanent Blackpool girl then?'

'Well...no. Not at the moment. But I am planning on moving here.'

'Really?'

Really? Was she? Louisa looked out of the window of the wine bar, to the crashing waves, and then back at Jimmy, his beard and his shirt that covered his snake tattoo.

'Really,' she smiled, as Mags set the drinks down on the table.

Later, as Louisa danced beside Jimmy, a tall, blonde woman appeared and tapped him on the shoulder. He grinned and gave the blonde a kiss.

'This is Penny,' he told Louisa over the music. 'My girlfriend.'

Louisa paused as the image of her and Jimmy together came careering back into her mind. Bed sheets. The scent of Jimmy: his skin, his breath, his hair. She felt Mags pull her from the dance floor.

'Sorry, Lou. I was going to tell you that he wasn't single. I knew that he'd make out that he was. He's a bit like that, but he's harmless. He is great with Penny. I hope you're not disappointed?' Mags asked, her pale blue eyes scrunched up in concern.

'No. No, I'm not disappointed at all. I'm just surprised.'

'Penny's used to it. She knows what he's like. But she'll put up with it because she knows he'll never actually do anything with anybody but her. Sweet in a funny way, isn't it?'

Louisa frowned. 'I suppose. Although who knows what's going to happen, really?'

'Psychics?' Mags guffawed.

'Yeah.' Louisa smiled weakly as she watched Jimmy's hand on Penny's waist. Penny danced well, her body bending and flexing in a way that Louisa's never could. Jimmy's eyes moved over Penny and then up to Louisa and Mags. He gave them a thumbs up. He wasn't unattractive, Louisa decided, as she examined the way he danced, his beard, his smile. But he wasn't Louisa's ideal type of man. She probably wouldn't have even thought about him in that way if it hadn't been for the image that had kept flashing into her mind all evening. The image that had made her feel invincible, as though no matter what she said, or what she did, she would end up with Jimmy as her boyfriend. She had almost begun to feel as though he already was, so that him dancing with another woman made her feel quite upset.

'It's almost eleven,' Mags said. 'Didn't you say you had to be back to the boarding house by eleven?'

Louisa nodded. She had imagined Jimmy walking her back to the house. Mags shuffled into her elaborate fur coat, which was far too thick for the balmy summer evening.

'I got it in the sale,' she said when she saw Louisa eyeing the coat. 'I'm boiling, but I look great,' she said with a laugh.

Louisa smiled. 'You do,' she agreed as she linked Mags's furry arm.

Chapter Thirteen

Grace, 2008

The morning after Grace dragged Eliot to the beach is frozen and silver. Grace cranks up the heating in her flat, thinking again of Elsie in the draughts of Rose House. It's Sunday, so Ash Books is closed. She flicks on the kettle and sits at her small kitchen table. She pours some cereal into a bowl but can't eat it. The cornflakes won't move down her throat, and eventually she pours the milk down the sink and scrapes the remaining orange flakes into the bin. Her flat is quiet, even with the radio on. Grace stands, and pulls her woolly cardigan around her tightly. She wants company, and there's only one place that she knows she will feel welcome so early on a Sunday morning.

Mags is cooking bacon when Grace arrives, and the warm, smoky smell makes Grace's stomach grumble.

'Want some?' Mags asks, after steering Grace into the kitchen and pouring her some coffee.

'Yes, please,' Grace says, thinking of her discarded cornflakes.

'Noel's just in the shower. He'll be down any minute. How was your evening?' Mags says, slapping some bacon on a roll and giving it to Grace.

Grace sighs. 'It was okay. I went out with Eliot.'

'I know. Elsie told me.'

Grace stops chewing her sandwich. 'Was she angry?'

Mags shrugs. 'She didn't say. I couldn't tell. You know what Elsie's like. I thought it was strange that you and Eliot were out without her though.'

'Elsie and I had a bit of a falling out. We can't seem to get along these days.'

'He's not for you,' Mags says, dolloping some ketchup on the side of her plate. They eat in silence for a few minutes, their eyes averted as they both chew.

Grace frowns. 'I don't know what you mean.'

'Eliot. He's not for you. You're too similar and you'd destroy each other. You know you would, Grace. Elsie is good for him. I know that probably hurts you, but it's true. You need to let them be. They'd be happy if you did. Elsie would be happy.'

Grace's mind is filled with the images of her future wedding day. It's always the same. It's real. Daisies, champagne, lace, Eliot.

'I don't want to hurt Elsie. I really don't.'

Mags wipes her mouth with the back of her hand. 'Then don't.' She takes Grace's plate and crashes it into the sink with her own.

'I might not have a choice. What if I'm meant to be with him?' Grace says quietly.

Mags turns from the sink so suddenly that it takes Grace by surprise. 'What did you just say?'

Grace feels herself colour. She's kept the secret of her vision, her gift, for so long. She scrambles through her thoughts, trying to decide if she wants Mags to know.

'We just get on so well. That's all. I think a lot of him.'

'You meant more than that by what you just said. I know you did. You have visions of the future like your mum used to have, don't you? You've seen something to do with Eliot, haven't you?'

Grace doesn't answer. She stares down at the knots in the wood on the kitchen table and prays for Noel to come down, for the phone to ring, for anything to happen except this.

'You *can't* live like that Grace!' Mags's voice is high-pitched and her skin has become mottled with pink distress.

Grace puts her head in her hands for a moment, then recovers, and looks at Mags again.

'I know I can't live the way I think I should. I know how dangerous it is. But it's so powerful, knowing what *should* happen, that—'

Mags is suddenly next to Grace, pulling at her arm. 'That's just it, Grace! You *don't* know! You don't know that it's true, or right, whatever you've seen. Just like your mother didn't know! I will not lose you to this, this...curse!' Mags finishes, standing and lighting a cigarette hastily.

Grace is silent. Mags doesn't understand.

It's a few awkward seconds later when Noel wanders in, bringing with him a fresh scent of shower gel. His hair is wet and looks darker than usual. Grace fights the urge to stand up and hug him, or hold his hand, or have any kind of contact with him.

'All okay?' he says, knowing very well that all isn't okay.

Mags nods, exhaling smoke slowly and leaning on the shiny black worktop behind her. Grace plays with a crumb on the table.

'Any more bacon?' Noel asks.

Mags motions towards the cooker. 'It's waiting for you. Help yourself. I'm off out to the shop. I need a few bits.'

Noel nods uncertainly and his eyes follow his mother out of the door. When she's gone, he turns to Grace.

'What's happened?'

Grace gives Noel a weak smile. 'Oh, you know. Just me, causing problems as usual.'

Noel grins. 'Well, it's true that you're trouble. Always have been. But that's what makes you so much fun.'

'Thanks for the compliment. I kind of needed one.'

Noel nods and takes a seat at the table. Grace watches him look at her with concern, waiting for her to speak.

Before Eliot, Noel was the one that Grace imagined kissing

when she lay in bed at night, the one whose initials she scraped onto her pencil tin with a compass, the one she felt an excited fear about how things might turn out with him one day. When the twins' mother disappeared, Noel came home to help Mags look after them. He was strong and calm when everyone else seemed high-pitched and hysterical. He had made Grace feel as though she might just get through the bog of sadness that pulled her down every time she thought of her mother. He'd said something about missing an interview and Grace could tell that he'd blown off the chance of a lifetime so that he could come home to Blackpool and look after her and Elsie because their mother had gone and they had nobody else. It had made Grace want to press her lips against Noel's, and be as close to him as she possibly could. But she was only sixteen then, and didn't know how to move towards somebody you wanted to kiss. So she had waited for Noel to move towards her, and kiss her, and make everything alright. But Noel had a girlfriend, and saw Grace and Elsie as sisters who he needed to take care of. He belonged to an adult world that Grace watched with interest but didn't quite know how to join.

So Noel didn't move towards Grace and kiss her, not then and not any time after. But even now, after all this time, and after seeing the future plainly before her, the ache to kiss Noel has not left Grace.

It probably never will, she thinks, as she gazes at him across the table.

'I keep having nightmares,' she says to break the silence. 'I keep dreaming about fire. It's terrifying. I've been awake since 4 a.m. I couldn't sleep, because the dream scared me so much. I wanted to ring Eliot, but I thought he might be with Elsie, and she isn't talking to me. So I waited until a decent hour and came here, to see your mum, and now she's fallen out with me too.' Grace sits back, exhausted and lighter for having said so much in one breath.

'I'm sure Mum hasn't fallen out with you. My mum never falls out with anyone. She just needed to go to the shop.'

Grace is quiet for a while before answering.

'I hope you're right. Noel, do you think what my mother saw in the future – her premonitions – do you think they were accurate?'

Noel frowns in concentration. 'I think they were probably images of what could have been. But I don't think anything about the future is set in stone.'

'But even if it's not set in stone, surely there's one outcome that's meant to happen. And those were the ones she saw?'

They haven't talked about Grace's mother for years, but after bringing her up last night with Eliot, Grace feels like she's not quite finished thinking about her.

'I think there's a danger in trying to follow what you think should happen,' Noel says. 'I think you should go with what you want to happen.'

Grace stares at him. 'But aren't the two things the same?'

Noel shrugs. 'Not necessarily, no.'

Grace shakes her head in confusion.

Noel pats Grace's hand. It's a clumsy movement but it makes Grace smile. 'I think that whatever it is you're worrying about, you'll make the right choice.'

Grace looks at Noel. His face is handsome. The tubbiness that plagued him through childhood has turned into quite an athletic shape. Although he isn't tall, he looks strong. His dark blonde hair, already beginning to dry after his shower, has a slight curl to it like Mags's. His eyes are the kind that people trust: round, blue and bright. Grace wonders what it would be like to see those eyes when she woke up in the morning, when she was scared, when she was upset. She wonders what it would be like to be Bea.

'So what do you think your nightmares about the fire are trying to tell you?'

'I have no idea. I've looked in all the dream books we've got in the shop,' Grace says as she slumps back in her chair.

'And?'

'They all say slightly different things, which I suppose could all make sense. The dream could mean something about creative energy and something new in my life.'

'Well, that makes sense. There's the shop, isn't there? That's new, and it must be taking up a lot of energy.'

'I suppose. But it seems more fierce than that. It seems to be warning me of something. It's more like a nightmare.'

Noel stands, and pulls Mags's laptop from the kitchen worktop onto the table. He taps on the keyboard, then after a few minutes reads out an online dream meaning. 'A dream of fire can symbolise sexual passion,' he finishes, the tips of his ears turning a subtle pink.

Grace looks down at the table.

'Well,' Noel says as he clicks the laptop shut. 'That's that cleared up.'

'I don't think that can be it,' Grace says, mentally suffocating her wandering thoughts. 'I wonder if the fire is something to do with my mum? I remember her telling us a story about a fire years ago. I think her own mother told her the story and she passed it onto us. But I don't know what it was.'

'Will Elsie know? Maybe we could see if—'

Grace shakes her head hurriedly. 'Elsie won't talk about Mum.'

'Okay.'

Noel is quiet for a while and Grace feels guilty for snapping. She stands up and touches Noel's shoulder. It's firmer than she expected: muscular and masculine. 'I'm sure I'm overreacting. I know my mum had nightmares a lot. I obviously take after her.'

'Well, from what I remember of your mum, that's not a bad thing.'

'Really? Nobody ever seems to remember Mum positively. Even I struggle, sometimes.'

'Your mum just had a difficult time with things, that's all. But she was a good person.'

'Thanks for saying that. It makes me feel a lot better. I think I'm a lot like her.'

'I think you are, too,' Noel smiles.

'Noel, your mum's worried about me because she worked out that I have premonitions like my mum used to.'

Noel stares at Grace for a moment, his eyebrows raised. 'Go on,' he says.

Grace sighs. 'Well, I don't think I have as many visions as my mum did. I certainly couldn't make money out of mine. But I do have them. That's why your mum was angry with me before you came in the room. She's worried that I'm going to do something stupid because of my visions. She said my mum lived her life all wrong. And she's worried I'm going to do the same. But I can't leave things, because I feel like I'm being warned about something, about leaving things too late to rescue. I have this powerful feeling that even if I don't pursue what's meant to happen, it will still be my future somehow. I'm not sure what to do...' she trails off, aware that she's speaking in code and probably not making much sense to Noel.

'It's simple. Do what you want to,' Noel says. He stands then, and seems to think about something as he puts his plate on the worktop beside the sink. 'I need to set off home really. Bea's got some work thing that she wants me to go to tonight, and I should beat the traffic.' He catches Grace looking at him and smiles. 'I'm not dismissing what you've said. I just think you should keep things as simple as possible and try to choose what you really want. Try not to be influenced by the visions you've had.'

If only, Grace thinks, as Noel gives her a quick, tight hug and wanders out of the room. She wants to run after him, to ask him to stay. She wants to ask Noel if he thinks she is meant to be with Eliot. She wants to take Noel's strong, safe hands and ask him who he wants her to be with. But she stays rooted to her chair, the scent of charred bacon lingering in the air, thick in her throat as smoke.

Chapter Fourteen

Louisa, 1968

'There's another one who wants to see you, Lou. Over there, by the bar.' Jimmy grinned at Louisa and rubbed his fingers together, his eyes widening greedily. He had taken the role of Louisa's manager since she had been telling fortunes, without any hint from Louisa that she wanted him to. He had her charging £1 per fortune.

'You'll be rich soon, Louisa. Really rich!'

Little did he know about the fortune from her father's house that had been sitting in the bank untouched since her eighteenth birthday, over two years ago. Louisa hadn't told anybody about her small fortune, not even Mags. Sometimes she wondered if she should give it away. She didn't see how she could ever spend it: she couldn't see how she would ever be able to choose a house that she loved enough to buy, or enough clothes and lipsticks to make the high pile of notes that she pictured in her mind flutter away to nothing. And now, because of Jimmy and her gift, she was making even more money. Fat gold coins collected in her purse after each weekend telling fortunes. People, it seemed, would pay anything to know their future.

'Tell her I'll see her after I've spoken to Jenny,' Louisa said to Jimmy, trying to sound grateful.

Jenny was a regular, always wanting good news, and Louisa never had the heart to give her anything but. The problem with this was that the good stuff never happened. Jenny was getting impatient. Louisa was going to have to tell her. One day.

'So, you know the tall husband you told me I would meet? I've still not found him,' Jenny huffed as she sat down heavily opposite Louisa. 'I met a nice man the other day and he wanted to take me out dancing. But he was short, so I told him I was already engaged. I had to pretend that I had dropped my engagement ring and lost it. So. Tell me when I'll meet him. Or where. Then I can get on with my life with him.'

Louisa looked down at the table. She fiddled with her bracelet. She did everything that makes it obvious that you're about to tell a lie. But then, at the last minute, the truth fell from her lips without warning.

'Jenny, there's something I need to tell you. When I said you'd marry a tall man, I really did believe it. But I think my reading must have been a little off. Because ever since then, I have seen something different for you.'

Jenny clutched at Louisa's arms so tightly Louisa's skin burned. 'Like what?'

'Well. I don't see a tall husband after all. I'm so, so sorry.'

'So it's the short man I'm meant to marry? Should I try to find the short man?'

Louisa looked up into Jenny's eyes. They were hazel and rounder than most people's, giving her the look of a child, or a doll. How could Louisa tell a child, or a doll, that she wouldn't live happily ever after? That all she saw was an empty, tidy house, with no husband and no children and no noise?

She peeled Jenny's fingers from her arms and smoothed out the wrinkles from her peach cardigan sleeves.

'Yes. Try to find the short man.'

Jenny's anticipation deflated with a gigantic sigh. 'Well! I must say, you frightened me a bit then. At least I'm going to have a husband.' She stood up, and checked her immaculate hair with her fingertips. 'You know, Pamela Fielding went and bought three cats the very day that you told her she wouldn't marry. I told her not to, but she said you've been right about almost everything you've told everybody. She said there was no point wasting time with men if she was never going to find one who loved her. But that makes me think she wasn't too bothered about a husband in the first place.'

Louisa nodded, remembering Pamela's too-intense gaze, the way she had stroked Louisa's arm for a little too long when saying her thank yous, her hair cut like a boy's.

'No, I don't think she was bothered about a husband at all.'

'Anyway. It's time for your next, I think,' Jenny said, smiling politely at the woman who had moved from the bar to Louisa's usual table.

The woman offered her hand. 'I'm Judy,' she announced aggressively. 'I want to know if I'm going to have any children.'

Louisa took Judy's hands. They were cold, even though it was summer, and Louisa could feel her bones through her papery skin.

She closed her eyes and waited, her spine rigid with nerves. She hated this bit. Hardly ever, but sometimes, Louisa couldn't see anything of the future. That was when she had to make something up. The last time she hadn't been able to see anything was when she was sitting with Pamela Fielding. That was quite an easy one to fumble through and come out unscathed. But Judy was different.

Suddenly, Louisa's body relaxed, and in her mind she saw Judy cooing over a baby with a pink toy rabbit in her cot. She was about to open her eyes and speak when she felt Judy's hands twitching under hers. She realised that she hadn't seen everything yet. There was more. This time there was a sound too. A dull, fast thud thud thud. The image was a flicker in warm red water.

'You're pregnant!' Louisa blurted out, her eyes flying open.

Judy smiled, but remained poised.

'Did you already know?' Louisa asked.

'I did. I just wanted to see if you would pick it up. And you did. So congratulations.' Judy's words were pleasant, but her voice was cool and tight.

Louisa sat back. She'd had people testing her before. And she'd always proved the skeptics wrong. She never normally minded when people questioned her. But today, she felt tired of proving herself.

'I'm glad you weren't disappointed with the service,' she answered Judy in an overly formal tone.

'My friends spend a small fortune on you. They act like you're some kind of royalty. I can't see the fascination, myself,' Judy said, reaching into her handbag for her glasses case. She snapped it open with her cold fingers and placed her glasses on the bridge of her pointed nose.

'Is something wrong?' Jimmy said as he collapsed onto the chair next to Louisa. Jimmy never just sat down quietly. He always collapsed, making a thud and a puff of Jimmy-scented air.

'No. Everything's fine,' Louisa said quietly, suddenly wanting to cry.

'I was playing a little game. You know,' Judy said, eyeing Louisa sternly, 'if you're going to make a business out of this, then you should be able to handle a little challenge now and again. It's human nature to suspect. People are always ready to find a fraud. I had quite a few people asking me to find out if you were for real.'

Jimmy frowned at Judy. 'She's not a fraud, if that's what you think. And even if you do think that, stay away. Leave us alone.'

Us, Louisa thought. Such a small word that said so much.

Later, after Judy had shrugged her haughty shoulders and left without paying, and after Louisa had eaten a portion of hot, salty chips on the promenade, she let Jimmy kiss her.

'What about Penny?' she asked, when Jimmy pulled away and carried on eating his chips.

'Penny's over with.'

So this was it, Louisa realised. She knew it had been coming. She knew that she would end up being Jimmy's girlfriend at some point soon. It had been like knowing which train she was going to board, but having no idea when it would come. Now it was here, she climbed aboard and took her seat, quite glad to be out of the rain.

Chapter Fifteen

Louisa, 1971

'Pass me that bottle, would you Lou?' Mags yelled over her baby's wailing. She flipped his little body over expertly so that he was suddenly nuzzled against her shoulder.

'Milk's coming, milk's coming, baby boy,' she sang. Noel was satisfied by his mother's rocking for a brief moment and his howls subsided, before suddenly rising again, his little scarlet fists clenched tightly against Mags's shoulder. Louisa watched as Mags lowered Noel carefully to feed him. His mouth clenched greedily around the teat and his tight little body slackened into rhythmic sucking.

'So,' Mags said, her eyes wide like they used to be when she told Louisa the latest piece of gossip. Louisa waited and sipped from her glass of water. There was a cloud of something on the rim and she wiped it away with her finger before looking up at Mags expectantly.

'My milk still hasn't stopped dribbling out of me. It's disgusting.'

That's it? Louisa thought, then immediately felt guilty.

'Oh,' she managed. She gazed at Noel. His eyes were half closed in a milk delirium and his little fists had unclenched.

'Daddy home soon,' Mags sang next, her voice cracking a little under the strain of the high notes.

'I'll get going then,' Louisa said, downing most of her water but leaving the last inch in the bottom of the glass.

'Oh no, please don't. Charles will be going straight out again as soon as he's home. And I can't put Noel down for more than a few minutes. I was wondering actually, if you'd stay and sit with him while I had a bath?'

Louisa thought of her flat in the centre of Blackpool. She didn't have a bathtub. But if she did, she'd be able to sit in it all day long without anybody to answer to.

'Of course I will. I'll put the kettle on, shall I?'

Mags sighed mournfully. 'I suppose. So you don't think I should have a glass of wine? I haven't had much since Noel was born. I'm scared I'll drop him or something. But really Lou, I'm gagging for a real drink. What do you think?'

Louisa shrugged. 'I don't see it doing any harm. I'm here too. I'll pour us one, shall I?'

Mags looked down at Noel and stroked his temple with her free hand.

'Oh, I don't know. I suppose Charles would see us drinking when he got home if we did that. He'd go mad. He hates me drinking when Noel's awake.' She raised her eyes again, the old twinkle back in them for a split second. 'We'll wait until he's gone out. You're so lucky having Jimmy, you know. He would never tell you off about things like that. In fact, he'd never tell you off.' Mags sat Noel on her knee and rubbed his floppy, rounded back ferociously.

'No, I don't suppose he would.'

Jimmy. Jimmy, with his scratchy beard and long thin limbs and rolled up cigarettes and green anorak. With his ex-girlfriend Penny, who just wouldn't go away. Mags was right: Jimmy wouldn't ever tell Louisa off, but she doubted she'd be too bothered if he did. Louisa had been planning to tell Mags that she'd been having doubts about Jimmy for a couple of months now, but every time she decided to get it out in the open that things weren't right between them, Jimmy did something sweet and changed Louisa's mind. One night when Louisa had been getting ready to go to Mags's house, mulling over what she would tell her about how much Jimmy irritated her, he had appeared in her bedroom and given Louisa a hug and told her that he would love her forever. Louisa had swallowed her lump of guilt and kept quiet all evening at Mags's, listening instead to all sorts of problems and worries relating to Mags's imminent labour. A few weeks passed, and Jimmy's sweetness turned sour and grating again, and Louisa had decided that she definitely did want Mags's advice. But by then, of course, Noel had arrived, and proper conversations had become even more difficult.

'Mags, I—' Louisa began now.

'Yippee!' Mags interrupted. She looked up from Noel, a stringy trail of milky mucus dripping from his mouth onto his mother's hand. 'A burp,' she announced triumphantly.

Charles came in, and went out again, and Mags disappeared upstairs into a cloud of bath salts and steam. Louisa sat herself on the stiff sofa, with Noel tucked into her chest. He stared up at her sternly.

'Oh, your mummy's having a bath,' Louisa began to sing, but felt too self-conscious to continue. If it was her own baby, she was sure that she wouldn't feel too self-conscious to sing, or to do anything. She wouldn't want a bath, and she wouldn't want a glass of wine, and she wouldn't care whether Jimmy wanted to tell her off or not. She stroked Noel's cheek, the peachy down on his skin velvety on her finger. He wriggled and grunted. Louisa stood, and had a sip of her wine.

'Shall we bounce?' she asked Noel. She bounced him against her shoulder carefully, imagining Mags upstairs in the bath. What was her friend's body like now? Mags had never been really slim, but now she seemed much bigger, as though she was still pregnant. Her flesh wobbled whenever it was revealed: through a popped button or a short sleeve. Louisa wondered if that would happen to her if she had a baby. Would Jimmy still love her?

'That's a silly question,' she whispered to Noel. 'Because we all know that he doesn't really love me now.'

Noel coughed at this and screwed his eyes up before suddenly bawling and drawing his knees up to his chest. Louisa rocked him and offered him more of the bottle of milk that stood next to her wine glass. He turned away, wailing, his face turning blood red with the effort.

'Oooohhh, you're a tired boy,' Louisa said. 'You're a tired boy and you need to go to sleep. Go on.' She fumbled on the table for his dummy, which immediately popped straight back out of his mouth. His anger swelled and he screeched inconsolably. Louisa stooped to retrieve the dummy and placed it back in his mouth, holding it down with her thumb. He sucked desperately, his eyes flickering with the promise of sleep. After a few more minutes, and a few more sips of wine for Louisa and what felt like a hundred more bounces and shushes for Noel, they lay curled up together on the sofa, the silence of exhaustion falling down around them.

It was the day after when Louisa saw the sign.

It hadn't been a pleasant walk. Louisa had walked with Mags and Noel every day since Mags had been home from hospital. Louisa took turns gently wheeling the navy Silver Cross that Charles had bought from his friend the night before Mags went into labour. Most of the walks had a pleasant feel to them, but today was one of those days that just didn't seem to glide by nice and smoothly: it had a sharp, uncomfortable feel to it. First of all, Mags had forgotten her keys and so Louisa (because Louisa hadn't given birth four weeks and two days ago) had been forced to climb over the fence and through the kitchen window to retrieve them. Louisa was wearing her pale green cardigan with the pearl buttons, and the arm had snagged on the rough wood of the fence. There was a loose thread now and a patch of angry wool right near her shoulder, which Louisa couldn't stop touching and feeling upset about. Today, she thought, would be the day she had snagged her favourite green cardigan. Noel was angry today too and bawled from his pram with no sign of stopping.

Mags was the same. Mags was always the same. She chatted about a new dining table that Charles had promised her.

'And before you start, I'm not turning into one of those women who talk about nothing but her home and what's in it. I want a new dining table so we can have card games at mine instead of the pub. Now Noel's here, our gatherings will have to be round at mine,' she was shouting over Noel's cries.

'Do you think we ought to get him out of his pram?' Louisa asked, wondering if Mags had managed to tune out the screams.

Mags shook her head. 'No. He'll go off to sleep soon.'

'Perhaps he's hungry,' Louisa pointed out, niggled. She was never normally niggled by Mags. Jimmy: yes, but never Mags.

Mags sighed and plucked Noel out from a bundle of white wool. She patted him and his little head wobbled against her shoulder. 'He was up six times in the night, you know,' she told Louisa, as though Louisa had no idea.

'Oh,' said Louisa, for what else was there to say?

'I think he would have gone to sleep in his pram. I shouldn't have got him out, but—'

Suddenly, Mags's words were nothing but a hum, as all Louisa's senses were snatched by what she saw ahead of her.

The house, her house, her mother's house. For Sale.

'—So I really do think that with me being so tired, and of course Noel up so much, that it's bound to affect even the smallest...' Mags was saying, her words suddenly reaching Louisa's ears again.

'Mags,' Louisa said, putting her hand on her friend's arm and suddenly knowing why the day seemed so unwilling to be like all the others. It was to be the day she had snagged her cardigan *and* the day she had been given her house back. 'I need to go to the bank.'

Mags frowned. 'What for? It's miles away.'

'I'm going to buy that house.'

Mags scrunched up her long nose. 'Isn't that the boarding house you stayed in for a few weeks when you first came to Blackpool?'

'Yes. I used to live there.' Louisa had told Mags that she had lost her mother a long time ago. She had mentioned that she used to live in Blackpool. But Mags didn't always listen properly: she was always looking for her lighter or rummaging in her purse or wanting to talk herself, or these days patting Noel's back and talking about burps and naps. She didn't appear to know she was doing it so Louisa didn't mind too much. Louisa just knew to tell her friend things that she really wanted her to know more than once.

She had told Mags about her past only once.

'You lived there? And you never said?'

'Well, no, I've not said much about it. It was where I lost my mum. That's where we lived before she went missing. It was my home.'

Mags shook her head. Noel, who was now back in his pram and had been quiet for a few moments, began wailing again. She picked him out of the pram and jiggled him about.

'I don't understand why you want to go back there then, if that's where you lived when your mum left. It might be upsetting. Are you sure about it? Why don't you have a think?'

So Louisa did. She stood for almost a minute, and watched Mags jiggle Noel, and listened to the gulls crying to one another over the screams and lurches of the roller coasters at the Pleasure Beach round the corner, and tasted salt on her lips. She thought of the blackberry stain on the kitchen floor and Mrs Williams' curtains that didn't quite meet in the middle, and the ghost of her mother and the thousands of pounds from the sale of her father's pretty house on the hill that were still sitting in the bank, untouched. She thought of running her own little boarding house, and calling it Rose House, after her mother.

'Yes,' she said, when she had thought for long enough. 'I'm sure.'

Chapter Sixteen

Grace, 2008

When Grace arrives at the shop on Monday morning, Elsie is lost in another world. Her eyes don't move from their fixed spot as the bell above the door tinkles and Grace moves towards the counter.

'Elsie?' Grace says, waving her arms in front of her sister's glazed eyes. The twins haven't spoken since Saturday, the night Grace went out alone with Eliot. Yesterday, Grace left Mags's house without speaking to her either. The day was lonely and empty, and Grace wishes now that she could snap her fingers and take back all the things she did at the weekend that seemed to upset everyone so much.

Elsie suddenly breaks out of her trance, eyeing Grace warily.

'Hi,' she says, before turning around to shuffle some papers behind the counter.

'Elsie, I don't want to fall out with you. If this—' Grace is interrupted by a female customer dashing in through the door. After the customer has browsed the children's books and quizzed Elsie and Grace about their stock of a series about a talking duck, she leaves without buying anything. Once the customer has gone, Elsie looks at Grace expectantly.

'I was going to say before, that if this is about Eliot, then I'm sorry,' Grace begins. 'I'm sorry that we went out without you on Saturday night. But the point is, we did invite you to join us. I'd never go behind your back, Elsie.'

Grace puts a hand on Elsie's. She half expects Elsie to shake off the contact, but she doesn't. Her sister's hand is cool, her skin silky. They have both painted their nails a glossy black and their fingers are exact. It's impossible to tell which fingers belong to which twin. They stand there quietly for a moment, hands interlocked.

Elsie squeezes Grace's hand. 'I'm sorry too. I suppose I just worry, because I know how much you think of each other. I really love him, you know. And I love you as well. I don't mind you spending time together, but I just worry that it might all end badly.'

'It won't,' Grace says. She gestures to the counter. 'Do you think we'll take any more cash today?'

Elsie smiles. 'We might. We're not going to be overnight millionaires, you know. And we've sold quite a bit since we've been here. I think we'll do okay.'

'It's not as busy as I imagined it to be, that's all. But I'm sure it'll pick up. Perhaps we should sell some things other than books. You know, trinkets and stuff. Kitsch things. They could all be book related. Like bookends, or collectables of characters from novels and things.' She waits for Elsie's response, feeling as though things might have been patched over. If they have, then it happened more easily than Grace imagined it would.

'That's not a bad idea. We could trawl round some vintage fairs and have a look for things to sell. We could go to car boot sales on Sundays, too.'

Grace laughs, relief washing over her at Elsie's apparent forgiveness. 'You're full of ideas!'

'Well, we can't magic stock out of thin air. Do you have any more ideas?'

Grace thinks for a moment, then grins. 'Yes! I do!'

It is late that night, after closing the shop and eating a stir fry that

Grace threw together from the contents of Elsie's fridge, that the twins balance a ladder up to the loft of Rose House.

'There are a couple of boxes up here, but not as many as I expected,' says Grace as she peers into the opening of the attic and climbs in carefully.

Elsie follows a few minutes later. Both of the twins are shaky and a little breathless. 'I don't know if I like it up here,' Elsie says, glancing around at the cavernous void, her head tipped forward to avoid banging it on the low beams.

Grace frowns and pulls some boxes towards her, yanking the tops of them open. 'Let's get started, and then we can get out of here. These are just our old clothes,' she pulls out the contents of one box and holds up a pair of jeans. 'They're tiny! I can't believe we were ever that small.'

Elsie gives a small smile and Grace stuffs the jeans back in the box, wondering if this is such a good idea after all. Nostalgia isn't something that she and Elsie often engage in.

'Right. You hold the torch, and I'll see which boxes I think we should take downstairs and look in. There's no point lugging it all down,' Grace says, keeping her voice light and cheerful.

She opens a few more boxes. One is full of meaningless bits: ashtrays, a chipped seashell, some fancy cutlery that was probably left over from when Rose House was a boarding house.

'Suppose we can see if there's anything in there,' she says as she slides it towards Elsie. 'All the others seem to be full of just clothes and stuff. Not really things that we can display or sell. I thought Mum would have kept all sorts up here,' she says, glancing casually at Elsie to gauge her response at the mention of their mother. Elsie's expression doesn't change, and she continues to sit still, her long black denim legs dangling down through the ceiling hatch.

'Oh, this one might be worth looking through. There's all sorts of things in here.' Grace kneels next to the box and the floorboards shift around her, moaning under her weight. She feels a shiver run through her body.

'Come on. Let's go back down,' she says, suddenly wanting to be anywhere but in that loft. Grace passes a few more boxes that look promising to Elsie, who climbs down the ladder so that she is near to the safety of the landing.

The twins lug the selected boxes into Elsie's bedroom. They dump them on the high, brass bed before clambering up themselves and sitting side by side. The bed is unmade: a knot of loose blue sheets that Grace wants to take off and replace with something neater and tighter. She tries not to think about Eliot in here with her sister, tries not to imagine what side of the bed he sleeps on when he stays over, but his things are scattered around the room. His forgotten watch is on the dressing table, tangled with some of Elsie's hairbands. An empty Coke can is on one of the bedside tables, a puddle of sticky brown residue seeping from underneath it. Grace knows it must have been Eliot's because Elsie only drinks Diet Coke.

Elsie doesn't mind the mess. She leans over to the side of the bed nearest to where Grace sits cross-legged, and hunts for the remote for the old, boxy television in the corner. Nothing about this room is modern. Apart from the clutter: the strewn clothes, the hairbands, the spilling pots of make-up, the odd stuffed toy owl, it isn't much changed from when it was Room 1 of the boarding house. It had been their mother's room once, but their mother had moved rooms suddenly one night, saying that she couldn't sleep in there any more. Grace had looked at her mother's wild, scared eyes at the time and wondered if the room was haunted. But Elsie obviously has no concerns about ghosts, because since living in the house on her own, she moved her things into this room without question. It's the biggest of the bedrooms, and although it's also the coldest because of the huge bowing window, it's the only room that you can see the sea from, if you crane your neck slightly and look out past the other tall Victorian terraces. Although Elsie has painted the room a bright, bubbled purple, and changed the furniture gradually over the years, she has kept

121

the layout the same, so that Grace, through narrowed eyes, can see straight through the 90s decor and the confused heaps of Elsie and Eliot's belongings to her mother's bedroom, from those days that seem a lifetime away.

Grace wraps her cardigan around her and watches as Elsie fiddles with the television remote, trying to get the ancient television to work.

'Come on, Els. We don't need the TV on. Let's find some things for the shop.' She delves into the box nearest to her on the bed. 'Look at this! We could do some themed displays,' she says, holding up a white porcelain rabbit who seems to have survived his time without being chipped or cracked. 'We could put him with that big hardback of *Alice in Wonderland* we've got.'

Elsie smiles. 'I like that idea. It would make the shop stand out a bit more.' She has a root through the box in front of her. 'There's an old Rupert Bear here. I remember him, he was mine.' She hugs the bear briefly, then tosses him next to the rabbit. 'We've got loads of Rupert Bear annuals.'

'This is great. We can do a kids' corner, with these displays and a couple of others.'

They search through the remaining few boxes, finding nothing else for the shop. In one, Grace sees the edge of a postcard in the corner, the blur of writing. She starts to reach in, to pull it out, but something stops her. She opens the soft cardboard flaps of another box.

Look at these!' she says as she pulls out matching burgundy velvet headbands. She puts one on and plonks the other on Elsie's head.

Elsie grins. 'You could probably get away with wearing something like this. I would look ridiculous.'

Grace touches the soft headband and jumps to her feet to do a twirl. She lands back down on the threadbare carpet with a thud.

'Hey, look what else is in here. It's our old school ties.' She attempts to put her tie on but overthinks it and gets it tangled.

Elsie leans forward and ties it for her.

'That's impressive. It's been ages since we had to do that.'

'I tie Eliot's sometimes,' Elsie says, her face colouring slightly.

There's a silence, and Grace pulls the last box towards her. 'I don't recognise any of this stuff,' she says. There's an old red toothbrush with tired, yellowed bristles, three small knitted cardigans, a brown skirt and two baby dolls with eerie painted eyes and flaked pink mouths.

'This must be Mum's box,' she says quickly. She realises that the headband is making her head ache, and she takes it off and drops it on the floor next to her.

'I'm tired. I think we should call it a night.' Elsie takes her headband off too and puts it back in one of the boxes. 'You can stay over here if you want.'

Grace thinks back to the last time she stayed over at Elsie's. She barely slept: she never does, here. But then she looks at Elsie's face, her own face, waiting patiently for an answer.

'Yes, that'd be great,' she says, banishing the sound of the sea from her ears.

Elsie smiles, pleased. 'I'll get you some pyjamas.'

After Grace has taken the spare pyjamas from Elsie, and brushed her teeth, washed her face and taken out her contact lenses, she lies under the ice cool duvet in what used to be Room 2 of the boarding house and waits for sleep to come. It takes time. Grace thinks and imagines and wonders, her mind whirring relentlessly. It offers her image after image; memory after memory. She thinks about the day her mother finally disappeared. Things had been strange for months. Their mother had been drinking more and more and wandering around from room to room each night. Grace heard her muttering jumbled things about love and babies, and Lewis and Mags and Noel. Grace knew that Lewis was hers and Elsie's father. She had always wanted to ask her mother about him, but she didn't dare upset her any more, or give her another reason to weep into the night. So she stayed quiet, and pretended that she hadn't seen her mother stare endlessly at a postcard Lewis had sent. Grace didn't see what was on the postcard, but it must have been something terrible for it to affect her mother so much.

Grace had hoped that the twins' sixteenth birthday might make things better. The twins would be adults, and surely that would help their mother survive whatever it was she was going through. She might confide in them; she might tell them about Lewis. They were all meant to be going to Wimpy for lunch, and then to Hounds Hill to do some shopping. Grace wanted a new black dress from Miss Selfridge to wear for the school leavers' disco and Elsie wanted a curling iron from Argos. Perhaps over cheeseburgers, or in the queue at Argos, their mother would turn to them and tell them what was bothering her. Elsie would see that their mother loved her enough to confide in her, and everything would go back to normal. The spell that seemed to follow them all around like a long, oppressive shadow would be broken.

But then she had gone.

'She's probably gone to buy you a last minute present,' Mags had said when Grace phoned her.

But Grace, who couldn't shake off the frightening sensation from her dream of drowning in thick, polluted seawater, knew that wasn't true. Elsie knew it wasn't true as well.

'She's gone for good, you know,' one of the twins had said to the other. Grace can't even remember which one of them said it now. But, she supposes as she lies in the blue darkness of Room 2, it doesn't matter who said it. Whoever said it was right.

The twins stayed with Mags for a while after their mother disappeared, although it wasn't long before they found out Rose House was paid for and belonged to them. They stayed there the odd night, after evenings out with college friends. But it wasn't until they started at university that they lived properly in the house, together. Grace knew that Elsie preferred it in their own home. Mags's house was always loud: Mags chatting, the television on full blast, fried eggs spitting out fat, the kettle boiling. There was always something to shout over. Grace didn't mind that too much, and she liked Mags. But from time to time, Elsie struggled with Mags's noise and her questions and her regular meals. Once the twins lived together in Rose House, Elsie began to talk a little more. She even laughed sometimes. Grace made them pasta with cheese on top and Elsie finished whole bowls.

But while Elsie settled back into the empty, tall house, and managed to blot the memories of their mother and her vanishing act from her mind, Grace missed the warmth and chaos of Mags's house. She struggled to sleep with the sea hurtling towards her, and then away from her again, and the sound of abandoned glass bottles rolling along the street. And then there was Eliot. Eliot, in Elsie's room, his deep voice reverberating through the walls and his laugh echoing around Grace's head, filling her mind with that agonising image of her own wedding day with her sister's boyfriend.

As soon as she had finished university, Grace found a job in a bookshop chain store in the town centre, and began renting her flat in Lytham. She left Elsie and Eliot alone in her mother's house and tried to let fate run its course.

Now, lying in the cheap bed Elsie bought years ago to replace the stained guest one that their mother left behind, Grace remembers her conversation with Noel. She wonders if leaving things to chance is really possible: if whether she did nothing, her future would still somehow hurtle her towards a marriage to Eliot. She wonders if her mother lost Lewis because of leaving things to chance, or if she was always meant to lose him anyway. Mags didn't seem to think so.

Grace always imagines that her father was dark haired, like the twins and their mother. She always wondered when she was growing up if their father had purple eyes, like the twins, and like the boy her mother always used to talk about. She wondered if they were related to the boy with the purple eyes who her mother mentioned sometimes. She wondered what his name was, and what had happened to him. But she never dared to ask.

She shuffles out of bed and pulls the duvet around her shoulders. It's thin, and the cool air seeps through it onto her bare arms. When she reaches the lounge, she flicks on the light and sits down beside the boxes of their mother's things that she found in the loft with Elsie. Elsie didn't want the boxes in her room while she slept, so they lugged them downstairs together before they went to bed.

Grace opens up one of the boxes and reaches in for the postcard she saw before but didn't mention to Elsie. As her hand rests on the shiny card, she realises that there is not just one card but a whole pile. A flutter of guilt lands in her stomach as she thinks of her twin asleep upstairs. Elsie wouldn't want to see them, she reminds herself. That's why it's best to look at them alone, and not say anything about them yet.

The postcards are in a neat little tower, stored in a way that Grace wouldn't have expected of her mother, who was always so haphazard in all matters of life. The first, with a picture of a Gondola on the front and a browned back, is stamped with the date: August 1979, when the twins would have been a few months old. The handwriting is rounded and neat.

I still love you, Lou

Grace takes the next postcard, a picture of a sunset on a beach in Mallorca. She turns it over gently. June 1980.

I still love you, Lou

The next is September 1981: a collage of Welsh castles. The years following are all dull illustrations of English cities: bridges, lakes, mountains.

I still love you, Lou

Grace pulls the duvet around her tighter. She flicks over each postcard to see the same.

On the front of one of the postcards is a nostalgic picture of Blackpool: a colourful promenade shining with people, green trams, seafood stalls, The Pleasure Beach, a man holding some donkeys. Grace smiles a little. Blackpool is so different now. She flips the postcard over, knowing what will be written, and jolting as she realises that it isn't as she expected.

The postcard is blank.

The address is that of Rose House. The faded date is April 1995, only weeks before Grace and Elsie's sixteenth birthday.

Weeks before their mother disappeared.

Grace thinks for a moment, before placing the postcards into a neat pile again. The memory of her mother's ashen face as she stared at what had obviously been this blank postcard for hours on end comes back to Grace and floats forlornly in her mind. She shakes her head to rid herself of the memory, and takes the last postcard from the pile. This one is from Blackpool too, but looks much older than the others. It's a picture of the North Pier, with its little ticket booth and the grand arch overhead advertising some long-forgotten show. Grace turns it over quickly. She can't look at North Pier without her nightmares of fire and fear flooding into her mind.

There's a spidery scrawl, faded with time.

'*Come back. I am your future. You cannot change what is meant to be*,' it says.

As Grace reads the postcard, Eliot flashes into her mind. Lace, daisies, champagne. She examines the date stamp. 1st April 1948. The day her mother was born. The address is somewhere in Yorkshire. Grace frowns as she stares at the postmark. She had thought her mother always lived in Blackpool. She thought that her mother had always been her mother: distant, anxious, full of love that she somehow didn't quite manage to transmit to the twins through her dreamy smiles and preoccupied head strokes. Now, it feels like she took more secrets than ever away with her, that she was somebody else entirely before the twins were born. Grace pulls another box, the one containing her mother's old things, towards her. She opens it slowly and takes out the first few items: the old red toothbrush, the clothes and dolls. She tips out the rest of the box's contents onto the floor of the lounge. There are a couple more cardigans, and a sealed white envelope, addressed to Grace's grandmother, Rose. On the back, there is a return address. It had been delivered from the same address in Yorkshire as the postcard dated 1948, but this one is dated September 1960. Grace stares at the surname of the sender, which is the same as her own.

Dr William Ash

Grace hesitates for a second. She notices that the envelope has some kind of stain on it, rather like dried blood. She shudders, and pulls the duvet around her. Then she tears the envelope open.

In it, is another postcard. Grace barely sees the imposing photograph of Blackpool Tower on the front as she flips it over to inspect the back, her mind racing. She heard Louisa mention Rose briefly as she was growing up. Rose has always been present in Rose House, simply because of her name. But Grace doesn't know anything about her. She fingers the yellowed card, noticing that the address on the postcard is to the same Yorkshire address and wondering why it had been sealed up, posted to Blackpool and left unread. She stares down at it, unable to believe that she might have been the only person to read it since it was sent.

The names and addresses of the recipient and sender on the envelope are written with a confident carelessness: looped, fast, and clever. The writing on the back is different. It is more laboured, square and littered with errors.

It's too late now. You have come back, but it's too late. You chose comfort over love, money over me. Our daughter will have my gift. She will see what should be and what will be. She must use it wisely.

Grace thinks of her mother wandering out of the house on her daughters' sixteenth birthday, in search of someone or something she had lost. She thinks of how her mother kept this envelope sealed for all those years, as though Rose might come back from the dead to claim it, when really, the advice that it contained was meant for Louisa. Grace looks at the envelope now: torn, discarded, silver in the moonlight that creeps under the doorway and through the curtains of Rose House.

Grace shivers and puts the all of postcards back, except the last one addressed to Rose, which she tucks under her arm. She wanders out into the kitchen, flicking on all the lights as she goes, the white duvet dragging along the floor behind her like a wedding dress. She pours herself some water and looks at the green display on the oven.

It's midnight.

She picks up the phone from its cradle on the windowsill.

'Hi. It's me.'

The next morning, as the twins eat cereal that tastes a little stale to Grace, and then drive to the shop together in Elsie's vintage racing green Mini, Grace is quiet. She wants to tell Elsie about the postcards, but she knows she needs time to tell her properly, and that first thing in the morning, when they are both drowsy and irritable, is not the best time. So Grace decides to tell Elsie later. Later, they will both be able to talk properly.

PART THREE

Chapter Seventeen

Rose, 1948

Rose lumbered along Blackpool's promenade in the chilly March breeze. The people around her shouted and laughed with the freedom of their spring holidays, but the way in which their arms were clutched tightly around their coats betrayed the hostile breeze. Rose wasn't cold: she was always, always too warm these days. As she moved towards the south of the promenade, she gazed at the fairground rides and the green trams and the stalls selling oysters and mussels. She looked up at the new maze of packed roller coasters that whirred over The Pleasure Beach, at the wide row of grand hotels. She squinted against the pummelling of sand in the wind to try and see if the little door from all those years ago was still there.

All of Rose's friends, if they felt they were in trouble, went to church. But church, with its high-beamed ceilings and glowing stained glass, made Rose nervous. It made her think of her wedding day.

Rose had married her husband six years before. It was rather an embarrassing story, really: he had been her doctor. She had only seen him three times before he asked her out, which was strange, as he was a very quiet man, not the type who would be expected to marry one of his patients. Rose had fallen on an uneven path near to her house and her ankle had soon ballooned up to twice its size. Rose wasn't going to go to the doctor, but her mother had insisted. He was new to the area, Rose's mother said, ever so good and old money rich.

'That's sprained,' were her husband's first words to her.

'Oh,' was Rose's first word to him.

She had hobbled out of his little white room, oblivious to the strand of her life that had just been pulled loose.

It was weeks later, after a check on Rose's ankle, that the doctor became somebody real, somebody who asked if she would like to have tea with him on Saturday afternoon.

'We could drive over to Harrogate,' he suggested, 'and go to Betty's.'

It didn't occur to Rose to say no. He was a doctor, after all.

After Betty's, and a walk around Harrogate, the doctor asked Rose to marry him. She looked up at him as he waited patiently for her answer, and saw that his eyes were a beautiful shade of green. Then she looked at his suit, which was dark grey, expensive and well fitted to his tall, wide frame.

'Yes,' she said, and he took her hand.

The night Rose accepted the proposal, she sat up in bed until the early hours, simply thinking. She thought about the boy with the purple eyes in Blackpool, and the gift that he was meant to have given her all those years ago. She thought about her wedding, and her wedding night, and felt sick and shivery all of a sudden. She sat cross-legged and bent over so that she could look closely at the ankle that she had sprained. It was matte again now, not shiny with anger, and the skin was looser: she was able to pinch it between her fingers, and did so a few times, just because she could. Eventually, Rose had lay back and tried to sleep. But for some time, she thought about how strange it was that her ankle appeared as though nothing had ever happened, and yet the rest of her life would always be changed because of it.

When Rose's wedding day came, she said her vows and wore a pretty veil, but knew deep down that this was not the life she was meant to be living. The life she was meant to be living was in Blackpool. Her gift was in Blackpool.

Every summer, Rose and her husband holidayed in Blackpool with Rose's parents. Every summer, Rose lay stiff in her bed at The Fortuna Hotel, tense with memories of crackling excitement and magic and fortunes. Every summer, she gazed into the crowds, searching for those purple eyes, held back by marital ties so strong she could almost see them.

Every summer, except one.

It was to be a typical holiday, and Rose expected nothing from it. But then her husband had fallen ill the day before they were due to depart, amidst piles of dresses and ties and dancing shoes.

'I will stay at home, with you,' Rose suggested to her husband in the morning, in a small voice. She knew that returning to Blackpool without her husband could only mean one thing.

'You shall do no such thing,' he had replied.

And so off to Blackpool with her parents Rose went, her husband waving her off gaily before sneezing into his soggy blue handkerchief and leaving Rose free to roam the beach at night. Her parents were old now and didn't want to dance or have a small drink after their dinner or go and see shows. They were both in their single beds by 8 p.m., wheezing from the change of air. On the first night, Rose lay in her own bed, wide awake, the scent of her home lingering on her nightdress, making her turn her head into her stark, odourless pillow. The sounds of pleasure rose from downstairs: glasses tinkling, guests laughing and shouting merrily to each other. So the second night, Rose thought she would join them. She sat alone in the hotel bar, a glass of white wine on the table in front of her. But it was no different, really, apart from the sounds of joy were right there instead of floating up from beneath her room: she could see couples and friends having fun, making the most of their holidays, making the most of being in love.

On the third night, Rose put on her favourite lavender dress, spritzed herself with Evening in Paris, and walked down the grand staircase of the Fortuna to the foyer and out into the balmy summer evening. The gulls were quiet, the lapping tide far away, the streets quieter than Rose had expected. She crossed the road, her eyes locked on the horizon beyond, which glittered with hope and magic.

When she reached the sand, Rose took off her shoes, wanting to feel the cool, soft sand beneath her. There was only one figure on the beach, and she walked slowly and certainly towards it. The gift she had dreamt of for so many years was luminous in her mind: no longer an image of a puppy, a hair ribbon, a book or a doll, but something more thrilling and exotic.

'It's been so many years,' the figure said as Rose reached him. He was a man now: a broad, strong, brooding man. She could see in the bright moonlight that his hair was the colour of oil, the purple of his eyes had deepened over time and his smile was still clever and captivating.

'I thought you were going to be in India,' Rose teased, her voice different somehow now that she was talking to him: lighter and louder.

'Oh, I lived the life of an Indian king for a while, but it wasn't for me,' he said, his electric finger tracing the veins that twisted beneath her wrist and along the underside of her arm. 'My life is here, by the sea, waiting for you to come back.'

'Me? You have been thinking of me for all this time?' Rose asked, suddenly hot.

'If it weren't for you, I wouldn't be thinking of anything. I would be ash,' he said, looking over to North Pier. Rose followed his gaze. It was the same as it had been when she had visited as a little girl. The pretty little ticket booth and the grand arch over the pier still advertised the same production that had been running when Rose had first visited Blackpool, all those years ago. If Rose squinted towards the end of the pier, she could see that the Indian Pavilion was still missing; devoured by flames and never to be replaced. If she breathed in deeply, she could still smell smoke and fire and fear.

'Stay with me,' he said to Rose. 'We have so much to talk about. I could make you happy here. You are not happy with that doctor. He's kind and rich, but that's not enough, Rose.'

Rose didn't answer for a while. Phantom smoke lingered in her nostrils and stung her eyes. The thrill of seeing this man, of his tough skin and bitter breath and soft lips, made a tingling sensation surge through her whole body. She turned to him.

'How do you know my husband is a doctor?'

'I know everything about you, Rose.'

'You know everything? You know what's going to happen to me?'

The boy looked straight at Rose, a stare so rare and piercing that it made Rose jolt backwards a little on the midnight sand.

'No. I only know what should happen to you. You should be with me, and laugh, and travel the world, and know real love. But you must make the right choice, Rose.'

Rose had kissed him then, and tasted his words. She had seen her future as clearly as a burning white star in the sky.

Now, as Rose fought her way against the Blackpool wind, her belly as round as a beach ball, she remembered the choice she had made. She closed her eyes for a second, picturing that tiny shadowy room that had ignited the rest of Rose's life. When she opened them again, she saw that the handwritten sign that had been etched in Rose's mind since she was eleven years old was gone. But the blue door was still there. She broke out into a run, despite her ripe, round belly, and burst through the door.

Gypsy Sarah looked up from her cluttered table as Rose suddenly appeared in the room. Her hair was dark brown, where it had once been grey, and her skin was white and smooth. It was as though she was becoming younger, not older. She smiled her crooked smile and bared three brown teeth that gathered like tombstones on one side of her mouth.

'Well, hello again, Rose,' she said.

Rose heaved herself and her belly into the velvet clad chair opposite the fortune teller.

'I found the boy you told me about, all those years ago,' Rose began slowly. There was so much to tell; so much for Gypsy Sarah to repair.

Gypsy Sarah nodded towards Rose's unborn child. 'So I see.'

'You told me he would give me a gift,' Rose's head fell into her hands, and she moaned softly as she smelt the smells of all those years ago: lavender and burning wood and raw meat.

'And he did give you a gift, Rose. He gave you the gift of a new life.'

'Yes, but now I'm afraid. I'm afraid that I will lose my big house and my husband. My husband will know the truth! He must know that the baby can't be his. We haven't had those kind of—' a ferocious blush roared over Rose's face 'relations for a very long time. I don't know what to do about it.'

Gypsy Sarah cackled, phlegm rattling violently in her throat and threatening to spill from her lips.

'You are worried about losing your big house before your husband? Did you list those things in order of importance?'

Rose flushed crimson again. 'No.'

'I think, Rose, that you need to find the boy with the purple eyes. He is a man now,' Gypsy Sarah prodded Rose's belly with a blackened finger, 'as he has proven. He will take care of you.'

Rose thought of the night in Blackpool last year that had made her body and mind bloom with colours and sensations she had never thought possible. Then she thought of her wardrobe filled with expensive dresses and her soft, warm bed. She didn't even know where the real father of her child lived, but she doubted that he could offer her what she would have to leave behind.

'Be brave,' Gypsy Sarah said. 'The boy with the purple eyes wants you, and he wants his child. The choice is yours, and yours only.'

Rose nodded, and stepped out onto the promenade. It had started to rain, and Rose had left her umbrella at home in its stand. Rain and salt soaked through her best court shoes, her stockings and her skin, making her bones cool and damp.

When the baby was born, slipping from between Rose's thighs and bringing with it a raw sting and a flush of scarlet slime, Rose wondered what her husband would make of this new little purple person, all wrinkles and skin. She knew that he wouldn't ever feel the heavy ache of love, or the slice of eternal worry that she felt from the moment she found out she was going to have her very own child. She wondered if he would feel anything at all.

He came into the room when Rose's face had been wiped and her bloodied bed linen had been whisked away. The baby was nuzzled into Rose's body, and her husband had to crouch awkwardly to bend and see it.

Rose tried to read his face, to see if he was as astounded as her at the sleek black hair on the baby's head, or the fact that she had perfectly formed little hands that looked as though they were made of pink porcelain.

He looked, and looked. And then he held out his hands.

'May I?'

Rose nodded, and smiled, and passed the little bundle to her husband. And as she lay back in her comfortable bed in her clean nightgown, her husband held the baby as though it was his.

'We'll give her anything she needs,' he said, and Rose, who knew that her husband only ever made promises that he intended to safely keep, thought about how very lucky she was and how lucky her daughter would be.

When the baby was a week or so old, a postcard plopped onto the large, clean mat in the hallway.

'A postcard from Blackpool,' Rose's husband said, placing the postcard on Rose's knee. Rose wasn't yet used to doing everything with one hand, and spent a few seconds trying to keep the sleeping baby still and retrieving the postcard from the edge of her knee.

The picture on the front was of the North Pier. Not an exciting picture, Rose thought, unless it brought back exciting memories of a fire and a boy and a night of love.

She flipped the postcard over to see a square scrawl.

Come back. I am your future. You cannot change what is meant to be, it said.

The baby woke with Rose's movement and began to fuss.

'This, my dear, means nothing to me.' Rose let the postcard flutter down onto the floor, jiggled her little baby and sat back in her comfortable chair.

Chapter Eighteen

Louisa, 1971

Louisa was glad that Rose House was finally empty of guests. The winter stretched out in front of her, blank and untainted by people's requests for lamb that was hotter or tea that was stronger or beds that were softer. Running a business was hard work, much harder than Louisa had expected it to be. Some days, she found talking to guests and dealing with their every need satisfying. But other days, she felt as though she had leapt into a huge, bottomless pool, pushed by an idea that bore no resemblance to reality. The idea of running a boarding house, of returning to the home that meant so very much to her, had filled Louisa with excitement and delight. But the day-to-day monotony of having clean knives and clean hair and a smiling face wasn't exciting at all. She wouldn't tell anybody that she was bored by her new business. She would keep this thought hidden, along with her other secrets that lay curled up in her mind like sleeping cats.

'Knock knock,' came Jimmy's voice from the door, stepping onto Louisa's blank winter and leaving prints all over it.

Louisa wished Jimmy wouldn't say 'knock knock' when he came into the room. Why say it instead of doing it? It was such a Jimmy thing to do.

'So, now you're finally closed up for the winter, can I please take you out for the evening? I have…' Jimmy cleared his throat, 'something to ask you.'

A moment's headache, a blur of the eyes, a flash: a sapphire engagement ring, a glass of warm champagne.

Louisa stared up at Jimmy. Was this really going to be the man who would make her happy for the rest of her life? Would she make him happy for the rest of his? She thought of Penny, still single, still eyeing up Jimmy all the time, still wearing her shortest skirts to make him see what he was missing out on.

'We can go out for the evening, if you like,' Louisa said. She felt a tugging in her abdomen, and suddenly wanted to throw up. She did a quick mental calculation. Four days late. More tired than usual. Could be.

The thought of having a baby of her own made Louisa ache. Every time she saw Noel, every time she held his little body against hers, she felt a physical pull in her belly and an ache behind her eyes, as though she wanted to cry. When Noel cried out for Mags, Louisa's whole body stirred. She watched Mags roll her eyes, or tut as she had to put down whatever she was doing to deal with her son, and knew that if she had a Noel of her own, she would be much more attentive than Mags.

Louisa touched her belly fleetingly and twinged with longing for whoever might be in there. Jimmy might be irritating, but if he had given her the gift she wanted so badly, Louisa would be forever indebted to him. She would see him in a different way. He would become her hero.

She stood up and kissed Jimmy briefly on his thin lips. He had hard lips and always pressed them too forcefully against Louisa's, but at that moment she didn't mind that so much. She felt a rush of pleasure as she remembered her vision of the sapphire ring, and patted Jimmy on the arm affectionately as she left the lounge and went up to her bedroom to choose her outfit for the evening that Jimmy would ask her to marry him and she would say yes.

Louisa managed to eat all of her prawn cocktail, which surprised her, because Mags had thrown up from day one of her pregnancy. Before the main course arrived, Louisa went off to the toilet to freshen up. Jimmy hadn't asked her yet, but she could see a bulge in his jacket pocket the size of a box and she knew that there was a sapphire ring in it.

Louisa didn't go straight into a cubicle when she reached the Ladies' but stared at herself in the mirror. She tried to see herself as somebody's mother, tried to see her face as the one that someone would look up to and care about and want to please. She smiled at her reflection, and noticed a shard of lettuce stuck to one of her incisors. As she leaned forward to check that she had scraped it away with her fingernail, her vision blurred and her head stung with the weight of a vision.

And then it came. Louisa saw an image of herself in the cubicle behind her, the cubicle she was about to go into. She saw herself sitting on the toilet, staring down at a smear of brown blood in her underwear and felt tears running down her cheeks, and suddenly she knew that there wasn't anybody in her belly after all, no magical being inside her, ready to justify a lifetime with Jimmy. She wiped her eyes, and took a breath, and pushed the vision she'd just had out of her mind, but still she knew that Jimmy wasn't her hero after all, and this wasn't going to be the night that Jimmy proposed and she said yes, and that there might never be such a night.

Chapter Nineteen

Louisa, 1972

About six months after Louisa and Jimmy broke up (for where were they going if not down the aisle?), Mags had one of her gatherings that had warranted a new dining table. Noel accompanied them and clambered up onto Louisa's lap when she arrived. Sheila came without her husband Jack, because Jack was in one of his 'moods'. Suzie, the little girl who Louisa had saved from the sea, was thirteen now and tagged along with her mother to the gathering, her hair parted severely down the middle and hanging either side of her small, bright face.

'Right,' Mags said, a cigarette drooping from her mouth, 'let's have a game of cards.' She leaned over and lit Louisa's cigarette for her. 'We could play for money for once and make it interesting.'

'You know Mags, you don't have to gamble for us to think you're still interesting. Even though you have Noel now, you're still the same Mags,' Sheila said. 'You're so desperate to still be fun.' She lit her own cigarette and inhaled, her eyelids half closed and flickering in nicotine bliss.

Mags bristled, and looked over at Noel, who was still wriggling about on Louisa's knee. 'I'm not trying to be interesting. Forget the money.'

'I don't know how to play any card games.' Suzie chimed in.

'Well, we could—' Mags began.

'I don't really want to learn,' Suzie interrupted breezily. 'I think we should play Monopoly. We always used to play Monopoly together. It'll be fun,' she said, sipping her wine as though she bossed around a group of adults and drank wine every day.

'I don't even know where my Monopoly board is, Suzie.'

Suzie stood. 'I'll help you find it.'

And so, it was after Mags had sighed and stood up to join Suzie in the hunt for a long-forgotten Monopoly board, and Sheila had lit another cigarette, and Noel had been moved from Louisa's knee to his bed, and the game had started to really get going, that the doorbell rang. Mags looked at Louisa and blushed at the thought of a guest who they didn't know very well finding them in the midst of paper money and property cards.

'I'll get it,' Suzie said. 'The game's not as fun as I remembered anyway. It's no good once you've missed out on Mayfair. I'll miss my turn.'

Sheila threw a little green house at her daughter as she left the table. 'You're only wanting to miss a turn so that you don't land on all my hotels!'

Suzie turned around and stuck her tongue at her mother cheekily.

'You're like friends,' Louisa said to Sheila, the noise of the front door opening and closing and excited voices drifting into the kitchen where they were sitting.

Sheila grinned. 'Yeah, Suzie's a good girl. She is like my friend. You know, there used to be a point when I wondered if...'

But Louisa didn't hear what Sheila had wondered, because suddenly the kitchen door opened and Suzie ran in yelping excitedly, pulling into the room a windswept Jimmy and Penny.

'They're engaged!' Suzie shrieked, apparently unaware of how this news might impact Louisa. 'Show them your ring, Penny!'

And Penny showed them her ring and, as Louisa knew it would

be, it was sapphire, and twinkled almost black as she held out her hand giddily for inspection.

'So when's the big day?' Mags asked, her eyes glued cautiously to Louisa.

'Well, this is why we've come round here now. We knew you were having a gathering and so we knew everyone would be here for us to tell,' Penny said, her big white pony teeth gleaming in the light of the candles that Mags had lit an hour before when everything had been different. 'We're getting married next week.'

Nobody said it, because nobody had the guts to. But everybody thought it; everybody knew it. Everybody looked from Penny's glowing face, down a little to her glittering sapphire, and across to her belly, which on first appearances seemed flat but actually, on closer inspection, was more rounded than it had ever been before, and certainly more rounded than Louisa's.

'Well! Congratulations!' Mags said brightly, and under the table her hand flew over to Louisa's and squeezed it firmly. 'Lou, would you do me a massive favour? I need to get these two a drink, but I think I heard Noel stirring. Would you pop up and see if he's okay? You're so good with him, he won't go back off to sleep for anyone else.'

Louisa felt a tug in her stomach at Mags's clumsy kindness, and stood up, suddenly ready to walk through the web of worried glances. 'Yes. I'll check on him.' She wandered out of the kitchen and upstairs to where Noel slept silently in his cot. She knelt down next to him, leaning her forehead on the wooden bars and staring in at the little face that had come to mean so very much.

Jimmy and Penny's wedding was rather thrown together. Penny's dress was an unexpected white, frothy affair.

'I thought she'd have gone for something plain,' Sheila said, her tone implying much more than the words. Jimmy's brown suit trousers were too short for his gangly legs, which made Louisa feel like Penny was definitely welcome to him. He had shaved his beard off for the occasion, which made him look quite different, and made it all easier for Louisa to bear.

'Shall we have one dance, Lou?' Jimmy said to her at the end of the night. 'For old time's sake?'

Old time. Louisa thought of old time, and Jimmy's snake tattoo on his wiry shoulder, and the way his feet stuck out of the bottom of the duvet when he was in bed, and the red marks the beard he used to have used to make on her skin. She thought of when he had first kissed her and he tasted of chips, and when she thought that she would have his baby and live with him until they were old and his beard was grey. She thought of even older time, when she thought she would have her mother forever.

'Old time doesn't want anything from us, Jimmy,' she said. 'Old time's sake is nonsense.'

Jimmy frowned, his new hairless face creasing in places Louisa had never seen before.

'I never did understand you,' he said, taking back his outstretched hand and placing it into his brown jacket pocket.

'I know.' Louisa replied. And then she thought of new time, of Mags and her loyalty and her determination to always be fun, and Noel with his eyelashes that were getting darker and longer each day and his perfect cherub's face and his high-pitched little noises. She thought of her boarding house and all the space she had every winter and how busy it was every summer. She thought of the things she might have to look forward to.

'I have to leave you now,' she said to Jimmy.

And just like that, she did. She wandered straight over to the bar, where she ordered a drink within seconds of an old man clanging the last orders bell. As she stood there, swaying and sipping, a man came over and smiled at her. He was shorter than Louisa, and his hair stuck out at odd angles. If he couldn't control his own hair, Louisa thought, what kind of a man must he be? He owned a shop in Blackpool that sold ice creams, so he and Louisa had, as he said, 'tourists in common'. He danced with Louisa for a couple of songs. He wasn't a good dancer. His name was Pete.

Pete took Louisa to his own ice cream shop on their first date. He let Louisa try seven different flavours of ice cream and they sat on the counter as they ate from little cardboard tubs, chatting about Jimmy and Penny and the wedding.

And suddenly, it was three months later and Louisa was seeing Pete all the time.

'He's not right for you, Lou,' Mags quite rightly pointed out as she plonked some fish fingers down in front of Noel. 'I don't know what you're doing. He's too old, for a start. And he's so boring!'

'He's alright,' Louisa said, gazing at Noel's fat little fingers squeezing the orange coated fish. 'I just want to settle down. I want a husband. And a baby. You know that.'

'Louisa, that is not a reason to marry the wrong man and you know it! Anyway, can't you see who you will end up with? Isn't that a perk of the job?'

Louisa shook her head and passed Noel a fork. 'It's not like that. I don't choose what I see. And I haven't had any visions since that one when I went out with Jimmy and I realised that I wasn't pregnant like I'd thought...' her voice trailed off and Mags looked up sympathetically.

'You have Noel, you know. You're like his second mother.'

'I know, and I love him. But it's not the same.'

'Well, just don't make a big mistake. It's not easy being married to somebody you don't even like,' Mags said as she picked up a pea from the floor and put it back onto Noel's plate.

But there must have been something wrong with Pete, Louisa thought. She wanted to do what Penny had done. There would have been nothing that would have excited Louisa more than to marry Pete with a telltale rounded tummy. She would have worn a tighter dress and had even practised the meaningful touch she would give her belly as a hint to her fascinated guests. But after six months of having Pete touch her and maul her, his lips squelching unpleasantly against her body, Louisa knew there was nothing in her belly to hide, except, perhaps, guilt that she didn't love Pete.

'I'm not the right girl for you, Pete,' Louisa said to him one day as he stacked up ice cream cones in his shop. His response was one of those cold, disturbing images that takes a while to fade: he lifted a cone back down from the shelf and crushed it in his giant paw. His face was expressionless, his mouth still and silent, and the flakes of cone fell softly onto the floor. For years after, Louisa imagined Pete on his hands and knees clearing up the crushed beige flakes after she had left. The image made her feel sick and sad.

There were other men. All of them were bewitched by her: none gave Louisa what she wanted. Louisa reached twenty five, twenty six then twenty seven. Noel toddled into childhood, leaving baby soft cheeks and cries and squeals behind. Louisa accepted that nothing was going to happen, that she would never wear a dress that strained over her belly, making people stare and whisper. She accepted that there might be a fault deep inside her that made her unable to create a baby like Mags had, like Penny had, like everybody did. She ran her boarding house. She drank some wine, and then some more. She invited some of the younger men into her bedroom at night. They had smooth skin and silky hair and smelt good. Still, nothing happened.

Louisa started to think it was too late.

And then she met Lewis.

Chapter Twenty

Grace, 2008

The slow, silent atmosphere that has settled over Ash Books seems, Grace decides, to be permanent. Aside from one well-spoken, headmistressy type of woman who marches in to enquire about antique editions of a famous mystery writer, and huffs out when Elsie tells her they don't have what she's looking for, the shop is dead for yet another day. Grace stands at the counter as Elsie searches for the mystery novels the customer had wanted on the laptop they bought with part of their business loan. The only noises in the shop are the intermittent clicks of the mouse as Elsie finds a website worth checking and the odd sigh when she doesn't find what she's looking for. The plan for the afternoon, when Elsie has finished searching online, is to begin the displays with the items they found in the attic with their mother's things last night. But this afternoon seems to be reluctant to appear.

Grace's eyes, wandering around the shop for something to do, fall to the old copy of *The Wonderful Wizard of Oz* in the window, and she wanders over and returns with it to the counter. It was one of her favourite books as a child, and she feels a pleasant flurry of anticipation as she turns the first yellowed pages to begin reading from the start.

The time sweeps by quietly, the noises of pages turning adding to Elsie's clicking and sighs. By the time Grace is disturbed by the front door opening, and the sounds of outside: buses, gulls crying, snatches of isolated conversations, Dorothy is well on her way to Oz.

It's Eliot. His tie is loosened and he looks tired.

'I've finished work early today. The students are on a trip to Stratford that I wasn't invited on,' he finishes, and Grace decides that his face isn't pale from tiredness, but that he is anxious, or stressed about something.

'Fancy lunch?' he says. Grace looks up, about to say yes, about to convince Elsie that they should shut the shop for half an hour, when she realises Eliot isn't asking Grace. His eyes are pinned on Elsie; he wants to take Elsie out for lunch, and only Elsie. Grace dips her head back down to carry on reading.

'Have a good time,' she says quietly, her eyes boring into an illustration of the Cowardly Lion.

'Are you sure you don't mind me going?' Elsie asks, looking uncertain. Grace feels a spike of guilt sear through her stomach.

'Honestly!' she says to Elsie, relieved to see Elsie start to relax. 'I think I'll start doing the displays with the stuff we found at yours last night. I'll be fine doing it on my own. You just enjoy a few hours off.'

Once they have gone, Grace pulls out the white rabbit that she found at Elsie's and places him with the pretty hardback copy of *Alice in Wonderland*. A pack of playing cards and a small print of the Cheshire cat that Grace bought years ago complete the collection that she arranges on a high table in the back corner of the shop. On a table a few feet away, she piles up their collection of Rupert Bear annuals, and sits their old stuffed Rupert on top of them. She sifts through the other children's books that they have acquired and makes some notes of things she could look for to display with them. The time finally begins to speed up, and Grace is surprised when she looks at her watch and sees that almost two hours have passed without her picturing Elsie with Eliot. Speaking to Noel last night has done her good: she can feel it.

Noel didn't mind Grace ringing him at midnight. She knew he would be up: he has told Grace before that he always stays up late. Bea had just left his flat after they had been out for dinner. Grace imagined Noel on a dinner date: quiet but attentive, interested in what Bea had to say. She wondered if he might do old-fashioned, romantic things for Bea, like pull out her chair and pour her wine. The thought of him with Bea wrenched her insides.

'Is everything okay?' Noel had asked, his voice popping the bubble in Grace's mind so that it pinged into nothing.

He'd listened as Grace told him about one of the postcards she had found: the strange blank one from Blackpool that had such an impact on her mother.

'She disappeared a few weeks after she got it,' Grace said, pulling her duvet around her whole body. 'Do you think that means something?'

'It probably means it was the final straw for her. She obviously thought Lewis had given up on her, that she had left it too late.'

Grace jarred slightly at Noel's choice of words and looked down at the postcard in her hand.

Grace hadn't told Noel about the two earlier postcards of Rose's, even though she held the one from 1960 – the one that had been sealed – in her hands as she spoke to him. For some reason, she wanted to keep that one to herself.

After Grace has piled children's books into the small sections she has created throughout the shop, she stands back to admire her work. It's starting to take shape. She turns to the front of the shop to gather more of the children's books she has decided to display, and sees the door open. Elsie and Eliot are back.

As Grace moves towards them, Grace feels something enter the shop with them: an uncertainty, an awkwardness, an expectation. Eliot looks at Grace awkwardly, almost as though he is apologising for something. Elsie gives him a brief glance, and then throws her arms around Grace. As she does, Grace sees a flash of gold and white. She stands still as Elsie hugs her, and then takes a step away, pulling at Elsie's left hand.

'What's this?' Grace asks, her voice a strange, strangled sound.

'We're engaged!' Elsie says, beaming nervously.

Grace looks down at the ring. It's beautiful: a glistening centre stone on a solid gold band.

'I'm really happy for you,' she says, hugging Elsie again.

'I had no idea!' Elsie says, as everybody who has just got engaged does.

Grace thinks of the image she has seen so many times. The weight of her wedding dress pulls at her body. She holds ivory roses. Eliot is by her side, whispering things she will always remember into her ear.

Grace remembers the crooked words on the postcard she found last night. *You cannot change what is meant to be.*

'No, me neither,' she says, her head feeling light, as though she might float off somewhere.

'He took me to the Hilton and ordered champagne,' Elsie says, still beaming. Grace tries to beam too. 'And then I knew what he had planned.'

'I thought it was rather obvious from the start. I was so anxious all the way there. I barely spoke!' Eliot says, his eyes darting over to Grace as though he is still anxious now.

'I suppose you were quieter than usual. The only thing you did say was that you felt a little queasy, and I was wondering why on earth you were taking me out for lunch!' Elsie says, and laughs.

She's happy, thinks Grace. This has made her really, really happy.

This is the first time, Grace realises as she watches Elsie talk and gesture with her newly decorated hand, that she has seen Elsie this animated in years. Ever since they were eleven, since the day of Rachel Gregory's birthday party, the day of the car crash, Elsie began to distance herself from who she had always been, from

Grace and from their mother, to step out of the light and into a darker version of herself.

The night of the car crash, the twins' bodies had ached with tiredness. Elsie's arm was wrapped tightly in a bandage under which dried black blood lurked. After watching some cartoons together, the twins began to feel a little more normal. When Mags arrived, and Elsie went out to say hello to her, Grace lay on the sofa, enjoying feeling as though things were okay again. Speaking to Noel on the phone had made her feel nicer. She was glad Elsie's arm didn't seem to be bothering her too much, and she knew that Mags would cheer their mother up.

But only a few seconds after Elsie disappeared out into the hallway to say hello to Mags, she returned to the lounge.

'What's the matter?' Grace asked, sitting up.

Elsie's face had been white since the accident. Now, it was red with anger, or humiliation, or something that Grace couldn't recognise, even on a face identical to her own.

'What's wrong?' Grace repeated, as Elsie stood frozen in the doorway of the living room.

'She was trying to save you,' Elsie said slowly, before standing in silence again.

'Who was?'

'Mum. She has just told Mags that she had a nightmare about the car crash before it actually happened, like a premonition. She knew it was going to happen. And she said to Mags that she tried to save you.' Elsie looked down at her bandaged arm. 'She made you move seats. But she didn't bother to move me. That's why I got hurt. She must have known I'd get hurt, but she didn't move me. She moved you instead.' Elsie's voice was rising now to an injured yowling sound.

Grace suddenly felt like she had eaten too much, as though she might be sick. She sat up and turned off the cartoons. The white light in the centre of the television faded slowly in the black of

152

the screen.

'Well, she probably got it wrong. You know how superstitious Mum is. She probably had a feeling that turned out to be all wrong.'

'No, that's not what she said. She said she'd had "one of her visions". It made it sound like she's had them before. And then she said that she was trying to save you. So you are fine. And I have been hurt. She chose you. You're the best one.'

Grace knew that her mouth was gaping open, and that she should say something. But she couldn't say anything. And then, suddenly, Elsie was flying around the room, stomping and trembling, as though a volcano had erupted inside her. Her skin was red and her black hair was flying behind her, loose from the braid that their mother had done for her that morning: so long ago.

'She hid my red dress. I know she did. I could tell, when I said I'd found it in the guest lounge. She didn't want me to look nice, and she didn't want to save me from the crash! She doesn't love me. Two daughters are too much for her. She wishes she just had you!'

'Elsie,' Grace said, words finally coming to her, 'you're being dramatic. As always. Go and ask Mum what she meant.'

Elsie stopped flying around the room and dropped onto the couch, suddenly exhausted. 'No. Why don't you? You're the one she wants.'

That was the moment Elsie changed forever. And now, Grace can see a little of the old Elsie, the colourful Elsie, seeping back, because for once, somebody thinks Elsie is the better twin. Somebody appears to have chosen her over Grace.

And so they stand, surrounded by children's books and pot animals and stuffed toys and other things that Grace had been enjoying displaying before Eliot and Elsie came back. Elsie beams and twists the ring around on her finger self-consciously. Eliot throws his arm around Elsie's shoulder and adds elaborate touches to the retelling of the event. Grace smiles and watches how excited her sister is, and wonders what it all means.

153

'It means that they're engaged,' Noel tells Grace later.

'I'm sorry I keep phoning you. I know it's not your problem.' There's a pause, and Grace imagines Noel shrugging.

'You know I said I've had premonitions?' Grace begins, her mouth dry.

'You think you should be the one who marries Eliot.' Noel's words are quiet, and calm.

'How did you know?'

'I've seen the way you look at him. I know you, Grace. I know you really well. And I also know that he's not the one for you, Grace. I've been telling you that for years. I bet if you'd never had that vision of marrying him, you would never have even wanted him for yourself.'

Grace feels her face burn. 'You're making me sound selfish, as though I've wanted to steal him. It's not like that.'

'I know it's not. I'm just saying that you're getting yourself worked up over someone who isn't right for you.'

Grace sighs, pictures Noel on the other end of the phone. The image of his face in her mind makes her prickle with a craving to see him. 'I don't know.'

But Noel hasn't heard her: he's on a roll, which is unusual for him. 'In fact, you're always getting worked up about Eliot. But he never seems worked up about you. I don't think that's right.'

'I need a drink,' Grace says. She wants to ask Noel to come and see her, or ask him if she can go and see him. She wonders what he would say if she did. Probably something about Bea. The heavy feeling that Noel is with Bea, that she will marry Eliot, weighs her thoughts down, making her head ache.

'You don't need a drink. You need to think about something else other than Elsie and Eliot.'

Grace has been lying on her neatly made bed for most of the conversation, but she gets up now and drifts over to her bedroom window. She pulls the slats in the blinds open between the fingers of her free hand. It's a grey day. The orange-brick, square flats identical to hers on the opposite side of the road are a mirror reflection of the block she's standing in. She half expects to see herself, peering through the blinds in the third window up, second in from the left.

'I haven't thought about anything else for years,' she admits. 'Not really.'

'Well, I demand that you do.'

'I've never thought of you as the demanding type,' Grace says, hearing flirtation in her voice and wanting to pull it back. Noel doesn't seem to notice.

'Oh, I'm full of surprises,' he says cheerfully. 'Think of something else, anything else, and let me know how you get on. I'll ring you tomorrow and you can report back.'

Once she's off the phone from Noel, Grace takes her laptop from her dressing table and sits cross-legged on her bed, loading up the internet. She wonders if Noel is right. Surely there is something else she can think about, something else she can do with her time. She types into a search engine, and waits. Within a couple of seconds, she's found the website of a local amateur dramatic group.

Grace has always loved acting. When she was at college, she won the drama award. The memory of being classed as the best in her whole year makes her smile even now. She was in every play possible whilst she was at college, and threw herself into the nightly performances until her voice was croaky and her limbs ached. She did some acting at university too, although fewer roles there appealed to her. Now, as she scrolls through the gallery of the society's webpage, she acknowledges that the only roles that she'd taken were the ones where she starred opposite Eliot. Eliot was always overly fussy about which roles he accepted (for he was always offered the main part). He liked modern, avant-garde plays, and so the involvement she'd had with theatre in the three years she was at university was a handful of Beckett and Brecht roles.

Now, clicking away at the dramatic society webpage, Grace sees that the local group meets every Friday evening, and that their next performance, due to be organised in the next couple of months, is *Macbeth*.

In their last year of university, Eliot was involved in directing an experimental performance of *Macbeth*. Grace played Lady Macbeth. On her opening night, Elsie surprised her in the makeshift dressing room with a huge bunch of pink carnations.

'I'm glad you're working so well with Eliot,' Elsie whispered as she hugged Grace just before the play began. 'I know that a lot of our friends think he's a bit arrogant. I love that you can see past it, like I can.'

Grace said nothing, just squeezed Elsie tightly and thought of her first lines.

They met me in the day of success: and I have learned by the perfectest report, they have more in them than mortal knowledge.

Grace clicks on the map of the drama group and sees that the venue is a ten-minute drive from her flat. She snaps the lid shut on the laptop, springs up and pulls the blinds shut.

Chapter Twenty One

Louisa, 1976

Louisa liked Lewis because he was connected to nobody. Louisa still had to see Jimmy and Penny at weddings and funerals and gatherings, because Jimmy was Mags's cousin, and Penny had known Sheila all her life, and Sheila was Mags's sister. Suzie was Sheila's daughter and Suzie's boyfriend Mark worked Saturdays in the chippy next door to Pete's ice cream shop. Suzie's boyfriend's sister lived next door to Penny's mum, Dorothy. Everybody was connected with sticky, tangled tape. But Lewis was different.

It was as though he had come from nowhere.

On the day that Louisa met Lewis, she noticed his eye colour before anything else: before his torn violet trousers, before the grease in his hair, before the way he gestured wildly with his hands when he spoke. She noticed all these things later, one by one. But firstly, she noticed his eyes. They were the exact green that her father's eyes had been.

She wondered for a few seconds when she met Lewis and noticed his apple green eyes what might have become of her father's apple green eyes, which were buried deep in the ground. Then she pushed the terrifying thought to the back of her mind and asked Lewis if he would like his eggs scrambled or boiled.

The first time Lewis arrived at the boarding house, it was morning. Most guests arrived in the afternoon, in time for tea. But Lewis was different from everybody else. Everybody else's tea was Lewis's breakfast. And so he arrived at 8 a.m. on the dot, on the seventh of July.

'I'm performing in the Tower Circus and need somewhere to stay,' Lewis said simply when he arrived.

'Ah. So you aren't staying with the other performers?' Louisa asked.

'No. I'm just temporary. I don't know anybody else. They've got me in to cover somebody who was in a car accident.'

'So, what's your trick?' Louisa felt as though somebody had opened a door somewhere, and a chill spread over her bare arms.

Lewis leaned forward and Louisa was suddenly in his world for a moment: animals and sequins and musty backstage smells and clapping crowds.

'That would be telling. Do you have a breakfast for me? Or shall I find somewhere else?'

And so Lewis had his eggs scrambled and slept in Room 2, and stayed for much, much longer than a week.

When all the guests had gone home for the winter, and Louisa's boarding house sighed with relief, Lewis stayed. He moved seamlessly from Room 2 to Louisa's room.

'I would have set up camp in here a long time ago,' he told Louisa as he pulled off his boots and wriggled into bed, 'but I didn't want your guests whispering behind your back.'

'I think they did that anyway,' Louisa said. She had seen their dubious, judging glances as she poured Lewis extra tea and gave him the biggest slices of cake. And she didn't care. They had talked about her when she had invited young men up to her room before, and so she was used to being the subject of speculation, but she didn't want to tell Lewis about that so she sat on her bed in her white silk nightgown and put her arm on his. Even Lewis's skin was different. Jimmy's skin had been fuzzy and pale. Pete's skin was thick and pink, like a piglet's. But Lewis's was darker, and rough, and strong.

Lewis kissed Louisa. He had kissed her before, briefly, in the dining room, but then Mrs Shingle had cleared her throat and pressed the bell in the hall for attention, and that was the end of that. This kiss was different. It was like gold, like melting gold that shimmered and sparkled and glowed all through Louisa, from her skin to deep inside her. She felt a longing for Lewis that she had never felt for anyone.

She pulled away from him. 'There's something you really should know if we are going to be serious about one another.'

'Who says we're going to be serious?' Lewis smirked.

'I do, because I'm psychic. I have premonitions about the future, so I'm actually very sure that things are going to be serious.'

'Is that it? Is that what I needed to know? Because I meet people like you all the time. Magicians, psychics, you name it,' Lewis said, ticking off the types of people with his fingers.

Louisa waved her hand impatiently. 'Oh no, not that. That's not important,' she said, although it was important, really. Just not as important as what she was about to tell him. She sat up in the bed and focused on the outline of her feet, way down at the bottom of the bed, under her mustard covers.

'I can't have children,' she blurted out. Her feet blurred and she looked up at Lewis, who was beaming. His teeth were off-white but shiny and clean. His face, even though she had watched him shave that very morning, was peppered with a fine stubble. He didn't have sideburns or a moustache like every other man in the world seemed to have. Just a nice, plain face with not too much detail. Louisa liked that.

'Even better,' he said, before clambering on top of her and kissing her again.

The next day, Lewis took Louisa for a picnic.

'But it's freezing!' Louisa said when he told her his plans. The

Tower was surrounded by silver mist, and the whole town seemed to shiver in the crisp November air.

'That doesn't matter. I have taken the weather into account,' Lewis said as he tucked a red blanket under his arm.

When they reached the beach, he shook out the blanket and gestured for Louisa to sit on it. Then he covered her with a second blanket and poured her hot black coffee from a flask.

'Do you think you will stay in Blackpool?' Louisa asked Lewis as he poured himself a drink.

'Now I have you? Of course I will.'

Louisa sipped her coffee and felt it warming her slowly. 'You make things sounds so simple. Don't you have anyone to return to?'

'No. My parents are dead. My friends have their own lives. So this can be my life: here with you.' Lewis chinked his plastic mug against Louisa's and a dot of coffee flew out and landed on her wrist. She wiped it away and sighed.

'You don't have a job.'

Lewis set his coffee down on the sand, and Louisa could tell that he was getting irritated.

'Do you love me?' he asked, his bright eyes fixed on hers.

Louisa had had an unpleasant dream last night and had woken up sticky with sweat and tears. Lewis had been shouting at her in the dream. He had pointed a finger at her, snarling, and Louisa had knelt on the carpet sobbing. There was blood on the floor and a broken glass next to Louisa's foot. Louisa had never had visions of the future through dreams before. Her visions had always happened when she was awake. But still, if it had been a premonition and it meant that there was a chance of this kind of thing happening between them, she wondered if she should spare them both the pain now. She wanted a baby, and warmth and contentment. She didn't want smashed glass and blood and sobbing, and she didn't want those things for Lewis, either.

She stared up at him, her eyes watering in the freezing air. His jaw was set firm, his face pale with the cold.

'Yes. I do love you,' she said. 'But I just—'

'—Don't. Don't 'just' anything. If you love me, then that's enough.'

They were both quiet for a moment then, the sound of gulls and the sea gulping up the silence.

'What about some work though?' Louisa asked quietly. 'I don't want to seem negative,' she added.

'Well, although the circus is done with me now, there are a few odd jobs I've seen advertised in the paper. Painting and decorating, that kind of thing.'

Louisa smiled, glad that Lewis seemed to be looking out for work.

'I still can't believe you made me think you were a clown in the circus. You had me fooled for weeks!'

Lewis laughed and the tension that had been between them shattered in one second.

'I never misled you on purpose. You just chose to assume!'

Louisa shook her head as she recalled Lewis's first few weeks at her boarding house. He had been rather reserved about his work at Blackpool Tower's circus and Louisa had eventually decided that he must be a clown, mainly due to his eccentric dress sense and theatrical ways. Lewis hadn't corrected Louisa, until they had bumped into somebody from the circus on the promenade one day who asked Lewis to have a look at the wooden stage where it needed patching up.

'Mending the stage is a funny job for a clown to have to do,' Louisa had mused afterwards, only for Lewis to hoot with laughter and admit that he was an odd-job man that the circus group had hired to keep their stage and props up to a good standard.

Lewis put his arm around her now and brushed a strand of black hair from her cheek.

'I can't believe you didn't know that I was an odd-job man all along. I mean, you're a psychic!'

'I know. But it seems like I spend so much time looking into other people's futures that I never see what will happen in mine.'

It didn't seem like an outright lie when she said it. It sounded like the truth. And if Louisa ignored the visions and dreams and whatever else she might have to make her think she didn't belong with Lewis, then it perhaps would be the truth one day: perhaps she would stop seeing into her future and be able to take each day as it came.

When Lewis had fed Louisa sweet strawberries and poured some fizzy wine into her coffee mug, and made her eat the last chunk of chewy, warm bread that he had brought, they stood and shook out their blanket. Sand sparkled as it flew into the air, and Louisa felt the icy wind slowly make its way onto her skin.

'I'm cold again,' she said, although she knew Lewis knew that.

'I know,' Lewis grinned. 'I can't keep you warm all winter, you know.'

But in actual fact, he did.

And then the spring came. Louisa's boarding house slowly filled up with returning guests, and Lewis worked at the circus again, coming home each night smelling of tangy paint and wood. He made enough money to buy himself a new purple jacket, because the one he had arrived in was threadbare at the elbows. He bought new raspberry pink blankets for each of the bedrooms, and a new frying pan for the kitchen, and a new set of wine glasses for the dining room.

'You shouldn't keep buying things for Rose House, Lewis. It's not yours,' Louisa said to him one morning as he unpacked a shining new cutlery set he had bought from a man on the promenade.

Lewis stood up, a teaspoon glinting as it fell from his knee. He bent to pick the spoon up, placed it quietly on the dresser and stalked out of the room.

'Lewis!' Louisa hissed, hurrying after him. 'Lewis, come back! I didn't mean that to sound the way it did!'

The door slammed, and he was gone.

An hour went by, and another. Dinnertime came. Guests commented on their new knives and forks, which Louisa found vaguely unsettling. These people were meant to be on holiday, having the time of their lives, and yet they all found the room in their minds to notice a change in cutlery. The house became lively as families gathered to set off out for the evening. It glowed with people, the smell of cigarettes, and the jostling of bodies anticipating their nights of dancing and drinking. As the guests left for their evenings of fun, the house became quiet again. Louisa shivered in the cool air of early summer as she locked the door behind the last guest. She gazed out along the road, where holidaymakers were dotted along the pavement, their voices merged and hazy.

Where was he?

A stone of unhappiness thudded down in Louisa's stomach. She had felt this way for most of her life, wondering and waiting. She had been missing her mother and wondering why she had left for so long now that Louisa had begun to feel lost herself. And now Lewis had disappeared too. She clamped her eyes shut, squeezing out the grey street and dusky blue sky. But she saw nothing apart from Lewis's face, as it was the last time she had seen it that morning: stained with the grime of the circus. She saw nobody's future, and nobody's answers.

She shook her head, went inside, and locked the door.

Chapter Twenty Two

Louisa, 1977

As suddenly as Lewis had disappeared, he was back.

Louisa was scrubbing the doorstep, which, she had noticed, was filthy with seagull mess and dropped cigarette butts and the yellowed rivers of an ice cream that a guest had dropped that morning. As she scrubbed, she felt a dark shadow pass over her where there had been sunlight. She looked up and pushed her black hair away from her eyes.

'You're back!' she yelped, stumbling to her feet.

'Of course I'm back.'

'But I thought you'd gone for good!' Louisa stood apart from Lewis and stared at him for a moment. She narrowed her eyes, her initial elation darkening. 'I was so upset.'

Lewis frowned. 'Why? Why would I leave you? Because everyone else has?'

'Not everybody. Only my mother,' Louisa argued, not because she thought that was true, but because she suddenly wanted to argue.

'Well, I'm not your mother.'

'I know, but if you walk out and don't tell me where you're going, and don't come back for two days, then what do you expect me to think?'

Lewis sighed and took Louisa's hand in his. 'I expect you to think that I love you, and I will always come back.'

'But where did you go?'

'Well, that's easy,' Lewis said, his face breaking into a grin. 'I went to buy you a gift.' He rooted in his purple pocket and brought out a red box. 'Here. Take it. Open it.'

Louisa took the box and opened it. Inside was a ruby ring, sparkling blood red in the afternoon light.

'It's beautiful,' she said shakily. She looked up at Lewis. 'Which finger is it for?'

'Whichever finger you think I bought it for,' Lewis shrugged.

Louisa thought for a moment. She didn't try to squeeze her eyes shut, or wait for the beginnings of a violent headache, or look into Lewis's eyes to try and see what he was thinking. She just thought. And then she eased the ring very carefully out of its tight velvet casing and slid it onto her finger: the fourth finger on her left hand.

To begin with, Mags was to be the only bridesmaid.

'But I'll look daft,' said Mags, after throwing her arms around Louisa in her initial excitement. 'Nobody has only one bridesmaid.'

'Alison Hall had one bridesmaid,' Louisa pointed out as she flicked through the Yellow Pages and jotted down telephone numbers of dressmakers. 'Do you fancy wearing green?'

'Alison Hall is not the woman to be inspired by. She doesn't like her husband, that's obvious. She put no effort at all into her wedding. She didn't even smile at her husband when they said "I do."'

'Well having one bridesmaid is no reflection on how I feel about Lewis. You know that,' Louisa said, replacing the lid on her pen.

'I do know that. But you don't want other people talking about you, and making comparisons, do you?'

'Mags, I don't care what people think. And I don't have any

other friends that are as good as you.'

'What about Suzie?'

Louisa considered it. 'Suzie's not my friend.'

'She adores you.'

Louisa let out a puff of amused air through her nose, and picked up her pen again.

'Suzie barely knows me.'

'Well, she still likes you. And we've never forgotten, you know.' Mags's voice suddenly became rather quiet. Mags's voice was never quiet. Louisa had to strain to hear her next words, even though she knew what they'd be: not because she could foretell them, but because they were the only words that Mags could possibly say next.

'You saved her life that day on the beach.'

Louisa drew a star next to the name of a florist. 'I know.'

'She'd love to be your bridesmaid. It could be her way of paying you back. So, are you going to ask her?'

Louisa waved her hand. 'Yes, I probably will. And while we're on the subject, I have something to ask you, too. I was wondering if we could have Noel as a Page Boy.'

Mags sat back and lit a cigarette. 'Of course you can. I'd already decided that he would be.'

'Oh, really? Are you suddenly in charge of my wedding day?' Louisa laughed.

Mags blew out some smoke from her nose. 'Well, somebody needs to take charge of the best day of your life. Might as well be someone who loves you almost as much as Lewis does. And yes, green will be beautiful.'

Louisa looked down at the Yellow Pages, at the starred numbers and circled names and the notes she and Mags had made next to each one, and felt a pleasant tug of happiness in her stomach.

Louisa didn't manage to find exactly the same colour green as Lewis's eyes for Mags's and Suzie's dresses, but she found a nice bright leafy green that the lady in the shop told her was this summer's bestseller for weddings.

'Mother of the bride outfits, bridesmaids, you name it,' she said as she plonked the material in a bag and tapped roughly on the till. 'Has your mum chosen her outfit, love? It'd be nice if she matched the bridesmaids. I'd do her a deal.'

Louisa stood, her mouth gaping open silently, thinking of her mother wading into the sea, tasting salt and sand and fear.

'Yes, yes. The mother of the bride has chosen her frock. She's wearing red,' Mags said hurriedly.

Louisa didn't speak again. She handed over her money in silence as Mags spun elaborate stories about the red dress that didn't even exist. When they left the sweet-smelling fabric shop, she let herself picture Rose: Rose in leaf-green, cheering Louisa on as she married Lewis.

'I'm so sad she won't be there,' Louisa said to Mags in the end, as they meandered through the back streets of Blackpool, the noise and delight from the promenade a distant blur of noise and colour. Mags paused and alternated the bags of fabric she was carrying to stop her arms from aching.

'I know.'

A couple of streets down, after they had walked for around ten minutes in uncharacteristic silence, Mags paused again. This time she put the shopping bags down beside her for a moment, put her arms around Louisa, and hugged her.

'I should have saved her,' Louisa muttered as Mags picked her shopping bags back up.

Mags shook her head. 'Don't be worrying about that. There's plenty of other people you can save.'

But Louisa wasn't listening. She was looking out, past the lines of houses and washing and children skipping, past the blur of holidaymakers, out to the glinting waves.

The wedding was held in the church near to Rose House. Louisa's dress was billowy and ethereal-looking with elaborate lace daisies stitched onto the sleeves. The guest list was rather compact. Lewis had no family and Louisa had no family. They had few friends between them. She still hadn't spoken to Hatty since her father had died. So Louisa and Lewis invited their small selection of friends, and friends of those friends. Suzie, who looked stunning in her leaf-green bridesmaid dress, brought her boyfriend Mark, who brought his brother Adrian. Jimmy and Penny came with their red-haired little boy who garbled a string of toddler gibberish throughout the ceremony. But even with the friends of friends and children of friends, the church still looked almost empty when the huge double doors were pushed shut.

As Louisa said her vows to Lewis, she felt a part of herself flutter up above them both, above the congregation, up past the myriad of sugary colours of the stained glass near the high church ceiling. She felt herself look down along the pews on the guests' heads, bobbing like buoys in a wooden sea. She felt herself fly out of the church and into the burning August air, and smelt the salt and the crowds of the promenade. She felt herself search and search for her mother, for a grey-haired woman wading back out from the sea with a faded dusting of copper freckles on her cheeks and shoulders, and for a boy with purple eyes who could tell Louisa why her mother had wandered out into the waves seventeen years ago. And then, suddenly, Louisa was back in the church, with Lewis clutching her hand and smiling at her and people applauding as he leaned in to kiss her. His lips were soft and kind, and tasted of black cherries.

At a few minutes past three o'clock, the small party moved from the church to The Fortuna Hotel in an assortment of cars. Louisa found that Mags had painted the car she and Lewis were to travel in with white hearts and smiling faces. 'Just Marreid', it said on the back of the car, for Noel had been given the job of writing. She smiled at Lewis as they drove the short distance to the hotel. She ignored what she knew, and smiled as though she was happy and thought she always would be.

As they moved around the dance floor to The Carpenters that night, Louisa looked up into her husband's apple green eyes before resting her head back down on his shoulder. She gazed around at the empty glasses and the paper plates of chicken bones and flakes of fallen pastry, at the other couples dancing with one another and the sleeping children sprawled on parents' knees, at the flashing disco lights and the relentless August evening light outside the window. She carried on looking and resting her head on Lewis and swaying with him until the music stopped.

Chapter Twenty Three

Grace, 2008

I can't believe she's done this to me, Grace thinks as she stares up at Rose House.

The FOR SALE sign is a garish yellow and is nailed ruthlessly next to the front door, where the guest house sign used to be. As Grace stands before it, unable to continue, for the moment, with her day, the front door opens and Elsie appears: all scarf and keys and shiny, wavy hair. She fumbles around a bit in her bag before noticing her mirror image standing before her.

'Grace!' she says, with a small smile. But then she glances to her left and sees the sign, huge and ugly. She clamps her hand over her mouth, her bunch of keys dropping to the floor and splaying on the concrete step.

'I'm so sorry,' she whispers eventually, but her words are carried away by the wind and the sea.

'Why didn't you tell me?'

'I was going to! I was going to tell you today!'

'That you're selling *our* house? How did you think it was okay to not tell me about this?'

'I was going to tell you today,' Elsie repeats, making a fury spread through Grace like fire.

'You are not the one who gets to make all the decisions! We're meant to be a team! Why do you have to have *everything* to yourself? Why can't you *talk* to me about anything?' Grace screams, knowing that she has lost control, knowing that she must calm down, but unable to stop her voice from rising and rising like a flame.

Elsie shakes her head.

'You hate this house, Grace,' she says eventually. Her voice is calm.

'I hate staying here, because it reminds me too much of Mum!'

'Oh, so I have to live here on your behalf? Has it ever occurred to you that I might hate staying here too? That I might not like the thought of being near anything that our mother touched?' Elsie says, bending down to retrieve her keys.

Grace is silent. She pulls her cardigan around her. She came here before work because she realised she didn't have a coat with her, and she was early, and she decided that borrowing a coat from Elsie and driving to the shop with her would be sisterly and pleasant. But then, of course, Grace had pulled up in front of a house that had a huge FOR SALE sign attached to it, and had immediately forgotten how cold she was. Now, she's suddenly freezing again, the winter wind snaking through the gaps in her loosely knitted sleeves and nipping her arms.

She turns from Elsie, shivering with cold and anger, and gets in her car. She ignores Elsie's face as she speeds away, and focuses on the narrow road so that she can't see whether her sister is upset or angry or, as usual, Grace thinks bitterly, indifferent.

When Grace arrives at the shop, she paces around, the door open half an hour early but no customers to take advantage of the extra shopping time. She kicks the counter, then wonders if her mother might have seen her from whichever ethereal world she is gazing down from, and feels instantly guilty.

When Mags arrives just after opening time, her brown curls that have lately been more and more grey flying behind her, Grace's body stiffens with apprehension. She hasn't spoken to

Mags since their disagreement about Grace wanting to follow her premonitions.

Why do I keep falling out with everyone? she thinks as she watches Mags rush in from the cold and slam the door shut noisily behind her. Mags holds up her hand as Grace begins to smile tentatively.

'Before you say anything, I'm sorry,' Mags says briskly.

'Oh, Mags I'm sorry too. I suppose I gave you a bit of a scare saying things that made me sound like my mother.'

Mags gestures to the back of the shop. 'Is the kettle on?'

'No. But I can soon sort that out.'

They walk to the back of the shop together and Mags sighs.

'Your mother was in a bad way before she disappeared. We both know that, Grace. But even years before that, she was always obsessing over what she should be doing, and how she should be stopping things that she thought were going to happen.'

Grace flicks on the kettle and thinks of the car crash. A dried red blood stain, the crunch of metal, the vanishing of Elsie's spirit and fun and noise.

'I know, and I really try to be different. I don't want to make mistakes or hurt people like Mum did. But she's in my blood, Mags. I'm the same as her. I try not to make the wrong choices the way she did, but having her gift is really difficult to ignore. It's so powerful,' Grace yanks two teabags from the packet, 'that I feel like I have to follow the visions. And I know that even if I didn't, they would probably still come true anyway. I can't forget them. It's too hard.'

'That's what Lou used to say. And it didn't do her any good.' Grace sighs and Mags holds her hands up in defeat. 'I'll drop it, for now. I don't want to fall out with you, especially over this. Don't forget my sugar.'

'Rose House is up for sale,' Grace says as she stirs some sweetener into Mags's drink.

Mags sits down suddenly on one of the chairs. 'Rose House? For sale? Since when?'

'Since I went to pick Elsie up this morning and saw the sale board. She didn't even tell me.'

Mags stands up and starts clearing away the tea things. 'I can't believe you're selling it.'

'I'm not. Elsie is.'

'Have you told her how you feel?'

'Yes. I'm furious with her.'

'You're always furious with Elsie,' Mags says. 'I wish you two could get on a bit better. You know, that was one of the things that always made Louisa anxious. She always knew you and Elsie would end up falling out over something.'

Grace stares into her scalding tea. How much had her mother known about the future, the present that they were all living in right now? Had she known about Eliot?

'She must have known everything about us,' Grace decides. 'She must have known that Eliot would cause problems between Elsie and me.' She pushes her hands through her hair. She washed it this morning and it is cool and satiny, too smooth to do anything with. 'I really wish she had stayed with us.'

Mags stops clearing up and stares into space. 'Me too.'

'She could have helped me make the right choices, if she was here,' Grace continues, and Mags shakes her head.

'That's the thing, Grace. You need to be the one to make the choice. Louisa didn't manage it.' She stands up and downs her drink. 'So it's up to you, now.'

Grace thinks of the postcard she found the other night, sealed in an envelope for over fifty years.

'Mags, do you think Mum would have taken advice if she'd been given it?'

Mags shrugs. 'She didn't take advice from me as much as I would have liked. Or your father. But maybe, if the right person had come along, with the advice she wanted, she would have taken it.'

Grace thinks of the scrawled, knotted letters, the clear warning, the message that echoes in her mind.

Our daughter will have my gift. She will see what should be and will be. She must use it wisely.

Why was the postcard never given to her mother? If it had been, would it have helped her to make better choices?

'Maybe.'

Mags stays with Grace for a while. A few minutes after she has gone, leaving the shop quiet and still once again, the door jangles open.

It's Elsie.

Grace stares at her sister accusingly; she can't help it, it's as though her features arrange themselves with no direction from Grace herself.

'Look,' Elsie begins quietly. She makes no move to unwrap her purple scarf, or take off her gloves or coat, or do any of the things that would suggest she might be staying. 'Eliot's friend is an estate agent. When he came round the other night, he gave us a valuation. We were chatting about selling Rose House and Eliot's flat and perhaps buying somewhere to live together after the wedding. I said I'd have to think about it, and that selling the house would be a big deal because of how much I think about Mum. I told him that I couldn't imagine cutting our final connection to her.

'I called into the estate agent's yesterday to ask for some more advice so that I could discuss it properly with you. I got these leaflets,' she pulls some crumpled papers from her bag and waves them around feebly, 'which I was going to show you today. But the agents must have made a mistake, and come and put the sale sign up before I'd properly confirmed it. I told them I'd need to get your go-ahead, so they shouldn't have done anything yet.' She stuffs the papers back into her bag, and then stares across at Grace. She's wearing more make-up than usual, Grace notices, or perhaps a different colour of eyeshadow. Her violet eyes glint in the weak winter light.

'You think about Mum?' Grace asks, unable to digest anything else Elsie has said other than the part about their mother.

Elsie shrugs. 'Of course I do.'

'But you never want to talk about her.'

'I talk about her sometimes now. With Eliot.'

Grace nods. 'I'm pleased that you talk about her,' she says, wiping her face with her hands. She can see her ghostly reflection in the glass of the shop's door, and realises that she has been crying, sees that her mascara has run in black scores down her face. She shifts her gaze to watch as Elsie takes her coat off and gives her a small smile.

The day inches by. The twins don't discuss Rose House, or Louisa. Grace keeps the secret of the postcards she found tucked away with the other things that she doesn't tell Elsie about. The shop is silent except for the squeaking of glossy pages as Elsie leafs through a bridal magazine.

The half term holidays are over. All the children are back in school, and adults are back at work. The only people wandering through the square are pensioners and their dogs.

'It's going to be a long winter,' Grace says as she stands and stares out of the big bay window at the front. The grey drizzle has chased the few stragglers of the day away, and the wide expanse of street is vacant and grim. Yellow lights have begun to filter through from the shops opposite. It's only 4.30 p.m. and already the sky is black.

'Well, it's not the end of the world if we don't make a huge profit in our first year.'

'I suppose not,' Grace agrees reluctantly. But it's not the money that bothers her. She has enough for rent and clothes that catch her eye and bottles of wine that are on offer. She saved some money after university, working at the bookshop chain in the town centre for over four years. After the monotony of working towards somebody else's targets, Grace thought that opening a business would be exciting. She thought that it would make her fulfilled, and happy to stay in Blackpool. But it doesn't. She is quite fond of Ash Books, and she wouldn't like to think that she

175

would desert her twin in their new venture. But the frustration of an empty shop and nothing to do in it rattles something deep inside her. She thought that having her own business would be exciting, but in fact it's nothing like she imagined it would be.

'Do you not need money for buying your next place with Eliot? Were you not hoping to make more?'

'We've been open a week, Grace. Give it some more time.'

Grace shrugs and wanders over to Elsie and her magazine, pulling it towards her and looking at the page filled with soft white dresses. She wonders how she will feel when Rose House is gone, and Elsie and Eliot are married. What will be here for her then, aside from the deathly quiet bookshop?

'When are you thinking of having the wedding?' she asks Elsie, whose face lights up at the question.

'We said perhaps in the summer. A lot of places might be booked up, but I'm sure we'll find somewhere.'

Grace's insides tighten. 'I'm sure you will.'

'And once the wedding's over, and the house is sold, we can focus on the future and Ash Books.'

Grace nods and looks around. The shelves are immaculate, the displays newly arranged. The till is empty. Even the twins' mugs are washed and neatly stacked in the room at the back. 'Yes,' she says, feeling her heart sag.

'Come on!' Elsie says brightly, leaping over to the door and twirling the 'OPEN' sign round to 'CLOSED'. 'Let's finish a bit earlier today. Eliot is taking me to the cinema, and you have your new drama group, don't you!'

Grace picks up her bag from the side of the counter, where she dropped it that morning.

'Yes, I do!'

As they walk through the sodden streets to her car, she thinks of stages and curtains and rehearsals and feels a buzz of excitement lift her spirits.

That night, after a quick shower and a change from her jeans to a casual tea dress and tights, Grace adds a layer of mascara to her already thick, black lashes and slicks some berry lip gloss onto her lips. She reaches for her phone in her pocket and types out a quick message to Noel.

Doing what you said. You'll be pleased with me. Chat later.

Grace clicks 'send', picks up her handbag and heads for her front door. A shot of nerves blasts through her as she starts up her car and drives to the centre where the drama group is held. She winds through the colourless streets and turns her radio up loud, enjoying the anticipation of something new and unknown. She pulls up in the car park a few minutes before the group begins.

When Grace pulls open the glass-panelled door, she sees the members of the group turn to see who has arrived. She smiles as she enters, and a few people smile back as she sits down on a free chair.

The woman next to her has huge hair and a wide, toothy grin. 'You're new, aren't you? I only started last week,' she confides, and touches Grace's arm conspiratorially. 'We'll be newbies together. I'm Shelley.'

Grace introduces herself, then quietens as she hears the organiser of the group ask for everyone's attention.

'Hi everyone. Lovely to see you all, and welcome if you haven't been before. I'm Kate. I run the group and direct most of the performances, although we encourage you all to be involved in as many aspects of performances as possible. Tonight we will be holding auditions for the next play. As most of you know, we'll be performing *Macbeth* in a couple of months' time. So, once the roles are decided, it'll be pretty full-on rehearsals until the opening night. I'll give out the scripts, and then let's see what you've all got. It's up to you which part you read. Do whichever scene you feel most comfortable with, and we'll cast according to who we see fit for each part.'

Kate wanders over to Grace and Shelley after the group has

started to break into smaller, hushed clusters.

'Don't feel any pressure tonight, Grace,' Kate says after Shelley has introduced Grace on her behalf. 'You can sit this one out, if you like. We'll be auditioning for our next play in a couple of months, so you can just do some observing and crowd stuff before then if you'd prefer.'

'Thanks so much, but I'd like to audition,' Grace replies quickly. 'I like a challenge.'

She looks down at the script in her hands and thinks back to the last time she played this part. The once-foreign words had meant a lot to Grace even then, but she feels like she can do an even better job of saying them now.

But when she steps onto the small stage to read her lines, she feels tiny pricks of sweat erupt on her forehead. What on earth is she doing? What made her think she could take the lead in a play?

She never used to feel this nervous. She always loved pretending to be somebody else. She takes a deep breath, and pretends that it is years ago, and that she is on the stage that she used to know so well, with Eliot watching her, and Elsie supporting her.

'I fear thy nature;
It is too full o' the milk of human kindness
To catch the nearest way: thou wouldst be great;
Art not without ambition, but without
The illness should attend it: what thou wouldst highly,
That wouldst thou holily; wouldst not play false,
And yet wouldst wrongly win...'

As Grace finishes speaking in the audition, she realises that although her limbs are trembling slightly, and her face is still a little clammy from the nervous sweat that has broken out, she feels more exhilarated than she has done in years.

'You were so right,' Grace says to Noel on her mobile a few days later. She's walking to Ash Books, and he is walking to the tube station. Their movements make the line hiss, and she has to strain to hear Noel's voice. She stands on the promenade for a moment, staring out to the grey expanse of sea, as she listens carefully for his words. She can't wait to tell him her news.

'Really? About what?'

'When you said that I needed to do something a bit different, to focus my energy on something other than Eliot and Elsie. I am so glad I joined that drama group, Noel. It was such a good idea.'

'So you're going to go again?'

'More than that! I'm making my debut in December!' Grace says, her excitement propelling her forward again in a brisk walk.

'You've got a part in a play?'

'Yes! *Macbeth*. And I know it really well, because I was in it years ago.'

'I remember that. You were Lady Macbeth.'

Grace smiles, the cold wind biting into her teeth. 'I was. And that's the part I wanted this time, but I didn't get it.'

'So what's your part this time?' Noel replies, his voice far away and almost lost in a chaotic buzz from behind him. Grace imagines him, suit on, laptop case swinging in his hand, moving under the London skyline with the other thousands of commuters. She gazes up at Blackpool Tower, which stands forlornly in the distance, and then drops her eyes to the ground.

'I'm just a witch,' she says, watching her feet move along the concrete, feeling suddenly as though the news isn't enough to make him proud of her. 'It's one of the smallest parts.'

'At least you got a part! That's something.'

'I know. And getting a part wasn't a bad result for my first meeting, was it?'

'I bet you'll love it. And you'll do so well that next time, you'll get a main role.'

'I hope so,' Grace says, but doesn't know if Noel has heard her, for the buzz behind him is louder now and the line crackles. 'I'll speak to you later, then,' she shouts.

She doesn't hear Noel's reply before the call cuts off, but she hears Bea's name, lost in the background noise.

Chapter Twenty Four

Rose, 1948

For a time, Rose enjoyed sitting in her comfortable armchair, jiggling her little baby about on her knee. She enjoyed taking little outings with her husband and her huge, bouncing pram that contained her perfect little girl. They walked to the park, the duck pond, the high street. Rose saved her clothing coupons so that now and again she could buy something she liked from Traver's Fashions. On those days, her husband would carry her parcel for her as they meandered home. They listened to *Mrs Dale's Diary* on the radio every afternoon and ate the sweet bread that they had talked about so very much during those ravenous, desperate years of the war.

Rose knew, when she walked hand in hand with her husband through the park, that she was the envy of so many women: so many of her neighbours who had lost their own husbands and fathers in the bloodshed that had ravaged the world. On account of his age and his profession, her husband had been allowed to stay home, stay alive.

But as time marched on, and the war finally started to feel as though it might become part of the past, Rose wondered how she would feel if her husband had disappeared mid-war, or had his face blown off, or returned with only one foot. Would she feel grateful to have him back in any form? Would she feel determined to make up for lost time? She had a frightening sense that had he been enlisted and shot to smithereens, or returned safely to her after five years apart, she would feel something better than the prickly frustration that gnawed away at her each day. For as comfortable as her life was, and as much as Rose's little girl brought joy to the pretty house that stood grandly on a hill, there just wasn't quite enough comfort and enough joy for Rose. There wasn't enough to cover the tedious silences between the two plates of eggs every morning, the lack of contact between a husband and his wife, the gigantic parcel of guilt and sorrow that sat between them every second of every day like a fat black cat licking its paws. There wasn't enough to stop Rose from lying awake next to the awkward bulk of her husband each night, thinking of the boy with the purple eyes and the feelings he had excited in her all those years ago.

So when Louisa was two, Rose packed their bags and left her big house and her husband. She walked to the train station, as it wasn't far. Louisa slowed them by stopping to splash in every puddle along the way, and Rose didn't have the energy to stop her. The walk took almost an hour. Rose carried her suitcase in one hand and held onto Louisa's podgy little hand in the other. When the train arrived, they climbed onto the hissing carriage, leaving their world behind in one step.

As the train wound through green fields and grey houses, towards the edge of the land, Rose stroked Louisa's soft black hair and thought about what they might do when they arrived in Blackpool. She fingered her hat, under which was crammed a handful of notes that she had taken from her husband's hiding place that morning. He'd thought his hiding place was a secret, but she had seen him through the crack in the doorway one morning, counting his money and then stuffing it into a shoe in his wardrobe. She didn't know what he was saving for. But Rose needed it more than him. She wouldn't be spending it on herself; every penny was for Louisa.

Rose's stomach squeezed at the thought of her husband. He had never done anything to harm Rose, and she cared about him very much. She wondered if he might find a new wife one day. Rose would write to him once she was settled in Blackpool with the man with purple eyes and explain that this was for the best. She would let her husband divorce her on whatever grounds he thought suitable.

And then they would both be free.

She settled back in her seat. Louisa was sleeping, her head heavy on Rose's chest. The pound notes in Rose's hat scratched at her head, nipping her scalp. She closed her eyes and imagined the cry of the sea and the colour purple and thought of all the magic still to come.

It was ten years later when Rose, who lived in a tall house where she could look out from her bedroom and see the roaring sea, was reminded of what she had left behind. As she clattered about in the kitchen, she heard the letterbox click open and shut. She rushed out into the hall and saw a bright white envelope flitting down onto the cool tiles.

The moment she caught sight of the handwriting on the envelope, Rose knew. She didn't need to read the sender's address written in blotchy black ink, or open it up and read what was inside. She knew it was from her husband. She picked the envelope up, turning it over in her trembling hands. How had he found her?

Rose had been making a blackberry pie for Louisa before the envelope had arrived, and now she saw that some blackberry juice from her fingers had stained the white envelope. She shuddered a little, for the stain looked like bright, fresh blood. She stood for a moment, still turning the envelope over, her fingers, purple at the edges, fluttering deftly. She looked up, out of the stained glass window of her front door. The blues and purples and oranges of the glass blurred the world beyond, making it impossible to see if somebody might be behind it.

There was definitely no need to open the envelope, Rose told herself. She knew what it would say:

'I have found you, Rose. Come home, I've bought you a new dress and a doll for Louisa.'

But Rose didn't want a new dress, or a new doll for Louisa, or to know that her husband had found her. She wanted to find the boy with purple eyes. She had been looking for all these years, but had still not found him. Now she must. She must, before her husband came to collect her. She trembled with frustration at not being allowed to live the life that was meant for her. It was bad enough that the doctor from around the corner was always trying to get Rose to take pills, to sign this form and that form, to stop talking about the boy with purple eyes. He was probably working with Louisa's father. Dr Barker said that Rose might not be very well, that he was worried about her. He said he was worried about Louisa, too, and made Rose sign a form with Louisa's name on it, although Rose had one of her headaches that day and couldn't make out the print. If only everybody would leave her, just leave her and stop trying to make her forget her true love. She couldn't let her husband or Dr Barker find her. They were coming. She knew from the letter that they were coming. They could be behind the coloured glass right now.

Rose squeezed her eyes shut so much that they hurt, and in that moment, she saw what she had to do. She heard the crashing of the waves beyond her house. The more she tried not to listen to it, the more she heard it, until it felt as though the shards of water were crashing against her head. She saw a figure in the calm, blue sea, waving her to join him, beckoning her to enter the life she should have had so long ago.

Rose moved towards the door, entranced by the image in her mind, deafened by the sounds of the water. If she didn't go now, then her husband would come for her, and Dr Barker would make her swallow those pills that sat in her bathroom cabinet, and it would be too late. She dropped the envelope onto the hall floor, and opened the front door, walking slowly to the beckoning waves beyond.

Chapter Twenty Five

Louisa, 1978

By the time they had been married for a year, Louisa was certain that Lewis was going to leave her.

She just didn't know when.

One week after their wedding, she had the dream again. She dreamed of that day in the future when her face was numb from tears, when she sobbed from where she was crumpled on the floor and she bled from broken glass and stared into a half-empty wardrobe. She awoke, sticky and breathless, and the images hung in her mind in the way that made her know it was more than just a dream. These things were definitely going to happen.

'Where are you going?' Louisa asked Lewis when he strode out into the concrete yard at the back of Rose House, when he put on his purple jacket, when he got out of bed and stretched his long hairy limbs, arching his back like an acrobat to get himself ready for the day.

When Louisa first started to ask Lewis where he was going all the time, when they were first married and fed each other cherries in bed, their limbs entwined, and walked along the beach together, their arms clamped around each other, Lewis ignored the edge in her voice, the tension in her face. He would cup her face in his large rough hands and kiss her with his cherry lips and tell her that he would never leave. Or, he would smile and shake his head affectionately like she was a naughty puppy; as though he didn't know what to do with Louisa but loved her anyway.

But now, a year on from their wedding day, things were different.

'Where are you going?' Louisa asked one morning when Lewis stalked into the kitchen holding his keys and wallet. Her voice was tight, stretched over a wail that threatened to emerge and drown them.

'Out,' he said simply.

'But out where? When will you be back?' Louisa was drying plates, and as she spoke the tea towel squeaked against the china, making her wince. Every unpleasant sound grated on her these days: it was as though the world was sharper around her and grazed against her skin. Soon, she would be scratched away to nothing.

'Louisa, I don't have to tell you everything about every place I go.'

'But I need to know. I need to know when you'll be back.'

'Why?' Lewis said, looking down at his key.

'Because I know that one day, you won't come back,' Louisa said simply. She continued to scrub away at the squeaking plate with her towel, even though it was completely dry, even though the noise tore at her ears.

'How do you know that? I don't understand how you can be so sure.'

'I had a vision. I saw our wardrobe with your clothes gone from it, I saw you leaving me. I know that you are going to hurt me, and it's driving me mad not knowing when it's going to happen,' Louisa admitted miserably.

'Well then, maybe you're not psychic after all. Maybe not everything you see is going to actually happen. You're in control, Louisa. You might have seen what *could* happen, but you can change it.'

'I hate it when you act as though my gift is useless. If I see something, then it happens. It *always* happens,' Louisa said as she slammed the plate down.

Lewis shook his head. 'You can't know that.'

'But I do know it! I know what happens. I know that you and I will break up! But I just don't know when.' Louisa was crying now, slow tears quickly spiralling into hiccuping sobs.

'Exactly!' Lewis shouted, banging his keys down onto the dresser.

'Shhh, the guests will hear!' Louisa said, wiping her tears with the tea towel, the rough fabric catching at her skin.

Lewis moved closer to her and whispered. 'You don't know when it's going to happen, because you don't know that it will. But the fact that you're so obsessed with it is making it more and more likely. You're pushing me away with all your doubt, Lou. You're suffocating me.'

'I can't help it,' Louisa said bitterly.

'So you can't help anything. You can't control anything. You're just going to sit about waiting for horrible things to happen.'

Louisa didn't say anything. She cried and cried.

Lewis swiped up his keys again and shook his head.

'You need to stop it. Stop using your gift as an excuse to not take control of your own life.'

Louisa sighed, a final sob escaping before she reached the weary state that comes after crying. 'I can't help it,' she whispered as Lewis stomped out of the kitchen.

That night, Louisa drank half a bottle of vodka. She had never liked the taste, and she screwed her face up as she swallowed to try and squeeze the unpleasant flavour from her senses. She just wanted to stop feeling. After four glasses, she did stop feeling. A pleasant, familiar dreaminess settled down over her like velvet. The world around her finally seemed softer and less chafing.

Most of the Rose House guests were out. A few were watching the television in the guest lounge. Louisa normally popped her head around the door of the guest lounge and gave the visitors her best guest smile, and asked if she could get anything for anybody. But tonight, after she tripped over nothing on the way from the kitchen to the lounge, she decided that she would leave them all to their own devices. When she heard Lewis climbing up to their bedroom just after ten o'clock, she flew from the bed to her dressing table and fumbled around for her lipstick. Her talc clattered off the table and puffed over the carpet, and her perfume bottle was knocked down with a clang by her clumsy hands. But eventually, she found her lipstick. She drew a big red smile onto her lips and ran her brush through her glossy black hair.

She watched in the mirror as Lewis entered the room. He stood silently, knowing she was watching him. She would make the first move: the vodka had made her brave.

'I'm sorry.' Louisa's words were clean and simple: a little slurred perhaps, but she couldn't help that.

Lewis didn't say anything. He raised his eyebrows slightly.

'Let's go out tomorrow night,' Louisa said.

'What about the guests? Have you forgotten that we have a full house?'

Louisa paused for a moment. She had completely forgotten.

'No. Of course I haven't forgotten. I am going to ask Mrs Brendan to watch the house after I've served dinner and the visitors have all gone where they're going for the evening.' Mrs Brendan lived next door. She had closed her own guest house last year, and lived in there alone now with four cats and not much to do. She wouldn't mind. 'As long as we're home for when everyone starts getting in. About ten. She'll do it, I know she will. I think it'll do us good.'

Lewis scratched his head and chewed his bottom lip. Louisa felt a flutter of irritation tickle her insides.

'I'm not asking the world of you, Lewis. I just want to go dancing or something. Or for a drink.'

Lewis looked at Louisa, then at her glass by the side of the bed, which was empty save for a few flicks of cigarette ash.

'I suppose we could go dancing.'

'Then it's settled,' Louisa beamed, her lips tight with the cheap lipstick. We'll have a wonderful time.'

It wasn't until the end of the evening of their night out that things went so horribly wrong. Because it was Saturday, Lewis took Louisa to The Highland Room for dancing and drinks. The subject of their future danced slowly beside them, but they both conscientiously ignored it. Louisa clung to Lewis, and tried to remember that he loved her, and that they were married. The image of the broken glass and the bloody sobbing and half empty wardrobe was pushed as far away as it would go.

'Shall I buy you another drink?' she asked Lewis, noticing that his beer bottle was empty.

Lewis shook his head. 'It's okay. I'll go to the bar.'

As he disappeared into the moving crowds of people, Louisa spotted a heart-lurching pair of eyes. They were violet: she was sure of it. It was the man who could give Louisa all the answers. He would tell her where her mother had gone, and why she had left, and why Louisa had seen it all too late. She scrambled over to him, elbowing her way past smooching couples and laughing friends.

'Hey, watch where you're going!' one woman called angrily as Louisa pushed her out of the way.

When she reached the man with the purple eyes, Louisa threw her arms around his neck, hanging from him and laughing in delight.

'I've found you! I've found you!' The words sounded so good to her that she kept on repeating them again and again. 'I've found you!'

The man frowned down at Louisa, and she saw disgust in his expression. A crack of disappointment clicked through her body: she thought that he would have been expecting her.

'You need to tell me about my mother!' Louisa shouted at the man. Once he knew who she was, he would remember Rose, and tell Louisa where she had gone, and everything would all become clear.

But the man didn't answer. He shook his head. Louisa tightened her grip around his neck. Even when she felt Lewis's arms around her, pulling her away, she closed her eyes and wrenched herself away from Lewis, closer to the man with the purple eyes.

'Get your girl off me!' the man yelled at Lewis.

Louisa heard Lewis shout something back, and then she felt herself propelled backwards onto the sticky, sweating floor. Feet thudded around her, and she felt blood drip down her face.

Later, when Lewis was packing his things, Louisa sat on the carpet, fingering her sliced skin and looking at the glass around her. She still didn't know how that had happened. She tried to recall if she had thrown the glass at Lewis, or dropped it, or if he had thrown it at her. It was only at that moment, as Lewis clicked his suitcase shut, that Louisa realised how stupid she'd been. The man's eyes had been purple from far away, but close up, they were an average cornflower blue.

'I don't know what's wrong with me, Lewis,' Louisa said.

Much later, as she lay alone in bed, their half empty wardrobe glowing in the darkness, she wondered if she had said it out loud.

Lewis didn't come back this time. Louisa knew he wasn't going to, so she didn't wait, and she didn't hope. Four days after he had gone, Mrs Brendan looked after the boarding house again and Louisa stood at Mags's cooker, sipping afternoon wine and cooking.

'Let's make dinner together. You look like you haven't eaten in weeks, and Charles is working late tonight at the office, so I want some company,' Mags said when Louisa arrived. She put a hand up to Louisa's hair and twirled a piece around her finger. 'Your hair needs washing too. Why don't you go up and have a bath and I'll start the cooking. You come down when you're ready.'

So Louisa had shuffled upstairs to the bathroom and sat in clouds of steam. The plopping of drips from the hot tap into the bath mingled with the clattering of pans from the kitchen below and Louisa covered her ears. She wanted quiet, but everywhere she went the noises seemed amplified, and even when there were no noises her mind was loud and full of screams and high-pitched thoughts.

Lewis had asked Louisa two weeks and four days ago why she married him in the first place if she was so sure that he was going to leave her. She said she didn't know, and that was true. She couldn't make sense of anything anymore. She dipped her head under the steaming water, and stayed there until the bath was cold and her fingers were wrinkled and Mags came and got her.

Now, Mags set out cheap cutlery on the table.

'Noel, move your book. We're eating at the table tonight.'

Noel didn't look up. It was the summer holidays, Louisa realised, and that's why Noel was at home. She loved Noel with all her heart, but had barely noticed him today: he was always so silent.

'So, Lou. Did Lewis say what his problem was before he deserted you?' Mags said, noticing a bit of dried food on one of the knives and picking it off with her finger.

'Oh, there were all sorts of problems. He felt like I was going to leave him, or go mad, or something. He said he was constantly frightened of me running off.'

'So he ran off instead?'

'I know,' Louisa sighed. 'It doesn't make any sense, does it?'

'He did really love you, Lou. He probably still does,' Mags said as she placed the knife down and stood gazing at her friend.

'But what's the point of him loving me if I just keep messing things up? What was the point of me loving him when I knew it was doomed?' What was the point in any of it, Louisa wondered, unaware if she was even talking out loud anymore. She stirred the casserole and eyed silent Noel, who sat poring over the book about whales Louisa had given him a few months ago. One of the guests had left it in their room, and Louisa had a feeling that Noel would like it. He liked any kind of book, as long as it was factual. He never said he liked them, but his constant reading gave him away. Mags didn't talk to Noel that much, and Louisa wondered if that was why he was so quiet, or if he was just that way anyway. She wondered if Mags had been different and chatted to him relentlessly about life and friends and the local football team and school and what was for tea whether he would still be sitting there so quietly now, leafing silently through his borrowed pages.

Mags gave a long sigh, which interrupted Louisa's thoughts.

'I don't know, Lou. I don't know what the point was. Come on, let's have dinner.'

'He didn't even leave me anything. A parting gift, or words to remember him by. He just went. And so it seems like there was absolutely no point.'

The point of Lewis became clear a week later, when Louisa couldn't drink her morning cup of tea for the fifth day running, and her period was two weeks late, and she felt as though she hadn't slept for weeks even though she went to bed at eight every night. It became clear when she felt a bubble of movement in her abdomen, when her breasts swelled like ripe fruits before her very eyes and a cloud of nausea followed her everywhere she went. It became clearest when she held in her arms her blue, screaming, brand new twin daughters. For when Lewis had disappeared, he had left Louisa not just one parting gift, but two.

When the twins were a few weeks old, their eyes began to change colour. Louisa had hoped that their eyes wouldn't change from their deep blue to green, because she wouldn't have wanted to always stare into apple green eyes that reminded her of Lewis and her father. But the colour they changed to wasn't green. It was a deep velvet violet that made Louisa think of her mother, and the boy with the purple eyes.

Louisa remembered how her mother had cried out for the boy with the purple eyes so many times before the day she had disappeared. Rose had been always searching for him, and now, in the violet eyes of her own daughters, Louisa saw whose blood coursed around her own body and the tiny bodies of her twin daughters, and why her mother had never been able to let the boy with the purple eyes go.

My father, she thought as she stroked the precious heads of her baby girls. She wept as she remembered the man with green eyes who she had loved for all those years, whose blood she didn't even share. She wept as she remembered the cake he had made for her fourteenth birthday, and the shell he had left on her pillow when she first arrived to live with him, and the way he had played and walked and talked with her as she stumbled along the path of childhood. She would have been alone without him. She wondered if he had known that they were no more than acquaintances, thrown together with only her mother as a link that was as fragile as a web.

Louisa continued to weep until she had let all her tears drip onto the babies' downy little heads and they awoke, howling with hunger.

Chapter Twenty Six

Grace, 2008

'So,' says Mags, eyes wide in anticipation. 'What's your news?'

Grace tears a piece of ham from her slice of pizza. The twins and Eliot are round at Mags's house for the evening. The night is an attempt by Mags at a celebration of Elsie and Eliot's engagement the week before. A banner hangs unevenly over the table, a dated wall clock poking out from the middle. There's confetti too, sharp little silver cupids and hearts that keep sticking to Grace's skin.

'My news?'

'Yes, Elsie said you had some good news too,' Mags said, before biting a huge chunk of pizza and leaving a string of unruly cheese to dangle on her chin.

'Oh, it's just a bit of news, really. I've joined a drama group. And I've got a part in *Macbeth* in December.'

Mags beams and wipes the cheese away, leaving a smear of tomato sauce in its path. 'That's wonderful! I'm so pleased you've got yourself involved in drama again.'

Grace pops the ham into her mouth and swallows it before answering. 'Me too. The group seems really nice, and I'd forgotten how much I enjoy acting.'

'What perfect timing for you to be distracted too,' Mags says, more quietly, although everybody can still hear her. Grace sees Elsie look up from her pizza questioningly. Mags is staring at Elsie's engagement ring.

'I mean with the shop being quieter now half term's over. So, Grace, what's the part?' Mags asks quickly, getting up from the table and going in the fridge for some ketchup.

'It's only a small part. One of the witches.'

'I still think you should have got a better part than that,' Eliot says, shaking his head sadly.

Mags looks at Eliot suspiciously as she dumps the ketchup on the table amongst the pizza boxes and napkins. 'Why?'

'You weren't even there when I auditioned,' Grace points out.

'I know you will have excelled. You deserved more than a witch's role.'

'At least I got a part. And if I do well, then next time I might get a main part,' Grace says, echoing Noel's positive words.

'That's such a cliché, Grace.' Eliot is smiling, but his words sting Grace like nettles. 'I'm sorry. I'm disappointed for you, that's all. You've played Lady Macbeth before. That part should have been yours.'

'Well, it's not mine, this time. And I'm fine with it. So let it go,' Grace says.

'Good for you, Grace,' Elsie says, poking Eliot in the arm. 'I think you'll enjoy it.'

There's a pause while everyone carries on eating pizza. After a few minutes, Elsie pushes her plate away and wipes her hands with a napkin. 'Mags, I'm really glad that you asked us to come round tonight. There's something I want to speak to you about. I can't really go on with the wedding plans until I've asked you about this. I need to know something.'

Mags glances at Grace so quickly that nobody else notices. Grace stops chewing, the pizza suddenly seeming inedible. She wonders if somehow, Elsie knows about the argument Grace had with Mags, and about the premonition of Grace marrying Eliot.

Out of the corner of her eye, she sees the *Engaged!* banner drift down on one side, the full clock suddenly revealed.

'Obviously, I won't be having any parents at the wedding,' Elsie begins, her eyes on her napkin, which she is tearing into tiny pieces. Grace starts chewing again. 'I don't even really know anything about my dad, or where he might be. So I wondered if you would give me away?'

The clock ticks, and the remaining side of the banner gives up, so that it falls down completely, swirling to the floor in a silver blur. Grace sees that Elsie is clutching Eliot's hand tightly. Speaking about their mum and dad must have been really hard for her. It's the second time in a week that Elsie has mentioned their parents, after over ten years of stony avoidance.

Mags's eyes become watery, her blue eye make-up blurring at the edges. 'Of course I will. I would love to, Elsie.' She looks down and clears her throat. 'I remember planning your mum and dad's wedding.' Mags waits for a second before continuing. There are no objections, so she takes a breath and carries on. 'It was exciting choosing colours and flowers with her. I was the chief bridesmaid, you see. Elsie, Louisa didn't have her mother there when she was organising her wedding, and I know that broke her heart.'

Elsie huffs, but her eyes fill with tears. She brushes them away savagely.

'I know I won't ever replace your mum, but I will be here for you. As little or as much as you'd like.'

There's a silence, and then Elsie sweeps the little pieces of napkin up with her hand. 'You knew my mum and dad the most. Do you think they'd like it if they knew you were giving me away?'

'Yes. Louisa would have been happy about it, I'm sure. Like I said, she hated that her mother had left her alone. That's why I can never quite believe that she...' Mags's words run empty. There are none big enough. 'Anyway,' she continues brightly, 'while we're on the subject of it all, what have you decided to do about Rose House?'

Grace glances at Elsie, who looks at Eliot, who shrugs and fiddles with his tie. 'The market's very unpredictable, but it's a very attractive house,' he says, sounding like an estate agent. 'It would sell quite easily.'

Grace picks up a little confetti Cupid and inspects him. She thinks of how she feels when she stays over at Elsie's: anxious and haunted. 'I suppose we could just put it on the market and see what happens. I know we haven't really spoken about it properly but I've decided I'm fine with selling up.'

Elsie raises her eyebrows in surprise. 'Really? I thought you were dead against it?'

'No. It was a shock. But you've explained what happened. I know you need to move on. We all do,' Grace says, thinking of Noel and wishing he was here to cheer her on.

'Well then, that's settled,' Eliot says, pulling his beer towards him and taking a long gulp. 'I'll contact the agents about it and confirm the sale sign can stay up. Then we can get the ball rolling.'

As Grace watches Elsie and Eliot exchange glances, she realises that she might not believe that the sale sign going up was a mistake after all. A small fire quivers inside her at the idea that Elsie might have lied to her, that this might all have been a plot. But as she thinks of Noel, and his demand that she stop obsessing over her sister, and how different Elsie seems at the moment, how much happier she is, she takes a last bite of pizza. The dough thuds down in her stomach, quelling the fire that wants so badly to take control.

'So, Elsie,' Mags says as quiet is descending again. 'Have you thought about your wedding dress? What kind of style do you want?'

She'll want something plain, Grace thinks, pushing her plate away.

'Oh I don't know, something quite plain, probably,' Elsie says.

'Haven't you seen anything you like yet?'

Elsie shrugs. 'Not really. There are a few nice ones in the magazines I've been looking in, but I haven't really been dress shopping yet.'

Mags stands up suddenly. 'I have something to show you two girls.'

She's back in a matter of seconds, after the twins and Eliot have heard her thud up the stairs, rifle and rustle through paper and bags, and then return down the stairs heavily and out of breath. When she returns to the table, she is holding a huge white box.

'Let's go in the lounge, girls, and I'll show you what's in here. Eliot, get yourself another beer. We won't be long.'

As they all move to the dark, cluttered lounge, Grace and Elsie look at each other, each wondering if the other knows what's in the box.

Mags flicks the lights on and places it gently on the oriental rug. 'I wasn't going to show you this, yet. I got it out of the loft when you got engaged. I suppose I felt a bit nostalgic, which isn't like me,' she sniffs. 'Anyway, as you've been talking about your mum tonight, I feel like you need to see this.'

Mags lifts the top from the box, and pulls out a wedding dress. It's crumpled, and the once-white netting and lace have an unpleasant grey tinge to them. But Grace can't see any of that: Grace is looking at the lace daisies that are stitched delicately over the arms, and seeing the vision she knows so well flash into her mind. She can't help it: she gasps and puts her hand over her mouth.

'I know,' Mags says, misunderstanding. 'Your mum gave this to me around the time your dad left. She didn't want it in the house, but she didn't want to get rid of it either. She said that if she threw it away it would be giving up hope of him coming back, and she didn't want to do that. I put it away when she gave it to me, and I haven't had it out since.'

Elsie pulls the dress from the box and holds it up against herself. She is kneeling down, so the tired fabric flows out onto the rug. The musty scent of slow decay lingers in the air.

'I'm sure your mother would love you to wear it on your own

wedding day. That's if you want to,' Mags says to Elsie carefully, eyeing Grace.

Grace looks down, looks anywhere except at the dress she knows so intricately: the way the sleeves would be slightly too long on her and cover her wrists, the velvety feel of the daisies underneath her fingertips, the surprising weight of the short train at the back. She looks at Elsie, and sees how her sister is actually considering Mags's offer. For the first time since she had the vision of marrying Eliot in this dress, Grace wonders if she might have got it wrong. But before she can feel the doubt, it has swooped away, and she knows that she, not Elsie, is destined to wear this dress.

'Well?' Mags prompts, sensitive pauses never her strong point. 'What do you think, Elsie?'

Elsie suddenly drops the sleeve she has been admiring as though it is burning hot.

'No,' she says. 'I'll choose my own. I don't want to wear this one. But thanks.' She shuffles to her feet. 'I fancy another slice of pizza, if there is any,' she says as she rushes back into the kitchen.

At about eleven o'clock, Mags's pronounced yawns and the thought of being at the shop all day the next day make Grace stand and clear the pizza boxes. Elsie has brought her car tonight, and as they drive away from the house, Grace leans forward in the back seat and touches her sister's shoulder.

'It's a really nice idea for Mags to give you away.'

'Well, it's what I want.'

'Talking about Mum and Dad tonight reminded me of something I found,' Grace says as the car swings onto the desolate promenade. 'There were some postcards in one of the boxes we brought down from your loft.'

Elsie nods, keeping her eyes on the road. 'Were they Mum's?'

'Yes. They were from our dad, I think. They didn't say a lot. Just that he still loved her. Then there was a last one, from around the time she left us, that was blank. That might have had something to do with why she left. The things she did might not have been to do with us. It might have all been because of him.'

Elsie nods again, and then turns up the radio. Eliot begins singing along to the song that has come on: a slow, pained Indie track.

Grace thinks of the other postcards to Rose. She thinks of the one that promises a gift and that talks of knowing what should be and will be. She watches Elsie and Eliot together in the front, Eliot singing, and Elsie smiling at his efforts to hit each note. She sits back in her seat, and decides to keep that postcard to herself.

When she lets herself into her flat, she picks up the mail from the mat in the hall. She went straight to Mags's house from the shop and so hasn't been home yet tonight. There's a bill, and a postcard. The postcard is from London, with four predictable pictures of tourist attractions in each corner: Big Ben, the London Eye, Buckingham Palace and the Tower of London. Grace smiles, knowing who it's from. She flips it over and sees Noel's handwriting: neat and masculine.

Another postcard to add to your collection. Saw it and thought of you. N x

Grace thinks of Noel buying the postcard, picking it from a rack, queuing to pay, finding Grace's postcode, finding a stamp, stopping at a postbox. Writing a kiss.

She flops on the sofa and takes her mobile phone out of her bag. Her mind races as she presses 'call', images whirling around: the wedding dress, Elsie's engagement ring, the postcards. When Mags eventually answers the phone, Grace takes a moment to respond, to push through the pictures in her mind and string together what she wants to say.

'Sorry to call so late. Thanks for tonight,' she begins with.

Mags is guarded. She doesn't want Grace to ruin everything. She thinks it's imminent. It's all so clear in her pauses, in her stilted replies. 'No problem.'

'Mum's wedding dress is the one I'm wearing in my premonition.

201

On my wedding day, with Eliot,' Grace bursts out. There's silence. Grace imagines Mags on the phone in her cluttered lounge, a lounge where their mother should sit with Mags and talk and drink tea with her friend like a normal middle-aged woman. But instead, her mother is buried somewhere, and nobody knows where.

'You didn't say there was a specific premonition like that,' Mags says.

'It's always the same.'

'You need to ignore it.' The control in Mags's voice begins to unravel.

'I know. I need you to get rid of it. The dress.'

'Really?'

'Yes. Elsie doesn't want it. Perhaps if the dress is gone, the visions will change.'

'I think it's the right thing to do.'

'I'm so sick of seeing that wedding in my mind, Mags. I'm tired of it controlling everything I think.' *I'm tired of not being able to just love Noel*, she adds silently.

'So, you don't really want Eliot?' Mags asks.

'I don't know, Mags. I saw the vision of our future within an hour of meeting him. I used to think that I would have fallen in love with him anyway. But these days I'm not so sure. It's so hard to know if thinking I'm meant to marry Eliot makes me want to. But I'm so frightened of getting involved with anybody else in case my future with Eliot ends up hurting them.'

There's a pause as Grace thinks of Noel, as Mags sighs, knowing the pattern of all this better than Grace.

'I just think that if I could somehow manage to get rid of the visions, or change them slightly, then things might be a bit clearer.'

'Then the dress is gone,' Mags says, and Grace can hear the lift of a smile in her voice.

It is a couple of weeks later when Elsie takes the phone call that makes everything lurch forwards, away from what they all know.

Her mobile, normally buried deep in one of her huge, bright handbags, has been sitting on the counter of the shop all morning. When it rings, Elsie springs forwards hastily, snatching it from the counter and answering within seconds.

She nods and hums her way through the short conversation as Grace watches. After a couple of minutes, Elsie hangs up. She places the phone back on the counter and stares at it for a while.

'That couple who looked round the house have put an offer in. It's the price we wanted,' she says eventually. Her voice is steady, but Grace can tell that its evenness is taking some effort. Elsie is even paler than normal and her violet eyes dart over Grace's face as she waits for her sister to answer.

Grace takes a deep breath. 'So, are we going to accept it?'

Elsie is still. She stares at the phone for a little longer, and then raises her face to meet Grace's gaze.

'It's the right decision,' she says eventually. 'I think it's something we all need to do.'

'I feel like we are letting our last link to Mum go,' Grace admits as Elsie picks up her phone and begins to dial the estate agent's number.

'Grace, we are always going to be linked to Mum. It's just a house.'

It's true, and it's not true. Grace shakes her head, unable to do much more.

'They're going to start up a bed and breakfast,' Elsie prompts. 'They're going to keep it as Rose House, which is quite incredible really.'

It's not incredible. Rose House is just a name, Grace thinks. But for some reason, the sentence Elsie has just uttered makes her feel like things are getting back to the way they used to be, the way she has craved for so long.

She smiles at her sister, at her own face which stares back at her, unblinking, waiting for an answer.

'Then let's do it.'

When Elsie has called the estate agent back, and the twins have had a celebratory latte from the café across the road, Elsie stands up and takes her car keys from the counter.

'I almost forgot! I have something for you! It's in the car. I'll just get it.'

When she returns, she is carrying a box that makes Grace's head pound. She lifts her hand to her temple.

'What's wrong?' asks Elsie as she hands Grace the box.

Grace shakes her head, making her mind knock against her skull. 'Nothing. What's this?'

'Open it.'

Grace tears at the hot pink tissue paper, and then inhales sharply. Her head thuds. 'Where did you get this?'

'From Mags's house. I went round the other week with some flowers to say thanks for the engagement gathering we had. I cut the stems for her because she was busy making us a drink, and I took them to the bin outside. I saw that she'd thrown Mum's wedding dress out and I felt weird about it. So I sneaked round the back when we left and got it. I didn't want to ask her why she'd thrown it out. It was obviously just upsetting her having it in the house.'

'So do you want to wear it on your wedding day after all?' Grace asks, hoping. Her throat is dry and the words burn her.

'No. I want you to have it. You'll get married at some point, and I think it's more your style than mine. And we all know Mum would have rather you had it,' Elsie finishes, with more weariness than malice.

'You should have left it in the bin,' Grace says. She's only had the vision once since Mags threw the dress out. She hoped that it was beginning to fade away. But now, it's more vivid than ever, the dress gleaming white and trailing behind her as she walks down the aisle with Eliot, married to him.

Elsie shakes her head, stuffs the dress back into the box. 'I'm sorry. I didn't want to upset you.'

'You haven't,' Grace says, wincing at the rustle of the dress as Elsie folds it down, the rustle she knows so well. 'It was a lovely thing to do.'

Elsie gives her a small smile and pushes the box towards Grace. Grace smiles back, feeling like a strand between them has been pulled tighter. But as she smiles, her head splits with pain, her chest is tight and the words she can't forget spin around in her mind.

You cannot change what is meant to be.

Chapter Twenty Seven

Louisa, 1983

Louisa took Noel's hand as they walked over the ornate bridge in Stanley Park. He was almost twelve: a little old to be holding anyone's hand, but he didn't seem to mind, and the twins would never give her the contact she craved.

Louisa's first guests weren't booked in until early August. Package holidays, she told anybody who might be interested, had a lot to answer for. Blackpool's popularity had changed in the years since she had moved back. It attracted different kinds of people now, and Louisa's boarding house was seeing more empty rooms each summer. The money that her father had left her when he died was dwindling down to nothing and the repairs needed in the house were growing like an overfed cat.

Still, she thought, swinging Noel's arm backwards and forwards with her own, she needn't worry about the guests and the repairs right now. It was a gloriously warm spring day, and she was with her family and friends.

Mags turned to Louisa as they walked. 'Where have the twins gone?'

'They've gone to look at the swans. They won't be far away. They're getting no better at walking along with me,' she sighed.

'They'll calm down with time. They're only four. It's still very young, you know.'

'I suppose,' Louisa said. 'I find them so hard to control, though. I thought it would be easier than this.'

Mags gestured to the ice cream hut and rooted in her bag for some change. 'I know what you mean. Noel, what flavour do you fancy?'

'I'm constantly thinking of what the right choice is. It's driving me mad,' Louisa whispered, almost to herself. She rubbed her temples. Her headaches were coming back these days, but with no visions following them. She normally took some aspirin before she went out anywhere, but she'd forgotten today.

'Lou, what flavour are you getting?' Noel asked, tugging on Louisa's hands.

'Oh. Chocolate, I think.'

Noel smiled up at her. 'I knew you would. Chocolate's the best,' he continued as they queued up to order. 'You always make the right choice. So don't worry.'

Louisa stared down at him. 'Thanks, Noel.'

When they had eaten their ice creams by the lake, they all settled on a patch of grass overlooking the water. Mags put on her sunglasses and lay back to read a magazine. She had rolled up her trouser legs in a bid to catch the sun, revealing stubbly white calves. Louisa lay next to Mags for a few seconds, but couldn't settle. She could hear Elsie and Grace squabbling over something, and Noel speaking calmly to them. She gazed across the grass and watched for a few minutes. Elsie was pushing Grace down the small hill, and Grace was co-operating by propelling herself down in joy. Louisa gazed at her daughters: their gleaming black hair, their porcelain skin and chaotic movements. Grace caught her mother looking and smiled warily. Louisa smiled back, hoping that her indescribable love would somehow be transmitted.

'So,' said Mags from behind the magazine. 'How are you?'

Louisa stared at Mags. 'What do you mean?'

Mags sat up and shrugged. 'Well, it's been a long time since Lewis disappeared. I know the girls can be hard work. It must be difficult on your own.'

Louisa narrowed her eyes. 'It's not like you to talk like this.'

Mags flipped the magazine shut. 'I know. I hate this type of conversation. But I'm worried about you, Lou. You seem preoccupied. You barely talk to me about stuff these days.'

'Like what?'

'Oh, I don't know. Men. The twins. Your psychic stuff. Anything.'

Louisa shrugged and stared out to the calm blue water. Swans glided over the surface as though it was ice. 'There's nothing much to say.'

'That proves it! You always have something to say, Louisa. So something's definitely wrong.'

Louisa picked a daisy and twiddled it in her hand. She thought of last night. She'd had the dream about the twins again.

'I'm not sleeping well.'

'Why?'

'I don't know,' Louisa replied quietly. She picked the daisy apart and stood, brushing its crushed petals from her jeans. She hadn't thought Mags ever really listened to her. But it was nice to know that she noticed when Louisa stopped talking.

'I've been having bad dreams. And I still miss Lewis so much. I just wish I knew where he was.'

'He's still sending you postcards, is he?' Mags asked, lighting a cigarette.

Louisa nodded. Every so often, Lewis sent Louisa a card from wherever he was staying at the time. Every time Louisa heard a postcard waft down from the letterbox onto the tiles on the hall floor, she rushed out to retrieve it. She would squint down at the postmark, trying to make out the blurred stamped letters. But even when she could make them out: Minorca, Herts, Beds, she still had no idea how to find him. He still didn't know about his twins, because Louisa had never been able to speak to him. His postcards always said the same.

I still love you, Lou.

Louisa hoped that one day Lewis would say it in person.

'At least you know he's out there somewhere, thinking of you.'

Louisa snorted. 'You don't mean that.'

Mags laughed a dry laugh, and tapped the ash of her cigarette onto the grass.

'You got me. I don't. I think you should forget Lewis, and find someone as boring as bloody Charles. Then you'll have more to worry about than bad dreams. Do you know, he's made me host seven dinner parties with his colleagues in the last two months? I spend half my life crumbling Flakes over trifles these days. I'm sure I'm destined for bigger things than that, you know.'

Louisa smiled but stayed quiet. She'd give anything to have Lewis back, and to be hosting dinner parties for him. She wished she hadn't lost him. Her gift hadn't helped her keep her mother, or her father, or Lewis. She gazed over at the twins. She would have to be more careful with them. Much, much more careful.

As it happened, the warm spring weather brought some guests to Louisa's boarding house that very night. It was a group of friends celebrating a thirtieth birthday. They had decided to extend their day trip to the evening and wanted somewhere to stay.

'It's all a bit last minute,' said one woman with wide eyes, clearly overexcited by the spur of the moment holiday.

Once Louisa had showed the group to three different rooms, she served them tea and coffee in the guest lounge. She breathed in the smell of polish as they entered. She had given it a quick wipe over and opened the windows whilst the guests had been unpacking. She hadn't been in there in months and the bright wooden surfaces had been fluffy with dust. She looked around as the group settled themselves in various chairs, and suddenly saw with an unpleasant shock how dated it all was. Orange velour curtains hung like two flames either side of the bay window, their colour merging with the pine and yellow wallpaper. Louisa hadn't changed the decor since she had moved in, and until this very moment, had never felt she needed to.

'I'm redecorating in here,' she found herself saying to the woman who had been excited upon arriving.

The woman smiled politely. The man next to her nodded, moving his head slowly around in order to survey the decor.

'What kind of thing are you going for?' another of the women asked.

Louisa waved her hand towards the curtains that suddenly offended her so very much. 'Oh, you know, something much slicker. Smoked glass, leather sofas, that kind of thing.'

'Must be expensive to keep on top of the trends. You know, with a big house like this?' said one of the men, smirking.

Louisa smiled. He was right. It was expensive. But what he didn't know was that he and his friends would begin the funds for the refurbishment of Rose House that very night.

It was past midnight when the friends returned from their night out to Rose House. They'd been walking along the beach, and they all insisted on taking their shoes off at the door, not realising that the last thing Louisa wanted was a collection of stinking trainers and stilettos sprinkled with sand jumbling up the hallway.

'Would you like any hot drinks? Or a nightcap?' Louisa asked. 'The only thing I ask is that you're quiet once you get upstairs. My twin girls are asleep, you see, and they might wake if you're noisy. But if you stay down here, in the lounge, you can talk as loudly as you like.'

'Wonderful!' said the excited woman. It seemed that her excitement was a permanent feature, as it was still in full swing. She stood swaying as if she was dancing, running her fingers through her crispy perm.

'Come on, Brenda. You've had too much to drink, love. Come

and sit down.' The man Brenda appeared to be dating patted his knee, but Brenda shook her head.

'No!' she pouted, reminding Louisa of Elsie. 'I want to have fun. Stop trying to ruin my fun.'

The man rolled his eyes, retracting his hand and the offer of his lap.

'Sorry,' he said to Louisa. 'She always gets like this. She never wants the night to end. But there's nothing for us to do now but have a quiet drink and go to bed.'

'Actually,' said Louisa, feeling all eyes suddenly on her, 'there's something I could do for Brenda, if she'd like. It'd be fun. But I'd have to charge.'

Brenda lurched over to Louisa and took hold of her hands. 'What is it? Tell me!'

'Well, I could tell your fortune. But I would have to charge extra, on top of the rate for bed and breakfast.'

Brenda's heavily made-up eyes gleamed with delight. 'Yes! Yes! Where shall we go? One of the bedrooms? I'll be quiet, I promise.'

One of the men snorted with laughter. 'What makes you think your future needs to be a secret?'

'You never know,' Brenda scowled.

'It's up to you. We can go upstairs if you want, or we can go and sit in the dining room if you don't want your friends to hear.'

'Of course I don't. If they know my future plans, then they might try to interfere in them. I'd hate that. Plus,' she whispered, bowing her head so close that Louisa could smell fried onions and cigarettes on her breath, 'you might tell us something that Brian doesn't want to hear.'

'I'm going to bed,' Brian said, stifling a yawn.

Another of the women shrieked. 'What, you're not having your fortune read? I'll go next, after Brenda.'

And so, Louisa sat in the dimly lit dining room until the early hours of the morning, until she had told each of the friends what she saw for them. It was the same as it had always been: weddings, babies, jobs, new houses, new hobbies, old flames. Brenda was the most excited by the news that she would marry Brian and have five children. Louisa wondered how she would take the news, since children had a reputation for spoiling adults' fun, but Brenda whooped with joy at the verdict. Another of the women, Maureen, was amazed to find that Louisa knew she was married regardless of the fact that Maureen didn't wear a ring. Maureen would remain married and would travel around the world with her husband on a boat.

'Yes! That's right! We're looking into selling up and buying a boat! Wow, you really are spot on,' Maureen gasped as she handed Louisa a creased ten pound note.

After the guests had gone to bed, Louisa cleared away their ashtrays and glasses and cups, and climbed the long, dark staircase. When she reached her bedroom, she undressed, before taking the duvet from her bed and clutching a pillow under her arm. She left her bedroom and silently opened the door of the twins' room.

The room was heavy with the sound of Elsie's and Grace's deep, rhythmic breaths. They were safe in here: the guests were all tired and there was no movement coming from the other rooms. But still. Louisa squinted in the darkness so that she could see her daughters. Grace lay on her front, her comfort blanket abandoned on the floor beside the bed. Elsie was curled on her side, mouth open, strands of black hair strewn over her cheek, falling and rising with each breath.

Before Louisa climbed beneath her floral bedcovers on the floor next to the twins, she did a mental calculation of the extra money she had made that evening. It added up to fifty pounds. She smiled to herself in the darkness.

That night, Louisa had the dream. Again, Grace was an inch taller than Elsie. Again, Elsie was slightly thinner and had subtle streaks of bronze in her hair. Grace's hair remained the glossy black of a raven. She wore a necklace of aqua stones, which lay flat against her collarbone.

The twins were in the guest lounge of Rose House. It was different somehow: beige and tired, empty. Candles flickered in the dim light and an exotic smell hung in the air.

The girls were in their twenties, just as they always were in the dream. They were beautiful. But there was something ugly in the atmosphere between them, something that made Louisa moan in her sleep, toss around in her tangled sheets. Elsie and Grace talked, their words clouded at first as the dream blurred into focus. Grace left the room, returned with a glass of something. Wine. Louisa could taste its acid, and could feel the alcohol deaden her senses.

Elsie spoke, her quiet, troubled voice so unlike the singsong chatter that Louisa knew so well. 'Grace, I really need to know that you're happy for me. I don't feel like you are.'

Grace closed her eyes for a moment. 'I just care about you.'

'That's not the same as being happy for me. I asked you if you were happy for me.'

'I want things to be good between us.'

Elsie rolled her eyes. 'So we're now talking about what you want? You can be so selfish, Grace.'

'That's not fair!' Grace's voice rose above the other, watery noises of the dream: the television, the clanking pipes, and some vague, aggressive music. 'I just mean I want us to get along. And I just want to do the right thing.'

Elsie frowned, her attractive features momentarily crushed. 'I don't even know what that means. I don't know why you can't just talk to me properly instead of speaking in riddles.'

Grace stayed furiously silent, a black tear rolling down her cheek. She wiped it away savagely. 'I just sometimes worry about what's meant to be.'

'Don't say things like that. You sound just like Mum. You look like her too.'

'We're identical twins! If I look like her, then so do you.' Grace laughed, and her frenzied laughter beat into Louisa's consciousness, waking her. Her heart was crashing against her ribs, her mouth dry. She wanted to stay awake, to never return to the dream, but her eyes flickered closed again, and she was pulled back, deep into the sleep she had just left. She saw the twins again, saw fragments of glass glinting in their hair, the floor an iridescent glass carpet. The candles burned on and on, their flames rising higher, threatening to spill out and lash the room with heat and terror.

Grace looked up at her sister, her crimson face streaked with make-up, her hair tangled. She pulled at her necklace, clawed at the round, bright aqua stones. 'I've done nothing wrong.'

'You've done everything wrong. You're too much like our mother. I will never forgive you for this, Grace. Never.'

The way Elsie said those last, cool words woke Louisa suddenly. She stumbled to her feet and squinted across the room. The milky light of dawn cast shadows over her sleeping daughters.

'I had the dream again.'

Mags looked up from dishing out Noel's plate of Smash and Bisto. 'The nightmare?'

Louisa nodded.

Mags moved over to Louisa and put her arm around her. It was a strange gesture for Mags to make, and her arm dangled uncertainly from Louisa's shoulder. Louisa leaned into Mags, smelling her friend's familiar scent of mints, cigarettes and hairspray.

'Why don't you tell me about it?'

Louisa shrugged. Mags took her arm away and turned again, busily clattering cutlery.

'I could take whatever it is, you know. Ghosts, goblins, blood, guts. Nothing gives me nightmares.'

'It's not scary like that. It's scary in another way. I suppose because I know it'll happen, and it's not very pleasant.'

The words ring in Louisa's ears as she speaks.
You're too much like our mother.

'Can't you do something to change it? Make sure that it doesn't happen?' Mags asked before hollering for Noel to come downstairs.

Louisa stared across the kitchen, until her gaze met Noel. He smiled at Louisa, and sat at the table in front of his mountain of mashed potatoes.

'Well?' Mags was demanding. 'Can you? Change it?'

'I could try. I just don't see how. I don't really know what will cause it. So I'll struggle to avoid it,' Louisa said. Why would Elsie come to hate her so much? She knew she'd had a few problems controlling the twins lately, but she had presumed that this was an issue that would be ironed out as the twins grew up.

'Perhaps one day you'll stop having the dream.' Mags banged down a cup of orange squash for Noel. 'And then you'll know you've stopped it. You'll know it's not going to happen anymore.'

Louisa shook her head, and thought of Elsie's words and Grace's tear-stained face. Why was Grace, usually the calm one, going to be the one crying and shouting? Where had Elsie's spirit gone? Why was she about to become so still and pale? 'I just wish I knew how to stop it all from happening,' she said as she sank down next to Noel.

Chapter Twenty Eight

Louisa, 1991

'Mum, where's my red dress?' Elsie shouted. 'I can't find it anywhere!'

'I'm not sure,' Louisa called back, on autopilot. She was engrossed in an unpleasant book about a man who was possessed by a poltergeist. It wasn't her usual type: Louisa had never read a horror story before. It was making her nerves stand on end, but she wanted to know what was going to happen to the hero, and if he would ever manage to shake off the damned spirit that was ruining his life.

'But I'll look ridiculous if I don't wear a dress! Everybody else will. In fact, everybody else has a new outfit.' Elsie was still yelling from upstairs, and Louisa closed her book with a sigh. She had no idea where the red dress was. The thought of it made her feel kind of irritable and upset for some reason, although she couldn't put her finger on why. She stood up, frowning at the mood that had descended on her from nowhere. It was probably the book: Louisa wasn't cut out for horror. This would have to be her first and last.

'I don't have a new outfit,' Louisa heard Grace point out sensibly as she climbed the stairs to the twins' bedroom. Louisa smiled to herself. Good old Grace. She always tried her best to calm her more fiery sister down.

'Okay, Elsie. I'm here,' Louisa said when she reached the girls. 'I'm not sure where the dress is, though. When did you last wear it?'

Elsie wrinkled her nose, and Louisa felt a twinge of maternal adoration. Although Elsie was beginning to emulate a teenager, she was still really a little girl. Grace didn't try half as hard to act or talk like an adult, and the ironic result of this was that she came across as more mature than her sister.

'I can't recall the last time.' Elsie frowned, and chewed on her lip. A theatrical tear hobbled down her cheek.

'Just wear your jeans,' Grace suggested. She already had her white jeans on.

Elsie looked at her sister in horror. 'Jeans are fine for you. But I want to appear as though I have made an effort for this party.'

'Well, if we're any later then it won't look like you've made an effort. The party started ten minutes ago,' Grace said as she tapped her watch.

The party was to celebrate Rachel Gregory's twelfth birthday. Rachel was a mutual friend of the twins, and lived in a very grand house in Lytham. Louisa was driving the girls there; Rachel's dad was going to drop them off home afterwards. They had planned to set off to the party twenty-five minutes ago.

'Come on, Elsie. Decide what you're wearing and let's hurry up and go. You don't want to be any later than you already are.'

Elsie sighed and turned to the bedroom she shared with Grace: currently a mass of upturned clothes and shoes.

'The consequences of this are going to be catastrophic,' she said, shutting the door behind her.

Ten minutes later, Louisa and the girls were strapped in the car and moving out of the parking space at the front of the boarding house.

'Stop!' yelled Elsie suddenly. 'I know where the dress is!'

Louisa sighed impatiently and gestured to her watch. 'Elsie, you do not have time to go back in again.'

But an excited Elsie was already unbuckled and climbing out of the car. She held up a finger to indicate that she would only be one minute. Grace sat quietly, rolling her eyes at Elsie's dramatics. Louisa thought about her book. She had borrowed it from Suzie, who had the whole series. Louisa gazed out onto the street and wondered if she should just ask Suzie what was going to happen to the possessed man, and if the story had a happy ending. That would be much less unsettling. The thought of the book made Louisa's blood fizz a little inside her. She supposed that people like Suzie loved that feeling: loved the extra adrenaline rushing through their bodies. But Louisa didn't. Yes, she decided, putting the car into neutral whilst they waited for Elsie. She would ask Suzie what was going to happen, and move onto one of her romance books instead.

Settled by this decision, Louisa glanced in her rearview mirror and smiled at Grace. Grace smiled back, then looked to her left. 'Yay. Elsie's back.'

'Oh, good. Let's get going then.' Louisa glanced out of the window to see Elsie in the red dress. A shiver ran down her spine at the sight of it and she wondered why. Elsie looked much happier, and the dress did look nice, although it was a little creased from being crumpled into God knows what space.

'It was in the guest lounge,' Elsie said breathlessly as she got back into the car. 'I don't know why. I remember seeing it in there and thinking that I should move it back up to my room, but I forgot.'

Louisa turned around in her seat and looked at her daughters. The red satin of Elsie's dress shimmered in the weak winter sunlight and Louisa's stomach turned. She frowned.

'What's wrong, Mum?' Grace asked.

Louisa shook her head. 'I don't know. Nothing, I suppose.'

She put the car into first gear and swung out of the parking space onto the road.

It was as Louisa was swinging out of a junction, and checked her rearview mirror, that she suddenly remembered it all.

She'd had one of her nightmares a few weeks ago. The red dress, crumpled with tears, and days of loss and fright and confused sleep. Elsie sitting on a hospital chair, waiting for news that Louisa could not give her. A gold Renault Five, as crumpled as the red dress. Grace dead.

As soon as Louisa had woken from the dream, she had crept into the twins' bedroom and taken the dress from the wardrobe. The twins hadn't woken, and Louisa had stood still for a moment, her eyes closed, listening to the steady breathing and the faint buzz of a draught at the window.

She had gone downstairs, still in a haze of sleep, and stashed the dress between the cushions of the chair in the guest lounge. Elsie never went in there. Louisa had planned to dispose of the dress the next day, but had returned to bed and slept a calm sleep that had made her forget those strange hours and her nightmare. She hadn't thought about the dream again, until it swooped into her mind now, its colours and screams vivid and frightening.

Louisa stopped the car and turned to her daughters.

'Grace. Come and sit in the front, please.'

Grace stared at her mother, her violet eyes wide and questioning. Elsie let out a sigh of exasperation.

'Mum, we've already established that we're late. We haven't got time to start playing silly games.'

Louisa ignored Elsie. 'Grace. Now. Otherwise we're turning around and going home.'

'Okay, Okay.' Grace clambered out of the back and flopped down into the front seat. Louisa smelled her daughter's subtle fragrance of banana shampoo. She glanced into the empty back seat next to Elsie, took a deep breath and started the engine again. She drove carefully, slowly, creeping along the promenade. The twins were groaning with impatience by the time they reached Rachel Gregory's road. Louisa's stomach flipped with relief as she saw the road sign that told her they had almost completed their journey, that the girls were going to be safely dropped off at the party.

And that's when the gold blur hurtled past them, and then swerved into them. Louisa heard metal crush metal, thudding, screaming, then silence. She squeezed her eyes shut, and when she opened them, she saw Grace next to her, her small body engulfed with shaking breaths. Louisa looked round to the back and saw Elsie sobbing, her arm glittering with glass and blood.

Rachel's father ran out then, followed by a number of well-dressed, overexcited children and alarmed adults. Somebody ran over to the car; somebody else ran back into the house to phone emergency services. The driver of the gold Renault was a mess of blood and soft moaning and glass.

'You were going rather slowly, looking for our house most probably,' Rachel's father said in his clipped voice, and Louisa wondered at his accusatory tone. 'I saw from the window because my wife had asked me to look out for you—'

'We were waiting to blow out the candles,' explained his wife, as though that mattered, as though it explained everything.

'I could see the Renault getting impatient, wanting to whizz past you. So he did, but then I think he thought he saw something coming towards him and swerved back into you.'

Louisa got out shakily. 'I need to see Elsie.'

'She's conscious. Don't move her. Let the paramedics see to her,' Mr Gregory said. 'What a bad bit of luck for you all. Ah well, these things can't be stopped can they?'

'Lou!' Mags threw her arms around Louisa that evening and held her friend tightly. They stood for a while, in the doorway of Rose House. The night was black around them.

'I'm okay. I'm okay,' Louisa said quietly, her warm breath floating outside in a puff of smoke.

Mags held on for a little longer before letting go. 'Where are the girls?'

'They're watching television. They're both fine. Elsie's arm and side are sore, but she's cleaned up better than I thought. She's not said much about it. And Grace is shaken, I think. But they're doing well. The driver of the other car is going to be okay too.'

Mags nodded and handed Louisa a bottle of white wine as they stepped from the hall into the kitchen. 'Get that open. I'm staying over tonight. You've had a shock and you need me. Charles is home from work, so Noel will be fine. It's about time his dad took care of him.'

Louisa took two glasses from the draining board and filled them to the top with the wine, too tired to argue.

'Noel said that Grace phoned him before. He said you'd made her move into the front of the car.'

Louisa stared into her glass, noticing a shard of cork clinging to the curve of the lip. She tried to get it out with her finger, but failed, pushing it into her drink instead.

'I was trying to stop it all from happening. I'd had one of my visions about the car crash. I saw it in a nightmare. I knew it was going to happen. I was trying to save Grace.'

'But the side Grace had been sitting on wasn't even touched, was it?' Mags was frowning.

'No. And worse, if I hadn't stopped to move her, then the Renault wouldn't have even been there when I was; things would have happened differently. I stopped to move Grace, and I drove slowly. I caused it, in a way. By trying to stop it, I caused it, and I harmed Elsie.'

'Louisa, you need to let the guilt go. You protected Grace. You drove carefully and did what you thought was right.'

Louisa sighed and gulped down her wine before pouring herself a second glass. 'I just have a feeling that I'm being tricked, somehow. By the nightmares and the visions. I can't ignore them, but the more I try to change them, it's as though I am messing things up. I know I did it with Lewis, and I want to do things right this time, but I don't know how.'

'Bloody hell, Lou. I love you, but you're driving me mad with

221

your feelings about what's going to happen and what should happen. Your gift was always a good way to make money, but now you need to accept that your dreams and your so called premonitions are not always accurate and try to ignore them. You're obviously just losing the knack, no big deal. There's nobody tricking you into changing what happens but yourself.'

Louisa looked up abruptly from her drink, startled. Tears suddenly prickled at her eyes and she saw Mags tense with guilt.

'I don't mean to be horrible,' Mags said apologetically. 'I'm just worried about you. You seem more and more preoccupied these days.' Mags lit a cigarette as she finished speaking, inhaling slowly and plucking a stray hair from her jumper, watching as it floated to the floor.

She doesn't understand, Louisa thought. The strength of the premonitions, the terror when they dawned on her and the need to try and change them, it was all too much to ignore.

But the day suddenly took its toll in one split second, as big days often do. The adrenaline emptied and Louisa leaned back against the worktop, exhausted.

'You're right,' she said to Mags. 'Come on, let's have another drink.'

Chapter Twenty Nine

Grace, 2008

Despite Elsie's optimistic predictions, the shop fails to become any busier towards Christmas. November ends, the nights turn blacker and icier, Christmas trees and white fairy lights begin to appear in windows all around the town, and still the shop is mostly empty.

'It's really not a problem. None of the massive book stores are ever heaving. It's the nature of the business,' Elsie says, flicking through a glossy bridal magazine. The pages squeak as she turns them, making Grace shudder. 'And don't forget we sold that first edition last month. That met our forecast alone. So we really are doing quite well.'

'I know. I suppose I thought we would always be busy doing things. It's different to how I imagined it to be,' Grace admits.

'There's plenty to do. You could create more displays, or you could do a stock take. Or you could always go off for an afternoon and look for some more stuff for us to sell.'

Grace shrugs indifferently, unable to summon much enthusiasm, then feels guilty. She walks out to the back of the shop and checks her mobile phone. There's a missed call from a number she doesn't recognise and she presses callback, wondering who it could be.

'Hello?'

Grace feels as though the voice is familiar, but can't place it. She pauses.

'It's Kate. From the drama group.'

Macbeth is meant to be going ahead the following week, and Grace wonders if there is some kind of problem.

'Hi, Kate. Is everything okay?'

'Well, not really. You see, Marion has had a fall. She was skiing in the Alps, and down she went. She's broken her leg. Lady Macbeth in a full leg cast isn't really what we were going for. So that's poor Marion out of the question. And her understudy, Viv, has pulled out altogether because she's been offered a last-minute cruise with her sister. The Baltics, apparently.'

'Okay,' says Grace, trying to still the excitement that is fizzing up inside her.

'So, I know it's completely last minute, and you must think we're very disorganised, and you don't have very long to learn the lines, but I wondered if you would like the part of Lady Macbeth? You really did do so well on your audition. A witch part doesn't do you justice, and we all know that, but it's just that we have all sorts of politics to think of, and it was your very first evening with us, and I—'

Grace holds up her hand in the air even though Kate can't see her. 'Kate, stop! It's fine. I would absolutely love to do it. I know the lines pretty well because I have played Lady Macbeth before. I was just thinking that I needed a new project, so your call came at a perfect time. It's an honour, honestly.'

Grace hears Kate heave a suitably theatrical sigh of relief. 'Oh, Grace! I can't thank you enough. So I'll see you at rehearsal tonight then?'

'Of course.' Grace grins as she slides her phone back into her bag.

'Who was that?' Elsie asks, joining Grace in the back. 'You look like you've had some good news.'

'I have!' Grace fills Elsie in on her new part in the play.

'Congratulations! I'm pleased for you. It's been years since you did any drama stuff. I think it will do you good,' Elsie says, turning as she hears the shop door open.

It's Eliot. He is wearing a suit, and a bright green tie that purposely betrays his eccentricity.

'What's the matter? Why aren't you at work?' Elsie asks.

'I had to have some space. I've got a free session, so I thought I'd come and see you.' Eliot's slim face is dark with annoyance. 'We've just had a departmental meeting, and we've been told that they are restructuring the whole Creatives department to make some savings.'

Elsie rushes over to him. 'You're not losing your job, are you?'

Eliot sighs in irritation as he stalks over to the chair behind the counter and sits down.

'No, not entirely. I do have to reapply for my full time position, though. All of us do, and then hours will be split according to who appears to be the best candidate. So it's likely that my hours will ultimately be cut, which isn't particularly good news.' He looks up at Elsie. 'I'm sorry. It looks like the wedding might have to be a small one.'

'That doesn't matter at all,' Elsie says, and Grace wonders at her sister's serenity. Eliot seems grateful. He reaches out and takes Elsie's hand.

'Thanks. I'll do my best in the interview.' His fleeting moment of calm passes again then, to make way for another explosion of resentment. 'It's so infuriating! I'll bet that Stacey gets all the bloody hours. You know what it's like there. If your face fits...' he finishes sullenly.

'Stupid Stacey,' Grace offers. Eliot looks up and smiles at the childish gesture. Stacey is a frequent source of exasperation for Eliot: constantly showing him to be the poor relation of the department with her long hours, her wise contribution to meetings and her pristine lesson plans.

'I need a drink,' groans Eliot.

Elsie starts to shake her head, then relents.

'Why not?' she says, and Grace sees her sister glance down at her twinkling engagement ring as she speaks.

Less than ten minutes later, the three of them are in the pub opposite Ash Books. A lone man with grey hair and a dipped head nods from his bar stool as they walk in. Other than that, and a girl drying glasses behind the bar, it's empty.

Elsie orders a lemonade. 'Too early for me, it's only 2 p.m.,' is all she says, but Grace knows what she's thinking.

'I'm going to have a small glass of wine. I need to calm my nerves for rehearsals,' Grace says, and orders her drink.

Eliot leans on the bar and gazes along the selection of bottles behind. 'I'll have a bottle of Bud. I've only got one lesson to teach later and it's a timed exam so I barely have to do anything.'

'Eliot, I don't think you should. I hate to be a nag, but if anyone at the College catches a whiff of alcohol on you when you're meant to be working, you're not going to stand a chance. I really don't want them to think Stacey's better than you.'

Eliot doesn't look at Elsie, but Grace can see him digesting the words. 'Okay,' he replies eventually and gives Elsie a quick peck on her forehead. 'You're completely right.'

They make their way to a small table near the window. Grace gazes outside as Eliot and Elsie chat about Eliot's job. She sips her wine and watches out of the huge leaded windows at the few passers-by, holding their hoods against the freezing wind or battling with rebellious umbrellas. She sits back in her seat, glad to be inside.

'So, when will the interviews be for the full time role?' Grace asks Eliot when there's a pause in the conversation.

'That's the worst bit. It's next week. I'm going to have to spend all evening writing out my application for my own job. I don't know what I'll do if they cut my hours.'

'You can help in the shop,' Elsie says.

Grace drains her glass. The thought of being in the bookshop all day with both Elsie and Eliot sends a shot of panic straight through her body.

Eliot, however, appears to be placated a little by Elsie's proposition. 'That's true. I'd like to get stuck into helping you out. And whilst we're playing "The Glad Game", I suppose a smaller timetable would free up more of my time to get involved in directing, too. Do you think they need anybody at your drama group, Grace?'

Grace stares across the pub, at the empty bar. The lone man is ordering another pint and shuffling a newspaper about to get the pages to crease in the right places. She really is trying to distance herself from Eliot, from what she knows about her future, and his, but even when she turns the other way, Eliot seeps into her life. 'I'm not sure. There are other drama groups, though.'

Eliot doesn't seem to notice the subtle rebuff, but Elsie catches Grace's eye and smiles.

Thank you, she seems to say.

The next weeks pass in a blizzard of rehearsals and late nights, which then merge into early mornings at the shop. A few days before the opening performance of *Macbeth*, Grace stands behind the counter at Ash Books, tapping through online auctions for book collections. The last ordering date before Christmas is looming, and Grace wants to order some new stock before the holidays begin. She is sending a message to enquire about a collection of boys' annuals from the 1950s when Eliot arrives. He's cleanly shaven for once, and his tie is a sober brown.

'I didn't get the teaching hours I was hoping for,' he says, before Grace has said anything.

'Oh, Eliot. I'm sorry. Hang on, Elsie's in the back.'

Grace leaves Eliot standing forlornly at the entrance and dashes to the little office at the back of the shop.

'It's Eliot,' she hisses to Elsie. 'He's come from work. He didn't get the full-time post. He looks really upset.'

Elsie drops the pile of receipts she is holding and they flutter to the ground like petals. Grace waits until Elsie has gone and kneels down to pick them up. She hears Eliot sigh, and glances up to see Elsie wrapped around him, his arms around her. They are locked together and Grace feels as though she shouldn't be there. She stifles a yawn: rehearsals and full-time working are beginning to take their toll. She hosted some after-rehearsal drinks on Saturday night, too, which turned into a party at her flat. She can barely remember who ended up there in the end, just that most of the group went home and Grace stayed up drinking with a couple of eighteen-year-olds who have the roles of extras in Macbeth's battle with Macduff. She's getting too old for all-nighters, she realises as she rubs her forehead and shuts her eyes for a moment.

She stands up, and places the receipts neatly on the desk behind her before going back out to the shop. Elsie and Eliot have stopped hugging now, but are standing holding hands. Grace clears her throat.

'I really am sorry, Eliot. It's so infuriating. I'm really angry for you'. She wonders if she should hug him, and decides against it, touching his slim arm fleetingly instead.

'He's still got half a timetable. He's got pretty good part-time hours, so he obviously did well,' Elsie says reassuringly, stroking his back, her calm words making Grace feel too loud and out of control.

'It's all a huge conspiracy,' Eliot says, then exhales loudly and tugs at his tie. 'Like something out of a George Orwell novel. I'm starting to wonder if I want to be there at all.'

'But you love the students, and you're great at teaching drama. Stick with it, and help out here too, and then reassess it all over the summer,' Elsie says. She motions behind the counter. 'Sit down. I'll make us a coffee.'

Eliot drops down onto the chair behind the counter and eyes the open laptop that Grace has been working on.

'Tiger Annuals, eh? Cute. I like it.'

'I'm on the lookout for some others. We want to create a retro cosy corner, over there,' Grace gestures to the back of the shop. 'I've just sent a message to the people who run this website asking if we can buy all the annuals they're selling at a discount.'

'That's a pretty hefty price they want for them individually. And it says here that some of them have torn covers. Can't you find some better ones?' Eliot says as he stares at the screen.

'I suppose so. I'm tired of looking now, to be honest. I've got Lady Macbeth's lines buzzing in my head too.'

Eliot rubs his hands together. 'Well, as we all know, I now have all the time in the world. I'll have a look. You go and have a run through your lines. We'll be fine, won't we Els?' he raises his voice to a shout at the end so that Elsie can hear from the back.

'Of course!' Elsie shouts. 'Is that just two coffees, then?'

'Are you sure?' Grace says uncertainly. 'I feel a little guilty leaving you to do something that I started.'

Eliot smiles. 'We will be fine, Grace. Do your own thing, and leave us to it,' he says, and his words float between them awkwardly until Grace turns away and goes to get her coat.

Chapter Thirty

Louisa, 1992

It was summer again.

Louisa's house was full of guests: loud, and grubby from their days on the beach and various tired attractions. Most of Louisa's guests these days were regulars, returning year after year. Some were impromptu visitors who turned up last thing at night wanting a spur of the moment stay. Neither kind of guest expected much from the decor or furnishings, so Louisa never did get round to swapping her orange velour curtains for fashionable smoky glass and leather.

Every evening of the summer, Louisa sat in the dining room, pouring drinks and staring into space and telling people their futures. Cash stacked on the table next to Louisa, and paid for Grace's extra maths lessons and Elsie's pencil crayons and Grace's friends' birthday presents. That is, until one damp evening in August when Louisa's gift disappeared.

It had happened a few times before, but this was different. When she took Maria Booth's hand in hers, Louisa didn't see black space or nothing or a vagueness that couldn't be put into words. She saw what she had seen in so many of her dreams: a blank version of the lounge of Rose House, Grace and Elsie arguing, Grace pulling at her necklace frantically, Elsie blaming her twin for something, her hatred for Louisa hovering in the room. Candles flickering, threatening to swallow the room in one ferocious flame.

How had this happened? Since the day of the car accident, the adorably precocious Elsie had withdrawn into a world that Louisa could not see or understand. Gone were her carefully selected 'adult' words; her peals of laughter. She was still and calm. And, as Louisa saw now, she always would be, even when war broke out with her twin. What were they going to fall out about? Louisa squinted to try and see or hear what the problem between the twins was, but the image was a hazy dream from which she could understand no reasons. She squeezed her eyes shut, seeing colours: blue and purple and orange.

'Excuse me. Is it meant to take this long? Last time I had my fortune told I was out by now,' whispered Maria Booth, snatching her hands from Louisa's grip and shaking her back into the present.

Louisa's eyes opened. Maria was glaring at her, arms folded, her fee beside her in a small, jumbled pile of gold and silver coins.

'I'm sorry. I'm feeling a little under the weather tonight, I'm afraid.' Louisa smiled weakly. 'Let me try again.'

Maria nodded curtly. 'Just tell me if it's true,' she said as she gestured impatiently for Louisa to take hold of her hands.

Louisa nodded, trying to remember what Maria Booth had asked her about when she first appeared in the dining room. She closed her eyes again, straining to try and see something, anything, related to Maria. At first, there was nothing. Louisa felt her head ache slightly, and then she saw the same image. Grace's adult face, wet with inky tears. Elsie, stony-faced.

Louisa shook her head. 'I can't do it. I can't see anything tonight. It's been a busy day and I—'

Maria stood up abruptly, causing Louisa to stop mid-sentence. She pulled back the pile of coins from the table and they jingled merrily as she returned them to her purse.

'I won't be paying for this, of course. What a disappointment.

I was going to stay in one of the hotels on the promenade with a swimming pool, but my friend told me about you. I paid your high rates because I thought that you could offer something a bit different. But it's all a big con!' Maria's voice, drenched in wine, became louder as she spoke.

'Look, come back tomorrow night. I'll try again then.'

'I'd rather not waste my time. I left the bingo early for this as it is. I'm not wasting any more of my holiday.'

Louisa sighed, wishing that this angry woman wasn't staying in her home for the next few nights, wishing that she didn't have to make her breakfast the next morning, wishing that it would all go away. The weight of seeing Grace and Elsie fighting and unhappy pulled at her insides, twisting them and making Louisa feel quite sick. She poured herself another drink, and pushed past Maria into the hallway, where the next guest waited for their future to be revealed.

'Don't bother,' Maria barked at the waiting woman. 'She's a load of rubbish. She would have taken my money if I'd let her, and she told me nothing.'

That night, Louisa thought of the days where she could sneak into the twins' room and watch them sleep. She wanted to do it now, to remind herself that she had family, that she wasn't alone and that the twins were still at peace with one another.

The twins might wake if she went into their bedroom. They weren't young enough to sleep through her visits now, and woke, suspicious, with every twitch and sound. But Louisa suddenly couldn't help herself. She found herself clambering out of bed and along the hall, past sleeping guests, past the clatter of bottle against glass in Maria Booth's room, to the bedroom that the twins shared. She opened the door slightly and immediately heard the girls' steady breaths, heavy with sleep. Stepping in, she saw Grace stir and sit up. The light from the landing spilled into the room, making it golden.

'Mum? What's wrong?'

'Nothing. Nothing at all. I wanted to see you.'

'What do you want?' Grace asked as she stared up at her mother with those violet eyes that said so much about where they had all come from.

Louisa stepped over clothes and magazines and a hairbrush, and sat next to Grace on the bed. She put her arms around her daughter and held her tightly, feeling Grace's cool skin, her long satin hair, her softly slept-in t-shirt. She wanted Lewis back, she wanted to know that she could stop Elsie and Grace from becoming enemies, she wanted to sell the house and go somewhere else where her family would all be together and get along. She wanted so much. But for now, holding Grace tightly in a bedroom drenched in darkness and sleep, would do.

Chapter Thirty One

Grace, 2008

On Sunday morning, Grace wakes early.

Typical.

She squeezes her eyes shut and tries to summon sleep back to her rousing body, tries to dull the feeling of the day around her. But it's no use. By 7.30 a.m., she's up, making coffee. She feels like she needs to do something, so she showers quickly, blow-dries her hair and then pulls on her warmest clothes, her boots and her gloves. She shuts the door softly behind her, knowing that everyone else in the block of flats will still be asleep.

The frozen air burns Grace's cheeks as she walks. The morning is silent and untouched. She moves away from the sea, from its grey whorls of secrets, from its stale, salty odour. She runs her lines for the play through her head as she walks. Eventually, she reaches the centre of St Annes. The bookshop watches her from the other side of the square, and she turns her head. There's a coffee shop open, and aching with cold, Grace heads towards it.

As Grace sips on a huge bowl of cappuccino, the gritty chocolate dust sticking to her lips like sand, she gazes out onto the small square of shops of restaurants. She can still smell the stale sea, even though she knows she should smell coffee and warm croissants.

Grace shudders, imagines herself in London, having breakfast with Noel in a smart coffee bar. Or perhaps – she allows herself the luxury of a rare daydream – if she were with Noel, she'd still be in his bed, luxuriating in sheets that were warm from being stretched over both of their bodies all night. Perhaps if she were with Noel, she wouldn't have felt the sharp need to be out so early in the morning. If she were in London, or a bright, buzzing city, there would be none of the ghosts that haunt her now.

As she drinks the rest of her coffee, Grace's eyes wander around the café for something to distract her from her thoughts. She jumps up when she sees a newspaper stand by the counter, and sits back down with a crumpled broadsheet from yesterday. She leafs through the giant pages idly. There's nothing that Grace finds interesting, until she reaches an advert for a vintage fair at the Winter Gardens in Blackpool town centre later today.

She swipes the paper from the table and jams it back in the stand, nods a thanks to the teenaged barista and rushes back out into the freezing morning.

Elsie is still in bed when Grace arrives at Rose House. Grace waits for a while at the door, looking down at her brown leather boots. Her hair lashes around her face, stinging her raw cheeks. She knocks again, louder this time, and the glass rattles threateningly. The colours of the glass spill into one another through their cracked leaded segments: blue, purple and orange merge as Grace stares through the window and waits for her sister.

Eventually, Elsie's silhouette appears, bear-like in a huge dressing gown. She yawns as she pulls open the front door. Her feet are bare and Grace winces at the thought of how cold they must be on the cracked tiles.

'What's the matter?' she says as Grace leads the way into the hall. The smell of the house that seeps from its depths: roses and the old green carpets stained with brandy and tears, greets Grace and momentarily transports her back to childhood.

'Nothing's the matter,' she replies after a minute. 'I've found somewhere we need to go today. I've been out for coffee, so I got the train straight to yours—'

'Out for coffee?' Elsie's words are stretched by another yawn. 'But it's still early.'

Grace shrugs. 'So don't you want to know where we're going today?'

Elsie pads into the kitchen and flicks on the kettle. Her hair is scraped back. Grace hasn't worn her hair up for years, and seeing Elsie's fine cheekbones, her delicate jaw, reminds her that she should try it.

Elsie nods, and takes two mismatched mugs from the cupboard.

'There's a vintage fair in town. I thought we might go and have a look for some books and other things for the shop. It starts at ten. What do you think?'

Elsie smiles. 'I think you've already decided on my behalf. But it sounds good. I'll have my coffee and then get ready.'

'Is Eliot here?' Grace asks after a few moments, not even sure why she wants to know.

'Yes. But he's still asleep. I'll leave him here, I think. It'll be nice to do something just us.'

Grace is touched by the words, momentarily stung with unexpected pleasure. She wants to reply, to give Elsie something back, but before she can, Elsie stands and picks up her mug.

'I'll get ready,' she says, leaving Grace to sit in the kitchen, alone except for the ghost of her mother, drifting around, unable to see, but there all the same.

The vintage fair is crowded and smells of must and dampness. Grace buys them each a cup of tea in a scalding cardboard cup. They wander around the stalls, their sleeves pulled around their hands to stop the burning.

As they walk slowly through the flood of people, Grace stares around her at the elaborate carvings above their heads, worn with age. The lost decorum of the building floats in the air like the spirit of a once grand, forgotten lady. A band is playing in the ballroom, throwing out drum beats and electric guitar notes that clash with the evocative grandeur of the ornate pillars and ceilings.

'This must have been a beautiful place once,' Grace says as she's jostled along. Elsie doesn't hear over the buzz of conversation, the music.

They stop at a stall that's crammed with vintage jewellery. Brooches, bracelets and earrings are all draped over exquisite, exotic jewels. Grace's eyes are drawn to a distinctive necklace, and she leans forward and lifts it carefully from its place on the table.

'Look at this, Elsie. It's beautiful.'

The chain is a worn, antique silver, with intricate clasps holding smooth, bright aqua stones. Grace tries to get the stall owner's attention, but she's deep in conversation with an older woman about a brooch. Grace clutches the necklace tightly, not wanting to put it down, the clasps biting into her skin.

'Come on, let's carry on looking and see if it's still there on the way back.'

'It might not be. I really love it.'

'But we've not even looked at any book stalls yet. All the good books will be sold if we don't get a move on,' Elsie says, beginning to walk away.

Grace sighs and places the necklace down reluctantly, before continuing to meander through the fair. Just as they reach the first book stall, Elsie looks around absently. 'Need the loo,' she explains. She flits off into the maze of people and Grace pushes her way to the front of the stall, picking up an old *Bunty* annual and leafing through it with the children's corner at Ash Books in mind.

Just as Grace is scanning over a comic strip called *The Four Marys*, wondering how she might do some kind of black and red themed display to match the colours of the drawings, Elsie reappears, her face unusually bright and hopeful.

'That was quick,' Grace murmurs, looking up briefly from the annual.

'Here,' Elsie says, pushing a paper bag into her sister's hand. The bag is pretty: pale pink with white polka dots. Grace puts the book down and opens the bag.

'Oh, Elsie!'

Inside is the necklace.

A rush of dizzy pleasure blooms inside Grace. 'I don't know what to say!'

'You don't have to say anything,' Elsie replies, her face flushed, her stance awkward.

'Thank you so much. That was a really amazing thing to do. Put it on for me, will you?'

And so, as tutting people try to pass them, and the clouds shift above them, casting a moment of bright light down through the skylit ceiling, Elsie moves closer to Grace. Grace feels Elsie twist her hair up from her neck and feels her twin's cool fingers against her skin. She feels the weight of the aqua stones, the cold silver clasps jagged on her bare collarbone, and a rush of hope and promise beams through her, bright as the momentary sun.

Chapter Thirty Two

Louisa, 1994

'Where's Elsie?' Louisa asked Grace as she lugged several carrier bags of food into the house. It was the Christmas holidays, and Louisa had gone to the supermarket early to buy a turkey and pretzels and peanuts and all those other things that Christmas expected of you. She had bought Elsie and Grace a magazine each: *Shout!* for Grace, and *Smash Hits!* for Elsie. She wondered if they'd swap and read each other's when they'd finished with them. She hoped so.

Grace flipped her hair over her shoulder. It was getting long, and seemed to get shinier each year. Louisa's own hair was beginning to become threaded with silver, but as long as Grace's hair stayed as shiny as this, Louisa didn't care quite as much about her own.

'She's gone to Mags's house.'

Louisa dropped the bags to the floor and winced as a glass bottle clanged against the floorboards. It will have been her brandy. She hoped the bottle hadn't cracked.

'She didn't mention to me that she was spending the evening with Mags. When's she back?'

Grace bent to pick some bags up and took them through to the kitchen.

'Tomorrow. She's staying over.'

'She's what?'

'Sleeping there. Did you get marshmallows?'

'But why? I know she's been getting on well with Mags, but why does she have to sleep there? Why can't she sleep here?'

Grace shrugged as she poked and prodded her way through the shopping bags.

'Dunno. Suppose she doesn't want to. She said something about Mags doing face masks and putting *Dirty Dancing* on.'

Louisa felt a flutter of apprehension and thought again of the brandy in the bag on the floor. She picked it out of the bag. It hadn't broken. She snapped the lid off and took a small sip.

'Mum!' Grace cried, horrified.

'What? It's Christmas! I just wanted to check that it was okay for making the pudding.'

'It's no wonder Elsie's run off to Mags,' Grace said as she pushed past Louisa to leave the kitchen.

'Grace! Come here. I'm sorry. The marshmallows are here. And look, I got you *Shout!* magazine.'

Grace stared at her mother for a moment, and Louisa noticed for the first time that day that her daughter's eyes were fringed with a light, hesitant coat of mascara. How long had Grace been wearing make-up? Louisa had no idea. She wanted to ask, but instead she waved the magazines about.

'I got you both one. Elsie can read hers tomorrow, I suppose.'

Grace's eyes fell to the magazines in Louisa's hands.

'We've already read those ones.' She snatched the marshmallows from Louisa's hand and stomped upstairs.

The rain came down heavily that night. Louisa sat in front of the fire with her brandy, unable to shake off the look of disgust in Grace's eyes. Grace had shut herself in her bedroom all afternoon. Louisa had knocked on her bedroom door several times, but Grace had avoided her pleas. Now, Louisa eyed the phone on the wall before standing and picking up the receiver.

Noel answered.

'Noel, is Elsie there? It's Louisa.'

Noel was polite and lovely, like he always was. Louisa cocked her head to one side to try and hear Elsie's response to Noel's coaxing. After a few seconds, Noel was back.

'She's a bit busy. She's making some mince pies with my mum. Can she call you back?'

Louisa let out a small 'yes' and gently put the receiver back on its cradle.

It was about an hour later when the phone rang. Louisa jumped up.

'Elsie?' she answered, thrilled.

'No. It's me.' The voice was deeper and more mature.

'Oh,' Louisa said, slumping against the wall. 'Hi Mags. How's Elsie?'

'She's fine. She's just having a bit of time away. She might stay a day or two. I hope that's okay with you.'

Louisa was silent for a moment. 'Mags, why doesn't she want to be at home with me? And with Grace?' she asked eventually.

Mags's sigh crackled through the line. 'I don't know. She won't say. But she has mentioned your drinking, Lou. I think she just needs a break. I think she deserves one.'

'You think she deserves a break from her own mum?' Louisa felt a wave of unexpected anger towards Mags. She wanted to say so much about how she had talked to Noel all those times when Mags had been too busy gossiping or applying lipstick or rooting in her bag to pay him any attention. How had it come to this?

'I didn't say she needed a break from you. She's fifteen—'

'I know how old my daughter is,' Louisa snapped.

'Look. I don't want to argue with you, Lou. Elsie obviously needed a change of scenery. I happened to be here. She thinks a lot of Noel, too. So she's having fun. She's safe. And you still have Grace. She can have you to herself for once. Is that so bad?'

Grace, upstairs alone in her bedroom with her door shut tightly. Louisa felt sharp tears prick her eyes.

'I just miss her,' she said, her voice cracking.

'I know. Of course. Tell you what, why don't you come round here on Christmas day? Bring Grace, and we'll all have dinner together. Noel and I weren't going to do much. But I've got a turkey, so we'll cook that, and we can play some games and make it a nice day. Yes?'

Louisa agreed, and put the phone down, and it was only after she had put her head back on the sofa and closed her eyes that she remembered she had bought a turkey to cook herself.

Darkness filled the lounge as Louisa sat sipping her brandy, listening to the sound of the steel-grey waves smashing against each other. The more she tried not to listen to it, the more she heard it, until it felt as though the shards of water were crashing against her head. When she could no longer bear the noises of the sea, and the heavy blackness around her, Louisa stood up and clicked on the television and the lamp. The room filled with pale light and sounds and Louisa thought of Grace upstairs and wondered if she had turned her light on too. She eyed the sugary brown liquid sloshing around in her glass. Then she stood, turned and ran up the stairs, tripping on the final step and spilling her drink on the swirling carpet. She ignored the unpleasant soaking of the brandy through her socks and banged on Grace's bedroom door.

'Grace! Grace! You have to come out! I need to show you something, and talk to you.'

There was silence for a moment, then a scuffling from behind the door.

'Grace, please,' Louisa said, more quietly this time as the effort of the stairs and her trip suddenly washed over her.

The door opened, slowly and narrowly. Grace stood behind it, the mascara blurred around her eyes after a whole day of wear.

'What?'

'Come with me,' Louisa said, clutching at Grace's arm.

Grace followed her downstairs into the lounge, where Louisa raised her glass to the air before re-filling it.

'Mum, can't you do anything without carrying a glass of—'

'Wait! Watch!' Louisa interrupted, pulling Grace into the kitchen. She raised her glass again, towards the ceiling where it twinkled in the fluorescent strip light. Then she swooped it down to the sink and poured it away.

'I'm done. I won't lose my girls.'

Grace smiled and Louisa's heart lifted.

'Do you think Elsie's very mad with me?'

'I think she's a bit mad with you. But she'll come round. She's seeming mad with everything lately. So it's probably not even you.'

'You're so honest, Grace. I'm so pleased about that.'

Grace blushed a little, then rolled her eyes. 'I've got some marshmallows left upstairs, if you want some.'

Louisa nodded, ecstatic. 'I'll get the toasting forks.'

Louisa turned off the television. They sat listening to the rain and sea and toasting the marshmallows on the fire. The spitting of the flames and pattering of rain and the chewing of gooey, warm pink and white marshmallow filled the room with magic.

Christmas day at Mags's house was full of creased foil decorations and cheap crackers: bad jokes and plastic nonsense spewing out onto the table. Mags had cooked her turkey with little sausages nestled around its wings and bottom. A Black Forest gateau sat on the wooden kitchen worktop, waiting for the dinner to be over.

When Louisa and Grace arrived, Suzie came to the door to let them in. She had black hair with blonde streaks at the front and wore heavy black boots.

'Where's Elsie?' Grace asked Suzie, beating Louisa to it.

'She's upstairs. Good to see you both. Merry Christmas.'

Suzie gave Louisa a hug before returning to the lounge. Noel appeared then, and gave Louisa a hug that made her feel cocooned and safe and happy. He smelled of a festive mix of new shower gel and roast potatoes. Louisa looked up at him.

'Happy Christmas, Noel. I'm glad you're here.'

Noel smiled. He had Mags's wide smile with big teeth. Louisa remembered Noel's very first tooth. She tried to summon the feeling of Noel as a baby, his bare gums showing a first little spot of brand new white, his light head resting on her shoulder, but before the memory had fully arrived, Noel moved past Louisa to give Grace an awkward Christmas hug and it blew away again like smoke.

'Where's Elsie?' Grace repeated to Noel.

'She's upstairs in the shower. I'll get Mum to go up and see if she's done.'

'I'll go up, if you like,' Grace said, stumbling past to climb the stairs. Louisa craned her neck to watch her daughter disappear into the upstairs of the house and then turned to Noel.

'Where's your mum?'

Mags was in the kitchen, sipping daintily at a tiny glass of sherry and chopping lettuce for the prawn cocktail. She gave a squeal as she saw Louisa and dropped her knife.

'Happy Christmas!'

'And to you. How is she?'

'Elsie? She's fine. She's absolutely fine. Here, wash these tomatoes, will you?'

Louisa took the proffered handful of tomatoes and moved over to the sink, which was overflowing with pots and pans and slithers of potato peelings.

'I've really missed her.'

'If today goes well then she might come home.'

Louisa nodded, feeling positive, as though anything was possible.

'I hope so.'

'Wine?' Mags asked as she twisted a corkscrew into a bottle

of red.

Louisa shook her head and looked for a clear surface to deposit the washed tomatoes.

'No? It's Christmas! Go on, here you are,' Mags said, pushing a full glass into Louisa's hand and taking the tomatoes off her in one skilful movement. 'Come on, it's all ready. Let's shout the kids and sit down at the table. Noel, move the telly into the dining room so we can watch the Queen while we eat. She's on at two. Noel!' she hollered as she manoeuvred her way out of the kitchen with a dish of prawns in one hand and the salad in the other.

At the dinner table, Louisa waited for Grace and Elsie to emerge before choosing her seat. They floated into the room together a few minutes later. Elsie glanced tentatively at Louisa before giving a weak smile.

'Happy Christmas, Mum.'

Louisa held her arms out to Elsie and was rewarded with a brief half hug. She sat down and beckoned for Elsie to sit next to her on one side, and Grace on the other. She pushed her wine glass away and saw the twins exchange a glance.

The conversation was subtle and pleasant to begin with. Suzie asked Noel if he liked the Christmas number one in the charts and he said no, causing mock outrage and good-natured lecturing from the twins that lasted well past the starter.

It was during the main dinner when things turned sour, when everybody had pulled crackers and wore gaudy paper hats and the table was littered with plastic treats from the crackers. Mags retrieved her wine glass from amongst the debris and held it into the air, the liquid sloshing over the side a little and dripping down onto her dinner.

'I want to make a Christmas toast. To family and friends.'

Noel took another piece of turkey. Grace smiled weakly and Elsie looked down at her still knife and fork. Louisa eyed her full wine glass that she had pushed away from her. Suzie chinked her glass against Mags's.

'I'll drink to that, Aunty Mags,' she said. 'I wouldn't have a Christmas dinner if it wasn't for you lot. Mark's still in the police, and he pulled the short straw at work so is doing all the long shifts in the cells all over the holidays,' she explained to Louisa and the twins. 'But staying with Mum and Dad in Spain with nobody else to talk to would have been painful!'

'We're lucky to have you here,' Mags said. 'Come on, everyone. Cheers!'

'Come on, Louisa. I especially want to clink glasses with you!' Suzie said with a laugh. Louisa smiled nervously.

'Here you go, Lou. Go on,' Mags said, passing Louisa her wine and not noticing the confused look on the twins' faces, or the look of tension on Louisa's.

'Why do you want to toast my mum so much?' Elsie asked, wrinkling her nose.

'Surely she's told you,' Suzie grinned, a stud in her nose twinkling in the weak winter light. But Louisa hadn't. She hadn't told the twins about her gift, or how she stayed up at night to try and earn the money to buy all the things they wanted on a whim. She hadn't told them anything about that day on the beach so long ago, about the blurring sight and the forceful images that made her head burn with terror.

'She saved my life!' Suzie continued mercilessly, like a steam train.

Elsie raised her eyebrows. Louisa wondered for a moment if Suzie might grind to a halt here, and leave things unharmed. If the twins knew that Louisa had kept her gift from them, they would be hurt and angry. If they thought she had happened to just save a life, then they would be moved.

'She saw into the future, and knew that I was going to drown. So she saved me!' Suzie was gushing, gathering a rapid pace. 'She has such a gift. You girls should be so proud of her, being able to stop things from happening to people she cares about. And think of all the people she has seen into the future for, and she never gets it wrong. Do you still do it, Louisa?'

The table was silent for a moment. Then came the question that she dreaded.

'Why didn't you tell us that you can see into the future?' Grace said, while Elsie sat glowering silently.

Louisa looked either side of her at her daughters and shook her head. 'I didn't really want to drag you both into it. Having this gift is unsettling. It makes you think you can stop bad things happening, and save people—'

But before Louisa could finish, there was an unpleasant screech of wood. Elsie pushed her chair back and stood to leave the table. Louisa started to follow but Grace leapt up instead. 'I'll go. You stay here. She's upset. You might make things worse.'

Louisa pulled her wine towards her as Grace thudded up the stairs after Elsie.

Just one sip.

One of Lewis's postcards arrived in April. This time, it was a postcard from Blackpool. Louisa flipped it over almost carelessly, expecting to see the words she knew so well. But this time, it was blank.

'What does this mean?' Louisa asked Mags, who shrugged and sucked on a cigarette.

Louisa couldn't understand it. Why hadn't he written anything? Was Lewis going to come back? She had bought some mints and ran a brush through her hair every morning now. If she woke in the night, which she often did, she looked at her reflection in the tall swinging mirror in the corner of her bedroom to check that her skin wasn't creased, that her mascara hadn't run.

She wondered what he would think of the twins.

He would know straight away that they were his.

They knew about him. Louisa had told Grace and Elsie who the postcards were from when one plopped through their rusty letterbox when they were about to leave the house one day. The twins were about eleven then. They hadn't talked much about it since. They were fine with it. Things were different, these days. Most of the girls' friends had divorced parents and parents they had never met.

'He was wonderful,' Louisa had said, but she knew the girls didn't believe her.

If he was that wonderful, their crossed arms demanded to know, *why is he not here right now?*

'Has he stopped loving me?' she asked, snatching Mags's cigarette and taking a gulp of bitty, smoky air herself.

Mags sighed. 'It's been a long time, Lou. The twins are sixteen soon, almost adults. They don't need him now, and neither do you.'

Louisa looked across at Mags's face. She was the best friend Louisa had ever had. Louisa saw now, as she stared at her friend's face, that her skin was looser than it once had been, that her eyes were lined and her hair was strewn with silver.

Where had all the time gone?

The night before the twins' birthday, Louisa tossed and turned in bed. She was having the dream again: the same dream that had haunted her for so many years. It was what, the third time that night? The image kept coming back and back, like a pin to a magnet.

Grace's face drifted before Louisa's eyes, then duplicated so that Elsie's was there too. Elsie was frowning, and Grace was smiling. Louisa felt herself being pulled into the dream, even though she flipped over and moaned, trying to avoid it, trying to wake, but it was no good. She watched as Grace threw the glass. It exploded into a thousand glittering pieces and its contents sprayed over Elsie.

Louisa kicked and grappled with the dream, wanting release, but she saw what she always did. Grace looking up at her sister, her crimson face streaked with make-up, her hair tangled; Grace pulling at her necklace, clawing at the aqua stones with trembling fingers. 'I've done nothing wrong.'

Elsie's voice, almost a whisper. 'You've done everything wrong. You're too much like our mother. I will never forgive you for this, Grace. Never.'

It was at this point that Louisa woke up with a start.

She knew now. She knew what the dream meant, and the choice she had to make to stop it from becoming reality.

She closed her eyes again, and lay back, her black hair splayed out on the pillow behind her like a fan. Another dream came, a different one now. This one was a slow-moving image, with no sound. It was the image of Louisa's mother stepping towards the sea, being pulled towards somebody or something invisible to everyone but her. She walked with purpose, her grey skirt billowing out like clouds as the water became deeper and deeper around her.

Come, the sea said. *Come, and it will make everything right.*

Louisa sighed in her sleep and her eyelids fluttered. She saw her mother walking further and further into the water, away from Louisa and away from pain. She saw the boy with purple eyes waiting for her mother on the horizon, smiling at her, wanting her to go towards him. And then the boy blurred into darkness, and her mother's figure was swallowed by the blue-black sea, and Louisa was awake again. Weak light like milky tea soaked through the curtains. It was almost dawn now, the dawn of her twins' sixteenth birthday.

Chapter Thirty Three

Grace, 2008

'What are you doing tonight?' Grace asks as Elsie's car swings onto Burleigh Road and alongside Rose House. The vintage fair was a success: Elsie's mini is weighed down with annuals and trinkets to put in the shop.

'Nothing. Eliot texted me before and he's got some work to do, so I was just going to have an early night.'

'I could come round for a bit if you want? I can bring some stuff and cook us something.'

Elsie tightens her mustard scarf before opening her car door. 'Yeah, if you want,' she says, her voice muffled by the cawing gulls that circle above them. 'Are you staying for a bit now? I can drive you home when we've had a coffee, then you can come back again later? It's only twelveish.'

Grace stands on the pavement and looks up at Rose House. It looms down, oppressive. The newly replaced Sold sign creaks with the effort of remaining up in the seafront breeze. It's already got a crack down one side. She touches her new necklace, finds it under the collar of her coat. It's cool and the stones are smooth. She feels again a flicker of excitement that Elsie bought it for her, that somewhere under the mounds of earthy memories and resentment, there lies devotion. She wants to keep this happiness clean and bright, before it's somehow bruised by a word or a look or a sigh of irritation.

Grace can see Eliot through the stained glass, making his way to the door to let Elsie in. She can make out every angle of him: his jagged black hair; his slim waist; his narrow, clever face.

'No. I'll walk home, and come back later. And I'll stay over, then we can go to the shop together in the morning.'

Elsie smiles and Grace waves goodbye, turning around and hearing the murmur of conversation as Eliot greets Elsie, the rustle of a brief hello hug, the front door of Rose House closing softly behind them.

That night, Grace catches the train to Elsie's house, laden with shopping bags. When Elsie answers the door, Grace heads straight for the kitchen and flicks on the kettle.

'I'm going to make us some pasta and cheese,' she says. 'Like I used to.'

Elsie smiles a little blandly, never one to get excited about food.

Grace unloads the bags: fresh pasta, mushrooms, purpling garlic bulbs, a bag of rocket salad, some mozzarella and a bottle of Chardonnay. She reaches for two wine glasses in the cupboard above her head and then pours the wine. It's warm, because it came from the shelf in the shop, rather than a fridge, but Grace wants a drink now, doesn't want to wait for it to cool.

They talk about the shop as Grace chops the mushrooms and boils the pasta. The aroma of the garlic in the pan is warm and lingers pleasantly in the air of the kitchen. Grace lists the items they still need to find to have a completed retro children's corner in the shop. She wants a vintage chair; perhaps an old school chair. Elsie talks about the small profit they have made and how she thinks they can build on it over the next few months. Grace watches her sister as she speaks, sees Elsie's eyes become calmly determined and focused. Elsie has researched running a business in

251

detail. Textbook phrases slip from her lips: phrases about forecasts and numbers and profit and loss.

Grace sips her wine. She won't feel bad that Elsie has done more research than her, because it's an unspoken agreement that Elsie will take care of the figures, and Grace's area will be aesthetics and marketing. After all, finding stock at the vintage fair today was Grace's idea. As she empties the pasta into a colander, steam puffing in front of her face, the thought of Elsie's wedding planning slices into Grace's mind. She wonders if Elsie is managing the aesthetics side of that okay. She puts the colander down in the sink and finishes her glass of wine in one gulp.

She'll ask her later.

They eat in the lounge with the bowls of buttery pasta on their knees, the television in the background flooding the room with a high drama soap opera: all yelling and drinking and crying. Elsie has lit some candles and incense sticks and the room glows with tiny orange flames and the scent of myrrh.

After they have finished eating, Grace takes the bowls out to the kitchen and then returns to the lounge, flopping down on the sofa next to Elsie.

'It will be so strange to have nothing to do with this house anymore,' she says, looking around the room.

She remembers their mother recalling her own childhood in the house, listening to her own mother's stories by the fire. She remembers watching a film with Noel in here, around the time of university. She remembers wanting to kiss him, but deciding then, as always, that her future with Eliot meant that it was an impossible thing to do. She remembers lying on the sofa with Elsie, entangled with her sister, the day of the car crash, moments before Elsie heard their mother admit to Mags that she had chosen to save Grace.

The memories flicker across the room like flames. Soon, the house will belong to someone else and the Ash memories will die out.

'I know. It all seems to be going through quite smoothly. Eliot and I have decided to rent somewhere until after the wedding. We can't see anywhere that we like, and we don't want to rush into buying something we're not sure about.'

What kind of home will Elsie and Eliot choose? It's difficult to imagine them anywhere other than here.

'That seems sensible,' Grace says, her words and thoughts wooden now that Eliot has drifted into the conversation. She touches her necklace fleetingly, then drinks her wine clumsily so that a drop lands on her jeans.

They sit in silence for a while. The soap opera finishes, its maudlin theme tune taking over the lounge.

'I've been looking at wedding venues,' Elsie says after a few minutes.

Grace takes a breath. 'Anywhere nice?'

'A few. Eliot wants somewhere in Blackpool.'

Grace pulls a face. 'Why?'

Elsie shrugs, her expression clamping shut like a trap, and Grace immediately feels a surge of guilt.

'I'm just glad he's taking an interest,' Elsie says pointedly, switching channels on the television.

Grace stands up, moves out to the kitchen and tops up her wine. The mood of the evening has gone sour, and it's her fault, but she can't help it. Talk of the wedding fills her with a sickly dread, a feeling that she is going to ruin it somehow. She drinks greedily and then fills the glass again before returning to the lounge, tasting acid.

'Grace, I really need to know that you're happy for me. I don't feel like you are,' Elsie says calmly as Grace sits down again. Her face is tense. All the brightness has been switched out.

Grace's blood freezes in her veins. 'I just care about you,' she says slowly, her head aching.

'That's not the same as being happy for me. I asked you if you were happy for me.'

It would be so easy to lie, to say *yes, of course I'm happy for you*. But Grace can't do it. Her sister is her own skin and cells and blood. She's part of her.

'I want things to be good between us,' Grace attempts, but Elsie rolls her eyes.

'So we're now talking about what you want? You can be so selfish, Grace.'

'That's not fair!' Grace's voice rises above the noise of the television, above the horrible clanking pipes and the vague sounds of a party next door. 'I just mean I want us to get along. And I just want to do the right thing.'

Elsie frowns. 'I don't even know what that means. I don't know why you can't just talk to me properly instead of speaking in riddles.'

Grace feels a jolt. She is so used to trying to prise the silent Elsie open that it hasn't ever occurred to her that she might come across as secretive too. Perhaps she isn't as good at hiding things as she thought she was. She stays silent, a tear rolling down her cheek. She wipes it away savagely.

'I just sometimes worry about what's meant to be,' she says finally.

'Don't say things like that. You sound just like Mum. You look like her too.'

Grace bursts out laughing, a manic sound even to her own ears. 'We're identical twins! If I look like her, then so do you.'

'No. It's more than that. It's the way you are. You share something with her, something that I don't.' Elsie's eyes darken.

'Why is that so bad? Not everything is a competition, Elsie. Not everything is about which one of us is better, or has more in common with someone we both love.' Grace's voice has risen again and she picks up her glass. She can feel energy in her, trying to escape, howling inside of her, fuelled by alcohol.

Elsie shakes her head. 'I don't want you to be like our mother, Grace.' Her words are soft, and Grace has to strain to hear them.

'And it's not because I'm competing with you. '

'Well then, why do you hate the idea of her being the same as me then?' Grace feels a resentment gnaw at her that Elsie cannot handle the truth. It's hard work keeping a secret. If Elsie knew, she wouldn't accuse Grace of being selfish. If Elsie knew what Grace went through each day, then she would surely come to life, her infuriating calmness would dissolve and fizz into the fury that had somehow become Grace's. Perhaps she should tell Elsie right now. Perhaps she should scream at her what she sees every time she closes her eyes, whose wedding they should really be planning.

She puts her hand up to her new necklace. Things seemed fine between them this morning. What was Grace thinking? Of course they weren't fine. Her fingers begin to pull, ever so slightly, at the aqua stones that hang around her neck, until she hears Elsie's next words, quiet and sad.

'I hate the idea of you being like Mum because I lost her. And if you're the same as her, it means that I'll lose you too.'

Grace's hands drop from the necklace, and she puts her glass down on the table gently.

'I didn't know that's how you felt,' she said, the energy inside her deflating in an instant.

Elsie shrugs. 'Come on. This was a stupid conversation. I didn't want to fall out with you. Let's just leave it. Let's go to bed.'

They stand, and Elsie blows out the candles, throwing the room into a peaceful, smoky darkness.

PART FOUR

Chapter Thirty Four

Noel, 1995

The drive back was long. It was May, but the roads were wet and sleek.

'*She's gone,*' Noel's mother had said that morning on the phone.

The small words circled round and round his mind like bombers as he sped along the motorway. As the road signs told him he was heading further and further towards the north, Noel thought of where he should be heading now.

There were four other people being interviewed for the news editor's position in the New York office. Four other people would be rehearsing answers to corporate questions right now, laying out their suits and running over their presentations while Noel was speeding away from it all.

He thumped his steering wheel in frustration, and the car swayed lightly, bumping over the cats' eyes.

What was he *doing*?

Jack, Noel's boss, would be furious. He knew how long Noel had waited for an editor's position to come up. He had watched Noel begin as a junior reporter, had encouraged his meticulous style and late nights at the grey office. Noel was the only one from the London office who had been shortlisted for this week's interview.

Jack had put in a good word for Noel at the New York office, and that meant that Jack's reputation was on the line as well as Noel's. Noel scanned through possible excuses he could give Jack as he moved further up the country, away from the success of London to the blustery, tired north.

Family stuff, he could say. But that was too vague. Jack would see straight through it. Noel could possibly get away with it if he told Jack that somebody had died. Who might he say had died? Or was that a bit sick?

Noel gazed out at the glossy road ahead of him, the car cruising underneath him as though he wasn't even in control anymore.

He'd have to come up with something.

He couldn't tell Jack the truth: it was all for her.

Even then, when she was sixteen, it was all for her.

Noel decided to ring Jack instead of waiting for him to find out from somebody else. He pulled into a service station about an hour from Blackpool and plopped a twenty pence piece into a worryingly sticky pay phone.

'Is there a problem?' Jack answered. He wasn't one for formalities like saying hello.

'It's just that something's come up. I can't make the interview.' Noel cradled the phone between his chin and shoulder while he fished in his pockets and wallet for more coins.

'Something urgent?'

'Yes. It's a family thing. And I can't really...I don't really have a choice, so I've had to come home.'

'Home?'

'Not my flat in London. I mean home to my family. My mum.'

'Has there been an accident?'

'No, not exactly.'

There was a long pause and Noel dropped another coin into the phone, imagining Jack sighing and rolling his eyes up towards his pristine white office ceiling.

'I'm not going to ask you what it is,' Jack said after a while. 'But deal with it, and get on the next flight. You can still make it to the interview. I can ask them to see you last.'

'Jack. I won't be able to. I'll have to leave it. I'm sorry, I know you put your neck on the line and I honestly appreciate it. But it's just not good timing.'

'Okay.' Another sigh. 'You've blown it, obviously. They won't reschedule your interview. You miss the interview, you miss the job. I'll see you Monday.'

'Okay. I—'

But Jack had gone. Noel stared at the receiver in his hand for a while, wondering if he should call Jack again and take it all back. His fingers slid over a twenty pence piece in his pocket, grasping it, then releasing it. He hung the receiver up and pushed open the door of the phone box.

Grey pellets stung Noel's face as he walked back to his car. The final stretch of his journey was silent and still. The roads towards the town centre were blank compared with the city ones he had left behind.

Noel's mother lived in the house he'd grown up in, a short drive from the town centre. The house was a copy of the one next to it, and the one next to that. Noel had spent so many years wondering what it would be like to live somewhere different to this bland semi. And now, as Noel pulled onto the kerb at the side of the house, he felt a tug of terror at what he had just turned down. The New York job had been his goal for years. He had spent the last week leafing through details of Manhattan apartments for rent that Jack had left on Noel's desk. He had been confident of his presentation and interview technique. He had bought a new suit and tried it on to check that it looked smart.

Noel gazed up at the house. His old bedroom was the biggest room in the house, at the front. When his dad had left, his mum had swapped rooms with Noel. She had wanted a new start. Noel had done as he was asked and quietly swapped his books for his mother's elaborate coats and handbags filled with forgotten lipsticks and crumbling tissues. He had liked helping his mother swap their rooms around. He could see that she was angry, could see her mouth puckered with the effort of not saying all the things she wanted to about the divorce.

As Noel stared up at his old bedroom, the light in there blinked on. Somebody was in there. His mother never went in that room. Although the curtains were closed and revealed nothing but a cool golden glow, Noel knew who had turned it on, who would be sitting on his bed, with Noel's childish old shark-patterned lamp beside her.

He stopped the engine, stopped thinking about what could have been, and let himself into the house. As soon as he opened the front door, Mags let out a whispered squeal and click-clacked in her slippers from the kitchen to the hall.

'I'm glad you're here!' she said as she gave Noel a faux-kiss on the cheek. 'Do you want some chips? I'm making the girls some,' she nodded towards the chip pan sizzling away on the hob, 'because they love chips. They've just gone upstairs though, so I doubt they'll eat any now. I've got a pork chop too, if you want it?'

'I'm okay with just some chips. How are Grace and Elsie?'

'I'll do you the chop as well.' Noel's mum busied herself with the fridge for a minute and then turned to him, her eyes welling up. It obviously wasn't the first time she'd cried that evening. The blue eye make-up she had worn every day since Noel could remember was sprinkled over her flushed cheeks.

'I still don't think Louisa's going to ever come back,' she whispered, her eyes darting upstairs in case she might be overheard. 'I don't know what they'll do. They're sixteen years old. I can't believe she's done it. I knew she wasn't at her best, but...' her voice trailed off and she began opening cupboards and pouring drinks of lemonade. 'I didn't think she'd ever actually disappear,' she eventually finished.

As Noel took his glass of lemonade, he gazed around the kitchen.

Nothing was out of place. Mags's house usually betrayed chaos and rushing, with letters and keys tossed on worktops and jackets and bags slung over chairs. But now, everything seemed to be immaculate. The worktops were desolate: a wide, wiped expanse of beige. The sink was bare, and the draining board emptied and dry. Noel imagined his mother tidying again and again, keeping busy. The thought pained him. He sat down at the table so suddenly that he banged his leg against the pine. He sat there for a moment, rubbing his leg, thinking of Louisa, of how much she had meant to him when he was young, and how wrong things had gone for her.

'It was their birthday, you know. She left them on their sixteenth birthday,' Mags said, peering into the oven, looking anywhere except at Noel.

'I know.' Noel had sent the twins a card each stuffed with a five pound note only the other day.

'She'd gone out in her pyjamas, we think. She wasn't well at all, in her mind. She had been getting worse for a while. I told her to go to the doctors a few months ago, but I don't think she did.'

'But you don't know for sure?' Noel suddenly felt a surge of miserable anger towards his mother. 'Why didn't you check?'

Mags's face collapsed and she began crying again, making Noel go cold with guilt. Of course it wasn't his mother's fault.

'I should have done, I know that now. I should have made her go and talk to somebody. But she was so bloody stubborn. Once she had an idea, it was like she'd been brainwashed.' Mags shook her head, then raised it towards the ceiling, waving her hands in front of her eyes to try and coax her tears back inside. She plonked a bottle of ketchup on the table and sniffed. 'Do me a favour, will you? The girls are in bed, in your room. Will you go up and pop your head round the door and check they're okay? The light is on. They won't have it dark.'

Noel nodded and made his way up the stairs, bracing himself for hearing muffled sobs. But when he looked around the open door into his old burgundy bedroom, all he heard was sleep. He stood there for a moment, feeling a little uncomfortable but unable to tear himself away. Nobody else would be able to tell which girl was which, but Noel could. Her hair was slightly darker, her skin slightly paler. She slept more intently, her limbs strewn, breaths deep and gasping.

It was hours later when Noel finally lay back on the sofa under the unzipped red sleeping bag that had accompanied him on various childhood trips. He lay quietly, hearing his mum shuffle around upstairs, running the water, rattling coat hangers, drawing her curtains. Finally, there was silence, but he still didn't close his eyes. Even in the dark, he could make out the room he knew so well. Woodchip wallpaper was punctuated by framed pictures Mags thought were artistic: women with umbrellas; children with dogs. The mantlepiece was home to the china mouse behind which letters were propped, the clock that was set six minutes fast so that Mags would always be on time (it didn't work: she always set off at least fifteen minutes late) and some unframed, curling photographs of them all over time. Noel was in fewer photographs than the twins. But they were girls, happy to pose, happy to pout. Noel was often in the background of the photos, head stooped, reading, wishing he could take himself less seriously but not knowing how to.

Impatient with his inability to settle and sleep, Noel threw the tangled sleeping bag off his legs and stood. He clicked on the standard lamp behind the sofa and the room was immediately drowned in a sickly peach glow. He wandered over to the mantlepiece and took a handful of the photographs before sitting back on the sofa. There were the pictures he remembered from various Christmastimes, one of his mum and her friends playing Monopoly while a baby Noel sat on Louisa's knee, one of Louisa and Noel at Stanley Park one summer. Noel held that one at an angle so that he could see the paused faces in the tepid light. He was shocked to find that tears ached behind his eyes as he stared at Louisa's pale face.

Now, in the strange night, the thought of what Louisa might have done, where she might be now, made Noel's stomach heavy. He remembered that day at Stanley Park, the day that the picture in his hand had been taken. Noel had liked Louisa a lot, and had felt an urge to please her. They had bought ice creams and Noel remembered wanting to buy Louisa's but having no pocket money left after spending it on a book about rockets. Louisa spoke to Noel more than anyone, then. The twins were too young to have proper conversations with, and although Noel didn't want to say much, when he did speak, Louisa seemed to be the only one who would listen to him. But this particular day at the park, Louisa seemed preoccupied. Even she didn't listen to Noel properly. So in the end he played with the twins. Noel didn't think they were particularly enchanting that day, or many other days after that. It wasn't until years later that Grace suddenly made Noel feel something click inside him every time he looked at her.

Once he'd returned the photograph to its place on the cluttered mantlepiece, Noel pulled the sleeping bag back over his body and closed his eyes. Sleep washed over him quickly this time, and he slept for much longer than he thought he might. It was light outside when he heard the kettle being flicked on in the kitchen next door to him. The clanking of mugs made him groan and lift up his head. Grace stood in the doorway, staring into the room, as though somebody had pressed pause on her.

'Hi,' Noel said.

Grace said nothing. She was wearing a thin t-shirt, and Noel could see her black bra through it. He tried not to look at her shape, at her hair which hung in thick black waves either side of her pale face, at her long, lean legs which were barely covered. He tried hard to remember that she was only sixteen.

'Grace. I'm so sorry. You've had a tough time, haven't you?'

Grace rolled her eyes. 'You sound like a teacher. You're saying what a teacher would say.'

So Noel stood up, even though he was only wearing his boxers, and he hugged her, and he tried not to smell her strawberry smell and feel her skin against his.

'She won't come back,' Grace said finally, her voice muffled into Noel's shoulder.

'You don't know that.'

Grace laughed, a sharp mean laugh. 'I do know it. I know it better than anyone. Come on. Let's have coffee. I've nicked one of your mum's fags too. Want to share it?'

'I don't smoke. And neither should you.'

More eye rolling. Suddenly it was very easy to remember that Grace was sixteen.

'Course you don't, sir,' she smirked. She threw a jar of Nescafé at him. 'Two sugars, please.'

Noel knew that Grace wasn't flirting, that she was just treating him like she might a weird older brother who she'd never actually considered as part of her world. He knew what flirting was now. Whatever it was that he had lacked at school, Noel seemed to have in the world of work. Women flirted with him in the lift and in bars and at office parties. One in particular flirted her way right into Noel's evenings, and somehow he was now in some kind of relationship with her. Cara was the same age as Noel. She liked going out to nightclubs in short skirts on Saturday nights and renting videos on Sundays. Sometimes they went to the cinema after work, sometimes they just sprawled out on the sofa watching television and eating microwaved meals. Noel remembered now, looking at Grace, that he hadn't even told Cara that he had left London and come to Blackpool.

'What are you thinking?' Grace said, her hands cupped around her coffee. She was wearing neon nail varnish that was chipped, and Noel thought of Cara's manicured hands that were begging for a big engagement ring to flaunt.

'I need to phone someone and let her know I'm here.'

Grace shrugged and put her coffee down on the worktop. Noel

tried to read her expression, to see if there was any curiosity about the female he'd just alluded to. But there was nothing. She began to pick at her nail varnish, lost in her own world.

Noel was drifting to sleep on Sunday night when he felt something weigh on the sleeping bag, near his feet. He opened his eyes and saw Grace's silhouette at the end of the sofa. She was sitting with her knees drawn up against her chest.

'Can't sleep,' she whispered when she saw that Noel had woken.

'That's okay. We can sit together for a bit. Shall I make you a drink?'

He could tell then, from the way that Grace shook her head, that she couldn't speak. She shook her head for much longer than she needed to. He shuffled up so that he was sitting next to her and put his arm around her.

Minutes passed while they sat in silence.

'People keep saying no news is good news. But that's shit,' Grace said eventually, her voice breaking. 'No news means that she's gone.'

Noel held Grace's shaking shoulders more tightly then, pulled her towards him and felt his chest become wet from her black tears. After a time, her sobs subsided and she disentangled herself from Noel and wiped her face on the sleeping bag.

'I'm sorry. I'm sorry,' she said.

'Don't be.'

'I'm so glad you're here, Noel. It's made it all easier. I can't even speak to Elsie about her. I can tell she's furious, and she's got things she wants to say, but she won't talk. She won't say anything.'

Noel thought of Elsie's distant, frowning face. She had barely spoken to Noel since he'd arrived. 'Everyone deals with things like this differently. She'll come round.'

Grace sniffed. 'Maybe. But I'm still glad you're here for now. Please say you're staying for a bit.'

Noel had planned to get up at 3 a.m. the next day and drive back to London in time for work. He thought of Jack's broad, annoyed face, of the line that somebody in a tall New York office had scraped through Noel's name in the interview list. And then he thought of how Grace had just crumpled into nothing, and how she had come to Noel to do it.

This was terrible timing.

'Course I'll stay,' he said to Grace. He saw her face change in the dark as she smiled. As she clambered off the sofa and left the room, he wondered what it might be like to kiss her, and if she'd kissed anybody properly yet, or done anything else. The thought made him ache, and he banished it from his mind.

Noel decided to go back to London on Tuesday night. On Monday afternoon, while they were sitting watching the news together, he told Grace.

'I do want to stay longer,' he explained. 'But my boss isn't great with the sympathy stuff.'

Noel had called the office that morning. Jack's words were still echoing in his ears.

'Noel, my sympathies are with whoever is suffering there with you. But we need you here, doing your job. We do have a policy on compassionate leave, but it doesn't cover family friends, I'm afraid.'

'Well, I suppose that's not how businesses are run,' Grace said now, lifting up her feet and plonking them on Noel's knees. She snuggled into the sofa. 'Is it a good job you've got? It must be, if you've moved all the way to London for it.'

'It is. I've worked my way up since I've been there. I started out having to photocopy and make drinks, but now I get to do interviews with different people in the finance industry and write them up. I always have a deadline to meet, so it's quite fast paced. But I enjoy the writing, and I love living in London. I've never wanted to stay in Blackpool,' he finished cautiously.

'I don't either,' Grace said quickly.

'What do you want to do after sixth form?'

Grace thought for a moment. 'Well, I suppose I need to pass

my exams first. But I want to move away. I want to go somewhere completely different. I sometimes imagine living somewhere like London. Or maybe New York, I'd like to live in New York,' she finished with a grin.

Noel hesitated for a minute, then spoke. 'I had an interview for a job in New York recently.'

Grace leaned forward and her deep violet eyes widened.

'Really? That's so exciting. Didn't it go well?'

'I didn't go,' Noel said, waving his hand dismissively.

Grace sat back and tapped him lightly on the head with a plump red cushion. 'You should have gone. You blew it. That's the kind of thing I'd do. I'd have a good chance at something then end up getting distracted and blowing it for myself. But I wouldn't expect you to do that. You should try again. As soon as there's another chance.'

'Chances like that don't come up very often, to be honest.'

'There must have been a good reason for not going. It must have been something important. Was it?' Grace said, looking at the television. The newsreader had a sombre expression, and then the scene shot to a field of people searching for something. A body. Noel snatched the remote from beside him and zapped off the news. The lack of television threw the room into silence. He realised he still needed to answer Grace's question about the New York interview.

'It was very important.'

They were both quiet for a minute, still staring at the blank television screen.

'So,' Noel said eventually. 'If you move to New York, what will you do there?'

Grace shrugged. 'Dunno what job I'll end up doing. I like English and I like drama. I might do a drama course and be an actress.'

Noel smiled, thinking of how he had always hated speaking in front of people.

267

'You'd make a great actress. I'll come and watch you perform if you like.'

'I'd love that. And why don't you write to me in the meantime? You know, when you've gone back to London. I love getting letters.'

Noel laughed. 'Write to you? I'm not great with words.' To his horror, as he said this, he felt the tips of his ears go red and wished he could hide them. He looked down, which seemed like the next best thing to do.

'Okay. Promise you will ring me then? You don't depress me like everybody else does.'

Noel smiled at the drama of Grace's words. He looked at her face: pale and tired and hopeful. He thought of how he hadn't even missed Cara since he'd arrived in Blackpool and how the first thing he would think of when he got back to London would be how much he missed Grace.

'I promise.'

Chapter Thirty Five

Grace, 2008

Grace decides to walk to the hall where the performance is being held on the opening evening of *Macbeth*. The air is icy and clear and she stuffs her hands deep into her pockets to stop them from tingling with the cold. She walks briskly, taking in the window displays in each house. Christmas is only a week away, and most of the houses burst with fairy lights and colour. Some display snowmen or plastic reindeer outside, their chaotic flashing adding to the jumble in Grace's mind.

Christmas always makes Grace feel the same: mostly dark and sad, with a tiny, glittering flicker of hope deep inside her belly that this one will be different.

When the twins were growing up, they usually spent Christmas day with their mother at Mags's house. Their mother and Mags would drink wine, and as the day moved into the evening, their conversations would become less clear to the children, and louder, punctuated more freely by blasts of laughter about things that Grace didn't understand. Noel was always there, quietly reading his new *Guinness Book of World Records* in a corner. One year, he didn't come home for Christmas. That was when Grace was about fourteen. He had just got his new job in London and he was spending the holidays there with friends. Mags mentioned him a couple of times that year but didn't seem too bothered. Grace supposed that, technically, things weren't much different, because Noel never said a lot. Still, Grace felt his absence and hoped that he wouldn't stay away from home the following Christmas. She couldn't imagine Noel with his friends. She wondered if he would laugh and chat to them like her mother did with Mags.

Noel returned home the following Christmas, and Grace thought that him being there might make things better. But that Christmas turned out to be one of the worst. Elsie spent most of the day locked in Mags's bedroom, furious with their mother.

Grace nuzzles her chin into her thick scarf and thinks back to that year as she walks towards the performance hall. That was the year that Elsie had taken another fatal step away from their mother by going to stay with Mags for a couple of days. Grace remembers wanting to go and sleep at Mags's house too, but feeling a thin thread of loyalty attaching her to their mother.

'Mags is going to teach me how to put eye make-up on properly. I think I've been doing it wrong. I can't get it to look right,' Elsie had said as she was packing her pyjamas and the next day's knickers.

Grace thought about Mags's make-up and wrinkled her nose. 'Mags wears blue mascara. Don't let her put blue mascara on you,' she said, remembering reading somewhere that blue mascara died out with the 1980s.

'I won't,' Elsie sniffed. 'She's bought us face masks, so by the time you see me I won't still have the make-up on anyway. And we're going to watch *Dirty Dancing*.'

Elsie didn't invite Grace to sleep at Mags's too. That didn't matter so much: if Grace had really wanted to go she could have phoned Mags and asked her. But she felt as though she should stay with their mother. Grace would ask their mother to teach her how to put make-up on properly. Then things would be as they should be.

But their mother went out all morning, so once Elsie had gone off to Mags's house, Grace drifted into Louisa's bedroom. The room was a mess, as always. The curtains were drawn, quivering slightly in the draught from the window. Grace pulled them open to let in the weak light, the sliver of sea in the distance catching her eye. She moved away from the window and looked around. Although there was a dressing table, it didn't look like the place to find make-up. Clothes were piled up in front of the mirror, which reflected the tangle of dull jeans and tops that seemed to be waiting for something: ironing, perhaps, or, judging from the stale scent of her mother's bedroom, washing. Grace shoved the pile of clothes to one side, but the pine dressing table was bare underneath. Reluctant to look in any drawers, Grace stood on her tiptoes to see what was on the shelf above the dressing table.

Bingo.

A frayed make-up bag, orange with spilt powder, sat opened on the shelf, its innards visible. Grace clambered up, leaning on the dressing table for support, and helped herself to a tube of sticky black mascara. Her mother didn't wear as much make-up as Mags. Some days she wore a streak of bright red lipstick, but most days she just wore some powder that smelt weird, and a bit of black mascara. Come to think of it, their mother was pretty, in her own way. But, Grace decided as she climbed back down from the dressing table, she could be prettier if she tried harder. Her hair was never freshly brushed, her clothes were always thrown on and her face constantly pulled together in apology or concern that she was late, or wrong, or, more recently, drunk.

Once she was back in her own, tidier bedroom, Grace eyed the mascara wand, then pulsed it in and out of the bottle. Although most of the girls at school tried to get away with wearing mascara, and Elsie had been wearing make-up for a year or so, Grace had never bothered with it. But now, she found herself wanting to join in with everyone else. She lifted the black, gloopy stick up to her eyes, wondering whether to keep them open or shut them. When she'd watched her mother put it on, she'd always have her eyes open, and her mouth would gape open too. Grace opened her mouth, and then stroked some of the mascara onto her lashes. Her eyes tried to close automatically to begin with, so on the first few goes Grace got a smear of black on her eyelids. Every time this happened, she washed her face and started again. She wanted it to be perfect.

Once she had finished her mascara, Grace brushed her hair and stared into the mirror. She looked different. She felt a wave of excitement as she realised that make-up made her prettier, and more adult. How would Elsie's make-up look? She lay on her bed for a while and thought about phoning one of their friends, but it seemed strange to ask them to do something without Elsie too. How long would her mother would be out for? Just as Grace was contemplating turning up at Mags's house, complete with her own mascara lashes and sleeping bag, she heard the key turn in the front door.

Her mother had been shopping. It would have been nice if she'd noticed that Grace was wearing make-up. They might have even put on some more, together. But her mother just dumped her bags and chattered on about some magazines she'd bought and asked where Elsie was. Grace, no longer wanting to dwell on Elsie's evening of fun with Mags, tried to keep the conversation as short as possible. She asked her mother if she'd bought marshmallows, even though she wasn't even too bothered about marshmallows. She did it to change the subject.

Then her mother had done the thing that made Grace feel uneasy. She had taken a sip of something straight from the carrier bag. It looked like brandy, and Grace caught a wave of its potent, nutty smell as her mother swung the bottle back down from her lips.

Grace didn't want to say it. She didn't even want to think it. But after being on her own all day, after teaching herself how to put make-up on with nobody to tell her how it looked, after thinking all about the fun that Elsie would be having at Mags's house, she felt brittle and angry.

So she thought it, and then she said it, before stomping off upstairs. *'It's no wonder Elsie's run off to Mags.'*

Grace can't remember how long she lay alone on her bed that day. She remembers that her mother poured some of the brandy down the sink and then they had toasted the marshmallows together, and she remembers being glad, for a few moments at least, that she wasn't at Mags's and that she was at home with her own mother.

It was a few days after that, Christmas day, that Louisa had admitted to the twins that she had a gift to see into the future.

'It's too late for her to tell us everything now,' Elsie had said quietly as the twins sat in Mags's bedroom. The room was full of carrier bags and bits of Sellotape and cut offs of red paper that betrayed last minute Christmas wrapping earlier on. 'She should have told us years ago.'

Grace thinks of Suzie being told everything about their mother; the twins being told nothing.

'I can't believe she wasn't honest with us,' Grace said, her voice shaking. She thought of the other night when she had sat in front of the fire with her mother. Something had shifted that night, and Grace had felt as though things might get better, as though her mother could be someone she might trust. But now, all those feelings melted away, leaving a sticky pool in the bottom of Grace's stomach.

'I've spent years wondering why she saved you and not me when we had that car accident,' Elsie said, her voice breaking into Grace's thoughts. 'I suppose I have been hoping all this time that I was wrong about her gift. But now we know for sure. She can choose who to save. And she chose you, and Suzie, and not me.' Elsie hugged her knees as she spoke, and her words were muffled.

Grace put her arms around her sister, who closed her eyes and was silent.

Now, Grace wipes her eyes as she walks: the cold air is stinging them

273

and making tears stream down her numb cheeks. She remembers holding a still, angry Elsie upstairs at Mags's house, the smell of turkey and trifle wafting up the stairs and making her feel sick. Grace had been so angry with her mother that day, for choosing one of them over the other to save, for not telling them the truth from the very start, for making her once fun sister become so sad and silent, for being so different.

But then, when Grace met Eliot and had her own first vision, she realised that she was different too.

Now that she knows she is the same as her mother, Grace understands: she understands how fierce the visions are, how impossible it seems to ignore them. She understands how alcohol makes everything less painful, and makes the visions less clear and sharp. And she understands how keeping a secret from Elsie, from anybody you love, is the most difficult thing in the world.

As Grace arrives at the hall for the performance, she feels an almost pleasant anxiety rush through her body. Although she has enjoyed the rehearsals over the past few weeks and has felt confident in her lines, she suddenly thinks of the audience as she passes through the art-deco-styled entrance and feels a little nauseous. Her head starts to ache as she gets changed into her heavy, musty costume and the familiar, lightheaded haze falls down onto her as she makes her way out onto the stage for her first scene. When it's time for her to say her lines, and she looks out into the audience, she does not see the bright lights above her, or a sea of faces, or the anxious expression of the actor opposite her as he waits for her to speak. She sees a vision: one she has never seen before.

She sees herself on a hospital bed, her legs flopping outwards, a murky pool of water between them. She sees Eliot next to her, cutting the cord of their brand new baby. He smiles at Grace and tells her it's a boy. He tells her that he is happier than he ever could be. The baby squeals for its mother, for Grace. And then, suddenly, the picture is gone.

Grace's mind instantly returns to her lines, and they spill from her lips, her hands shaking as she gestures to the other actor on the stage. She says each word she has practised, her voice lilting with the intonations she has decided upon over the last few weeks, makes all the movements she has rehearsed, but does not think of anything other than the vision she has just had. In between scenes, in the small dressing room that smells of old carpet and spilled drinks, she stares at her script, seeing no words: seeing nothing other than Eliot.

When Grace is saying her last lines, and rubbing furiously at invisible blood on her hands, she looks out into the audience. It's a mistake that she shouldn't make. Any decent actress knows that you don't look out into the crowds, because for one, you can't make out faces below the blinding stage lights, and because for another, if an audience member sees your face, instead of the character's, even for a split second, the illusion that they have paid to see will be shattered.

But Grace forgets all of this, and her eyes dart fleetingly, like quick swimming fish, over the people who are watching her.

And there, towards the centre somewhere, amongst an ocean of people who mean nothing, is Noel.

As soon as the play is over, the dressing room swarms with relief and excitement.

'Good show tonight, Grace!'

'Great first night! That's going to be hard to beat, eh?'

Grace has imagined the moments after the opening night's performance more than once, lying awake in her flat, unable to sleep. She has imagined chatter such as this: the 'well dones' and the 'good shows' from Kate and Shelley and the man with the alarmingly appropriate Scottish accent who is playing Macbeth. She had expected to join them for drinks somewhere, in a stylishly scruffy flat of one of the actors, and return home fulfilled and a little drunk. She had expected to linger over dressing as Grace again, over peeling away Lady Macbeth's clothes and bravado to reveal herself.

But in incongruous reality, Grace swoops her costume over her shoulders and hurriedly pulls on her jeans and bright pink jumper. She nods along to compliments and bats them back skilfully: 'you too,' 'well done, that was your best performance yet, you know'. And then she says a quick goodbye, and darts out from behind the stage, out into the lighter, brighter world beyond to find Noel. He is waiting for her, alone in a red sea of deserted chairs and sweet wrappers.

'You came!' Grace says, throwing her arms around Noel. He is familiar and foreign all at once. Normally, she is able to keep her feelings about Noel tightly wound together, but tonight, something seems to unravel: she feels something spring deep inside herself. For once, Noel, the thought of being with him, being his, shines in her mind and throws everything else into its shadow.

'Of course I came.' Noel usually hugs Grace for an instant longer than he should, but tonight he extracts himself from her quickly, making her feel on edge, as though nothing tonight, or ever, will be like she thought it would be. 'I've got some news.'

Chapter Thirty Six

Noel, 2000

'How's your day been?' Bea asked Noel as she sipped her white wine.

'Good. Really good, actually. I went to that opening of the new branch of Hersey's Bank and did some networking. I'm going to use it for an article next week. I enjoyed getting out of the office and meeting people.'

Bea frowned in surprise. 'You enjoyed a party? I hope you're not bailing on me and becoming all schmoozy.'

Noel shrugged and split open his bread roll. Bea said nothing more, and silence sat between them again.

After leaving Grace in Blackpool to deal with Louisa's disappearance, Noel had returned to London, to a stern Jack and a desk full of tasks to help him prove himself. He felt like he was still proving himself even now, almost five years on; the opening of Hersey's was the one event Jack had put Noel forward for in a long time. Jack never spoke of the New York transfer that Noel had turned down: not with words. But Noel saw traces of annoyance in the menial tasks he was given, and could feel resentment float towards him every time he entered Jack's office.

Noel had tried not to think about the choice he had made. He tried to carry on being there for Grace and his mum. He spoke to Grace on the phone quite a bit when he had returned to London, and even tried to write her a decent letter like she'd asked him to. She had replied to his first few notes, but eventually her replies petered out, and Noel tried to take the sting out of his disappointment at this with the thought that it meant Grace was doing okay and moving on. He continued seeing Cara, until she happily accepted a sudden job offer in Glasgow and moved away one damp March morning. Noel didn't feel what he thought he was probably meant to feel as Cara rooted around his flat, looking for things she'd left there in the past year or so, then left his front door for the last time. He mainly felt a sense of gloom and monotony. Some other girl would probably be leaving her mixtapes in Noel's drawers in a couple of months' time, and coming round to collect them a few more months after that. It had all seemed so pointless.

And now there was Bea.

'So,' Noel asked Bea now. 'How was your day?'

'It was okay. I have the workshop tomorrow for the school.' Bea shook her head and her green dangly earrings jangled against her blonde hair. 'I'm dreading it.'

Bea worked in the local library and was currently embroiled in a new initiative to give workshops on children's classics to large groups of loud, disinterested children.

'I mean, I'm not a teacher. I don't want to be a teacher. I'm not brave enough. I hate that things have to change all the time. The library was doing well without any of the workshop stuff. I don't see why we have to keep doing them.'

Their starters were placed down, and Noel spread a thick layer of pâté over his bread as Bea continued speaking.

'I've spoken to Pat about it. She doesn't like it much, either. But there's not much she can do, I suppose.'

'Hmm,' Noel said, and took a bite of bread. 'Maybe look for work somewhere else if it keeps changing and you don't like it,' he said when he'd finished chewing.

278

Bea looked hurt and Noel wondered why. 'It's not that simple. I've been there for years. It's comfortable there.'

'Well, just see how it goes then. Maybe you'll get better at the workshops. Maybe you'll even enjoy them if you stick with it.'

Bea shrugged and stabbed at her melon rather savagely. It was the most aggressive Noel had ever seen her.

It's not my fault, Noel wanted to say. But he didn't. He topped up the centimetre of wine she'd drunk since they had arrived, and finished his pâté. He didn't speak again, and neither did Bea. The silence wasn't awkward, but it was dreary. Noel wondered which was worse.

A tall, ivory candle flickered in the centre of the table as they ate their main courses. Noel ate out a lot with Bea these days. He did what he thought he was meant to do for Bea: he took her on nice walks out of the city and to nice restaurants with candles and wine and clean cutlery with each course. She wore fancy earrings and Noel always wore a shirt. It was all as it should have been, but there was something missing, and ignoring such an absence took more effort than Noel might have imagined, like trying to ignore a missing tooth or finger.

'Do you want to come and meet my family?' Noel suddenly asked Bea.

She looked up, and set her knife and fork down together on her plate, which was still half full of tarragon chicken and new potatoes that looked as though they were a little too hard.

'Your family?'

'Yes. By my family I suppose I just mean my mum. And the twins I told you about. It's their twenty-first birthday party this weekend, and I wasn't going to go, but I think I will. And you should come with me.'

Bea frowned. 'To Blackpool?' she said, screwing up her nose a little.

'Yes. It'll be nice. My mum's hired some sort of club for the party. We'll go Friday night, after work, and come back Sunday night.'

'I think I'll have a quiet weekend at home. Pat said she might need me in on Saturday. So I'll stay here. But you should go.'

Noel shrugged. 'Okay,' he said, as Bea sliced neatly into a hard potato and popped it into her mouth.

When he arrived back in Blackpool on Friday, Noel instantly looked up at his old bedroom window, as he always did when he pulled his car up onto the kerb. The window was open, the net curtains billowing out like smoke. He wondered if the twins could possibly be getting ready in there. Perhaps they would all go to the party together. He thought about inviting Bea here with him, and guilt mingled with relief as he realised how glad he was that she had said no.

Before he was even at the front door, Mags had rushed out, her hair in rollers, her blue eye make-up a little brighter than usual. She ushered Noel inside, and the scent of smoke and cooked meat and Mags's scent of mints yanked him back to the past, to Louisa, to the day when Grace had clung to him so tightly he had considered never ever going back to London.

'Where are the twins?' he asked as he put his bag down in the hall.

'Bring that up here,' Mags gestured to his bag and pointed upstairs. 'You might as well sleep in your room instead of on the sofa. Elsie and Grace aren't staying here so much now,' she explained as she retrieved the bunch of net curtains from their tangle around the window frame and pulled the window shut. 'I miss them, obviously, but they seem to be doing a lot better this year. That university course they're doing has really done wonders for them. They've made some good friends. Elsie's even got herself a boyfriend.' Mags puffed up the pillow on the bed. 'How's Bea?'

'She's okay. I asked her to come with me this weekend, but she had to work.'

'That's a shame. Maybe next time.'

'So, what time's the party tomorrow?'

'Eight. We'll get there early though. Auntie Sheila's coming in our car, and Suzie is meeting us there with the balloons.'

Noel felt a tug of anxiety at seeing everyone again. Being in London made it easy to pretend that Louisa had never disappeared, to tell Grace over a crackling phone line that things would be okay, that the huge hole Louisa had left could be somehow patched together. But now, here, Noel realised that being home with family and old friends would make Louisa's absence sharp and new all over again, even after five years.

'It will be so strange. Without—'

'I know,' Mags said, laying her hand on Noel's shoulder. She looked up into his eyes for a rare second, before pushing him gently towards the landing. His mother's eyes were tired. The skin around them was beginning to sag with the weight of time. 'Come on. Let's put the kettle on.'

The party was full of people Noel had never seen before, mainly female students with jutting hips and glowing cigarettes attached to their limp fingers. The twins still hadn't even arrived at 9 p.m.

'Fashionably late,' Suzie grinned at Noel. Noel had been sitting in a corner, huddled with Suzie and her husband, Mark, around a small table peppered with bent cardboard coasters, for an hour or so. 'They're late to everything,' she continued, after pausing for a second to sip her lager and lime.

'Well, Elsie is. Grace is normally on time to things like this. It's yet another thing that they argue about,' Mark added, using a generous smile to show that he was joking.

Noel stood up. 'I think I'll get another drink. What can I get you all?'

The bar was small, and Noel had to wait for some time to order the drinks. Before he'd ordered, the room gave out a united shout behind him. He turned to look at the door, but couldn't make out the twins because of the rush of people that had swarmed towards them. The arrival of the birthday girls made the bar suddenly quiet, and Noel was served. As soon as his pint was poured, he pulled it towards him and took a sip. It was warm and not particularly pleasant, but he had another gulp, and another, until he couldn't put off the inevitable any longer.

The twins had arrived with a tall man who stood slightly in front of them as they chatted to their guests. Elsie's hair was a bit lighter than it had been the last time Noel had seen her and she looked thinner than she used to be. Grace looked the same to him as she always had: somehow fragile and strong all at once. Her black hair was piled on her head, and she wore a long purple dress.

Noel made himself take a step towards her. He'd grown up with Grace, he reminded himself, and was entitled to go over and spend time with her at her twenty-first birthday party. Leaving his drink on the bar, he wandered over and stood quietly next to the friends Grace was chatting to. As he waited for her, slightly apart from the group, and watched her talk, the years Noel had spent in London having a flat and girlfriends and friends melted away, leaving him as awkward as an adolescent.

The man the twins had arrived at the party with, who Noel presumed to be Elsie's boyfriend, was in the midst of a histrionic anecdote. He flung his arms here and there, and Noel could hear wisps of various theatrical accents over the music. Elsie laughed hard and clutched the man's tweed elbow. Grace laughed too, and a strange mixture of emotion gripped Noel: pleasure at seeing her laugh and sorrow that it wasn't with him.

Finally, once the man had finished his story, and the small crowd that had grown during the little performance had dispersed again, Grace's eyes moved across the room and stopped when they reached Noel. She smiled: a small, angular smile that was slightly sharper than her twin's, catlike and delicate. She weaved through the friends who remained next to her. Noel held out his arms and Grace hugged him fleetingly. She smelt different to how she used to, of musk and adulthood, and Noel had a sudden disloyal thought that Grace's scent was more pleasant than Bea's, which was always a little too sweet. He hadn't even known until that moment that he had ever even registered Bea's scent. But Grace made it impossible not to compare.

'Noel, I'm so glad you could come. I didn't know if you would. It's been absolutely ages since I saw you.' She turned and beckoned Elsie over. Elsie moved over to them and kissed Noel's cheek with a professional air about her.

'Lovely to see you.'

Noel realised then that he'd forgotten to buy the drinks he had offered Suzie and Mark before the twins had arrived. He looked over at them, sitting and waiting politely. He loosened his tie a little, then straightened it again. 'Can I get you both a drink?'

Elsie nodded. 'I'll have a lemonade, please. I'm pacing myself,' she added, when Grace looked at her incredulously. She took the hand of the man Noel had presumed to be her boyfriend.

'Eliot, this is Noel, a family friend. Noel, this is my boyfriend, Eliot.'

'Hello, hello,' Eliot said. 'So you know my girls?' He dropped Elsie's hand in order to shake Noel's. He reminded Noel of the salesmen who worked on the same floor as him in London: a smooth, assured face uncreased by any kind of self-doubt. His tweed suit jacket gaped open to reveal a bright green shirt and matching slim tie.

'I do know them. Our parents were friends,' Noel said, immediately regretting mentioning Louisa so early on, or at all. But if Eliot thought Noel was insensitive then he didn't show it. He put an arm around each of the twins.

'I was just asking Elsie and Grace if they wanted a drink,' Noel said to Eliot. 'Can I get you anything?'

'That'd be magnificent. What are you drinking, Elsie?'

Elsie tucked a strand of hair behind her ear. 'I'm sticking to lemonade for now.'

'I'll have a double vodka,' Grace said, before high-fiving Eliot, who held two fingers up at Noel to indicate that he wanted the same.

When Noel had delivered everybody's drinks to them, Mags beckoned him over to where she had saved him a seat. He sat down and they watched the party for a while. The venue was a squat, rather stark rugby club. Old photographs of the twins were stuck on the orange walls along with 21st birthday banners, and jostled with faded photographs of rugby teams for attention. The unattractive brown tables were sprinkled with metallic confetti and balloons bounced from the low ceilings. Grace, Elsie and Eliot moved around the room as one, Elsie shadowing Grace and Eliot, basking in their light.

'So, are you doing okay?' Noel asked Mags eventually.

She sipped her gin and tonic and shrugged.

'Are you getting out much?'

Mags laughed. 'I'm not an invalid, Noel!'

'I know. I just want to check that you're happy. I know you still think about Louisa a lot, even after all this time.'

It wasn't even half an hour since Noel had berated himself for mentioning Louisa in front of the twins, and here he was again, pulling her into the room, pulling her wistful, worried face from the past into the present. But he couldn't help it. Now that he was in Blackpool, Noel's mind was filled with Louisa and Grace and the past. Now he was here, he couldn't even remember what he talked about in London with his colleagues and friends. Things that didn't matter, he supposed, as he waited for Mags to respond. He watched her lined face crease up with emotion before she answered.

'I'm okay.' Mags squeezed Noel's hand. 'I do think about her, all the time. I wonder if she'll ever come back.'

Noel swallowed and scratched his head. He watched Grace across the room. Her expressions and movements showed a small but perceptible growth in confidence since her mother had disappeared.

'The twins seem to think she won't come back. Elsie thinks she left, and I think Grace believes she's dead,' Mags paused at the black, unthinkable word. 'I just don't know. I still don't know. Louisa talked to you a lot, didn't she?' Mags said, suddenly facing Noel.

'A long time ago, yes. When I was much younger. She used to talk to me about whatever book I was reading.'

'So you didn't talk about anything else?'

Noel frowned. 'Nothing she won't have told you. You were her best friend. I was just a little boy.'

'You were like a son to her,' Mags said as she downed the last of her drink and pushed her glass to the centre of the grimy table. 'I don't know where that left me.'

'Like a mother to the twins, I suppose.'

They sat there for a few moments longer, watching, thinking, remembering.

After sitting with Suzie, Mags, Mark and Noel picking at a luke-warm buffet and talking about their university courses, Grace and Elsie were pulled onto the small dance floor by their friends. They both moved self-consciously, Grace a little more freely, their faces and bodies pocked with garish disco lights. Eliot danced with them, twirling them around alternately. The dance floor was full and occasionally spewed out a few unlucky dancers onto the carpet beyond, out of the spotlight.

When the chaotic dance music changed without warning to a slow set of songs, Grace wound her way through the couples to the bar. Eliot began to follow, but was pulled back by Elsie. He put his arms around her, his face in an expression of mock torture, and they danced slowly, hanging onto one another, smiling out at the people who watched them. Grace stood still on the side-lines, watching her sister. Her mouth was in the shape of a smile but there was something missing in her expression, a blankness, until a girl drenched in tattoos threw her arms around Grace and dragged her to the dance floor to dance to the last part of *I Will Always Love You*. Grace grinned widely then, but Noel could see that no matter which way she was pulled by her friend, her eyes were always on her sister and Eliot.

'Noel, it's been so lovely to see you. I'm going now,' Suzie said, after tapping Noel on the shoulder and giving him a brief hug. She yawned and wriggled into her coat. 'I'm at work early tomorrow.'

Mark stood and shook Noel's hand. 'Nice to see you again. You up here much these days?'

'No. I always mean to visit Blackpool more,' Noel said, glancing over at Grace, who was being spun around wildly by her friend to the last song. She caught Noel's eye at that moment and he patted Mark on the shoulder in farewell, then began to move towards her.

When Grace saw Noel, she beckoned for him to join her. He took her hand as she held it out.

'I'm so glad you came!' Grace yelled in Noel's ear, then moved her face level with his. Her breath was heavy with alcohol, and Noel saw a haze in her expression. Her eyes were heavily made up with black make-up which had begun to fall in crumbs under her bottom eyelashes.

'Me too.'

Grace held onto Noel tightly and rested her head on his shoulder. As he swayed with her, he knew that she was facing Eliot and he knew that she was staring at him. They continued to sway for a while, until Eliot and Elsie began to kiss and Grace snapped around and pushed Noel away.

'Another drink?' Grace asked. The lights flicked on and she rubbed her left eye, causing a smudge of black to dart across her cheek.

Noel craned his neck to look at the bar. Sullen staff waited, their bar cleared and ready to be closed. 'I think your party's over,' he said as gently as he could. He knew people got upset about the end of their own parties, although having never thrown one, he couldn't say that he really, fully understood.

Grace looked up at him and Noel found himself wanting to touch her, to wipe the smudge of make-up from her cheek. He lifted his hand, not caring for that moment about Grace being younger and apparently consumed by Eliot, about him having Bea waiting for him at home, just aching to touch her warm, powdery cheek. But in the instant that Noel raised his fingers, Grace turned her head to see if Eliot was watching them. Noel's hand fell away, back down to his side, and Grace, her gaze fixed on her sister's boyfriend, noticed nothing.

Noel slept late at his mum's the next day, and by the time he had showered and eaten the huge cooked breakfast that Mags insisted on making him, it was near to 1 p.m. The blank day stretched in front of him as he realised with a jolt that he had no plans. When the phone rang, Mags jumped up from the table and rushed out of the room to answer it.

'Yes, he's still here,' Noel heard her say from the hall after a few seconds. He stood, wondering if Bea had somehow got his mum's number, but before he reached the phone, Mags returned to the room.

'Was the phone for me?' Noel asked.

'Yes. Grace. She's on her way round.'

Noel suddenly felt as though he'd eaten too many sausages, or that perhaps the bacon his mum had proudly piled on his plate had been out of date. 'What for?'

Mags shrugged. 'Probably just wants to see you.'

Noel thought of Bea, and their stilted conversations. He thought of the too-sweet-smelling lotion that she kept by her side of the bed and spread over her hands each night. Her hands were always so soft and immaculately manicured. She said that handling the library books all day dried out her skin if she wasn't careful. Even if she stayed over at Noel's, she brought the hand lotion with her and set it on the bedside table. It irritated him like mad, and he didn't even know why.

'Best do your hair, love,' Mags said, interrupting Noel's thoughts and making him feel sixteen again.

When the doorbell rang about half an hour later, Noel could see Grace through the frosted glass in the front door. She was holding something, although he couldn't make out what it was. When he let Grace into the hall, the item in her hands revealed itself as a black lever arch file.

'Noel, I'm so glad you're still here,' Grace said as he gestured for her to come in. 'What with our birthday party and everything, I totally forgot about an essay that I have to finish by Monday. It's 3,000 words on *A Streetcar Named Desire*. I know you did really well at uni. Will you help me?'

Noel sunk onto the sofa and Grace dropped down next to him and he could smell smoke and the heavy, musky perfume she'd been wearing the night before.

'Did you have a good time last night?' he asked Grace as she opened the file.

'Yeah. I did. Feel rough now though, and I can barely remember any of it. I'd planned to stay in bed all day,' she wrinkled her nose, 'but unless I want to fail my module on American drama, I can't do that.'

'Grace, I have to say that I know nothing about the play you just mentioned, or anything you'll be expected to write about in your essay. Why don't you ask Elsie? Or Eliot?' he added, the thought paining him.

'Because Elsie's already handed hers in, and I told her that I'd finished mine too, so I didn't look bad. And Eliot won't even start his till Sunday night. He'll be in bed all day today, and my essay will be the absolute last thing on his mind,' she finished with a dry laugh. 'He can get away with writing his essays at the last minute. He'll finish his in an hour and then get a better mark than anyone in our group. If I leave it any longer, then I'll fail, but I'm not inspired to do it,' she ended, putting her head in her hands. Her hair spilled through her fingers in black tangles and Noel wondered if she had brushed it since last night.

'I really want to help you. I've nothing else to do anyway, and

I obviously want you to pass. But you just need to write it, Grace. You did so well at college. You need to try as hard as you did there.'

'I know, I know,' Grace sighed, then suddenly sat up straight, her expression bright. 'I have an idea! Maybe we could watch the film together!'

Noel laughed and shook his head. 'Isn't that the worst thing you can do as a student? Watch the film instead of reading the book?'

Grace laughed too. 'No! I know you think I'm being lazy, but I'm not. This is for one of my drama modules. The essay is about its portrayal on screen and on stage. We went to watch the play last month in Manchester, but I haven't watched the film yet. I was going to try to manage without, but I'll never pass then. Watching the film is the perfect way to get me in the right frame of mind! Would you mind? It might not be your kind of thing...' she trailed off, slumping a little again on Mags's velvet sofa.

'I don't mind at all. Do you have it with you?'

'No. It's at home. Elsie's probably in, but she won't mind if we watch it there.'

'Then I'll get my keys.'

Grace smiled, and Noel's heart jumped a little, and he thought what a shame it was that he was never this excited about watching a film with Bea.

When they pulled up outside Grace's house and Noel looked up, a pain seared through him as he remembered all the times he had visited Louisa here with Mags. The house was unchanged: the bay windows still had their original worn leading and watery stained glass. The burgundy hood over the front door flopped down weakly as a reminder of the house's past as a busy bed and breakfast.

'Don't you fancy starting it up again as a hotel someday?' Noel asked as Grace swung open the front gate and fumbled in her huge bag for her keys.

'Nah. The hours are ridiculous. Our friend's mum has a hotel on the prom and she never stops. She's up till midnight working the bar and then up first thing to cook the breakfast,' Grace said. 'I told you, anyway. Don't you remember? I'm going to be an actress,' she grinned as she unlocked the front door, the heels of her boots clicking on the tiles in the hall.

'Not if you don't get your essay done first,' Noel said as he followed Grace into what he remembered as the dining room. It still had one of the original mahogany dining tables in it, which was overflowing with loose sheets of paper and biros, and a fruit bowl filled with change, paperclips and the odd hair scrunchie. A couch sagged in the corner, with a navy throw drooped over it, and a pizza box that appeared to be a couple of days old rested on the floor next to the gas fire.

'Not as nice as you remembered?' Grace asked, wincing at Noel's possible response.

'Just different. But hey, it's a student house now, isn't it? You're living exactly how you should.'

'Elsie and Eliot think so,' Grace smiled as she grabbed a couple of the papers from the table. 'But I hate it being so messy. I sometimes think of moving. It's sometimes just too hard to be here after…you know.'

Noel looked around the room, as though he would see Louisa drifting past somewhere. 'I can understand that.'

'Anyway. I'll go and get the film from Elsie's room. It seems like she's out. We'll watch it in the lounge, so go in if you like, and make yourself at home.'

Grace disappeared upstairs and Noel moved into the lounge, which he couldn't remember ever going in before. It had always been saved for the guests in the times when he used to visit Louisa with Mags. It was a small room that smelt of incense sticks and brandy. Sitting in there was like being swept back in time, to a place where orange velour curtains were the height of fashion. A huge, ripped couch spilled out from the back wall, and Noel sat on it, wanting to take off his shoes and put his feet up but not feeling it would be appropriate, even though the room was crumbling with neglect.

'Got it,' Grace announced as she burst into the room. 'I'll put it on.'

As Grace knelt in front of the video player, Noel realised how much she was starting to look like Louisa. Even though Elsie was Grace's identical twin, her attitude towards things and manner somehow excluded her. Grace's hair hung down in the same way that Louisa's used to, untamed, and more beautiful for it somehow. She pulled her lips tightly together when she was thinking, in the same way Louisa used to, as if she was scared of her thoughts spilling out of her mouth. Her eyes, although a different colour, for Louisa's had been blue, were beginning to share the same fearful glaze that he saw in Louisa's as he was growing up.

Grace turned from the video player self-consciously, as though she could feel Noel watching her.

'Are you sure you don't mind watching this?'

Noel wanted to tell her that there was nothing he'd rather do, and the words almost slipped out, but then he remembered with a jolt the way Grace had looked at Eliot the night before.

'I don't mind at all.'

Grace stood still for a moment, taking all of Noel in, as though she was deciding something. Then she crossed the room and yanked the curtains shut, before pressing play on the remote control, throwing the room into an eerie orange darkness.

Chapter Thirty Seven

Noel, 2008

Noel looks down for a minute before he tells Grace his news. He wants to blurt it out, which is a feeling he isn't used to, one that takes him by surprise. But he can tell she has rushed out to see him, that she still has Shakespeare's lines whizzing around her mind, and he wants to give her time to consider what he is saying, and to see what it could mean for them both. So he stares at the carpet, which is a deep red and stained with years of shoes and spillages and sticky wrappers.

He has never been to a local performance like this before; he's never been to anything like it before. Seeing Grace on stage was strangely exhilarating, almost as though he was performing himself. The very thought of performing makes Noel feel nervy, and as he watched Grace tonight, gesturing grandly to the other actors and throwing out her lines with that theatrical twang, the uneasy knowledge that Eliot and Grace have this passion in common crawled through his mind like an unexpected spider.

But, Noel reminded himself as he sat alone in the stale red chair and waited for Grace to come out from backstage, their similarity was the very reason for Grace and Eliot's incompatibility. Together, they were destructive. He remembered Bea then, and the thoughts in his mind began to scurry, building tangled webs of frustration from nothing.

Things had been stale with Bea for a long time. They'd had another disagreement just before Noel had left for the opening of Ash Books, a few months before. This one had been about the washing machine, which needed fixing. Noel had forgotten to buy the spare part he needed to fix it. Bea lashed out, angered by wearing the same trousers twice in a row.

'How did we get to the point where we're arguing about washing?' Noel had attempted to joke. But Bea had shaken her head sadly, as though that question, unfortunately, proved everything she had ever suspected about him.

'I think we need to talk,' he'd said in the end. Bea had explained patiently that she couldn't always remind him what needed doing, what needed fixing, Noel had interjected when defending himself was necessary. Bea didn't cry, or shout. Her eyes were still and unblinking as they discussed the necessity to not give up on so many years. The whole conversation reminded Noel of a particularly grim meeting at work: objectives that had to be tackled, the delegation of tedious tasks, the unified sighs at what lay ahead.

They'd had the same conversation over and over again for the last few years. One of the early conversations had resulted in a couple of promising changes. Bea had even gone out and got her hair cut to kick start a new her, a new them. It had swung neatly just below her ears and it suited her more than Noel thought it might. Noel had joined a gym. They made an effort to go for coffee after work every Thursday afternoon, which had been pleasant to start with, but then Bea had started working late on Thursdays. Eventually, her hair grew to her shoulders again and looked much the same as it had a year before. The silences grew, and then turned sour, until they weren't even silences, but clumps of bickering.

'I think we have to call it a day,' Noel said last week.

Bea had shrugged curtly. 'If you say so.'

And that had been that. She had packed up her things that

night, and gone. Noel had stared out of the window and watched as she leaned into her Fiesta to place the boxes of her things in neat stacks. She was wearing a floral dress and a white coat from M&S, and leaned carefully to avoid touching the car with her clean white sleeves.

Twelve years, boxed neatly away within two hours. It said a lot, but Noel didn't want to dwell on exactly what that was. He moved away from the window and went into his bedroom. *His* bedroom, not theirs.

Bea had cleared out her drawers, which had always been painfully tidy. She had left a few things of Noel's that had made their clandestine way into there on the top of her bedside table. One was Noel's watch: he was wondering where that had gone, and felt a spike of irritation poke his insides. She would have known it was in there, but instead of telling him, she waited for him to check: punishment for his carelessness. But now, with the battle over, the neat stream of punishments flowing into a wide sea of insignificance, the watch sat winking at him. Beneath it was a piece of card. Noel put his watch on and then turned over the square card.

You are cordially invited to the wedding of Eliot and Elsie, it said.

Noel's first thought, ridiculously, was about the style of the card. It was thick, purple and shimmering. It was nothing like a traditional cream wedding invitation.

Typical Eliot.

Noel's next thought though, waiting patiently behind the larger, but less important dithering ideas about card colour, was about Bea, and why she had kept this in her drawer for so long.

It didn't matter. It didn't make any difference. Grace had told him about the wedding more than once. But Bea didn't know that; she didn't know that Noel spoke to Grace on the phone. She didn't know anything about those conversations, charged with love and caring.

Well that's precisely the point, isn't it Noel, he heard Bea's voice say in his mind. *If I'd have known you spoke to Grace so very much I wouldn't have bothered to hide the invitation, would I?*

He strode into the lounge and propped the invitation up on the mantlepiece, an action that reminded him, disconcertingly, of his mother. As he digested the idea that Bea hid the invitation so that he wouldn't have a chance to see Grace, the icy edges of his irritation melted, turning to liquid guilt. He should have ended his relationship with Bea a long time ago. They both knew that. He had done the right thing today. But he had left things too late. He hoped, so much, that Grace wouldn't do the same.

Now, Grace takes his hand. He wants to pull her towards him, wrap himself around her. But he stops himself. He lets himself compliment her on her performance, but she is impatient with words that do not reveal anything. He looks at Grace's face, thick with stage make-up, waiting, wide with confusion and doubt and fear, and he begins to tell her the news: not that it's over with Bea, but the other bit of news, the same bit of news that he should have had all those years ago, when Grace was sixteen and had just lost her mother.

Chapter Thirty Eight

Grace, 2008

Grace feels her flushed cheeks drain to white. Marriage, or babies, or both, with Bea. It has to be. She remembers the vision of having Eliot's child that she had as she walked on stage, and her head aches with confusion. She searches Noel's face for a clue to what he's about to say, not able to wait, powerless for the few agonising seconds that he takes to reply. There's nothing to go off. His eyes are wide, sincere. He isn't smiling, but his face doesn't betray any unhappiness either. His features are tight with anticipation, but anticipation of what, they do not say. So Grace has to wait. She takes his hand. It's warm and solid and pleasantly big around hers.

'You were amazing in the play. I'm so glad you ended up with a main part.'

Grace smiles, but is impatient. 'What's the news?'

Noel takes a breath and squeezes her hand.

'I've had a job offer. In New York.'

There's silence. Grace stares into Noel's eyes, which are fixed on her, unblinking and steady. She feels his hand around hers. She feels as though she is falling, and only grasping Noel's hand will stop her. She fumbles for some words, but all the words in her head are Shakespeare's, useless now she is off stage.

'Is Bea going with you?' she eventually manages. At least, she thinks, she has got the question over with.

'Bea's not going anywhere with me. It's over with Bea.'

Grace watches the tips of Noel's ears turn pink. He never seemed besotted with Bea, but the break-up must have ripped up what he knew of his life.

'It's a good time for you to go, then. A good time for a change.' Grace wonders what has happened to her articulation. It's stunted and inadequate for such an important conversation. Her lines have washed over her own selection of vocabulary, making them wet and unable to grasp.

She can't think of what else to say, or do, so she falls towards Noel, and hugs him tightly. Having Noel's arms around her is always the same, always make her feel safe and as though she won't ever be alone. Ironic, considering his news.

'When do you go?' she says when she steps back, refreshed and ready to continue trying to talk.

'Not for a couple of months. I need to work my notice in London, and sort out somewhere to live in the States. It'll probably be somewhere tiny, but that doesn't bother me. It's a great opportunity. I'm pleased it's come around again.'

Grace nods, the thought of a life without Noel making her sting, the thought that because of her, he's had to wait years for this move.

'I am happy for you. It's such an amazing opportunity. I'll miss you, though. I'll miss you being here,' she gestures around the empty hall. 'Nobody else comes to things like this. It's always you. You're my best friend, Noel. '

Noel nods and a little bit of Grace's heart breaks.

That's the way it should be though, surely. Eliot should be her husband, and Noel should be her best friend. Even if she doesn't pursue Eliot, she's not meant to be with Noel.

You cannot change what is meant to be.

He's safer in New York than with Grace.

Grace is suddenly exhausted. She yawns, and Noel hugs her again, and drives her home.

Christmas passes quickly, leaving, as it always does, heavier waist-lines, a disappointing selection of strawberry and coffee creams rattling about in a chocolate tin that once promised so much, and a subtle despondency. January promises new beginnings and fresh-ness, but brings only rain and grey skies. The shop, after a brief flurry of business during the Christmas holidays, is quiet again. *Macbeth* runs its course, Noel returns to London, and Grace's drama group continues to meet weekly, holding Grace in a higher esteem than it did before her role as Lady Macbeth.

Grace stands behind the counter on the last day of January, watching torrents of rain batter the world beyond the window of the bookshop. Elsie has gone for her final wedding dress fitting: the wedding has been booked for April. Eliot is due any minute to deliver some boxes of vintage magazines that the twins found at a book fair the day before. There has been one customer in today, two if Grace counts the dog that joined the elderly lady who wandered around as though she was lost. Grace stared at the terrier and it stared back, daring her to expel it.

'Nice dog,' she said to the customer in the end, who ignored her and pulled at the door to leave without buying anything.

Eliot turns up just before lunch, shaking his wet head and making himself look rather like a dog.

'Careful,' grins Grace, 'we don't want soggy magazines!'

Eliot doesn't smile back. 'I really think you should have gone with her, you know.'

Grace feels a stab of guilt. Elsie didn't ask Grace to go with her to the wedding dress fitting, but Grace knows that she should be there regardless.

'She didn't ask me to be there,' Grace defends herself and takes the box from Eliot. She places it on the counter and begins to unload the magazines. One is a tattered copy of *Cosmopolitan* from the 1960s. She flicks it open and looks down at the comical advertisements featuring shapely domestic goddesses sporting this dress and that fridge. She can feel Eliot's dark brown eyes boring into her but refuses to look up.

'You are utterly aware that Elsie wouldn't ever ask you to go with her, but you also know that she wants you there at her fitting. You're her twin, Grace, and this is her wedding.'

Grace stares down, her eyes glazing over at an article on keeping husbands happy.

Eliot takes a step forward. 'I have to ask, Grace: is this some kind of rebellion, some display of jealousy?'

Grace's eyes shoot up from the yellowed page. 'Jealousy?' she spits. 'Oh yes, because I simply must be jealous of Elsie if she's marrying you.'

Eliot throws his hands up in despair. 'So what the bloody hell is it? You should be there each step of the way with her, and she's told me you've had nothing to do with it! She's chosen the flowers, she's chosen the colour scheme, her dress,' he ticks off items on his slender fingers, 'and she's done it all without her best friend making any kind of comment on any of it. Doesn't that seem wrong to you?'

'It's not like you're making it out to be. It's more complicated.' Grace barges past Eliot, slamming the magazine down on the way.

'What is?' Eliot is shouting now and Grace shuts her eyes for a minute. She wonders if she should just tell him. What would he say if she did?

It's me you're meant to marry. You have the wrong twin.

She contemplates for a moment, her head burning. Then she snatches her bag and coat from the floor next to the counter and pushes the keys into Eliot's willowy chest, hoping that they jab him and hurt him.

'Fine. Look after the shop for me then.'

She walks to the wedding dress shop, her breaths short and sharp with adrenaline. She doesn't know why she didn't just stay calm when Eliot asked her about her lack of interest in the wedding. Grace used to be so good at staying calm when she was young. Now, her temper is her worst fault. It is as though playing the part of Elsie for all these years, since Elsie began to be sadder and quieter, has made Grace actually morph into her twin.

The rain drives down onto Grace's hair. She pulls it and twists it down one side of her head and into her red coat as she edges closer to the wedding dress shop in the square. She knows its exact location: Elsie points it out every single day. The moment that Grace enters and is surrounded by cream, rustling trains and cabinets of glittering tiaras, and the huge, luxurious changing room that Elsie has described so many times, Grace knows that Eliot was right and that she should be here.

She asks the blonde woman behind the counter if Elsie is having her dress fitting, but before the woman can answer, Elsie is shouting her. Grace can hear her voice, even though she can't see Elsie anywhere.

'Grace, is that you?'

The curtain of the changing room sweeps open and there stands Elsie in her wedding dress. Although Elsie looks more beautiful than Grace has ever seen her, although the simple ivory tulle and veil stitched with tiny, blinking stones make Elsie look like somebody Grace never thought her sister would be, it's the expression of happiness and hope on Elsie's face that makes Grace's eyes fill with tears.

'I thought I heard your voice! I can't believe you came,' Elsie says, taking a step towards her twin.

They hug, in a distant way so that Grace doesn't get Elsie's dress wet, and Grace notices that Elsie smells different to how she usually does: more gentle and floral. She's suddenly somebody that Grace doesn't recognise. She's the person that Eliot could make her, if Grace wasn't here to ruin things.

After a moment, Elsie steps back, suddenly self-conscious. She motions down to her dress. The train isn't long, yet is unmistakable.

Elsie's hair, normally falling around her face in layered chunks, is piled in an elaborate coil.

'What do you think? Is it okay? I know I probably should have told Mags I would have Mum's old dress and worn it instead of trying to give it to you, but I didn't want to spend my wedding wearing something old that reminded me of the past. I took the dress home like you asked me to, but I definitely don't want to wear it. I want to move on.'

'You look incredible, Elsie. It's all perfect. I completely understand about you not wearing Mum's dress. We should have talked more about it when I made you take it home, but I couldn't bear to bring it up for some reason. I'm so sorry I haven't been much help lately.' There, Grace thinks, she has said it. And it didn't even hurt. She feels a tug of anger at herself for being so reluctant to get involved in the wedding, and an equal reluctance to apologise for all these months.

Elsie snorts, ruining, for a moment, the image of the perfect bride. 'Don't be ridiculous. I prefer doing things on my own.'

'But this is your *wedding*. And I should have been there with you, planning. I'm sorry. Things will change, you know.'

Elsie takes Grace's hand, and as she pulls it towards her, Grace feels the brush of her sister's soft wedding dress. 'You're here now. So they already have.'

Elsie wants to leave it there, Grace can see that. But Grace wants to pull some more at their wound, and tell Elsie everything: about the visions, about how Grace is going to try to ignore them and not be led through a life that might not even be hers. She wants to tell Elsie about the old postcard that she found with her mother's things, and the words on it:

Our daughter will have my gift. She will see what should be and what will be. She must use it wisely.

She wants to tell Elsie that she has tried to use the gift wisely, but that it's just too difficult when she knows she should marry Eliot, and that the person she wants to be with is Noel, and Noel is nowhere in the visions of her future, because he is moving to New York.

But Grace doesn't do any of this. For once, she does what Elsie needs her to do, and wants her to do, and leaves it.

Chapter Thirty Nine

Grace, 2009

The wedding flies towards them all after Elsie's final dress fitting. The wedding and reception are both booked at The Fortuna Hotel on North Promenade. Elsie likes the echoes of grandeur in the hotel: the sweeping staircase, the high, ornately coved ceilings and the Victorian furniture. Some of the rooms are a little tatty, but Elsie doesn't care about that, and Eliot thinks that it adds to the hotel's charm.

The morning of the wedding, Grace arrives at The Fortuna early to help Elsie get ready. Elsie and Eliot stayed the night at the hotel together, together, flouting tradition.

'Eliot's gone for the morning,' Elsie says as she ushers Grace into the shabby bridal suite. Grace tries not to notice the peeling wallpaper and concentrates on what Elsie is saying. 'He said he might go to the bar and have some Dutch courage. I hope he doesn't drink too much. You don't think he will, do you?'

'I don't think he'll let you down, Elsie,' Grace says. If Eliot were marrying her, she thinks, and not Elsie, he would probably drink all morning. And so would Grace.

'I don't think he will either, to be honest. He's been so much help in the shop the last few months. Things have gone quite well recently. I really think he's the one who is meant to be my husband.'

Grace is silent. Today is the day that they will both move on. Grace wonders what Noel is doing, and wishes that she was moving on with him.

'Anything from Noel on his big America move?' Elsie says, making Grace's head shoot up from the faded swirling roses on the carpet.

'How did you know I was thinking about him?'

Elsie taps the side of her nose, and Grace notices her sister's manicured nails. The tips are pearl white, which contrasts with the glossy pink nail.

'Perhaps Mum isn't the only one who had a gift.'

Grace swallows and stands nervously, until Elsie prods her.

'Grace, relax. I'm the one who's meant to be nervous today! I definitely don't have any kind of weird gift. All I know is that for years and years, I have known that Noel is in love with you. And now I get the feeling that it's finally mutual. But I didn't have to be psychic to work it out,' she laughs, 'I just had to get you thinking about weddings and future husbands!'

Grace feels light and relieved. 'Okay. I'll admit it. I care about Noel a lot. But he's moving so far away, I'm trying not to think too much about it.'

Elsie nods and sighs, and Grace knows that it's a sigh of relief that she has found a husband and isn't in the murky water of uncertainty that Grace is always swimming through.

If only she knew, thinks Grace, *that I am certain of who I was meant to marry, and that she is marrying him instead.*

But as she watches Elsie glide over to her wedding dress and admire her naked wedding finger in anticipation of the ring it will soon bear, the gradual realisation that Elsie is the one who is really meant to marry Eliot rises up through Grace. She knows, as she watches Elsie descend the once regal staircase of The Fortuna towards Eliot with her wedding dress sweeping behind her, that Elsie brings out the best in him, and that Grace brought out the worst. She knows that Elsie is going to be happy, if Grace just manages to let them have their own wedding day without claiming it as hers.

As she sits and eats her chicken and seasonal vegetables, and toasts the bride and groom with her water, Grace wonders why she was given the gift that her mother had. She reaches in her little purple bag that matches her violet bridesmaid dress and pulls out Rose's postcard as everybody else taps into their flaky pools of meringue. She places the card onto her satin knee and looks down at it discreetly.

It's too late now. You have come back, but it's too late. You chose comfort over love, money over me. Our daughter will have my gift. She will see what should be and what will be. She must use it wisely.

Grace doesn't know why she brought the postcard with her: she can remember everything on it. But something made her want to keep it with her the night she found it, and she's been carrying it with her ever since.

Her mother hadn't used the gift wisely. But how could she, when it sent her spiraling into a dark, frightening madness? Perhaps it wasn't a gift after all. Perhaps it was a curse.

Grace takes a short, sharp breath and then tears the postcard into two. The paper rips easily, softly, weakened with time.

She takes out her phone and taps out a short message, hoping it's not too late.

I love you.

After the first dance, which would have been awkward were it not for Eliot's smooth confidence, and the cutting of a leaning white cake, Grace sits in a corner of The Fortuna's Empire Room with a Coke and wonders if she should order something stronger. Mags, Suzie, Sheila, an old couple who are apparently Mags's cousins – a wiry man called Jimmy who Grace remembers meeting when she was very young, and a woman called Priscilla, or Penny, or something similar, and their son, a man with hair the colour of carrots – are all swaying about on the dance floor, all pretending that they are much younger than they really are. Usually, Grace would lead a chaotic takeover of the dance floor. Usually, Grace would slosh her drink over people's toes and slur apologies. But tonight, Grace sits quietly and observes. She feels better for it. She remembers when she was a child, when she always used to be the quiet one. After Elsie fell silent and cross for so many years, Grace learned to talk more than she wanted, to cover up her sister's sullenness. And as soon as Grace had found the things that made her feel like doing this: Eliot and alcohol, she had clung to them like a possessive toddler clings to his favourite toy. Now, watching Elsie swing about with Eliot, clutching her tulle sides and laughing, Grace sees that she no longer has a sullen sister to make up for.

So she sits quietly, feeling like herself once more, until she sees somebody that makes her forget who she was and is and will be.

There, shaking Eliot's hand and kissing Elsie on the cheek, is Noel.

Grace shoots up from her seat, leaving the torn postcard behind on her table and rushes over to him. He smiles at Grace when she reaches him and takes his phone from his pocket.

'I got your message,' he says. Grace can see from his dishevelled hair and stubble that he didn't think through coming here. He didn't plan it out. He just came.

'I was on my way here anyway when I saw it. I realised how hard today would be for you,' he says in her ear as she slowly puts her arms around his neck. They sway about to a slow song that has come on, and Grace sees Elsie and Eliot watching Noel, looking at the way he is holding Grace. She shuts her eyes for a moment to block them out. All she wants to think about is Noel, and that he came here for her.

'I can't get in the way of New York again. I know you didn't go last time because of me,' Grace says after a few moments.

'You won't get in the way, Grace. We'll work it out.'

Grace rests her head on Noel's shoulder and wonders what will happen. She wonders if she will go to live in New York with him, or if she will go for long holidays, or if Noel will come back in a year or two. She wonders if she will give her share of Ash Books to Eliot and find work in America or somewhere else. She wonders if she will become an actress. She wonders if she will be with Noel until she is an old lady, and manage to be a wife to him and a mother to his children. She wonders if she is doing the right thing, for herself and her twin and their mother and her mother.

But as Grace moves next to Noel with the lights dimming around them, there are no sudden flashes of pain and knowledge, no visions of the future, no certainties.

Everything, for this moment, is as it should be.

Outside, the sea purrs and the glimmer of purple dances happily on the waves.

HANNAH EMERY

I studied English at the University of Chester and have written stories for as long as I can remember. I especially love writing about how fragile the present is and how so much of it depends on chance events that took place years ago.

My favourite things in life are my family, my friends, books, baking on a Saturday afternoon, going out for champagne and dinner and having cosy weekends away.

I live in Blackpool with my husband and our little girl.

Find out more about me at hannahcemery.wordpress.com and follow me on Twitter @hannahcemery.

Printed by RR Donnelley at Glasgow, UK